The Hollow Queen

The Hollow Queen

BOOK EIGHT OF
THE SYMPHONY *of* AGES

Elizabeth Haydon

A TOM DOHERTY ASSOCIATES BOOK

New York

THE HOLLOW QUEEN

Copyright © 2015 by Elizabeth Haydon

Maps and ornaments by Ed Gazsi

A Tor Book
Published by Tom Doherty Associates, LLC
175 Fifth Avenue
New York, NY 10010

www.tor-forge.com

Tor® is a registered trademark of Tom Doherty Associates, LLC.

The Library of Congress Cataloging-in-Publication Data
is available upon request.

ISBN 978-0-7653-0567-1 (hardcover)
ISBN 978-1-4299-4297-3 (e-book)

Tor books may be purchased for educational, business, or
promotional use. For information on bulk purchases, please contact
the Macmillan Corporate and Premium Sales Department at
1-800-221-7945, extension 5442, or write to
specialmarkets@macmillan.com.

First Edition: June 2015

Printed in the United States of America

0 9 8 7 6 5 4 3 2 1

To the great Ward Evers, who was the godfather of this series,
who dreamt it into being at NOLA in the French Quarter
during the ALA Conference of 1993 over uncounted
Dixie Blackened Voodoos, and who insisted that medieval music,
string theory of physics, archeology, anthropology, herbalism,
and linguistics could, in fact, be the basis for a fantasy series.
Thank you forever, my friend.

ACKNOWLEDGMENTS

With greatest respect and gratitude to the two editors who have shepherded this series through its birth and its upcoming completion: Jim Minz, who saw it in the raw in a different era and served as its midwife putting an enduring stamp on it, and Susan Chang, who inherited it in difficult circumstances and has, through kind patience and expertise, brought it to the summit of the mountain overlooking the valley beyond.

Thank you.

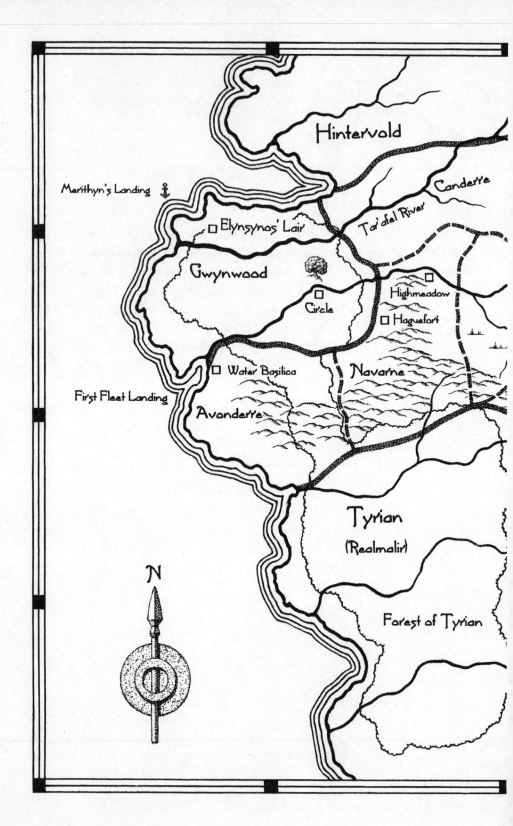

Hintervold

Canderre

Merithyn's Landing ⚓

Elynsynos' Lair

Ta'dal River

Gwynwood

Circle

Highmeadow

Haguefort

Water Basilica

Navarne

First Fleet Landing

Avonderre

Tyrian

(Realmalir)

N

Forest of Tyrian

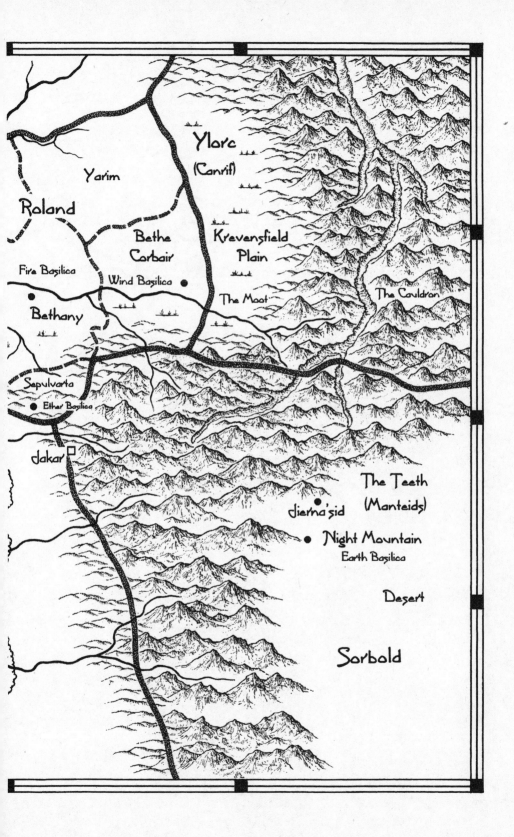

THE WEAVER'S LAMENT

Time, it is a tapestry

Threads that weave it number three

These be known, from first to last,

Future, Present, and the Past

Present, Future, weft-thread be

Fleeting in inconstancy

Yet the colors they do add

Serve to make the heart be glad

Past, the warp-thread that it be

Sets the path of history

Every moment 'neath the sun

Every battle, lost or won

Finds its place within the lee

Of Time's enduring memory

Fate, the weaver of the bands

Holds these threads within Her hands

Plaits a rope that in its use

Can be a lifeline, net—or noose.

1

Ylorc
(Canrif) ★

Bethe
Corbair

Krevensfield
Plain

THE FORGES, YLORC

𝕿he ring of steel against anvil was always a lovely percussion line
for a song, and Sergeant-Major Grunthor was in the mood for singing as
he pounded away, shaping the new pick hammer he was making.

The fires of the ancient forges of Canrif, designed and built a millennium and a half before by Gwylliam the Visionary, splashed light over the
enormous smithy, adding a dance of shadows to the heat and smell of the
place, increasing the Sergeant's already considerable pleasure. Gwylliam,
an ancient king he had never met, was a genuine anus of a human being
in Grunthor's estimation, but an undeniable genius at smithing and architecture. Therefore he thought it only right and fitting to shape his new-
est song in tribute to the long-dead inventor, whose mummified remains
he and his comrades had come upon a few years before, splayed out on a
table that was hidden away in the vault of a secret library in the bowels of
the citadel the man had literally carved out of a mountain range in what
now was the kingdom of the Firbolg, known as Ylorc.

Grunthor threw back his head between swings of the forge hammer
and let his glorious bass, often a few notes flat, fill the high-ceilinged chamber with song.

Oh, Gwylliam was a piece o' shit
But that don't matter none,
'E liked ta build and loved ta smith
'Cause makin' stuff is fun.

It isn't nice ta beat yer wife
Ya shouldn't if you 'ave one,
But anyone would wanna smack
That bitch that they called Anwyn.

Yen the broadsmith, the Archon responsible for the forges, stood in as close an approximation to attention as the wiry Firbolg body was capable of and tried to maintain a placid expression, when what he really craved was to go to bed.

"Join in, Yen," the Sergeant instructed as he turned the pick hammer on its side. "That's an order."

"Don't know words, sir."

"Hmm. Could be a problem, then. Once Oi get the chorus down, Oi better 'ear ya."

"Yezzir."

"Hmmm, now—where was Oi?"

" 'Bitch that they called Anwyn,' sir."

"Ah, yes." Grunthor opened his mouth to begin a second verse but, struck suddenly by decorum, he removed the shield from his eyes with great drama and stepped momentarily away from the anvil. He turned and looked furtively around the smithy floor.

"Where's me pint?"

"Base of anvil, sir."

"Ah, yep—'ere she is." Grunthor scooped up the amber bottle, pulled the cork with his back teeth, spat it out, and held it high to the towering ceiling above, adding its shadow to those that were already dancing there.

"'S'only proper we drink a toast to Annie," he said solemnly. "'Ere's to Anwyn, dead, *again*, a third an' 'opefully final time. You was a worthy adversary, Annie. Well, not really. You was a craven, manipulative nightmare with far more opinion of yerself than you ever deserved. May you writhe in the Vault o' the Unnerworld in unceasin' agony for Time Immemorial, amen."

"Amen," said Yen automatically.

The Sergeant-Major, who stood fairly close to eight feet tall with shoulders as wide as a one-ox plow, waved the bottle aloft for a moment longer, then downed the contents, following up with a resounding belch that echoed through the smith chamber.

The guards atop the ramparts applauded politely.

Grunthor acknowledged their applause with a tip of the empty bottle, put it back at the base of the forge, then picked up the tool he'd been smithing and held it out for the broadsmith's inspection.

"Yer opinion, Yen?"

The Archon examined the hammer.

"Not one of your better ones, sir."

The Sergeant's enormous amber eyes narrowed. He held up the newly crafted pick hammer to them and inspected it himself.

"You best be talkin' about the song, sonny. This 'ammer's a thing o' beauty."

"Yezzir."

The manic light went out of the Sergeant's eyes, and his face grew solemn.

"Really? The truth now, Yen, no jokin'. This is important."

The broadsmith signaled silently for Grunthor to turn the hammerhead over, and leaned closer to look at it again. The tool was approximately three times the size of the pick hammers that were routinely produced in the kingdom's commercial forges for mining and rock climbing in the peaks of the Teeth. Grunthor himself had designed the original model for the routine hammers several years before, and it had become one of the kingdom's most successful goods of sale, sent in trade around the world. In addition, its contribution to the expansion of the kingdom to new heights, literally, and the mining of the gemstones and rare minerals that he and the Firbolg king, Achmed the Snake, had discovered in the depths of areas unexplored in Gwylliam's day, was significant.

His expression at the moment could only be described as hurt.

Yen thought carefully and cleared his throat.

"You said big one for smashing."

"Yeah," said the Sergeant-Major. "What's wrong with it?"

"Head too long compared to height. Need to be shorter." Yen cleared his throat again. "Not by much."

"'Ow much?" Grunthor demanded.

The broadsmith looked at the head of the tool again. Then he held up his fingers with an infinitesimal gap between them.

The Bolg sergeant's face lit up again.

"Oh! Well, if that's gonna make the difference, let's put 'er back in the forge, then, Yen. Gotta be perfect fer what Oi got planned. Oi guess what ol' Brenda usta tell me at the Pleasure Palace was true, then. Longer's not always better. Oo'da believed it? Take yer time, Yen.

"An' besides, it gives me a chance fer two more verses, maybe three."

Yen merely closed his eyes.

Several hours later, when the massive head of the pick hammer had been shaped in proportion to Yen's satisfaction, and the handle adjusted to accommodate it, Grunthor went down the long hall that was one of the major horizontal air vents for the forges and opened the gated doorway. He stepped out onto the sheltered ledge, into the night wind, and stared westward, over the steppes at the Krevensfield Plain and the rest of the Middle Continent beyond.

What had been a pristine vista not that long ago was now speckled with light and smoke from what the Lord Marshal of the armies of the Cymrian Alliance, Anborn ap Gwylliam, had termed the Threshold of Death.

Grunthor and the Firbolg king had taken great amusement in the melodramatic name, but appreciated the concept nonetheless; Anborn had established a battle line, an interconnected series of fortified encampments that had once been farming settlements, designed to prevent the army of the southern nation of Sorbold from crossing, unrestricted, into the central regions of the Middle Continent. Most of the major provincial seats and army garrisons of the Alliance were positioned in the northern third of that area, and the great gap between the helpless farmers and the bulk of the army was now in the process of being evened out.

Tactically, Grunthor was pleased.

As pleased as one could be when an ally was defending a vast open landmass that bordered an attacking nation quartered in mountains, an enemy with an eye on assets north of that enormous open field.

Not good plannin' fer our side on the part of the All-God, he thought, watching the last moments of the sunset. *Or 'ooever it was what planned it.*

Just as the last of the turquoise light left the sky, he felt a shadow fall upon him from behind.

Grunthor smiled.

"Good evening, sir. Got a new joke fer ya."

There was no response, but Grunthor could feel the shadow grow a few steps closer.

"Whaddaya get when ya cross a Firbolg soldier with a Dhracian assassin?"

There was a moment of silence. Then a sandy voice spoke.

"I don't understand."

"Either an unbeatable combination of milit'ry might, or the ugliest, deadliest prostitute *ever*."

Silence echoed up the vent.

"I still don't understand."

Grunthor sighed. "'Ave a seat, Rath."

With almost no disturbance of air whatsoever, the space on his right was occupied with the thin body of the Dhracian demon hunter, a man with whom Grunthor had had little interaction and even less conversation.

The man who now was the only person in the Bolglands with a chance of killing the adversary for which they were preparing.

2

NORTHERN SEACOAST, TRAEG

The waves that crashed along the rocky coast carried with them the thinnest sliver of fading moonlight, shining waveringly at the seam of the sand and the depths.

Gwydion ap Llauron stood for a moment in the sea wind as he broached that gleaming edge, up to his knees in a rolling surf. The heir to the legacy of some of the most famous mariners in history, he had felt the sea in his blood all his life; his earliest memory was of being held suspended within the gently swirling tides, most likely in the arms of his father, long before he had the ability to walk on his own, the salty water swelling and ebbing around his infant body. There had been a comfort in the waves then that he remembered still, when all other memory of those early days was lost to Time and age.

Gwydion, or Ashe, as the high lord of the Cymrian Alliance was known to his intimates, waited for a few moments with his feet buried in pebbled sand disappearing relentlessly into the Deep and watched the moon until it set. Then, when all trace of light was gone from the sky, he waded farther out into the burgeoning waves.

In his hand he carried an ancient blade known as Kirsdarke, a sword of elemental water forged in another age, on the other side of the world. It was a deeply magical weapon, said to have been tempered in the cold, boiling icefire of an undersea volcano. Its frothing blade was raging with excitement, running in shining rivers from the tang to the tip as he walked deeper into the surf.

As the water crested his thighs, Ashe allowed himself a final thought of his wife and infant son, the former now engaged in the war that was taking root in the land behind him, the latter hidden deep within distant mountains to keep him safe from that conflict and from those of dark intent who hunted him for darker reasons. Ashe whispered a prayer for their safety skyward to whatever beneficent force might hear him as he separated himself from the realm of air.

Then, inhaling deeply, he submerged his body into the arms of the sea.

The rippling sound of the wind vanished from his ears as the water closed over his head, replaced by the heavy thrum of waves and the dark tides beyond them. Ashe closed his eyes, knowing that when he opened them again he would see no more than he could with his eyes shut; the falling moon had taken the very last illumination beneath the surface with it, leaving only endless darkness.

He waded, blind, out farther until his feet could no longer brush the sandy bottom, hanging suspended in the drift. The sensation harked back to his first memory, as he had intended, and he allowed himself a moment to revel in the comfort he remembered as his body went vaporous. Kirsdarke's blade turned formless as well; he could feel the heft of the weapon lighten in his hand as it became nothing more than hilt.

With the fading of his corporeal body came a strengthening of his will; the power of the elemental sword of water vibrated through him with a roar, attuned now to the most overwhelming source of power, strength, and vibration in the world: the wild ocean, the Wide Central Sea at the edge of which he was now hovering.

Eyes still closed, he loosed his last bond to the part of himself that was anything but water, and felt his flesh dissipate, falling away like a diaphanous garment in the tide. Then he focused his thoughts and tied his mind to a particularly strong current and let it pull him, with the receding waves, out into the dark world of endless water before him.

Walking through the ocean.

Heading west.

Passing below the keels of the pirate ships, armed merchant vessels, and warships that plied the waves above him, an enormous armada that had destroyed and then blockaded the harbors of the Alliance, effectively sealing off the western coast of the continent to any seafaring vessel not belonging to that argosy of death.

Unnoticed.

3

THE RAVEN'S GUILD, YARIM PAAR, PROVINCE OF YARIM

*Y*abrith was by rights a petty thief, a thug, and a modestly talented killer.

Other than a reputation for a cool head, he had little to recommend him as second-in-command of the Raven's Guild, the famous coterie of assassins that also operated one of the most celebrated tile foundries on the Middle Continent, doing business in plain sight while the darker element of the guild hid their dealings from the light of the sun. So while many of his fellows were more gifted in the arts of larceny, intimidation, graft, pickpocketing, and murder most foul and for hire, Yabrith had achieved a fairly easy place in the guild's hierarchy, essentially holding down the fort whenever the guild scion, a hollow-faced, narrow-eyed man known as Dranth, was away.

As he had been for some time now.

Having Dranth's trust was something Yabrith never took for granted. He had known from a very early age that position was essential within an organization like the Raven's Guild, and had been similarly aware of his shortcomings when it came to the thuggery normally necessary to achieve such position. He was gifted with a blade, though many others were more so. He had no compunction about fulfilling contracts on women, children, or the clergy, but neither did anyone else in the Raven's Guild. Among the roster of soulless murderers, brutal beaters, and vicious torturers in the ranks of the organization, Yabrith could almost have been mistaken for a rank amateur rather than actually considered an assassin at all.

So rather than scrapping in back alleys or slitting throats in the dark, he instead became a student of organization and procedure, gaining a knowledge of protocol and the inner workings of every office, business, barracks, and noble house in Yarim Paar, even up to and including the Judiciary, the capitol that was the provincial seat of Yarim and the home of its duke, a dullard named Ihrman Karsrick. There were, in fact, more men working in the Judiciary on the payroll of the Raven's Guild than not on it.

Even so, the longer Dranth remained away from the guildhall, the more nervous Yabrith became. Given that the scion had taken an out-of-town job, traveling overland with three others of superior skill and minimal ethics, to the realm of the Firbolg in the neighboring mountain range known as the Manteids to the human population of the continent, and as the Teeth to their current occupants, Yabrith was finding himself growing a little more nervous with each day that Dranth did not return.

The guild scion was known as a man of speed and alacrity of purpose.

Finally, when Dranth unexpectedly stepped through the fireshadows that coated the floor near the table in the guildhall where Yabrith was finishing his supper one evening, Yabrith choked on the sausage he had swallowed before chewing it properly.

"Welcome back, finally," he said as he wiped his mouth clear of spittle with his linen napkin. "I don't believe you have ever been this late in returning from a journey before; I hope all went well."

"Swallow your tongue," Dranth replied darkly as he crossed to the sideboard beside the fireplace, seizing the bottle of brandy with hands that shook and splashing the ruby liquid into a crystal glass. "If you need help I can assist with that."

Yabrith's eyebrows rose into his hairline, but he said nothing. His jaw clenched shut with a resounding *pop*.

Dranth turned his attention to emptying the decanter of brandy, after which he heaved the glass into the fireplace.

Yabrith knew better than to comment. He brushed the glass fragments surreptitiously from his doublet and waited for the guild scion to speak.

He sat quietly while Dranth paced in silence in front of the glowering flames, finally dropping into the armchair at the head of the table.

Yabrith continued to wait.

At last Dranth looked up.

"The others are dead," he said. His voice was hollow. "Like bottle flies."

Yabrith exhaled, still saying nothing, but clenched his intertwined fingers together even more tightly than they had been since the guild scion's first order of silence.

The three men who had ventured forth with Dranth into Ylorc, the mountainous realm of the Firbolg monsters, were the most skilled members of the Raven's Guild. Trentius, known for merciless interrogation that bordered on artistry, was said to be part bat, able to hang upside down in the darkest of alleys and caverns until a victim passed by below; Sandon, an albino who was all but invisible in direct sunlight and an unerring marksman with everything from a crossbow to a throwing knife; and Dhremane, a mute who had successfully erased all sound from his passage, and all odor from his flatulence, who could stand, undetected, for more than eighteen hours, in plain sight—each of them a master dispensary of death.

Gone.

Yabrith would have sooner believed the sun would voluntarily refuse to rise than those men be lost to the guild, their expertise unmatchable, irreplaceable.

"Who—how—?" His words trailed off.

The guild scion interlaced his long, thin fingers and pressed them to his lips.

Yabrith waited nervously.

"It was the ruler of the Bolg himself, our most grievous enemy, the man the rulers of Roland call the Assassin King," said Dranth, finally breaking the silence. "The target of our mission. At least for us—the emperor of Sorbold was expecting us to retrieve the Child of Time and its mother, whom Sandon was able to paralyze with a dart shot, but the Bolg king killed him and everyone else—I alone escaped."

Yabrith swallowed dryly.

"There was no possible way he could have known we were there," Dranth continued, uncharacteristically talkative. "I watched our three other guildsmen conceal themselves, as well as the two that came from Golgarn, and even I could not find them once they took cover. When I saw him kill Sandon before his crossbow had even stopped reverberating from the dart shot, I knew we had no prayer of a chance."

"Lucky you were able to escape."

"You have no idea how much." Dranth's sallow face was glowing red in the firelight, either from the heat or the drink. "Pack for a journey. We are leaving at foredawn tomorrow."

Yabrith nodded. "Where are we going?"

"Back to Sorbold, to Jierna'sid. I need to return to our friend the emperor, report that our attempt did not go well, and ask him to help me find another way into the Bolglands."

Yabrith could not suppress his shudder.

"I imagine Talquist will not be pleased with this news."

"No, he won't," Dranth agreed. "So I will need to bring him a gift to mollify him. Fortunately I have one."

He rose from the table and left the room without another word.

4

HIGHMEADOW, NAVARNE

Seventeen-year-old Gwydion Navarne stood nervously outside the door of the library next to the chamberlain, who looked even more nervous than he did. The tray in the man's hands was shaking so violently that the young duke felt the need to seize it and remove it from the chamberlain's grasp before its contents shattered onto the floor.

"It's all right, Manus, you may return to your tasks," he said, trying to approximate the tone of voice his late father or his godfather might have used, and failing miserably. "I'll take the Bolg king his after-dinner cordial myself."

The chamberlain, new of hire at Highmeadow, looked relieved and bowed. "Thank you, m'lord."

Gwydion nodded politely and watched as the house servant scurried away back to the buttery, then sighed. He tapped ever so lightly on the library door, and, hearing no response, quietly let himself in.

The fire that had been blazing merrily on the enormous hearth when he left to obtain the cordial glass had burned down to sleepy coals while he had been away, working up the courage to come back into the room.

In front of that fire at a small portable desk sat the previously mentioned Firbolg king, a man known in the common tongue as Achmed the Snake. Gwydion was aware that among the Bolg king's subjects, the ferocious race of demi-human beings known as the Firbolg, he had other titles too—the Glowering Eye, the Merciless, the Earth-Swallower, the Night Man, and a host of others that Rhapsody had humorously shared with him long before—but as King Achmed sat at his godfather's desk, an empty plate and neatly folded napkin beside the large open ledger he was studying, the young duke was certain that to his Firbolg subjects, the comic names were signs of the utter respect and sheer terror in which they held him.

Given that the Firbolg were themselves the stuff of nightmares to the human population of the continent, Gwydion was loath to disturb him.

In silence, therefore, he placed the brass tray down on the lower table between the great leather settees and took the glass, with its three fingers of dark gold liquid catching the firelight, over to the Bolg king's desk.

And waited respectfully.

For far longer than he wanted to.

Finally the Bolg king spoke, not breaking his gaze away from the ledger.

"You're a generous man," he said in his strange, sandy voice. "That vintage is remarkable; the bouquet has a pleasant sting to it. Is it from Canderre?"

"Marincaer," Gwydion corrected. "It was one of my father's favorites."

"If that be the case, it was worth you risking disturbing me with it. Thank you."

"I am sorry if I've disturbed you," Gwydion said, his nerves rising again. "I will leave you to your reading once more."

The Bolg king did not look up, but gestured impatiently at one of the settees. "Sit."

The duke of Navarne complied.

When nothing happened for a long stretch of moments, he ventured a question.

"Have you found anything of use in Ashe's notes?"

"Yes."

Gwydion made himself more comfortable on the settee. His discomfort was not at the presence of King Achmed, a man he had an extraordinary fondness for while much of the Middle Continent found him either intimidating or terrifying, but rather at the memory of what had transpired a few hours before.

The Firbolg king had arrived unexpectedly earlier that night at Highmeadow, the central military fortress of the Cymrian Alliance and home of Gwydion's godfather and namesake, Gwydion of Manosse, his late father's best friend. King Achmed's presence in the western lands of the Great Forest between the provinces of Navarne and Bethany was a shock from which Gwydion had not yet recovered; the Bolg king had an almost pathological aversion to traveling in the human realm, and with the war beginning to spread across the continent, Gwydion knew that only the most severe of necessities would have brought him out of Ylorc, the name by which the Firbolg called their mountainous kingdom.

Gwydion had remembered, just before dinner was about to be served, that before Ashe left he had asked for the request to be made of Achmed to assess a prisoner being held under the tightest security in the stockade. The Lord Cymrian had declined to name the prisoner, but requested that Achmed try to determine if the taint of demonic possession could be discerned on that prisoner, if the Bolg king ever happened to be at Highmeadow.

Gwydion Navarne had made the request, and the king had agreed to do so with only the slightest of annoyances obvious in his reaction.

Gwydion had accompanied him down the stairs, carefully sprung the seven-lock trap, and waited for the guard to open the door.

He could not believe his eyes when the man in the center of the cell turned around.

The prisoner was none other than the Lord Roland, Tristan Steward, regent of Bethany, his own first cousin once removed and the highest-ranking noble in Roland behind the Lord Cymrian himself.

He was just beginning to recover from his surprise when the Bolg king seized the guard's crossbow and fired a bolt into the Lord Roland's forehead, cleanly bisecting his brow.

Then King Achmed had handed the weapon back to the stunned guard, instructed Gwydion to leave the body there for several days to make sure that no demonic detritus would be passed to anyone else, signaled impatiently for the door to be closed and locked again, then trotted back up the stairs, intent on returning to his study of Ashe's research materials regarding the emperor of Sorbold.

Several hours later now, Gwydion was still shaking. He took a deep breath, deciding to risk the Bolg king's ire again.

"So what did you find?"

Finally Achmed looked up.

"Ashe has done a credible job of assessing and enumerating the reasons that the armies of the Alliance should not launch a frontal or flank attack on Sorbold."

Gwydion nodded. "He allowed me to review the intelligence reports and battlefield communiqués with him almost every day," he said, squeezing the arm of the settee to try to quell his trembling. "Each time I did, it was more and more apparent that Talquist and the basic terrain of the empire have insured that the realm is invulnerable to our armies. Anborn will have a busy enough time defending the Middle Continent from their legions."

"True enough."

"Then what is it that you've decided to do?" Gwydion asked, struggling to keep the panic out of his voice.

Achmed picked up the cordial glass. "I'm going to enjoy this libation you've kindly provided."

"And then?"

The Bolg king took a deep draught, then looked the young duke over with his mismatched eyes.

"I understand you saw combat recently."

"Yes."

"How did that go?"

Gwydion sat up a little straighter. "It was terrifying, but rather successful. And surprising."

"Surprising in what way?"

"Well, given that it was my first experience in battle, I suppose it's fair that anything would be surprising. I am certainly glad to have lived through it. But Anborn seemed, well, a bit confused by it all."

"Confused? Anborn? Interesting. Would you care to explain?"

"The garrison he had quickly established was nothing more than a series of farming settlements barricaded and manned by eight thousand or so volunteers, recent recruits, and civilians, mostly the inhabitants of those settlements. Some of these were even children, boys younger than me. Ashe has been training and conscripting continental garrisons, mostly deployed in the major citadels and provinces—" His voice trailed off suddenly. "I beg your pardon, Your Majesty," he said sheepishly. "You clearly know all this."

"Of course I do. Why do you think Anborn was confused?"

"The battle turned far too easily," Gwydion amended. "There was absolutely no reason for the army of Sorbold to be defeated so cleanly and quickly, given how vastly outnumbered we were and the fact that they had iacxsis with them. Have you seen these beasts in person?"

Achmed took another sip of his drink. "No, but I've seen the battle-field reports from their attack on Sepulvarta."

The young duke shuddered. "Wingspan of about fifteen feet, part lizard, part bat, it appeared, seemingly carved from stone. Jaws like a plague locust. Terrifying."

Achmed waved his hand dismissively. "You had two ancient elemental swords with you—Daystar Clarion and Tysterisk—that alone could have stood to eradicate Sorbold's advantage numerically. You also had the Iliachenva'ar bearing one of those swords, and she is competent with her weapon, even if you are new to yours. And of course you were under Anborn's command. I don't find your victory surprising *or* confusing."

"Nonetheless, the Lord Marshal said that it was far too easy."

"That's because Talquist was baiting him. That attack was merely for show. It's a shame the soldiers who were committed to it on their side did not know that. But in the end, that deception will be Talquist's undoing."

Gwydion rubbed his temples, trying to ease the headache that had crept behind his eyes. "I don't understand."

For the first time since he had arrived, Achmed smiled slightly.

"Wars are won by will, by individual determination. Not soldiers, not even generals, but don't tell Anborn that if you are within range of anything he might throw at you. It is will that powers an army, will that wins a sea battle. Will is the heart of any conflict. If you can destroy the will, the conflict will end.

"Talquist has been putting this invasion, this worldwide conquest, in place for a very long time. I have not yet traced the roots of every betrayal, every complicit deception, every nefarious dealing he has undertaken in setting up this monstrosity. There is no question in my mind that he has made alliances with those who have similar intentions of conquest, but what I wonder more about is who has been deceived, who is part of his coterie by accident or by deception. It matters little; once the war began, all mercy, all forgiveness was off the table for anyone who joined the wrong side by accident, who was deceived into believing what they are doing is right. But there's an art to knowing where the will really is in a war.

"Those that defend a continent, an alliance, a people, even a family are blessed to have will already on their side. But the will that leads an evil man to destroy nations, enslave populations, make deals with demons— that is a will that needs support to survive, to triumph. It is like a chain with many links. Such a chain can be incredibly strong, and when the will to conquer is joined by similar will, that sort of support can be formidable.

But when that support has been coerced, or misled, or intimidated, there is sometimes an opportunity to cause a break in the links of the chain. If you can determine what part of that chain was made under false pretenses, sometimes those links fall away on their own."

He drained the rest of his cordial and set the glass decisively down on the desk again.

"Then, of course, you can always go for the manacle first."

"The manacle?"

Achmed rose and began to gather Ashe's materials into an organized pile. "The head of the chain. The reason it was formed in the first place."

Gwydion blinked. "I'm sorry, I don't understand."

"Talquist must die." The Bolg king opened one last scroll.

"Understood. How do you plan to bring that about? Especially since you've already acknowledged that it would be a mistake for our armies to attack Sorbold?"

Achmed spread the scroll out and weighted it down at the edges. "I said nothing about armies. I'm going alone."

Gwydion swallowed the bile that had risen in the back of his throat. It took him a moment to form calm words.

"While I have no doubt that you know what you are doing, it would be highly enlightening to hear how you intend to do so."

"Do you see this?" The Bolg king displayed what Gwydion saw was a detailed map of the terrain surrounding Jierna Tal, the towering palace in which the emperors of Sorbold had reigned for centuries uncounted, and pointed to the mountainous surroundings that served as natural defenses to the city of Jierna'sid, Sorbold's capital seat.

Gwydion nodded.

"What exactly do you see?"

"A place designed by the All-God to be unassailable," Gwydion said.

Achmed snorted softly. "If you say so." He ran his leather-gloved finger across a particularly savage-looking part of the mountain range, where jagged peaks ringed a vast chasm that had been carved by an ancient river in a long-forgotten age, separating the inner part of the highlands from the guardian ridge at the edge of the Krevensfield Plain with a seven-league-wide gulf two thousand feet deep.

At the top of the inner ridge of that gulf stood the palace of Jierna Tal, its fabled thousand-foot-high tower facing the southwestern vista.

"Truly brilliant planning," Achmed said. "Position a tower on the edge of an interior chasm two thousand feet deep, the tower itself a thousand feet high, the only place in the land that needs no human guard, because the terrain is so forbidding. Inexpensive to guard, but a vast view if one is needed."

He smirked at the blank look on Gwydion's face.

"Send me your best leathermaker, a tanner with an eye for color."

When Gwydion's expression turned quizzical, Achmed handed him a sheet of parchment on which the strata and geologic compositions of the Sorbold mountain range had been carefully annotated.

"Have you studied the rock formations of the Teeth?"

"Modestly," said Gwydion. "Why?"

"The bedrock of those mountains is sedimentary—limestone, dolomite, and silica."

Gwydion nodded. "Pyrite and metallic copper as well," he said. "Some of Sorbold's greatest treasures are the minerals that slaves are mining at this very moment. Anborn and I saw great ships full of them being off-loaded in the Nonaligned States, in Windswere and the like, ships and wagons containing entire cities full of people."

"Indeed. Back now to the rocks. In the fireborn strata of those mountains, feldspar and mica are plentiful. Granite, slate, and serpentine bands make up the Inner Teeth. Are you familiar with the colors of these rocks?"

"Many of them—the metallics mostly."

"Good. Wake up that tanner and tell him to bring me color samples of everything he has available in the colors of the stones."

Gwydion nodded again, rose, and left the room for a moment, returning forthwith.

"A deliveryman will be here shortly with the samples, sire."

Achmed went to the coatrack where his cloak hung, and pulled it from the hook with a sweep. He crossed the room quickly and laid the garment in Gwydion's arms.

"This tanner—I assume he has an assistant? Staff?"

The young duke nodded. "Actually, the tanner is a woman, and extraordinarily gifted. She has a full staff of cutters, assemblymen, beamers, embroidery men, swabbers, buffers, and bucktailors. While my knowledge of geology is minimal, my father saw to it that I understood leathermaking from an early age, as it is one of the major industries of my province."

"Good. Then please identify the most trustworthy of them, and command them to prepare for an evening shift stretching into night. Take the cloak and have them pattern it to one and a half times its current size. Hooded, with an internally seamed tie."

"Should I send for more food, then?" Gwydion asked humorously, trying to compensate for his sweating hands. "It sounds like you are looking to double your size."

"Clearly not, or I would have asked that the pattern be twice the current cloak, not half again. It is very important that the leather also be as water-resistant as it is possible to make it. The workmanship should be judged by its solidity, not its appearance, except for its color. I'm not looking for pretty work, just strong—and in the right colors. As soon as the samples get here, I'll make selections and they can get started at once. I will need two cloaks, to be finished no later than two hours past midnight. And be certain, once again, that you choose only those workmen whose silence can be trusted."

"It will be done."

Achmed nodded, satisfied. "Thank you. And while that is being undertaken, because even the best-laid plans sometimes go awry, I will tell you the story of MacQuieth's Wings. Just in case."

"Just in case what?"

"Do you have any more of that brandy?"

"Absolutely. I'll ring for the chamberlain."

"Leave him to bed. He is a dolt, a poor replacement for Gerald Owen. What happened to him, by the way?"

"Gerald?" Gwydion asked. "He died in his sleep, actually, while I was in battle north of Sepulvarta. His heart gave out, I imagine, though it was so big and strong it's hard to believe. He was an elderly man, of course, having devoted so much of his life to three generations of our family. I miss him terribly. I am grateful that Melly is not here; he was the one constant in her life. I'm glad to be able to spare her the pain of his loss for a short time, anyway."

"Hmmm," the Bolg king said noncommittally. "I hope that was the case."

"You've reason to doubt that it was?" The young duke went suddenly cold.

"I always doubt that convenient natural death is natural. There's nothing you can do about it now, so if I were you I would not spend too much time contemplating that possibility. Now, if you would kindly attend to what I've asked of you with the leather mistress—"

Gwydion was already on his way out the door.

5

When the duke of Navarne returned sometime later, another glass of the cordial in his hand, Achmed had already returned each of the documents he had read to the shelves and drawers of Ashe's library and was sitting on one of the settees in front of the fire, lost in thought.

Silently, Gwydion handed him the drink.

"Do you remember the bay gelding I had delivered to you two years back?" The Bolg king's voice was full of memory.

"Of course." Gwydion sat down on the other settee and glanced at the fire. It was burning low, almost to the stage of coals.

"Have you looked in on him as I asked of you?"

"Not recently," Gwydion admitted. "I did so regularly before I went into battle."

Achmed nodded. "And I assume he is still stabled separately from all but your elite bloods?"

"Yes, of course. Just as you asked. I admit his presence has always been strange to me; a horse of that caliber, groomed meticulously and exercised regularly, but never ridden formally or called in to any use."

"He is one of MacQuieth's Wings," the Bolg king said, still staring into the fire himself.

"MacQuieth's Wings?"

It took a long time for the Bolg king to speak again. When he did, his voice was dry and soft.

"In the old world, the hero named MacQuieth was known for many skills, but the one I was able to assess and figure out was his ability to fly."

"Fly?"

"It was believed that he actually could, because he seemed to be able to pass through great distances in befuddlingly short amounts of time. It was really quite extraordinary; he could traverse the island of Serendair, which was almost half the size of the Middle Continent, in little more than three days."

"Three days? That seems all but impossible. No wonder it was believed that he could fly."

"At least some of his remarkable speed was due to a carefully built and maintained network of outstanding horseflesh, quartered in secret at various points across the island. MacQuieth knew the terrain of Serendair better than all but the most accomplished of foresters, and his brain was uniquely mathematical. He was able to synthesize the logistics of time and distance with an understanding of the lay of the land.

"He had determined a route of hubs that allowed him to travel not as the crow flies, obviously, but very close to it in terms of its efficiency and speed. I have to admit that, while *no one* would think to accuse me of being a fanciful man, I was secretly disappointed to discover the reality of MacQuieth's Wings. But that was a long time ago, long before I was named king and had a population to guard, a realm to protect. Now I am grateful for the knowledge of that ancient hero's system, which I've duplicated as best as I could in this new world. It took me less than a sennight to arrive here from Ylorc, in spite of the fact that the regular journey along the trade route is a fortnight and a half in good weather and conditions."

"Remarkable."

"Not really," said Achmed. "It is merely good planning. Good planning usually pays off, though not always, of course. It is in those times when it doesn't that I am most aware of how vulnerable we all are in the world. The best you can do after the last plan is carefully laid is to lay your wager well, and be ready for the time your card doesn't come up when the deck is cut."

He rose slowly and stretched his body meticulously, like a patient cat.

"Now, if you will be so kind, I would like to see that guest room you promised me for the night. Wake me the moment the cloaks are done."

"I will," said Gwydion. "I shall await their completion and bring them to you myself." He stood and rang for the chamberlain.

"Thank you. Remember—no later than two hours past midnight. I need to be gone beyond the sight of anyone at Highmeadow before Firstlight."

"Sleep well." Gwydion hesitated, then blurted out the question he had pondered for hours.

"Er—Tristan Steward?"

Achmed turned and looked at him coolly. "Yes?"

"What—what should I tell Lady Madeleine? His wife?"

"I would leave that to your godfather when he gets back," Achmed said. "He's a much better liar than you are. And if he doesn't come back and you judge intervention to be necessary, I would tell her that he died bravely serving the Alliance. All those Cyrmians wouldn't recognize the truth anyway."

He turned again and followed the nervous Manus out the door.

OVER THE NORTHERN BORDER,
STEPPES OF SORBOLD

Dranth was dreaming, something he could not remember having done in so long that it was as if it were the first time.

He was wrapped in a dark camp blanket beneath a brindleberry bush, his unconscious mind methodically making schematics and escape routes for a panopoly of situations that might occur within the palace of Jierna Tal. Had Dranth been conscious, he would have been undertaking the same chain of thought.

He had already determined that he was prepared to sacrifice Yabrith if worse came to worst, though that would be an unfortunate turn of events. Though no one in the Raven's Guild considered Yabrith to be a solo operator, he had the long-term memory of the organization at the edge of his consciousness, and he had been a favorite of Esten, the legendary guildmistress, when she was still alive.

It had never ceased to amaze Dranth that a man of such little repute as Yabrith would be welcome in the guildmistress's bed, but then, Esten had cravings for which even the most cold-blooded of men had reservations. At one time or another, virtually every member of the guild had serviced the guildmistress, often as a rite of initiation, and on many more than one occasion, a poor performance in that regard had led to a quick burial later in the night.

Apparently Yabrith had been satisfactory, at least.

The image of Esten's rotting head, worm-ridden eye sockets and beetles in her hair, stuffed summarily into a small packing crate and wrapped casually in paper, delivered to his doorstep, still haunted the guild scion. Because his dreams were rare, he was spared the thought of it at night. But during the day, when his mind had finished all the calculations and algorithms that kept him routinely alive, when his thoughts had free space, the memory of her face would return, staring at him blindly, hissing at him with a mouth where the tongue had rotted out.

Avenge me, it whispered.

Dranth rolled over to free his shoulder of the rock that was bedeviling it on the cold, sandy ground and groaned in his sleep.

He had tried.

He had failed.

But until his last breath, he would continue to prosecute the blood oath.

Until his last breath.

Already he had begun to suspect that the furor for revenge was beginning to wane in several of the other guildsmen. While in life Esten had their love and loyalty without question, the cost of his crusade to bring her murderers to tribal justice was adding up to a ledger that was hard to balance.

But that was because none of them had seen her as he had when he had first become aware of her.

Dranth, who was old enough to have been her father, potentially her grandfather, had first come upon the little murderous prodigy in a back alley in Yarim when she was only eight years old. He had seen her first from behind, her dark, ragged hair bouncing across her shoulders as she systematically removed the organs of a soldier who had fallen asleep, drunk, between the taverns he had been frequenting earlier that night. She managed to eviscerate him so quickly, so cleanly, that Dranth had stood frozen in nothing less than awe at the sight.

Then, when she was finished, she wiped her nose with her sleeve and turned to see him watching her.

And smiled.

That smile, glittering teeth below eyes as dark as the night sky within a face framed by matching hair, had caused him to silently swear his soul into alien slavery, to vow to protect and promote her for the rest of his life.

Never even imagining that hers would end so soon, before his.

She was the only person he had ever loved.

He had never tired of doing anything Esten needed, unquestioningly answering every demand, undertaking any job, even willingly allowing her to deflower herself upon him at the age of eleven, something that even he found mentally abhorrent but physically irresistible. The image of her young face, still missing some of the adult teeth, staring down from atop him, carefully watching his reaction, was burned uncomfortably into his memory, and it returned now, her eyes narrow in observation, sparkling as she forced him into fondling her in ways she knew made him uncomfortable.

Even in his sleep, acid rose in his throat at the memory of her insistently putting his hand on her prepubescent nipple, a place that a breast one day would be, guiding him in techniques of stimulation she should never have known so soon. He knew that her physical immaturity could not be allowing her any sexual satisfaction at the things she was making him do. He knew exactly why she demanded them of him.

Because they made him uncomfortable.

She had even told him so.

He had taught her what she wanted to learn, how to use her body to entice and control men, and in turn, she had used that knowledge as a weapon of impressive potency to gain her what she wanted, when her other weapons—a brilliant, quick mind, savage beauty, deadly aim with a blade, and the complete and utter lack of a soul—were insufficient.

Avenge me.

Suddenly, as a chill night wind swept under the bush, dropping thorns on his face, Dranth woke and sat up carefully, shivering.

Returning to Talquist, having failed, was one of the riskier things he had ever undertaken.

But at least he felt he had the winning card in his pocket not only to survive, but to gain another chance at killing the Bolg king, the man who had taken Esten from him.

And, more specifically, the giant Sergeant-Major who had done the actual killing.

He passed a thin hand over the hollows of his bald head at the memory of the voice of the woman in the meadow where the assassination attempt had gone wrong, the woman who had been the target of the initial paralytic.

Whom they had planned to take, along with her infant child, to the emperor of Sorbold, after killing the men they sought.

Meridion, shhhh, now. Shhhh.

Meridion.

He had the name.

The name Talquist craved above all other pieces of information.

Dranth reached over and shook the snoring Yabrith awake.

"Get up. We are almost there."

"It's not dawn yet," Yabrith muttered, yawning widely and farting loudly.

"All the better," Dranth said, slinging his pack to his shoulder. "A few more hours of darkness will serve to get us all that much further to Jierna Tal. Let's go."

6

BENEATH THE WAVES OF THE WIDE
CENTRAL SEA

𝒜she could feel the sun on his face long before he deigned to open his eyes to it.

The water around him was lightening to a hazy green as morning came to the world above, a world with no boundaries or landmarks, nothing to break the endlessness of the sea.

He had been traveling for less than a sennight. This was the fifth sunrise he had experienced since leaving the dry world; it was now bringing the watery realm to wakefulness again. A nominal amount of sleep was still necessary to sustain his consciousness, but it was only enough to rest his mind a little, and did not interfere with his progress into the depths.

The first two days had been a disturbing confirmation of everything he knew from scouting reports on the coastline blockade. The waters north of Avonderre Harbor where he had waded into the sea were clogged with debris and bits of broken ships, caught in the current and floating in the waves, even now, weeks after the assault and raid from the air that had destroyed one of the greatest and busiest ports in the Known World.

Talquist's forces had managed to eradicate in a relatively few hours what had taken centuries to build.

The sunlit realm of the first hundred or so fathoms of depth, the part of the sea in which vision was still useful, was full of fish this morning. He had passed through them in his sleep; now, awake and conscious as he had become with the morning light, he was aware of the song of a large cetacean, a whale in all likelihood, somewhere nearby. Ashe knew his wakefulness had made him more corporeal than he was in his sleep, and he hovered in the drift, waiting for it to pass, along with the swirling schools of its prey.

As the huge creature's wake rumbled through him, he thought back to the time less than a year before when he had met his most illustrious ancestor not very far from this place in the sea, back on the same cliffs that towered above where he had entered the water.

In his search for Rhapsody when she had been captured by the demon known as Michael, the Wind of Death, he had come upon MacQuieth Monodiere Nagall, his mother's ancient forebear and hero of the Seren War two thousand years before. In the sight of history and the whole of the world, MacQuieth was believed long dead, but Ashe had learned some time before that reports of the deaths of ancient Cymrians were occasionally overrated. And while he had witnessed the hero's actual demise, had been told that his heartbeat, which Achmed the Snake, a man who could track such things from the old world, had said rang like a great bell, even below the waves, was now silent, there was more than enough memory in the sea, especially those places near where the great man had lived, that carried his essence, even now.

The longer he spent, vaporous and formless, beneath the waves, the harder it became to fend off strong memories that would creep over him in the quiet depths.

The most difficult ones were memories of loss: the death of his father, Llauron ap Gwylliam, a complicated man with a painful past, but who had risen above it in later years to be a steady religious leader and caring, if somewhat manipulative, father.

He had regretted more than anything his rejection of Llauron, his unkind, brusque refusal to allow his father the one thing in the world Llauron craved once he had forsworn his humanity and become, like his great-grandmother Elynsynos, a dragon in elemental form.

The simple knowledge that he would be allowed to know his grandchild.

That unkindness to the man who had taught him everything he knew about forestry and the wilderness, who had floated him in the tides as an infant, taught him to swim in them as a child and had taken him to the sea as a youth, had engendered in him a love of the earth, taught him the lore of places that were natural and the cradle of history ate at him now as he walked the sea, formless in it, as his father had once held him in his earliest memory.

Perhaps one day I will understand what it truly means to be a father, he thought as he passed through the wreckage of ships, the burning barrels of magnesium and pitch, the body parts that had still not been consumed by fish and other creatures of the Deep.

All he knew was that the child who had been secreted away for his own protection, the infant his wife had carried in pain and love, had pled with him to have, was now so deep a part of his soul that he could not imagine the possibility of taking a single breath more if he were not able to reclaim him, to protect him and keep him safe from a world that threatened him.

It was too much to contemplate and still remain sane.

Ashe let the thoughts flow out of his amorphous mind, concentrating instead on one thing, and one thing only.

The White Ivory tower of the Sea Mages in Gaematria, the mystical island wrapped in fog and secrets, to which he was traveling.

The Isle of the Sea Mages was a place of scholarship and mystery, where many beings of elder races like the Ancient Seren, the Liringlas, the Gwenen, and the Gwadd had chosen to make their home when the Second Fleet of the Cymrian exodus had been sundered at the Prime Meridian by a great storm in their passage from the old world. Magic was studied as a science there, and his uncle, Edwyn Griffyth, served as High Sea Mage, lending his brilliance in the areas of engineering and smithery to the knowledge that was said to be hoarded as treasure there.

He had beheld the legendary tower on both of his previous trips to the Isle, and had been so clearly impressed by its power, its height, and the reverence with which it was spoken of by the Sea Mages and anyone who came to Gaematria. Ashe knew that if any instrumentality, any tool was capable of seeing beyond the nefariously deep magic that was obscuring an oceanwide blockade, a naval undertaking that had allowed the pretender to the throne of Sorbold to all but shut down sea trade around the world, it was the tower.

Ashe cleared his mind, fixing his vision on the image of it, and pressed on, formless in the waves of the ocean.

7

PALACE OF JIERNA TAL, JIERNA'SID, SORBOLD

Talquist Rev-Penthor, the recently crowned Emperor of the Sun in the desert realm of Sorbold, lingered on the top step and allowed himself one quick look from the inspiring heights of his beloved tower that faced southwest out of the palace of Jierna Tal before turning to address the entity that had arrived just moments before him.

Given that entity's power and genesis, it was impossible not to be at least a little intimidated.

"Good morning, Faron."

Talquist took a moment to catch his breath. The stairs to the tower room were steep, and the emperor was still recovering from the night before, which had been especially fine. As the borders of the empire continued to expand, the bedwenches supplied to him were growing in appeal, a fine variety of the most exceptional and beautiful captives from exotic places on the shipping routes and across the continent. Additionally, the captured liquid stock of the distilleries of Canderre and Argaut was even more plentiful, leading to more and more regular overindulgence of a different sort. And the successful fulfillment of his plans was giving him copious reason to celebrate.

Paying the price each following morning in the coin of headaches, mild nausea, and light sensitivity.

A minuscule price to pay, he thought as he stepped more fully into the room.

Good morning, Majesty. The shrill voice made Talquist's head feel as if it were about to cave in. *You smell of the horse that apparently shat on you as you slept beneath it.*

Talquist suppressed a belch. "Interesting that a stone nose is capable of smelling horse shit," he said as pleasantly as he could. "I believe this is a new development. I'm glad to see that you are evolving and becoming more and more—er—sophisticated each day."

He walked over to the massive map of the Known World inlaid in countless types of wood and displayed on the wall next to the window, the shipping lanes detailed in extraordinary accuracy. The sting of the wind through the aperture was dry and sandy, the fragrance of this desert land. For just a moment Talquist missed the tang of the sea wind he had been dreaming about a few moments before. He examined the map.

Each port, harbor, and trade stream was meticulously annotated with customized pins indicating shipping assets, military vessels, and product bound for market in all corners of the Known World. Talquist nodded, satisfied. Then he turned to the enormous globe that stood beside the map, the three-dimensional representation of those places he had marked on the wall.

"What's the good word this morning?" the emperor asked pleasantly.

He finally deigned to cast his sight to the other side of the window.

On that side of the round tower room stood an enormous statue, half again as tall as the tallest human man in his nation. Formed of Living Stone, once primitive and rough in its casting, the titan now resembled a natural-born soldier in all aspects but its massive size and the startling blue eyes that could occasionally be seen when it chose to display them.

Talquist was never certain, but it seemed to him that there was menace in those eyes that ran even deeper than the smirking tone the animated statue generally employed since recently finding its voice.

Hmmm. The good word. Any good word? This morning I think I'm liking "defenestration." The smirk widened into an almost menacing grin.

Talquist, who knew the definition of that word, stepped away from the window and glared at the titan.

"I'm not sure why you delight so in taunting me," he grumbled.

Maybe it is because I despise pretenders, said the titan lightly. *Perhaps to Sorbold now, and to the Known World soon enough, you are a godlike figure, immense in power with a reach that spans the endless sea. But you and I both know that you are merely a common man in a king's garments, limited in life span as you are in vision. You seek to eat the beating heart of the Child of Time for the purpose of making yourself immortal, while you ignore what is truly important in your own plans.*

"Toss me out the window then," said Talquist. "Hurl me from the parapet into the chasm below, if you are so intent on defenestration. See what becomes of you then, you arrogant pile of animated mud. You may be able to destroy any army that comes *at* you, but you will never be able to build an army to come *with* you to seek the Child of Earth that you crave to capture in the Bolglands. Do it. Defenestrate me. It will put an end to this headache and spare me from ever again having to listen to your voice, which makes the mating screams of alley cats sound like orchestral music by comparison."

Now, now, don't get peevish, said the stone statue. Its tone rang with amusement. *I said maybe. It is also possible that I actually like pretenders. I certainly have been willing to work with one long enough now.*

"Well, that is so very much more reassuring, thank you."

The look of amusement in the statue's blue eyes faded into something darker.

Do you wish me to continue to obscure your blockade or not?

Talquist sighed dispiritedly. "Yes, of course."

Then step aside. The gigantic titan walked forward as the emperor moved quickly out of the way until it was standing in front of the globe. It opened its hand.

Between the index and middle fingers was an oval object, slightly convex and tattered around the edges. At first glance it resembled a large piece of carapace, gray in color, otherwise unremarkable. But as the sunlight shining through the aperture came to rest on its surface, the object began to gleam with a blue radiance that skittered across its scored face.

Faron turned the object over, so that the concave side was ascendant.

Inscribed on that side was the primitive image of an eye occluded by clouds. Had he been holding it with the other side up, Talquist knew, a similar picture of an eye clear of similar clouds would be seen. Talquist was not certain what magic allowed the scale to see through disguises and over great distances when the convex side was employed, but he was grateful for its concave side's ability to obscure wide swaths of the world when passed over the map that had been made from ancient trees originating in the places detailed on it.

Knowing that it was a scale of an ancient dragon, he was hardly surprised at anything it could do.

Just as the violet-colored one in his own possession had made it possible to take the throne of Sorbold.

He watched, fascinated as always, as the titan exposed the concave side to the sunlight, then carefully moved it over the route his multitude of pirate ships, merchant vessels, and warships was following across the Known World, crippling the Middle Continent and isolating it from contact with the rest of an unknowing world.

As Faron applied the scale, it seemed to Talquist that mist, thick and white, formed along the pathway the titan drew across the map. From experience he knew that this was merely a sign that the powers of the scale were at work; as far as he knew, no real mist was hanging at that moment in the sea, literally obscuring his ships and their wares.

But it might as well have been.

By all accounts across the Known World, the only faction that was aware of his plans for the coast of the Middle Continent, which his navy had already summarily destroyed in a glorious display of military superiority and the aerial attack of iacxsis, were the surviving inhabitants of the Middle Continent themselves.

And they were in no condition to send out word to anyone beyond their broken and smoldering harbors.

The titan turned back to the emperor. The unsettling blue eyes looked down at him thoughtfully.

There you are, the statue said pleasantly. *One more day your plans are hidden from the sight of the world. Enjoy this day, Talquist. This is the last time I will undertake to use the blue scale in this manner.*

"What are you talking about?" the emperor demanded. "It is far too soon for the western reaches of the Known World to become aware of the blockade of the continent. The Diviner's armies of the north are not in place in the Middle Continent yet."

That is unfortunate. The titan's smile grew wider. *But I have no doubt a manipulator of your skill will be able to cope with this small setback. It is long past time, Talquist. I tire of leading your armies in pointless exercises. Had I been able to participate in the hurling of the orphans and infants into the sea at Nikkid'sar, that might have provided some momentary entertainment. But, like you, I seek a very important child. Unlike you, the child I seek will serve to benefit many, rather than just myself.*

"My immortality and yours are irretrievably tied together, Faron," Talquist said disdainfully. "I hate to keep having to remind you that without me, you would still be nothing more than a freakish glob of gelatinous goo, with a mouth fused in the center and gaping lips on either side, boneless and without the ability to stand, let alone lead an army on the Bolglands. It was I that harvested this magnificent body of Living Stone for you, that rigged the Scales to bring you into life within it. I have taught you everything you know, and yet you continue to threaten our alliance."

The towering statue looked down at him amusedly. *That's an interesting perspective on the world. Well, may it keep you warm at night. Goodbye, Talquist.*

"What—what you mean?" The emperor's swarthy face went suddenly pale.

It means that I am taking the fifth, eighth, and twelfth regiments, and marching on the Bolglands.

"No," Talquist stammered. "No. It is too early, Faron. Be patient. All will come to fruition in the appropriate time."

Well, you know what they say, said the titan. *There's no time like the Present. And that's especially true ever since you hurled the Seer Rhonwyn to her death out that very window into the great chasm below the tower. No time like the Present at all anymore. A shame, really. Your impatience has cost us a rather important tool that could have been used to achieve our ends. But no matter. Best of luck with your pursuit of immortality and earthly reign. May that keep you warm at night as well.*

"You—you can't possibly leave to take the mountains yet," Talquist whispered. "The scales must remain together—"

The statue smirked. *We can do that, by all means. Give me yours.*

The emperor drew back in horror.

I thought you'd see it my way.

"Faron," Talquist whispered, "what are you doing? We have an almost-complete set of the scales, only missing two for a complete spectrum! I have the violet scale of the New Beginning. All we need is a yellow and indigo—"

We do have a yellow, do we not? The titan's voice was wry and cracking with sarcasm. *Oh, wait, no, that's right—what you thought was a yellow dragon scale of ancient origin, a part of Sharra's Deck spared from the sea when the Island sank, for which we diverted our resources and risked our ultimate goals, turned out to be a* cookie, *didn't it? I do not have time for this, Talquist, for your pathetic plans, your endless quest for a longer life you do not deserve. I have the red, blue, orange, and green scales; they are more than sufficient to aid me in my quest. Which is going to begin right now.*

"Please—"

But just to be sporting, I will tell you what, Talquist—I'll give you one last reading through the blue scale.

The titan pulled out the scrying instrument again, which, like the others, had long ago been a scale in the hide of an ancient dragon, a gift given to save the Earth from just the sort of demonic beast that now resided within the statue of Living Stone. Faron held it up to his unnaturally blue eyes and stared at it, then moved it until it was in front of the Merchant Emperor.

Then he smiled broadly.

This is your lucky day, Talquist—there is a timely warning for you. The scale says that there are two assassins coming for you. Hmm. What is that expression again? Oh yes. Forewarned is forearmed. Very well, you've had your last reading ever from the scales in my deck. Best of luck with whomever is hunting you.

The titan turned to leave, blotting out the sun from the window as it did.

"Faron—"

With surprising alacrity for something of such great height and heft, the giant statue turned and glared down at the ruler of the Empire of the Sun with such surpassing hate in its searing blue eyes that Talquist had no choice but to leap away.

Be silent. The command was spoken in a voice shrill with menace, scratching against the emperor's eardrums. *Do not tempt me, Talquist. I have wanted to kill you from the moment I became aware of you. At best you are a colossal waste of time. At worst, you are in my way. And that is an utterly unacceptable place for you or anyone else to be. Now, for the last time, stand aside and I will see if I can restrain myself from pounding you through the granite floor of this tower. If you had any idea what a struggle that restraint is at this very moment, you would defenestrate yourself rather than risk being torn limb from limb alive.*

The emperor stepped rapidly out of the way.

The anger in the titan's eyes cooled somewhat, but the look of hate remained.

Wise choice. Goodbye.

A cruel shine glazed the look of hatred.

And, by the way, the name of the child you seek is Meridion. *If only you had a blue scale in your possession to find him with, now that you know it. Oh well.*

The giant stone statue turned its back on the emperor of Sorbold and hastily made its way with remarkable flexibility down the long staircase that led to the palace proper below.

As soon as its footsteps could no longer be heard echoing on the marble floors, Talquist's knees collapsed beneath him and he crumpled to the ground. He remained there, supporting himself with his hands, then made his way on his knees to the open window overlooking the deep canyon below the tower.

He could see the statue exiting the palace on the other side of the tower. In a voice that Talquist could not hear but that scraped against his skin nonetheless, even as high up as he was, Faron called for his chariot, a four-wheeled heavy cart drawn by a team of eight horses, and it was brought around.

As the stone monstrosity stepped into the cart and took the reins in its giant hands, it looked aloft one last time at the tower window a thousand feet above. Talquist could not be certain, but he had more than an inkling that a smile was decorating its face.

Then it slapped the reins against the backs of the horses and rolled out of sight.

8

Fhremus Alo'hari, supreme commander of the army of Sorbold, stepped off of the ascendant staircase and onto the polished floor of the second level of the palace of Jierna Tal.

As always, a sense of awe passed over him as he beheld the tens of thousands of candles in the giant chandeliers that lighted the towering ceilings of the hall, opening into beautiful rooms built of fine marble quarried from Sorbold's immense mines, appointed in glorious linen draperies and silk carpets, also a major product of export from the land. It never had ceased to amaze him, even from childhood, how many riches the All-God had blessed his native land with.

The Creator, he corrected himself, eschewing the name for the deity that had been used throughout the realm since his birth, recently replaced by law with an older title from the animist times of history, before the Cymrian landing, when the indigenous peoples who were his ancestors were the rulers of the empire.

His forebears.

And Talquist's.

"Fhremus! Oh, good, you're here! Excellent." The emperor's voice thudded against his eardrums, sounding nervous.

"Is everything all right, m'lord?" he asked, noting that Talquist's swarthy skin was flushed and sweating, his hair damp and his eyes gleaming in what appeared to be concern.

"No, Fhremus, no, everything is most certainly not all right," Talquist stammered. "I have it on good authority that two assassins, most likely from the Raven's Guild of Yarim or possibly from the Spider's Clutch of Golgarn, are on their way here at this very moment, intent on killing me."

Fhremus's forehead furrowed.

"On whose good authority, m'lord?" he asked. "I have seen no such briefings, and I made a very careful review of all your security, as well as the field reports, just before I came."

The emperor shook his head violently.

"No—no. I can assure you, the source of my information is irrefutable." He took out a handkerchief of fine Sorbold linen and wiped his perspiring brow. "I am glad you are here, Fhremus. If I recall, Hjorst has just been told to deploy from the Hintervold, and you are about to return to Sepulvarta for the next stage of the assault?"

"Yes, m'lord."

"Well, belay that order. Who was the young man who led the raid on the Abbey of Nikkid'sar?"

Fhremus tried to keep his lip from curling in disgust. "That would be Titactyk, m'lord."

"Well, elevate him in your absence for the time being. I need you here, beside me, in the palace, until these assassins have been captured. They know ways into Jierna Tal that may prevent them from being picked up by your security forces."

The supreme commander blinked in surprise.

"They—they do? How in the world would assassins have that sort of information?"

Talquist swallowed the answer that was about to fall out of his mouth—*because they have been here before, because I summoned them, because they have been in my hire on more than one occasion—because I am in league with them, and worse*—and coughed.

"I don't know, but as I have previously stated, the caliber of this intelligence is extreme. You are to remain with me, Fhremus, at all times, day and night, until they are apprehended. I am the emperor now; I deserve the best soldier in the realm as my guard."

"Yes, m'lord."

"Good." Talquist exhaled, letting loose of some of the panic that had gripped him. "So, set about making my defenses impenetrable. They may get in, but I obviously want to make certain that when they are here, they are unable to harm me."

"Of course, m'lord," Fhremus said. "No one would want that."

For the first time in his career as a soldier, he did not speak the truth to his superior.

9

THE CAULDRON, YLORC

Grunthor had walked through the entirety of the armory, the hallways of each of the forty levels of barracks, and the breastworks that lined the fields below the steppes of Ylorc, his Dhracian shadow in tow, and still had not managed to lose him. His intent had been to ensure that all of the new blunt weapons he had ordered had been manufactured and distributed, and had noted only five instances where the proper armaments were not in place. The offending parties who were not up to code were upbraided with threats so caustic that one of them, a Firbolg soldier of impressive accomplishment who had been commended for valor in a number of intense battles, had lost control of his water and urinated at the Sergeant-Major's feet.

Grunthor was delighted.

"Glad to know Oi still got it," he said to Rath as he left the barracks.

"Why have you taken their knives, the axes?" the Dhracian asked. "Their bolts?"

"Because what's comin' can't be taken out by anythin' sharp," Grunthor said, kicking his boots against a nearby wall to clear them of piss.

"No, but what is coming with him can be," Rath said, sidestepping the urine pool and following the Sergeant-Major up the passageway to the Great Hall.

"Pshtt," Grunthor scoffed. "Any army that comes is a diversion or a suicide mission, whether they knows it or not. My forces got that 'andled. They's just as competent with blunt objects and weapons as with slashers, some o' them, like the Guts clans, even more so. Whatever Talquist's armies get 'it with, they'll bleed, poor bastards. Sad thing is they prolly think they're dyin' fer king and country. Oh well."

He opened the recently repaired golden door that had been crushed in the explosion that had taken down Gurgus, the mountaintop that hovered in the peaks above the Great Hall, in a rain of boulders and picric acid, the final gift of the mistress of the Raven's Guild in Yarim when she had infiltrated Ylorc. Grunthor strode inside, Rath behind him.

They crossed the vast hall in silence except for the thudding echoes of Grunthor's boots on the polished floors, beautifully inlaid with mosaic tiles, passing the thrones of Canrif where Gwylliam and Anwyn, the first Lord and Lady Cymrian, had held court eleven centuries before, until finally they came to a small room behind the dais on which the thrones stood.

That room contained a glass funicular of a sort which transported passengers between floors by means of a system of ropes, next to which a redundant staircase stood, connecting the floors by more traditional means.

"Oi 'ope bein' in the Lightcatcher ain't gonna bring back any bad mem'ries fer you," Grunthor said as they ascended the stairs. "You was in pretty bad shape when we carried you in there last."

"Indeed, thank you for your efforts on my behalf," said the Dhracian, as if the effort to speak was painful.

"Oh, our pleasure, indeed," Grunthor said smugly, with a wide grin. He led Rath through the massive room that housed the instrumentality to the far side, where a long, broad window looked out onto the breastworks of the steppes and the Krevensfield Plain beyond.

"Omet," he called. "You 'round?"

From the shadows of the round tower's exterior, a young human man emerged, wearing a full beard and a weary expression. Omet was the Archon of the Lightcatcher, the only one of Achmed's elite council that was not Firbolg.

He had been a slave child working in the forges of the tile foundry run by the Raven's Guild in Yarim when Rhapsody and Achmed had rescued him, destroying an important tunnel the guildmistress was building under the streets of the city, looking to commandeer water from the obelisk of Entudenin. The thwarting of Esten's plot had given the Bolglands a master tilemaker and grateful worker, who had followed Rhapsody's advice to him to the letter.

Go carve your name into the unforgiving mountains for the world to see.

It had also provided the province of Yarim with life-giving water that was, even now, rejuvenating the drought-stricken region.

"Here, sir," Omet said. He nodded to the Dhracian, who was the only other person to be healed as he had been, with the aid of the Lightcatcher in its new incarnation through the red light of the color spectrum.

"Good. Oi came to check in before we deploy."

"Deploy?" Omet looked suddenly nervous. "Where are you going, sir?"

The tusked smile of the Bolg sergeant grew wider. "Well, that all depends on what you tell me, Oi suppose."

He walked back to the instrumentality and looked up to the dome above, set in the peak of Gurgus, the highest of the mountain peaks within the Teeth, surmounted in height only by Grivven Peak, the towering mountain at the tip of the range that stretched out in a peninsula-like configuration at the very edge of the steppes leading down to the Krevensfield Plain. Grivven served as a watchtower to the west, and an oversight post for the breastworks, a series of inground tunnels that scored the Krevensfield Plain itself, where the Bolg routinely ran incursions at the border of their lands.

The dome in Gurgus Peak was a perfect circle, divided meticulously into seven sections, each of which was inlaid in heavy glass, each in one of the seven colors in the light spectrum. The dome was perched above a table, an altar of a sort, above which an enormous, multifaceted diamond had been suspended.

Encircling the table at a distance of approximately thirty feet was a circular track on which a large metal wheel stood on its side, scored with holes that, when the wheel was moving, emitted different pitches of sound. It was an instrumentality Achmed had named the Lightcatcher, redesigned and rebuilt from drawings of a similar instrumentality that Gwylliam the Visionary had installed in Gurgus Peak more than a thousand years before, powered by a flamewell vent to the fire at the heart of the Earth. Achmed had objected to the use of that power source, knowing the risks it posed, and instead redesigned the instrumentality by making use of the sun as the source of its energy instead, either timed to shine through individual glass panes as it made its way across the sky, or storing its light in the diamond.

Grunthor had been privy to the use of the Lightcatcher on several occasions. The first was the use of the red section of the spectrum to heal Rath's horrific injuries sustained in a Thrall ritual gone wrong.

The ancient demon hunter had trapped a F'dor in the complex web of tonal attack when he had been assaulted by a stone titan that had rescued the demon at the very last moment. The attack had injured Rath to the point of death on a physical and metaphysical level; only the Dhracian's ability to navigate favorable gusts of wind, which returned him to Ylorc and the Lightcatcher's power of healing, had spared his life.

Grunthor had also stood at the table beneath the diamond at night and watched as Rhapsody used the stored light within the stone through the blue spectrum to scry into Lianta'ar, the basilica dedicated to the element of ether in the currently occupied, formerly holy city-state of Sepulvarta to the southwest of the Bolglands, on the northern border of the nation of Sorbold.

He, along with Achmed, Rhapsody, and Constantin, the exiled Patriarch of Sepulvarta, had witnessed acts of defilement taking place on the basilica's high altar, including the human sacrifice of the basilica's own sexton to obtain an augury that told Talquist what he needed to know to gain the immortality he was seeking above all other goals on his ambitious and bloody agenda. The answer to his question had caused the Lady Cymrian to quake with fear.

It involved the eating of her infant son's beating heart.

Grunthor had never been fond of the concept of magic in any configuration. His truest confidence was placed in the ring of steel against bone, of strength, planning, and skill against that of a foe, toe-to-toe, in glorious, bloody battle, something the race of his mother, the Bengard, a gigantic breed of oily-skinned desert dwellers who celebrated the preparation for war in gladiatorial arenas, had engendered in him. But having seen the Lightcatcher in use, and having been forewarned of plans that they would otherwise never have had an inkling of until they were in the fray, he was beginning to see it as useful, to understand Achmed's obsession with this ancient machine that had kept the armies of Anwyn, Gwylliam the Visionary's hated spouse, at bay from the mountains for almost five hundred of the seven hundred years' war.

Being a fond godfather to Rhapsody's son, Meridion, he was particularly happy to have advance notice of anything nefarious planned against the baby.

"Do you know 'ow to use this thing to look into places, see what's goin' on in 'em?" he asked Omet.

The Archon shook his head.

"I can set it up, calibrate it," he said. "I have the calculations as to when the sun will be in the right place to use individual elements of the spectrum. I can even deploy the wheel to make use of the musical tone that is needed to blend with the light in order to make the Lightcatcher function. But I have no knowledge of true names or an understanding of how to scry.

"A Namer, or someone with the Right of Command, like a king or a benison, usually is needed for something like that. I imagine Gwylliam used it himself when he was defending these mountains against Anwyn; he certainly knew her true name, as did the rest of the world. So scrying is something above my pay grade, sir. Anyone can use the red spectrum for healing, if they time it right, however.

"When I was healed after the mistress of the Raven's Guild poisoned me, all Shaene and Rhur had to do was put me on the table in the light from the red section of the spectrum." The young man's voice caught in his throat; Grunthor was silent for a moment in the knowledge that those two glass artisans had been crushed to death a moment afterward, when the glass dome had exploded, having been trapped with picric acid by the guildmistress.

Whom he had already beheaded at the time.

"Is there anythin' else you know 'ow to make it do?"

Omet considered.

"His Majesty has banned the use of the yellow and orange spectra, which affect fire, heat, and light, in all but dire emergencies, because their use is still experimental. He has ruled out the use of the Indigo section, known as Night Stayer, and the violet, the New Beginning, altogether, because there is no information in the literature about how they were applied except to warn of the wide-ranging and potentially dangerous risks of their misapplication."

Grunthor was counting.

"What about the green? Constantin made use o' that when the Duchess, the king, an' Oi were ambushed by assassins in the meadow at Kraldurge. They was 'idden in ways we neva' would o' seen 'em, except that the green light appeared and 'Is Majesty took 'em out as if they was standin' right in front o' us."

Omet exhaled.

"I'm not sure how to scry in grass, which is the negative aspect, the flat of the green note, through the Lightcatcher," he said, somewhat nervously. "I did, however, see the Patriarch apply the positive, the sharp, which is translated as Grass Hider. He used it to shield Rhapsody and the women she traveled with to the Deep Kingdom of the Nain, as much as possible. That I might be able to do; it's not an exact application. I could set it to green sharp, *Kurh-fa*, and put it on a continuous cycle. I'm not sure if that will help confuse or misdirect any attack that's coming, but it's the only other thing I can think to do."

"Unnerstood. If Oi'm not mistaken, that was 'ow Gwylliam kept Anwyn out—and if that's the case, Oi see no reason not to give it a try. We're gonna need every bit of 'elp we can muster."

"So, now that I've answered, where do you plan to deploy?" Omet asked nervously.

The Sergeant-Major looked at him seriously, his large amber eyes solemn beneath the grassy brown hair on his head.

"Every single soldier will be on full guard across the kingdom, and we're gonna need every bloody one o' them," he said, his face a mask. "If, as we think, Talquist is sendin' the titan you saw in the forest of Navarne, Rath, to find the Earthchild, he can strike anywhere—'e's not bringin' the army for that. It's a distraction, to keep us engaged, while 'e finds a way in."

The Dhracian nodded.

"But 'ere," the Sergeant said cheerfully, digging something out of his pocket. "Maybe this'll 'elp."

Rath looked at the object in Grunthor's hand.

It was a pick hammer in the same configuration as the one the Sergeant had been forging earlier, only a tiny fraction of the size.

"What is this for?"

"It's a weapon," Grunthor said indignantly.

"Hardly. I don't need this."

"Whaddaya mean, ''ardly'? It's a perfeckly nice pick 'ammer, an' Oi imagine you know 'ow to to use it—well, *anyone* know's 'ow, ya smack whatever ya can. Aim for 'is rocks, if you can forgive the play on words."

"Actually, that was fairly unforgivable." The words were spokenly flatly, without humor.

Grunthor looked solemnly at the Dhracian.

"Ya got a dagger. You may as well 'ave a weapon o' last resort. You an' me, Rath—we are gonna be right in the doorway to 'er chambers, right in the eye o' the storm, shall we say—'cause we don't got no other choice. You an' me—*we* are the last resort, the final fallback. Which means it's all up ta us in the end. Half a million Bolg may 'old the line—but we will be in the teeth of it, whenever it comes. An' if we fail, that's all she wrote. The game's over, and there won't be nothin' left. Nothin' in this world, and the next."

The Dhracian nodded again. He had already known that as well.

10

The moon had risen at last. Wrapped in fog and brittle clouds that raced across the cold sky, breaking apart in their passage, it floated at the horizon, hovering over a night that seemed to grow bright as day within moments of its rising.

The Icemen of the Hintervold had gathered at the edge of the fjord in response to the call of the gyldenhorn, a long and deep-bowled instrument known for its deep, resounding voice and capability of piercing even the thickest night wind. When the horn sounded, it took less than the time it had taken for the sun to descend one hand of sky for them to assemble, clad in the heavy furs and leather armor that provided warmth as well as dark cladding, shielding them from ordinary sight.

The Icemen were quiet warriors. In their realm of endless winter nights and unnaturally long summer days that left outsiders feeling itchy and unnerved, they remained year-round, living silently off what the land could provide them in winter, harvesting the bounty of the forests and towering mountains in summer.

The residents of the Hintervold that inhabited cities were cousins to these men. They shared the same ancestors, the same empty history, the same love of the cold. The sparse city dwellers, unlike their self-sufficient cousins, had come to rely on other parts of the Known World to provide them with food to span the short growing seasons, bad weather, and years when the animal herds were elusive. Their reliance had proved to be their undoing now.

A leader in a nation south of the Riverlands had violated his trust, had interrupted their shipments of grain and foodstuffs, poisoned them with rat droppings, mold, and toxic substances that caused many of the women of the Hintervold to lose their babies in the womb, children to starve, and men to grow sick and die. The righteous wrath of the survivors had built into a growing storm that was completely natural.

It was just aimed at the wrong leader.

The gyldenhorn sounded again. In answer, glaciers calved in the distance, raining hillsides of snow and ice down into the dark valleys below.

As if of one mind, the Icemen turned in the direction of its call.

Standing at the rise of the tallest swale on the fjord stood a man clad in a robe of heavy polar-bear fur, a leather hat with a carved matching representation of the ursine beast crowning his head. His magnificent beard, gray and curling at the ends, hung down almost to his waist, and his black eyes were crowned with equally dark brows. In his hand was a staff with a horizontal crossbeam of blackthorn sharpened to points at the ends.

Hjorst. The Diviner of the Hintervold.

Although one side of the Diviner's line was descended from the same Cymrian refugees from which their hated foe had come, he was also a descendant of an even more ancient indigenous people, ice dwellers who had lived in the cold mountains and frozen seas of the Hintervold for a thousand years before the Cymrians even thought to leave their doomed island homeland.

His primitive bearing and warlike demeanor belied the fact that he had been educated in the modern capital of Marincaer half a world away, a place where he had grown fond of elegant potables, whiskeys, brandies, and rums from the finest distilleries in the world, as well as flaky pastries, fresh fruit, and dainty finger sandwiches with the crusts cut off.

But even if he had been modernized in his education and experiences, the Diviner's heart belonged to the primeval earth. He not only loved this glistening land of almost year-round snow and ice, where elk, mountain goats, and tirabouri wandered the permafrost in thunderingly gentle herds, but he believed unwaveringly in the animist beliefs and sacred rituals of the earth that were practiced by these people.

Bloody, uncultured, and violent as some of them might be.

As he stood atop the rise, the Diviner looked down for a long moment at the troops gathering at his feet. The cold of winter had abated; Second Thaw was here now, the earliest days of spring which the more southerly parts of the continent had been enjoying for several months. With the spring came the melting of the barriers that the Icemen carried around inside them. They were stoic in the winter, a time when anger or distress cost more energy than it was worth, but in spring the blood ran close to the surface, spinning rivers of rage and the lust for vengeance in their hearts and bodies.

As it was running now.

Quiet as they were, the Diviner could feel the black anger building on the fjord in front of him.

An anger he shared.

Hjorst had not undertaken a specific divination to confirm the circumstances over which he was about to launch bloodshed. Divinations were only safely performed at Yule, in the depths of a frozen winter, when the sacred teachings were proscribed, for divination in any other time was considered risky at best, and at worst, offensive to the animist spirits.

It was a gift to be able to access knowledge that one's own senses were not entitled to by the spilling of blood; to expect to be able to do it on a whim was arrogant and insulting to nature. The Diviner had already bent the rules by performing divination at the turn of spring for a friend, the recently crowned emperor of Sorbold. He did not wish to anger nature and the upcoming war by spilling blood intentionally for other reasons, even if they were sacred ones.

In the back of his mind he recalled the divination of Yule at the beginning of this past year. It had warned direly of treachery, but the specifics were uncertain. The only hint that the holy augury had offered was that the traitor to his nation was one who presented himself in the guise of a friend. Hjorst had immediately guessed who the only person was to which the augury could apply.

Gwydion of Manosse.

The Lord Cymrian, the leader of the Alliance to which the Hintervold was a friendly confederate, though not a member, spanning the vast bulk of the Middle Continent.

And who, by circumstance, was therefore the holder of the majority of the grainfields and vineyards, orchards and foodstuffs of most of the continent.

The Lord Cymrian himself had traveled to the Hintervold to offer the friendship of the Alliance upon his investiture, bringing with him his new wife, a woman of surpassing beauty and wisdom. She was herself trained and experienced in agriculture, having been responsible for the rehabilitation and expansion of the vineyards, rice bogs, and vegetable fields of the realm of Ylorc, where the first-era Cymrians had built their great civilization, Canrif, a thousand or more years before.

In addition to making suggestions that had been implemented with great success in the sparse farms and hatcheries of the Hintervold, the Lady Cymrian had offered songs of growing and harvesting which had helped the Riverlands, the only part of the Hintervold with reliably tillable soil, produce crops with almost double the yield. The Lord Cymrian had offered a tariffless delivery of grain and other foodstuffs as a sign of friendship to help the Hintervold recover from some of its worst droughts that had occurred over the previous three years.

Hjorst was a man who took such offers reverently and seriously. The Hintervold valued its independence enough to be judicious in accepting contracts or partnerships. The violation of a promise of peace and friendship with the Hintervold was an offense of deep insult and threat, one that could not be overlooked the way the provinces of the Middle Continent and the nations of Ylorc, the Bolglands, and Undervale, the mountainous realm of the Nain far to the east, had forgiven the ancestors of these new leaders, put old enmities aside, and reunited.

But there was such sincerity in the visage of the two handsome leaders of the Cymrian Alliance that he could not overcome the way his heart rose in hope at their offer of peace and friendship. Hjorst, by nature a skeptic almost from birth, put his nagging doubts aside and signed on as a friend of the new Alliance.

So when the shipments of grain did not arrive on time, or did not arrive at all, the Diviner was enraged. When the ones that did arrive were laden with poison or rat feces, or showed signs of widespread mold, and his communiqués to the Lord Cymrian demanding explanation were met with silence, the Diviner could not stand by in similar silence.

Not when his people were being starved.

And not when he had learned that the Alliance was secretly planning to attack and annex the Riverlands at the end of spring. It sickened Hjorst to realize that the tour he had given the Lord and Lady had merely been a scouting trip for them, which he had supplied and hosted.

He had clandestinely thrown in his lot with the leaders of two other nations who had each been similarly injured by the deceitful leaders—Beliac, the king of Golgarn, whose southern coastlands shared a northern border with the Bolglands, who had discovered his lands were about to be invaded by the Firbolg, also signatories to the Alliance. Beliac had an almost obsessive fear of being devoured by the Firbolg who had been his distant neighbors for five hundred years, and had been relieved to find friends among the enemies of the Bolg.

And Talquist, the regent of Sorbold, about to be crowned emperor, who himself had been betrayed by the Lord and Lady, though in the back of his mind, Hjorst had still not completely put the pieces of that betrayal together.

Talquist's taking of the holy city-state of Sepulvarta, an independent nation between the borders of Sorbold to the south and Roland in the Cymrian Alliance to the north, had been confusing to the Diviner, even after he and Beliac had been given a carefully guided tour by the emperor himself.

But it didn't matter.

If revenge was not struck soon, if action was not taken, within the short growing season the Riverlands would belong to the Alliance, and all foodstuffs to his mysterious and ancient land would be gone.

In the gutteral tongue of their indigenous forefathers, the Diviner spoke.

As with most other things the Icemen undertook, there was silence. Unlike the armies of the men to the south, there were no war screams, no roars of approval, no shouted cheers in response to their leader's quiet commands.

The place, the fjord where they had chosen for centuries to meet was a natural amplifier; the Diviner's words, spoken in his gravel-toned voice, solemn, stern, and with deadly intent, made their way through the permafrost itself, through the soft leather boots wrapped around their legs and feet and tied with rawhide, permeating each individual soul.

So that every man present heard and understood him without question.

We leave, this night, to destroy those that are killing our people and our land.

Even in silence there was unanimous consent.

The Diviner's instructions and Rule of Engagement were clear: no women were to be raped, no children were to be killed if at all possible. Any material goods, spoils of war, were to be gathered by commanders and returned to the central command center behind Hyvensfalt glacier, where they would be sorted through and distributed as needed.

When the specifics of the attack had been laid out, the Diviner summed up his commands with a final spoken thought.

"The Lord Cymrian, Gwydion of Manosse, is a liar and a traitor. Despite professing his friendship and support in alliance to us, he has undertaken to starve and kill our people. The evidence of this is clear. He who finds this man and returns him alive to me will find entrance to the Afterlife upon death. Anyone who brings me his body or a recognizable part thereof shall be rewarded handsomely in this life.

"May the moon hide you from the enemy. May the Earth give you strength. Should you die, die bravely."

In silence, each Iceman raised his arm in assent.

From the rise, looking down at the fingers of seawater reaching into the coastland of the fjord, Hjorst thought, they looked like a vast and innumerable forest of strong trees, pointing to the sky.

Then, just as silently, they turned, thirty thousand strong, and began their long journey over the warming permafrost to the Riverlands in the south.

And beyond.

WESTERN PASS, KRI'SAN PROVINCE, SORBOLD

One hundred seventy leagues away, in an entirely different clime, an entirely different set of circumstances, similar instructions were being given, though they varied in several critical places.

Titactyk, second-in-command of the western division of the army of Sorbold, was indulging in the exact opposite of the Diviner's vocal artistry.

Upon receiving his orders from Jierna Tal on the day prior elevating him to command of the first through fourth divisions of the imperial army of Sorbold, Titactyk had crowed with delight, startling the soldiers who were standing nearby.

The orders were dated effective the next day, so their new commander-to-be had immediately encouraged any of them willing to do so to join him for some celebratory rambles. As many of the soldiers in his presence at that moment had been part of the division that he had led, along with the stone titan sent to accompany them by the emperor, to the Abbey of Nikkid'sar, where the wanton rape and murder of the women and children of the sanctuary, the sodomizing of the abbess, and the flinging of the eleven infants present into the sea via catapult had all been a sanctioned part of their mission, there were few that did not enthusiastically follow him off into the flesh markets of the province in which they were quartered, awaiting deployment.

"Men, it is our mission tonight to prevent the rampant robbery that has been happening across the city," Titactyk called in great exaggeration from the back of the wagon in which the rabble had ensconced him, a skin of wine in each of his hands. "Women's purses have been stolen in broad daylight, if you can imagine that! Let us be certain that we not only keep those purses from being taken, but that we spend as much of our coin in them as it is possible to ram in there!"

Raucous laughter and hooting cheers followed his wagon up the street.

One of those who did not choose to join in the merriment toasting Titactyk's new promotion was the nephew of the man who still officially held that post.

Kymel Alo'hari Fyn, a young lieutenant in the second division, was the son of Fhremus's sister and the fifth generation in the family to serve the Empress Leitha, whose passing had elevated Talquist to the Sun Throne. Kymel had been a zealous soldier, following proudly in his uncle's footsteps.

Until the raid on Nikkid'sar.

Now the young lieutenant, who had been a pleasant conversationalist, generous to his fellow soldiers about taking unpopular shifts and duties, and proud of his service to the royal house of Sorbold, had gone quiet and taciturn, appearing occasionally hollow-eyed and unkempt, though he was still reliable in arriving on time for muster and completing any duties assigned to him in a satisfactory manner.

Kymel had confided the details of the raid on the abbey to his horrified uncle, had interrupted Fhremus's subsequent rantings about execution and courts-martial to assure Fhremus that the unit had been acting under the direct orders of the emperor to leave no inhabitant of the abbey alive, even knowing that its purpose was to be a sanctuary for the poorest and most vulnerable of the continent's children.

Upon bearing witness to Fhremus's own shock, Kymel had gone mostly silent, responding regularly, if slowly, to questions and commands, but otherwise keeping to himself.

Fhremus, delayed in Jierna Tal, had tried to find a way to keep a quiet surveillance on his nephew, but to no avail. *There are no secrets for long in the army* went one of the most common expressions in military rapport, and to be seen as overseeing or providing special treatment for a family member was one of the most dangerous games that could be played. The supreme commander did not have enough experience or connections to do so without endangering Kymel even more, so he kept his distance and continued to pray silently to the All-God for his nephew's safety, an action that in itself was punishable as treason by the crown if the authorities were aware of it.

So on the eve of deployment into battle, a few short weeks after the rout in the fields of Roland just north of Sepulvarta that the unit had already experienced, Kymel was sitting alone on the rampart of the city wall, staring north.

He knew the next day would bring a muster, a palpable excitement in which he would be expected to partake enthusiastically. He had already overheard Titactyk practicing his call to arms, his rhetoric of defense of the nation and retribution for wrongs perpetrated on Sorbold by the Cymrian Alliance and its leaders, the Lord and Lady Cymrian, his inflammatory speech designed to whip the soldiers of the first through fourth divisions into a frenzy of war-hate and rage, exploding into violence of both sanctioned and unsanctioned kinds.

It would certainly be effective, he knew.

What he did not know was what *he* would do upon witnessing it.

Kymel watched the sun burning orange on its way down the welkin of the sky to the horizon.

Wishing to be anywhere than where he was.

11

IN THE DEEP KINGDOM OF THE NAIN, UNDERVALE, NORTHEASTERN MOUNTAINS

*L*ady Melisande Navarne, all of ten years old, stretched wearily and yawned.

This day, like each day, had been long and dark, even with the luminescence of the sconces that brought the equivalent of daylight into the underground kingdom built into the forbidding mountains beyond the Teeth, north of the Bolglands, that she was now residing in.

At the very end of the world, as far as Melisande was concerned.

Logically, she was very glad to be where she was, happy that her life was what it was, given what she assumed was going on in the world beyond those mountains.

But as time passed, as the days went on, as she assumed they did in the world outside, Melisande was growing bored.

Boredom was not a bad thing, she reasoned. Safety and boredom went hand in hand for her these days, unlike her recent exploits, which were exciting but highly dangerous.

She had been sent into the Great Forest by her adoptive grandmother, Rhapsody, the Lady Cymrian, on a mission to discover what had happened to the dragon Elynsynos, an ancient being of legendary stature and a beloved friend to Rhapsody. Elynsynos's terrifying rampages had been recorded in famous ballads like *The Rampage of the Wyrm* and *The Burning Fields,* epic songs studied by every Cymrian child. Melisande, who in her heart had craved excitement tinged with danger from a very young age, had discovered that the fantasy of dangerous adventure and the reality of it were very different.

Even though, if the truth be told, she had enjoyed a good deal of it.

And was even more grateful to have survived it.

After agreeing to accept Rhapsody's offer of the mission, she had been packed into a carriage, surrounded by soldiers from her brother's forces, and sent under guard due west to the Great Forest with the ultimate destination of a sacred, untrod area north of the Tar'afel River known as Gwynwood. She was expecting to be looking for Gavin the Invoker, a man she had never met but who was known to be the religious leader of the biggest population of believers on the continent, those nature worshippers called the Filids, numbering more than three million.

Instead, Gavin had found her.

She had not recognized him when she met him after her carriage was attacked by highwaymen and set on fire. She had been lost in the virgin wood and wandering helplessly, just a few days short of her tenth birthday. She had thought him a vagrant, at best a forester, and had traveled grudgingly with him to what turned out to be his own center of power, the Circle, the central place of religious observance for the nature priests of the Filidic order.

Only to discover that he was their leader.

Gavin had guided her successfully from the Great White Tree to the sacred lands where Elynsynos's cave was reputed to be, then let her go on alone as the Lady Cymrian had instructed them. She had found the dragon's lair, had entered it bravely, in her own opinion, only to find it empty, with no sign of the beast.

But at least she had been able to find Krinsel, a Bolg midwife who had been badly injured in a battle of dragons between Elynsynos and her vicious daughter, Anwyn. The sight, upon discovering her, of the midwife's eye, white like a poached egg, still haunted Melisande's dreams.

So while she had been able to rescue the midwife, instruct Gavin to seal the dragon's cave as Rhapsody had ordered, and make it back safely to Highmeadow where her brother and the Lord Cymrian were waiting for her, planning to send her off again, Melisande could not help but feel like a failure.

Especially since immediately thereafter she had been packed off on a journey to the Nain mountains, mostly for her own safety in the upcoming war, but also because she was accompanying Rhapsody's oldest friend in the world, a First Generation Cymrian named Analise, and the Bolg midwife she had rescued, who was being sent for healing to the Lady Cymrian herself, who herself was planning on going into hiding with her baby in the Nain mountains.

Melisande's tenth year of life so far had therefore consisted of missions into forests, over mountainous terrain, witnessing yet another dragon battle between Rhapsody and Anwyn in the steppes that led up to the Nain kingdom, and observing an impressive negotiation with Witheragh, a wyrm with a sour attitude who guarded the entrance to the Nain kingdom on the other side of the Molten River. In the presence of four of the most impressive women she had known in her life, Melisande had loved her travels, had loved being of aid to her adoptive grandmother and her little cousin, who, in spite of being very young, was already fun to play with.

And being allowed to explore the kingdom of the Nain with its very own princess was an opportunity that no one she had ever heard of had been granted.

It therefore seemed petty and selfish to be missing the excitement of the outside world after settling into a routine of tending to the baby, attending to her studies, and listening to tales of the three women in her company. Melisande had been raised by an extraordinary father, a cheerful and selfless man named Stephen Navarne who had taught her to be grateful and appreciative of all she had, so in her own mind she was quite possibly the luckiest child in the world.

But that didn't keep her from feeling bored.

"Busy?"

Melisande jumped.

Smiling down at her was one of her fellow caretakers of Meridion, Analise o Serendair. Like Krinsel, Analise was a midwife, and had a fondness for children, so of the three women who were sharing quarters with her, she was the easiest to be with.

"No, not at all," she said quickly, putting her unread book aside. "Can I help with something?"

"Hmmm. Indeed I think you can. Come with me."

Melisande stood and smoothed out her skirts before following Analise up the corridor.

The ancient Liringlas woman led the little girl out of their section of tunneled hallways, where guards stood watch constantly, out of the palace, and into the streets of the capital city within the mountains.

At the north end of the town, a tributary of the watercourse of fiery lava known as the Molten River ran through the rocky interior walls, at the edge of the granite streets. A huge natural stone bridge crossed the river, and today it was packed with children, giggling and pointing into the molten liquid that was moving quickly along the riverbed, shining so brightly that it cast shadows all the way to the towering ceiling of rock above them.

"What's going on?" Melisande asked Analise in alarm.

Analise smiled. "To the north of here, there apparently be a waterfall—or, more accurately, a firefall that is calving."

"Calving?"

"Breaking apart, splitting the rocks with its extra force today. And I believe many of the rocks that have spilled into the river have been causing some amusement to the children of the kingdom."

"Why? Why would that be funny?"

The elderly woman smiled.

"Well, I still be struggling with the pronunciation of their language, but if I be translating it correctly, I believe that quite a number of the floating rocks resemble buttocks."

"Buttocks? You mean like—"

"Yes."

"Really?" Melisande suppressed a giggle.

"Aye, big fat ones, if I'm translating correctly. Sticking up in the river, waggling themselves at the palace. Occasionally making some fairly horrifying noises, probably from the release of gas from the calving. Would you like to go see?"

"Well—I suppose so. Are you coming too?"

"I think not," said Analise, smiling broadly. "I think my presence would cause the Nain children to scatter, and that would be a shame. But I think that you would be welcome."

"You do?"

"I think so. There be nothing like sharing a good joke to aid in making friends quickly. And what be a better joke than a river full of rocky butts and fat fannies bobbing in liquid fire and farting?"

Melisande burst into laughter. "I can't imagine one."

"Nor can I," said Analise. "I will wait here for you. Go to the bridge, and see if you can catch sight of a few hindquarters in the river. Perhaps you can make a few new friends as well." She winked. "Hopefully those things will be easy to tell apart."

Melisande gave the woman a quick hug and hurried off to the bridge, where, after a few moments of initial surprise, the Nain children rapidly made room for her. She spent almost an hour among them, giggling madly and pointing to particularly plump posteriors as they floated by in the Molten River.

When finally the parade of posteriors appeared to be over, she returned to Analise, who, as promised, was waiting where Melisande had left her.

"I take it the calving be over? Did you see many passing posteriors going under the bridge?"

Melisande nodded, grinning. "There was an enormous one with dimples that was making strange and grotesque sounds as it passed under the bridge. If I understood him, and I'm not sure that I did, but one little boy seemed to think it looked a lot like his father's. Apparently it sounded like his as well."

"Was that the best?"

"Undeniably."

"Well, I be sorry to have missed it. Why don't you tell me all about it on the way back to our rooms? It be almost time for my shift, and once we be back, you can regale Princess Gyllian and Krinsel with tales of your exploits."

Melisande slipped her hand inside the crook of her elderly friend's arm.

"I think not. They have been on diapering duty for the last several hours. They may have seen all the buttocks they wish to already today."

BENEATH THE WAVES OF THE WIDE CENTRAL SEA

*A*nd then, on one afternoon just like every other afternoon since he entered the ocean, Ashe heard a sound.

In the ever-present noise of the sea, the sound was faint; had Kirsdarke itself not made note of it, he never would have been aware of it. But there was something ancient and devastating in its call, a sadness that could not be measured, a pain that reached down into his heart and broke it.

He willed himself to take on more form, more heft than his vaporous body had held since entering the waves, and, with renewed strength and muscle, kicked down to the ocean floor below him.

The diffuse light of the sun hovered in the water and lit the undersea for a hundred fathoms or so. Below that bright realm was a realm of twilight, dark water in which visibility was all but impossible, even for the Kirsdarkenvar.

Ashe closed his eyes, following the call he felt through the hilt of the sword down into the darkness.

The ocean floor was not too far below the end of the realm of light. The rippling blade of the elemental sword of water glowed blue in the gloom as Ashe crossed the threshold into the twilight. He held Kirsdarke aloft and searched the sandy bottom of the sea, ghostly in the sword's light.

At first there was little of note; pale fish darted away from the glow, scattering into the shadows, leaving nothing but the emptiness of the open sea. Ashe's eyes scanned the sandy ocean floor, scored with deep ridges and dotted with seaweed waving in the drift.

The mournful noise hung in the water, echoing weakly.

Ashe followed it.

There was a familiarity to the tone, which seemed almost impossible in the vast breadth of the ocean through which he was walking. And yet it called to a memory deep in his brain, something long before his own birth that existed in the blood of those like him, cursed by Fate to be born into families of immense power and ridiculous longevity.

He cast a net of thought back into the past to see if he could find a connection to that sound.

And, after a moment, thought he might have.

Then went utterly cold at the possibility.

Gods, he thought. *Oh gods.*

For a moment he hesitated speaking the name, fearful that to do so would make the being even more vulnerable than it appeared in the depths of its rocky shelter. Then he shook his head to fend off the shock that was dulling his senses; any word he could thrum down in the depths as he was, away from the light of the sunwater, would drown in the weight of the ocean.

And, if he was right in his assessment, there was little more that could be done to destroy it than had already been done.

The occluded light glowed dully in the darkness of the Twilight Realm.

Ashe hovered in the heavy drift, the rippling blue waves of light from Kirsdarke splashing over what lay at the bottom of the sea. Finally, words came to the forefront of his mind.

Great-Grandmother? he whispered in thought. *Elynsynos?*

Only the echo of the all-but-infinite water answered him.

12

ON THE ROAD EAST TOWARD CANRIF,
WESTERN SORBOLD

As the titan's chariot rolled along the road, followed by the mounted fifth, eighth, and twelfth regiments of the army of Sorbold, an inner conversation was taking place within the enormous body of Living Stone, inaudible to anyone around it.

Even if the words and thoughts that were being exchanged within the body of the titan were spoken aloud, in the free wind, they still could not reasonably be expected to be heard over the clatter of the horses' hooves, the shouted orders, the creak of the wagon wheels, and the lumbering of the wagons themselves along the primitive road. Even on the smoother, more sophisticated trans-Orlandan thoroughfare which bisected the continent farther to the north across the lands of the Middle Continent, noise was unavoidable in the passing of a caravan of that size.

But the conversation had no chance of being overheard primarily because the entities undertaking it were formless beings, traveling together in the stone body.

The secondary traveler was a far more ancient and powerful being than the first. A F'dor spirit named Hrarfa, a member of the Older Pantheon of demons born in the Before-Time of the world, by rights was the senior of the two residents of the body, but circumstance did not allow for the dominance of her intent. She had lost her host body a number of months before when she had been so unfortunate as to have come across a Dhracian; she had been caught in the Thrall ritual that was the death knell for her kind, and as her host body expired, leaving her spirit formless and on the brink of dissipation, the titan had come into her presence.

Seeking another of its kind.

The spirit who actually occupied the body was an entity called a Faorina, one of the rarest forms of being in history. It was the child of a F'dor demon who had willingly allowed the breaking open of his spirit in order to procreate during the brutal rape of an Ancient Seren woman centuries before. The offspring, which its father had called Faron, had been a freak of epic proportions, a gelatinous monster with a humanoid head and a body comprised of soft bones and proto-limbs that had barely been able to support life out of the comforting pool of water its father had provided for it to live in.

Faron had, within the last several years' time, endured a long and painful ocean voyage, the death of his father and the sundering of his ship, and imprisonment in a carnival of freaks, finally falling into the hands of the newly nominated emperor of Sorbold, who was humbly serving a regency year before being crowned.

The emperor had placed the battered body of what the freak carnival had called the Fish Boy onto one plate of the Scales, a massive instrumentality brought to the new world from the Island of Serendair, on which all major decisions of state in Sorbold were made. By balancing the dying monster-child against a primitive stone statue of an ancient warrior formed of Living Stone, the element of earth still alive from the dawn of Creation, the statue was animated with a life force whose significance and power the emperor could not possibly have understood.

The desperate plea from a dying F'dor, accepted by the simple mind of the Faorina, had led to two beings occupying a body that at one time had been that of an ancient indigenous man, a soldier in the era before the Cymrian exodus, who had died in battle and had been buried in the temple of Living Earth, Terreanfor.

In the dark mountains of Sorbold.

Hrarfa, the being with higher-level abilities of reason, had been worrying since the statue's exit from Jierna Tal. All of the conversation with Talquist had been in her voice, and at her instigation. Faron was the owner of the titan body, but his thought processes and abilities to act on his intentions were still in development. Hrarfa was frequently frustrated, having to accommodate the slow thoughts and actions of her Faorina living partner, but she swallowed that frustration in the face of two thoughts.

The first being that, without Faron's agreement to take her on as a host of a sort, she would have been snuffed out on the wind.

The second thought was a far more exciting one.

Hrarfa, like all demons of her race, had one overarching goal, one single-minded need.

To let her fellow fire demons out of the Vault of the Underworld, where they had been trapped since the Before-Time.

In spite of many carefully planned escape attempts, there had only been two ways discovered of opening the Vault over the course of history. The first happened by accident, when a star known as the Sleeping Child fell from the heavens into the depths of the sea and shattered the Vault, itself made, like the titan's body, of Living Stone. When that had occurred in the First Age of history, a number of F'dor, Hrarfa among them, had been ejected or been able to escape, while the rest remained trapped when the Vault was resealed.

The second way of opening the Vault had been discovered later in history. A race of beings known as Children of the Earth, entities that were magically conjured by dragons seeking to extend their progeny by sacrificing some of their life force, or soul, and housing it in a body also formed of Living Stone, like the statue that had eventually become the titan.

Unlike the primitive statue, however, Earthchildren were living beings, though most of them had passed from the world in long-ago ages. They had souls, and features, and even earthen bones and internal organs. One of those bones, the rib, was the perfect size and shape to serve as a key of Living Stone.

A key that would open the Vault of the Underworld.

And, as luck would have it, the one last known living Child of Earth was here, on the Middle Continent.

Deep within the Firbolg mountains.

And Hrarfa, like the rest of her race, knew it.

The F'dor had been biding their time for ages, waiting to find such an opportunity. Hrarfa herself had passed from host to host, searching for a chance to take the rib from the Earthchild's body.

But the challenges and barriers to finding that child and doing so had been mammoth.

Now, however, that two distinct beings, each with a similar goal, resided in a titanic body of Living Stone, the challenges had been minimized.

Perhaps, even, eliminated.

*A*s the caravan set out for the Bolglands, Hrarfa sought her living partner in the darkness of the earthen body.

Are you angry with me for leaving him, Faron?

At first, and for the longest time, there was nothing but silence.

Finally an answer, sensed, unspoken.

No.

Hrarfa was relieved. *Good,* she whispered. *He was unworthy of us. Wasting our time.*

For a long while there was silence. Then, at last, a thought conveyed in the darkness of their stone residence.

I want it to be over. I want to be with my father again.

I know, Hrarfa thought soothingly, desperately hoping to impart comfort to the childlike entity she shared the statue with. *I know, Faron. Do not despair.*

We are on our way now.

Silence answered her.

13

SOUTHWESTERN BORDER OF ROLAND AND SORBOLD

*Y*abrith raised his eyes to the sun.

The morning was late in coming, it seemed to him, heavy clouds hanging low enough in the sky to delay any real light. Dranth would return from his morning scouting soon, he knew, and was no doubt appreciating the shade.

The sweet richness of spring in the Middle Continent was fading into summer's dry heat as they approached the southern ring of the Teeth. Yabrith was secretly pleased; moisture in the air, wet grass, and color were foreign notions to him, and while the desert clime of Sorbold was much sandier and drier than the cold clay of Yarim he was used to, he was more comfortable approaching it. But that was the only reason he was more comfortable.

He had not been with Dranth when the guild scion had secured the order to enter the Bolglands and capture the Child of Time, as well as the information of how to do so. Dranth had returned to the guildhall in what, for the acerbic master assassin, could rightly have been deemed a good mood, something Yabrith did not recall seeing in the several decades of acquaintance he had shared with the man. Dranth had been so excited, so certain about their mission and the intelligence he had received, that Yabrith had been almost sad not to have qualified for the unit assigned to carry out the mission.

Now, of course, he was secretly relieved to have been overlooked. But at the time, when Dranth had summoned the top echelon of assassins to select the participants, and had included him in the meeting only so that he would know his stewardship of the guild and hall were required, it had stung. He had always known that Dranth did not consider him a true assassin, but more on the order of Paddy the barkeep, Janil the weapons-maker, and Leopold the poisoner, all critical to their operation but never actually a part of it.

Having been made in his youth, with the stabbing out of the eyes of one of Yarim's town guards in a back alley while he slept off his drink, Yabrith had always thought he was at least considered an assassin, if a non-practitioner. He had taken part in mass stabbings and ritual torture that led to killings whenever the opportunity presented itself, just to subtly remind his mates in the guild that he was one of them. He had even been chosen by Dranth to accompany him to Golgarn, another mission under-taken for the new emperor of Sorbold, to meet with the Spider's Clutch, that seaside kingdom's guild, to undertake the setup that had frightened Beliac, Golgarn's king, into handing over every warship Talquist requested without resistance. At the time, Yabrith had taken the assignment as a sign of Dranth's faith in him, a show of respect.

But now it was clear that he was really only being tolerated, appreci-ated for his administration skills, an emasculating feeling if ever there was one. It called his very brotherhood into question.

Knowing that Trentius, Sandon, and Dhremane did not even see death coming in the Bolglands was easing the injury a bit, however.

Beside him the dust in the air shifted, a subtle way that Dranth had for letting him know he was back. No one who was unfamiliar with the ways of the guild scion would even have noticed. The thought raised Yabrith's fallen spirits a bit.

"Done movin' yer bowels?" he asked politely.

Dranth said nothing, but took up the pouch he had left behind in his scouting and affixed it to his waist.

"We're only one day out of the steppes," he said, his voice grainier than the sandy wind. "Two more to the official entrance road. It's heavily guarded, and while I utilized it when I came for the emperor's second Weighing and coronation, I suspect I would be welcomed less hospitably now. So we will take the back way and get there in three."

Yabrith nodded and took up his own provisions.

"No time like the present," he said pleasantly.

Dranth stopped in his tracks and stared at him. "I was just thinking that same adage," he said suspiciously. "What is the likelihood of that?"

Yabrith shrugged. "Don' know," he said. "But if we don' heed it, we will be arriving in four, and that's a far less lucky number 'n three, as far as I'm concerned. Let's be off."

They blended into the shadows cast by the finally rising sun and were gone.

TYRIAN FOREST EDGE, NEAR THE BORDER OF JAKAR, SORBOLD

The end of his hidden passage on the way to Sorbold was about to come to an end, Achmed knew.

And, when it ended, he expected it would end in a goodbye, said to someone from whom he hated to part almost as much as he hated to meet up with her.

At least now that her husband was out in the ocean somewhere, attempting to rally support from the Cymrians who lived across the Wide Central Sea, the reason for his dislike of meeting up with her had been eliminated.

And so the meeting of the two old friends in secret in the forest of Tyrian had been the only pleasant thing either of them had experienced in recent memory. Rhapsody had been for some time in the Lirin wood where she reigned as their titular queen, making preparations for its defense and coping with the loss of Port Tallono, the Lirin harbor; Achmed had managed to get word to her through the first of the Lirin stables where he boarded a horse upon arriving in Tyrian at the northeastern fringe of the forest, just south of Navarne.

The roan that he had quartered in the private livery there was nervous upon seeing him at first: a strange thing, given that he had trained it personally, but after an hour or so in the forest, he came to understand that its discomfort had not been with him, but with being taken out of the thinner forestlands for the deeply forested greenwood. Roans were forest horses; once they had traveled for a short time in the uninhabited woods, no other people in sight, the animal had settled down and had virtually flown over the untrimmed ground.

Outside of Tyrian City in the central part of the mighty forest, he traded the roan for a Mondrian, a horse of the same bloodline as that of the late Llauron the Invoker, Ashe's father, who had been knowledgeable about and fond of the breed. He had been pleased enough with the animal to get over his initial distaste for agreeing on something with Llauron; it was one of the nimblest mounts in his network.

Rhapsody had met him a few hours outside the stable. Her own responsibilities only allowed her the span of three days to travel with him before she needed to return to the front in Roland, but they had met up without incident and traveled speedily and silently together, covering ground that should have taken twice as long in Tyrian, arriving at last in a thick glen near the southeastern forest edge, through which the towers of the bloodsport complex of Nikkid'sar in Sorbold could be seen in the far distance.

It was a place of bad memories for the Lady Cymrian; she had followed some foolish advice from Llauron long ago and made her way in, without reinforcements, to that complex to capture and steal a gladiator who turned out later in life to the be the Patriarch, now in exile.

The memories must still be fresh, he knew, judging by Rhapsody's eyes, which glittered more noticeably the closer they came to the end of the route.

She said nothing, however.

As they came to the terminus at last, Achmed dismounted and, waiting until Rhapsody's mount had come to a halt, took the bridle in hand while she did so as well.

"You're moving better," he observed as she came off the horse one-handed, avoiding the arm that had been bound to her chest in a cloth sling. "How's the wound?"

"Almost healed, but Ylsa has been after me to allow it as much of what she calls 'gentle time' as it can have; the muscle mends less rapidly in that area of the body than others, so improvement can be deceptive as to how much strength is really there." The Lady Cymrian turned her head and whistled a quiet trill, then glanced about the forest and turned back to him. "It's so strange to be here on horseback."

"Why?"

She smiled slightly. "I've been here many times since, usually on foot and in the open, but the first time I ever came through here I was escorted by Oelendra and a few of her most trusted scouts, in secret and mounted, just before I made my way clandestinely into Sorbold, as you are about to attempt."

The Bolg king's sharp gaze flickered for an instant in surprise.

"Attempt? You doubt my ability to make my way clandestinely into *Sorbold?* What have I ever done to you to merit such a vicious insult?"

"It's not meant as an insult or a lack of confidence. I am not worried about you getting in at all. I just hope you can get out again. And I am also just trying to keep as much clarity of speech as I can these days. Without possession of my true name, my entire identity is contained in 'Rhapsody,' which is the Namer part of me, the one sworn to truth in speech. So while I believe you will make it to Sorbold, just as I believe it will be a fine day, I can't be sure, and so I say 'attempt.' I know, however, that in spite of evidence to the contrary this morning, the sun will eventually rise, and your passage will be riskier, so if you want me to return your mount to the way station for you, I will be happy to do so. I know you like to check on each of your Wings personally after riding them, but I suspect you know that the border guards who tend to that livery have it well in hand."

"I do. Thank you."

The woman who was at once the Lirin queen, the Lady of the Cymrians, and his second-oldest living friend smiled a little more broadly at him.

"It's strange; I can remember virtually every detail about you, or at least what I've known and experienced with you—Grunthor too. But I only remember Ashe, who I have been told is my husband, from the time when we met him in Bethe Corbair on our initial journey to the Bolglands, and the journey he and I made to find Elynsynos. And I can barely recall the fact that we have a child at all—some days I am shocked to be reminded of it. But I met you as Rhapsody, and as a result, all those memories are intact. It's amazing what memories are tied to different parts of one's nomenclature."

Achmed swallowed his initial comment and smiled in return.

"Well, I'm glad you remember what is *important*, at least," he said lightly. "Thank you for the unnecessary escort. I should be off. Did you bring the floating lanterns?"

"Of course," Rhapsody said. "They're in the left saddlebag, if you don't mind getting them yourself."

"Not at all." The Bolg king slashed the rope on the saddlebag and affixed it to his pack.

"Would you mind telling me why you wanted objects the Lirin use in religious celebrations over the sea, and that for humans are mere toys? Floating lanterns. It seems a strange thing to bring into Sorbold. Are you planning to use them to signal for help?"

"Perhaps."

"I don't think I will see them from here—or from Roland."

"Oh well. Another idea into the Great Latrine of Life." He glanced around the glen. "I should be off."

"Travel well," she replied as he turned to the Mondrian and slashed the bindings of the rest of his gear. "The liverymen should be here momentarily in response to the call; do you want me to delay them so they do not see you?"

"They won't see me," the Bolg king said as he shouldered his packs. "I perceive no breakage of branches or changes in the wind—I have more than enough time to be clear of this glen before they arrive."

"Good." Rhapsody patted his arm. Then, as her smile faded, she let the hand of her good arm encircle his elbow, pulled him closer to her, and pressed a soft kiss onto his cheek, letting it linger there for a moment. "Be careful. I know it's not a necessary warning, but take it as a sign of friendship."

Achmed exhaled. "Given that you are about to go back into Bethany soon, and into the heat of the war, I would offer the same advice. In your case, I think it's a similar sign *and* a necessary warning."

"Why? Do you think me suddenly foolish just because I got injured in battle?"

"You've always been foolish; there is *nothing* sudden about it. And no, not because you were injured. You are not yourself, Rhapsody. And while I have to admit I find this aspect of you oftentimes preferable to the woman I met in Easton long ago, I grudgingly admit that when your instincts were your own, misguided as they often were, you knew yourself enough to keep yourself safe most of the time. Even though I did have to sing you back to life once back then."

She grimaced. "I beg you not to remind me. My body recovered, but my eardrums never did."

Achmed's expression grew even more solemn.

"You have used your only chit given to you by the house for free," he said seriously. "You have tricked Fate one too many times; you have no fixes left. Now everything counts, especially when you are not with Grunthor or me. We have been in truly dangerous situations together, but now you are more or less alone and in the center of a continent at war, as well as being the mother of a child that is the sole obsession of a soulless man who rules the sea, and a good deal of the continent. We Three are spread more thinly than we have ever been before; if you recall, all our greatest victories in and out of battle have been together, not apart. All I am asking is that you try to remember not to take risks. You've never been especially good at it, but now you are working, quite literally, with one hand tied behind your back."

"Actually, it's in front of my chest."

"Well, there is little enough difference in the topography of those places on your anatomy that one can be forgiven for not noticing the arm placement. One day, one hideous and eventual day, we face the possibility that the Three will become Two, or even One. I just don't want that day to be any time soon."

Rhapsody shrugged with her one good shoulder.

"You are a believer in the myth that we may live forever," she said. "Until this moment, I've never even heard you entertain the notion that we Three might die. I didn't realize it was an option."

"It's not. Especially not for you. You are, after all, someone's mother now. Even if he is irritating and smells bad. And even if you don't remember him." He exhaled deeply, as he often did when words were difficult. "I apologize for being unduly offensive about him."

Rhapsody shrugged. "No need. I feel no insult anymore, if I ever did. It's amazing how little I feel at all." A thought occurred to her, and she opened her pack, pulling forth the box of Black Ivory given to her by Faedryth, the Nain king, and containing strange, translucent strips of a filmy material, burnt at the edges, that she had not been able to identify. "Does the name *Werinatha* mean anything to you, by any chance?"

The Bolg king, a man who was almost impossible to surprise, blinked in astonishment.

"Yes," he said tersely. "Why?"

Rhapsody shrugged. "Anwyn said something to me in the broken vault of Kurimah Milani, when I followed her down and killed her some months ago. It has been nagging at me, and has something to do with this strange substance that Faedryth unearthed in the mines of the Nain kingdom."

The Bolg king looked over his shoulder, listening for the approach of the liverymen, then silently motioned for her to continue.

"She told me that history, Time itself, had been altered for me. She made reference to a figure I have mentioned to you that I had seen in the realm of the Lord and Lady Rowan, behind the Veil of Hoen—the Weaver, the manifestation of Time in history. She said that there was a flaw of some sort in the Weaver's tapestry, where the threads of Time had been cut and rewoven—a thread removed that affected all of the rest of history. And that, for some reason, it was done to improve my lot in life in the Past—though she had no idea by whom or why. She said it had something to do with my grisly death in childbirth that was unnatural."

"As in the prophecy Manwyn threw at you in Yarim?"

"Perhaps. Anwyn said that this filmy substance was the only record of it."

Achmed glanced into the Black Ivory box, then shook his head. "Go on."

"Apparently she heard one word when scrying into the Forgotten Past, as she called it, though I don't know if it was connected in any way to that whole 'death in childbirth' episode. She said it was a name that connected me to another person in my life, earlier than I had come to know that person in this second iteration of Time. It was the name of someone that this person and I had both cared for, and whose death brought us together. Then she spoke the name—Werinatha—and that was all she said."

Silence filled the forest glade.

"I was wondering if that 'another' was you."

"Perhaps," Achmed said, "since Werinatha was indeed someone I knew."

"Who was it?"

The Bolg king lasped into silence again. Rhapsody stood quietly awaiting his answer. Finally he spoke.

"A fellow student at Quieth Keep—the place I met that infernal idiot Jal'asee, from Gaematria."

"It sounds like the name of a woman."

"Yes."

"Did she—did she die in whatever accident happened at Quieth Keep, that you and Jal'asee argued about when he came to Gwydion Navarne's investiture?"

The Bolg king was silent again for a long moment. "Yes."

"Hmmm. Well, Anwyn said that supposedly I knew this woman too, or in some way she connected me and someone else who knew her, and who also knew me. So that may indeed have been you. Anwyn was a vicious liar, but she, like her sister Seers, was supposedly unable to lie about the realm that was her domain, the Past, without losing her power to see into it. So while I have no idea what any of this means, at least it is good to know that the prophecy about death in childbirth is something that may have already occurred, in the Past, and that Time, for whatever reason, was altered to spare me from it."

Achmed glanced over his shoulder again.

"I hear the liverymen," he said. "They will be here in a moment, and I don't wish to be seen."

"Very well," the Lirin queen said. She squeezed his arm affectionately. "Be on your way."

Achmed looked at her for a long moment. He let his free hand cover hers that encircled his elbow, then took it from himself, raised it, and pressed it to his lips, releasing it a moment later. "Goodbye."

Her slight smile returned. "Goodbye. I hope when I see you again we will be celebrating victory."

"Well, if you are still acting as a Namer, your words of hope may be a good contribution to that. They certainly can't hurt."

He turned and slipped into the shadows that the rising sun was allowing to break into the trees, casting dusty light all around.

14

Hrarfa was starting to become worried.

During the course of their journey the Faorina spirit whose host body she was clinging to had grown even more distant and quiet. Hrarfa knew, or at least suspected strongly, that it was still there, still aware; there was a testy, almost hostile mood she could sense in the dark of their walking stone prison.

The inability to successfully manipulate her demonic co-conspirator was disturbing to Hrarfa. Her most recognizable characteristic throughout the entire history of her time in the upworld, free from the Vault and able to take on human hosts that were weaker than she was, or willing, was the ability to manipulate and deceive even powerful host entities, or their associates, into doing whatever it was she wanted.

In her last body, that of a beautiful First Generation woman named Portia whom she had caught unaware and had violently overtaken, eating the poor woman's soul alive in an orgiastic fever of glee, Hrarfa had easily managed to successfully seduce Tristan Steward, a weak man but nonetheless a powerful one, into giving her everything she wished for, the price for which was the repugnant but necessary surrendering of her host body to his lascivious needs. *What's a little repulsive knobbing if it achieves the desired end?* she told herself while he continuously gripped her thighs painfully as he rode her up against closet walls, fornicated her, facedown, in piles of stable straw, groped her in the backs of carriages and insisted on sliding his insufficient tarse into her mouth at any available opportunity in a variety of uncomfortable positions. *He has no idea his conquests of me gave me control of his soul long ago.*

He certainly had not been the first man, nor the hundreth, to succumb to her will while assuming she was his toy into which to pound himself.

But the young misfit she had convinced to share the body of the stone titan was another matter.

Hrarfa did not understand the motivations of the Faorina spirit, the demonic child named Faron. Obviously charms of the flesh had no power over him, nor, it seemed, did her constant promises of reunion with his dead father always mollify him.

It was, however, the only reassurance that ever seemed to work.

Now, after a long period of silence while they were leading the combined regiments across the northern border of Sorbold on their way to the Bolg kingdom, Hrarfa tried once more to make contact with Faron.

Faron—once we have the rib of the Earthchild, we will have the key to the Vault. And then our kind will be set free, after millennia in bondage.

After a long and customary silence, she finally heard a response.

And then?

Hrarfa hesitated, recalling that the Faorina spirit was only half F'dor, that it had a sense of existence that the Older and Younger Pantheons had never embraced. The insistent, overarching need for sweet destruction, even unto that of the Earth, and Life itself, might terrify him. She took the equivalent of a breath, then made her thoughts as gentle as was possible to make them.

And then, we will be free. All the souls, our family, that have been imprisoned unjustly from the beginning of Time, will move about the world, unfettered. And your father will be with you once again.

There was silence within the vault of Living Stone, a tiny reflection of the one which held their race.

Then, after a long absence, a thought made its way into Hrarfa's awareness from the primitive mind of the being with whom she shared the stone body.

I do not know if I believe you.

Hrarfa's consciousness lapsed into silence. Finally a question.

Why?

The Faorina spirit did not answer.

Faron, Hrarfa thought desperately. *Tell me what is troubling you. Please.*

She searched the blackness inside the titan's body, but could not even feel the other consciousness.

IN THE OPEN SEA

𝒪n spite of being in the middle of the moving, evanescent water of the ocean, Ashe had the distinct feeling of standing above an open grave.

The seafloor was littered with pieces of a broken ship, ancient but not rotten. The detritus was covered completely in barnacles and limpets, more than a millennium in residence on decking that had been built from trees of Living Stone in the shipyards of Serendair in the days preceding the great exodus long ago.

The pieces of that ship had been lovingly gathered and lay, carefully positioned, in the approximate places they would have occupied in the time when that ship was whole. Ashe could feel its name reverberating in his head, as if the shipwreck was singing it.

Lysandra, it sang.

Though his body was largely vaporous, Ashe could feel the sensation of his throat constricting. It was a name from the annals of history, known to every Cymrian descendant.

The name of the ship of Merithyn the Explorer.

His great-grandfather, dead almost two thousand years.

The leader of the First Fleet and the expedition of the Cymrian populace fleeing the Cataclysm to what was then the new world, the continent they now inhabited.

The lover of the dragon Elynsynos.

In his thoughts, he whispered the dragon's name again.

This time, a flicker against his barely corporeal cheek answered him.

Quickly Ashe kicked down into the depths, holding the sword above him. Its blue blade cast ghostly shadows on the seafloor, bringing the shipwreck into better view. The parts of the *Lysandra* that remained in the ship's grave were long boards of decking and rails, with a broken mast amidships, wedged at an angle in the sand. A few random items, metal plates, wooden barrels, and the lids of sea chests, lay amid the skeletal remains of the vessel, like an exhibit in an enormous underwater museum.

Ashe willed his eyes to adjust in the darkness illuminated by the light from Kirsdarke.

He thought he could make out a form wrapped around the base of the mast, even more vaporous than his own, the copper scales of the memory of its skin striped with black ash. His eyes followed the line of deep metaphysical burns farther out into the sand at the depths of the sea and found that some of what he had assumed were swales in the ocean floor was actually a partially buried wyrm form, entrenched in the center of the reassembled ship pieces.

Elynsynos? he thought, fighting back the panic charged with hope that now was threatening to consume his mind.

The drift pressed heavily around him, clogging his senses. He could catch no sign of life save for the infinitesimal song the ship was singing; there was no repeat of the flicker against his cheek.

Elynsynos? he thought again. *Please—is that you? Please, please let it be you.*

After an agonizing moment, he thought he saw a slight shifting of the sand. A few grains rose into the heavy drift.

Then he heard, or more correctly *felt* a thought, weak and distant, almost dreamlike, in reply.

Begone.

Ashe's mind felt as if it had caught fire. He held the sword closer to the mast, taking care to maintain as respectful a distance as he could.

Great-Grandmother? he thought, trying to keep the impact of the vibrations gentle. *Are you there?*

Nearer to him than he imagined, the sand shifted again, and in the gauzy light from Kirsdarke he saw what appeared to be a vaporous eye, closed and wrinkled, reveal itself from a barrel-sized mound that a moment before had been covered with sand and open slowly before him.

The filmy lid drew back, revealing a translucent blue iris scored with a vertical pupil.

Much as his own irises were.

A command, directly from the gaze of that eye, formed clearly in his mind.

Go away.

Ashe recognized the threat in the thought. He let the heavy drift carry him backward a few yards. *Are you injured?* he asked as quietly as he could make his thoughts. *Tell me how I can help you.*

The lid of the filmy eye closed slowly, an extended blink. When it opened again, there was slightly more light and focus in it.

You can do as I ask. Go away—you are interfering with the song.

Ashe felt a sense of exhaustion wash over him when the command was completed.

Do you remember me, Great-Grandmother? he asked.

There was no reply.

The eyelid closed once more.

I am Gwydion, son of Llauron, Ashe thought desperately. *Grandson of—*

He stopped short, remembering that his grandmother, her own child, Anwyn, who had attacked her with dragonfire, was dead.

By his wife's hand.

Then an idea occurred to him.

Pretty's husband, he finished, naming himself with the title the dragon had referred to him by when Rhapsody had introduced him to her in the Cave of the Lost Sea, the wyrm's lair in the forest of Gwynwood.

The eyelid opened once more. The enormous pupil expanded noticeably.

Pretty's husband?

Yes, thought Ashe eagerly. *Yes.*

The seafloor shifted again, and the other eye and a large part of the dragon's ethereal maw rose slowly from the seafloor, shedding sand.

Is she here?

Ashe's throat tightened again.

No, he thought, fighting back despair and focusing on the discovery.

The eyes took on a fond glow.

I am listening to the songs she found for me. The thrum echoed in Ashe's brain. *Merithyn's songs.*

Ashe's mind cleared. He recalled Rhapsody telling him, when he and Achmed had retrieved her from her imprisonment in a sea cave along the western coast of the continent, how, in her captivity, she had heard the songs that Merithyn had sung into the wind above the waves two millennia before, missives of love for the dragon to whom he had given his heart, who had invited the refugees of Serendair to take shelter in her primeval forest lands. The ancient sailor had left her reluctantly to return to the Island of Serendair and lead the Cymrians back to the Wyrmlands, only to have his ship sunder at the Prime Meridian in a great storm on the return voyage. Merithyn had apparently sent her love songs of farewell as he was dying.

He looked at the pieces of the ship around him.

Merithyn's grave, he thought. *This must be the spot where he died. In all the vastness of the sea, she has located exactly where he met his end.*

Indeed, the dragon replied dreamily. *Here is where I lost him forever.*

Ashe blinked in shock, having forgotten in the awe of the moment how thrum was carried in the drift.

I am sorry, Great-Grandmother, he thought in the direction of the vaporous beast.

Are you? said the thrum of the dragon. *For the first time in ages, I am finally not sorry. Pretty was right; she told me the key to finding peace is not where your body rests, but where your heart remains.* A rolling wave of bubbles washed over and through Ashe's body as the ethereal wyrm sighed. *In this place, both his body rests and his heart remains. And his songs—his songs are here as well.*

Are you injured? Ashe thought, trying not to disrupt her reverie.

For a long time there was silence. Finally the gleaming eyes focused on him. Had his body not been composed largely of thickened water, the light from those eyes would have burned his flesh away.

I had no bodily form for Anwyn to attack in the forest. The beast's thoughts were stony. *But even an ethereal form, which is the closest thing a dragon has to a soul, can be damaged by an elemental attack—and dragon's breath can burn it. I was in agony when I fled Gwynwood, every nerve seared, on fire. All of my own child's doing.*

Ashe closed his eyes, remembering the feeling of that kind of agony, having lived through it for twenty years himself.

In the beginning, when those who traveled with Merithyn came to my lands, my invited guests, they sang stories of their homeland, and of the exodus. But later, I heard the tales they told of me—not about the love that Merithyn and I found together, nor of my generosity, my hospitality offered to them in their time of need. No—they sang songs of lies, The Rampage of the Wyrm,

The Burning Fields, *all the epic tales of my evil nature, my destructive actions, every one of which was untrue. I loved the Cyrmians, so I forgave them. I assumed they manufactured those lies because they never knew the truth.*

Pretty told me of the songs she heard that Merithyn had sent to me over the sea as he was dying. The people that landed on my shores had heard those songs too. They had sailed across the world with him, had been saved from death by him, heard him singing them as he was dying himself, and yet they still lied. The lore of my life is polluted by those lies.

I came here in search of my lover, looking as I should have long ago. And I found what remained—a few fragments of his ship that had not washed up on shore or been ground to dust, the place where his bones had fallen to the ocean floor, and the songs. Here, finally, I have found comfort. I have found my love. I have found home.

Ashe tried to keep the wildness out of his thrum.

Elynsynos, he began quietly, *on the continent, you are thought to be dead. The Shield of the Earth is compromised. The Wyrmril are struggling to keep the Unspoken at bay—the Great Forest is vulnerable. I have done my best to maintain the Shield while waging the war, but—*

The vaporous eyes narrowed menacingly.

Be on your way, Pretty's husband. Leave me in peace.

Caught in the chasm between joy at the discovery that the wyrm was alive and desperation at her intransigence, Ashe fell silent.

The ethereal beast stared at him a moment longer. Then the gleaming eyes closed, and the insubstantial form began to sink into the seafloor again.

Please. The word rose, unbidden, from Ashe's viscera. *Elynsynos, please help me. My wife is in battle. My son—your great-great-grandson—is in the hands of strangers, being sought by those who would kill him. The entire coast is barricaded, on fire. Millions are at risk of dying an eternal death, the Afterlife itself in danger of extinction—*

Enough. The word was soft against the walls of his mind. *Enough, son of Llauron. I am sorry for you, for Pretty, for your son, for the millions who are about to die. But I am finished with this life, with this world. Unlike them, unlike you, I am pure wyrm, formed from primal Living Earth, born without a soul. I will never see my love again in the Afterlife, where his soul waits, forever alone. Perhaps you and those you love will meet again one day beyond the Gate. But I am done with all of you. I remain here, in the arms of the sea, at the last place where I can remember the man I loved. Be on your way. You are out of place here.*

Ashe hovered in the heavy drift as the mounds of sea sand settled back into swales in the cold depths of the black ocean. The elemental sword of water trembled in his hand, its light diminished ever so slightly.

Then, when the silence began to echo in his ears and the hollow of his heart, he closed his eyes and kicked up to the Sunlit Realm again.

Leaving his forebear's grave, and the dragon who guarded it, behind him.

15

THE ALTAR OF ULTIMATE SACRIFICE,
THE CIRCLE, THE GREAT FOREST

The end of spring moving to summer had filled the trees of Tyrian and the rest of the Great Forest with heavy leaf cover, the lacy patterns of newborn foliage that had shadowed the ground when winter had ended growing heavier with the increase in sunlight.

Under normal circumstances, Rhapsody had always been wistful when the baby leaves matured, filling the Great Forest with shade, blotting out a clear view of the sky. As a Liringlas Singer, it was her custom and religious practice to salute the daybreak and the appearance of the first star at sunset with song, so being in the forest in summer was a complication to her morning aubades and her evening vespers. But now, with an occupying army encamped along the destroyed harbor of Port Tallono, just beyond the forest's edge in the west, and a series of raids being undertaken from Sorbold in the southeast, the heavy foliage was a blessing, masking troop movement in the interior of Tyrian and serving as a detriment to their enemy's intentions of sacking the forest.

It was, perhaps, the only advantage the kingdom had.

Now, having said goodbye to her viceroy, Rial, her friends, her commanders, and her people, and having left her contingent, her guards, her mount, and every weapon she had save for Daystar Clarion, the elemental sword of starlight and fire that was affixed by a simple belt of leather to her waist, she stopped in front of the Altar of Ultimate Sacrifice, a relic of great significance to the Filidic religion, waiting. She was attired in the simple, undyed robes of the nature priests, with a hood covering her gleaming golden hair, which now reached only to the base of her neck.

The new-summer wind rustled the leaves around her, billowing through the silent glen.

The Lady Cymrian and Lirin queen closed her eyes, breathing in the rich green scent of the trees mixed with a tinge of smoke. She felt no longing for the time of lacier foliage, both for the practical purposes of the heavier cover and the fact that the part of her that would miss it was far away, in the Deep Kingdom of the Nain.

The Great Forest was the massive woodland area that covered all but the seaside fringe of the western coast of the Middle Continent. In the north above the Tar'afel River and a bit south of it the area was known as Gwynwood, a pristine white wood, as its name implied, that was largely uninhabited and often considered sacred lands. It was known to be the home of the dragon Elynsynos, the ancient wyrm that had allowed the original Cymrian settlers refuge and sanctuary in her previously unsettled lands.

Before she disappeared.

South of Gwynwood in the center of the western coastal region was the Circle and its surrounding towns and villages, the holy lands of the religion of the nature priests known as the Filids, as well as the place where the Great White Tree stood. This area was the most densely populated part of the Great Forest, home to nearly half a million people.

Finally, the southern half of the Great Forest encompassed the realm of Tyrian, known in the ancient language of the Lirin that lived there as Realmalir. Almost twice as many Lirin occupied Tyrian than lived in the Circle lands, but the enormous size of the southern part of the forest made the settlement sparser. It was this land over which Rhapsody had been invested as queen, and where she felt most at home on the continent.

A land to which she had said goodbye with great reluctance.

There was a soft rustling in the trees, an intentionally made sound.

Rhapsody turned and looked behind her.

A figure appeared, a tall man in a forest-green cloak and forester apparel, holding a whitewood staff topped with a golden oak leaf. He came forward and bowed politely.

"Your Majesty."

She suppressed a smile and took down her hood. "Your Grace."

Gavin, the Invoker of the Filids, grimaced.

"You're right. Formal address in the mouth of a friend does sound awful, doesn't it?"

"No worse than 'Your Majesty.' How are you, Gavin? How are Gwynwood and the northern forest faring?"

"Thus far there has been no real incursion, just skirmishes in the thinner forest lands to the west. Most of those inhabitants have taken refuge at the Circle. The invading forces have set up barricades between the forest edge lands and the sea. The barriers are movable, so I suspect the plan is to continue to creep forward until siege can be undertaken."

Rhapsody nodded. "We are seeing the same tactics. It's most likely going to be a coordinated attack. If it is, though we have some advantages, our forces will be outnumbered eight to one or more. The slaughter will be immense."

The Invoker shook his head.

"I never would have believed a few short years ago that we would be in this place, defending the Great Forest from attack from Sorbold and its allies. It seems inconceivable."

"Well, King Achmed and Anborn have always expressed a common contention that there is no such thing as peace, merely episodes of calm between outbreaks of war." She smiled slightly. "And then, of course, there is Grunthor. He calls those episodes of calm 'the Boring-as-*Hrekin* Times.'"

"*Hrekin?*"

"In the human tongue, uhm—'shit.'"

Gavin's smile, spare and considered, matched hers. "Well, with any luck, at least he is entertained by what is going on now."

"Oh, endlessly. As he was outfitting the Bolglands for the invasion we expect there, he was singing as I haven't heard him in years. He averages two new songs a day, most of them grisly, all of them martial."

"Someone should be enjoying himself, I suppose," said Gavin. "Are you ready? Sufficiently fed and rested? Your hands most recently washed in the moving water of a river or stream?"

Rhapsody's smile faded and she nodded solemnly.

"Short of invasion from the air, we shall not be disturbed; I have seen to it," Gavin said.

"Good. If we are interrupted, the best we can hope for is to have to begin all over again. At worst, both your heart and my mind will suffer damage."

Gavin looked at her steadily. "Are you ready?"

"Yes."

The Invoker stepped nearer to her and brought his palm to rest on her forehead as she closed her eyes. In turn, she brought her hand to rest on his chest over his heart.

For a long moment they stood, silent, clearing their thoughts.

Then, quietly and methodically, Gavin began speaking the names of each of the forest's tree species and most plentiful plants, using the Old Cymrian words, the language of Rhapsody's childhood. At each invocation, the forest floor seemed to grow warmer, the air vibrating in a clear wind.

Amastiscas. Small-cone pine.

When the vibration from his words quelled, the Lady Cymrian sang an incantation of protection in return.

Vrith lei malinus mantre kohs—Fire shall not harm thee.

Slowly, methodically, they sang the soft song of each major living entity's name, the Invoker speaking each title, the Namer following with the protective chant. After a moment, the named species sang in return, its true name vibrating in the air when the protective song had successfully wrapped around it.

With her eyes closed, Rhapsody's mind was wreathed in memory. The song she was wrapping around the forest's trees and plants was the same incantation she had used to protect the Great White Tree, at the previous Invoker's request. Through a sapling of Sagia, the tree's Root Twin that had grown in the enchanted forest of Yliessan in the old world, now in the courtyard of Highmeadow, she had blessed both trees with the melody she had heard the Root singing when she and her two Firbolg friends were passing along the Axis Mundi through the heart of the world itself.

Over and over again she called to the meteorological elements and the characteristics of fire itself, the element from which she wished to protect each species.

> Green Earth below thy roots, guard thee
> Wide Sky above thy branches, shelter thee
> Cool Wind buffer thee
> Rain fall down upon thee
> Fire shall not harm thee.
>
> Light of early spring, illuminate thee
> Heat of summer sun, warm thee

> Leaves of flaming color, bejewel thee
> But fire shall not harm thee.

With each new protection, the air of the world in which they were standing grew thinner, the heft of their bodies lighter, until, for all intents and purposes, they had become almost nothing but the sound they were generating, ancient and enduring as the Earth itself.

Hours passed. The morning sun moved high into the vault of the sky beyond the thick and cool green leaves, then began to descend toward afternoon. No birds sang, no animals approached; the vibrations they were generating were sufficient to frighten off any creature that might have come within the sound.

Finally, the Invoker named one last plant.

Hymialacia. Highgrass.

In spite of the exhaustion that was racking her body and spirit, Rhapsody smiled slightly.

It was the name of the species of scrub that she had first Named in front of Achmed and Grunthor, a tall field grass that, in one of her first major acts of Naming, she had used to hide them from a field of Lirinved soldiers in the old world.

Its namesong rang, clear and true, in return.

The Lady Cymrian and the Invoker remained standing, touching each other, until the warmth of the ground had faded, the wind had grown thick with dust again, and the song of birds and the scurrying of forest animals could be heard once more.

Finally they opened their eyes.

The creases around Gavin's eyes seemed deeper now; he looked down at Rhapsody intently.

"Are you all right, m'lady?"

"Yes. You?"

The Invoker nodded slightly. "Come back with me to my house; you must rest."

"I must go. Thank you, however."

Gavin shook his head. "With respect, while you are my sovereign, I entreat you to yield to my wisdom in this matter. There is less of you— us—incarnate at the moment than you may believe, and unless you wish to be defenseless and weak on the journey to wherever it is you are going next, you would be well advised to heed me. One turn of the sun will make a great deal of difference in your strength and stamina, Rhapsody."

The Lady Cymrian nodded, suddenly overwhelmed with exhaustion.

"Well, since you have seen fit to name me properly at last, I will accept your kind offer of hospitality and rest within your walls this night. Thank you."

The Invoker offered her his arm, and she took it, shaking slightly.

"At least whatever devastation Sorbold wreaks upon the forest, it will not burn."

"No, it will not burn," Rhapsody agreed. "That may or may not be a blessing; in a forest fire, your citizens and mine are more likely to prevail than desert and mountain dwellers. But nonetheless, it will not burn."

"Where is it you are off to now? Back to Tyrian?" he asked as he led her toward the Circle.

"No," Rhapsody said. "I'm off to meet up with Anborn in Canderre. The troops Ashe has been recruiting and training are finally ready, and it is time to deploy them. As it is, with Talquist's advantage of time, cover, and numbers, it's well past time, very likely. The Lord Marshal plans to leave skeleton garrisons in the cities, emptying them of all save a few soldiers to guard the women and children, and send the rest to the front."

Gavin guided her carefully over a rut in the forest path.

"So you will be at the front, helping to lead that assault on Sepulvarta?"

Rhapsody shook her head.

"I'm not certain, but I have a suspicion I am going to be left behind this time in one of the cities as well."

The Invoker swallowed, suddenly even more exhausted than he had been a moment before.

16

WEST OF THE PRIME MERIDIAN,
WIDE CENTRAL SEA

If that was Merithyn's grave, then I'm closer to Gaematria than I thought, Ashe mused as he rose closer to the surface, allowing his ethereal form to pass through the soft sunlight shining in diffuse rays in the ceiling of the sea. *Merithyn's ship sundered at the Prime Meridian, so I have passed the centerpoint of the Wide Central Sea.*

He closed his eyes as the sun broke over his face and listened as he hung in the brightening drift. He had been following the lead of the elemental sword of water through the darkness and endlessly similar sea vistas since he had entered the Deep, but now it was humming in an entirely different way.

Instead of singing a harmonic with the element from which it was born, there was a decided difference in its tone, a greeting or warning of a sort that indicated it was noting the presence of magic of another kind than its own.

Ashe's head broke the surface.

It took a moment for his eyes to adjust, for his body to thicken enough for his organs to begin to work again. He floated in the drift, in the rising swells of the open sea, and stared west, following the sun.

It took a few moments, but then finally he saw it in the far distance.

Clouds of what looked like steam rose from the sea in thin wisps, thickening as they ascended into low-hanging vapor that swirled in beautiful patterns, as if an entire sky of thunderheads had plummeted from above into the sea. Beyond that mist, the twisted shell-shaped spires of the university that was the largest building on the island of the Sea Mages could be barely made out at the edge of his dragon sense, piercing the clouds at a distance of approximately five nautical miles.

Ashe took a deep breath of the sea air, a sensation he had not experienced for some time. Bobbing now in corporeal form, he thought back to the one time his father had taken him to the Isle in his youth, on the first of only two voyages he had ever made to the place. It was a rare moment of fond remembrance in this time of war, when his mind and soul were tormented by the absence of his family and the looming death he could feel in the very air of the continent.

The Sea Mages were refugees of the Second Fleet who had chosen to remain on the mist-wrapped island in the middle of the Wide Central Sea when their ships had been beset by the backlash from the storm that had sundered Merithyn the Explorer's ship and many of those of the First Fleet that he was leading. The leader of the Second Fleet, another of Ashe's ancestors on his mother's side, MacQuieth Monodiere Nagall, who led the Second Fleet, offered the survivors a choice of staying on the uninhabited island, which had been called Gaematria by sailors for time uncounted, or continuing back west to the continental landmass that lay at the other side of the Wide Central Sea.

The majority of those survivors chose to sail west with MacQuieth, eventually landing in Manosse, a well-developed nation where they found an easy existence and had blended into the culture, their Cymrian heritage of minimal notice until their ridiculous longevity began to entrench them in the peculiarity and introspective oddness that often accompanied a vastly extended life span bordering on immortality.

The rest had chosen to remain on the all-but-hidden, utterly deserted island, turning their backs on the civilized world and immersing themselves in endless study and invention, which they sometimes shared with the outside world. More often, and increasingly more completely, they had chosen to eschew that outside world altogether, becoming a closed society of immortal but elderly adults, avoiding the contact and open borders that were necessary for subsequent generations to be recruited and propagated.

There are worse things than death, Ashe thought as he sank back beneath the waves, preparing to embark on the last leg of his journey. It was a notion he had been well aware of for much of his life, but now even more so that he was a father himself.

The concept of living forever without his family was too much to even consider without being driven mad.

*O*f he had thought that sighting the Isle of the Sea Mages was the beginning of the end of his journey to their realm, Ashe could not have been more wrong.

In sufficient time to have come to the beaches of the island repeatedly, he was still finding himself floating in currents leading out to sea, rather than to shore.

After the third time that the sun had risen and he had still not landed, he began to realize that the magic of the Sea Mages had been entwined with the natural geography of the island in preventing strangers from being able to approach the shores. He was beginning to roil in frustration when he felt a song vibrating through his hands. After a moment he recognized the call; had he not been holding the elemental sword of water, he would never have been aware of the song at all.

He had lived with Rhapsody long enough to understand that each living entity in the world sang a song of a sort, a vibrational signature known as a true name, but often the vibrations of those songs were heard only by Namers and were inaudible to the rest of the world. With Kirsdarke in his hand, however, he could hear the unmistakable song of the island before him, ringing through the sea air, shouting its name into the wind, where it was whipped around among the clouds of mist.

Gaematria.

His heart a little lighter than it had been within the darkness of the depths, Ashe sank once more into that darkness and went vaporous again, attuning the sword to the song of the island, pointing its tip away from him and closing his eyes.

Then he allowed the current to carry him toward the Isle of the Sea Mages.

*T*he louder the song of the island grew, the warmer the current ran. Ashe could feel the temperature change while he was still a good distance away; indeed, it seemed to him that the increase in both the heat and the strength of the churning waters that surrounded the base of the island in the depths was possibly artificial in nature, that the Sea Mages themselves may have taken action to disrupt the natural rhythm of the waves as a deterrent that would keep most ships from landing there.

Something about the ferocity of the underwater churning made Ashe recall words that had been spoken to him about the place sometime before, when a First Generationer named Barney, a barkeeper who had known Rhapsody in the old world, revealed to him that the legendary hero from the Third Age, MacQuieth, was, contrary to popular belief and reasonable assumption, still alive. As he was battered about by the ferocious waves, the words came back to him.

How do you think that Gaematria, the island of the Sea Mages, has remained unmolested all these centuries there, alone, in the middle of the Wide Central Sea? MacQuieth guards it from the depths. There is a whole world beneath the waves of the ocean, Majesties, a world of high mountains and deep chasms, of unimaginable wonders, of beings that rarely, if ever, are seen on the drylands. Do not assume because something is not within your senses that it is dead; there are many places in the world for a man to hide if he does not wish to be found.

Inwardly Ashe sighed. While he had found Barney's words to be true regarding the wonders of the Deep, he knew that the original revelation was no longer in fact the case. He and Achmed had witnessed the hero's end as the great warrior wrestled Michael, the Wind of Death, and the F'dor demon that clung to him into a boiling sea.

I am glad for him, he thought. *The heartbeat that rang like a great bell is silent. He has finally found the peace he longed for. But such an incalculable loss for the world.*

Finally, when the raging water began to successfully bar his landing, he let go of all physical form and allowed the current to carry him where it willed. He imagined himself curled up like an infant in the womb, awaiting birth in the warm waves, and gave a mental command to the sword to bring him to the shore.

Moments later, he felt a cessation of the heat, of the spinning and thrashing of the waves. Formless as he was, he sensed a solidity that indicated his presence on a beach or dry land of some sort. A cool wind whipped over him, tickling his solidifying body.

Ashe opened his eyes.

The sky above him was hidden by the formidable mist he had seen from the sea, but beyond that haze it appeared a different color blue than the ocean had been. Ashe inhaled deeply; the air still had the taste of the sea, but was cleaner, calmer. He lay still, allowing heft and weight to return to his bodily form.

He was lying thus when his dizzy dragon sense picked up the thudding presence of steps coming nearer in the sand.

Ashe lay still as two men approached. He had almost regained his solid form when they reached him. The tightly fitting clothing he had worn into the sea was all but dry when he felt the tip of the spear against his neck.

"Who are you?" The words were spoken in a dialect of Old Cymrian, a dead language everywhere else in the world. Ashe smiled in spite of himself. "How did you come to land here? Where is your ship?"

"I am Edwyn Griffyth's nephew," Ashe replied quietly in his best attempt at the dialect. "I respectfully request that you take me to see him."

The two men above him stared down at him as the first removed the spear from his neck. They looked at each other, then began to laugh.

"Are you the *Lady* Cymrian, then?" the man without the spear said. "If so, your appearance does not live up to your reputation." He chuckled at the confusion on Ashe's face. *"Zinkyn,* not *zemkyn.* You just announced yourself as Edwyn Griffyth's niece."

"My apologies for my poor knowledge of the grammar of long-dead languages," Ashe said in the Orlandan tongue, irritation rising. "I am not the Lady, but the Lord Cymrian. My business with my uncle is of an urgent nature. Again, I request that you take me to see him. *Now.*"

The unintended ring of authority was in his voice, punctuated by the threatening multivoice tone of the dragon.

The two men, who were attired in loose cassocks, knee-length trousers, and solid sandals, exchanged a glance. "Stay here, please, m'lord," the one with the spear said. From the folds of his cassock he removed what looked like a long thin shell with the curvature of a conch and stepped away into the wind.

He raised the shell to his lips and began to blow what sounded like a series of half-spoken, half-whistled pitches into it.

Ashe closed his eyes again. He knew that the man was sending a message to the High Sea Mage on the wind, just as he had known that the spear the man had carried was the least of the weapons that man could have used against him, the rest of them magical, so he rested, allowing his body to become accustomed to being solid again.

In what seemed like only a few moments, the man was back.

"My apologies, m'lord," he said, abashed. "Edwyn Griffyth awaits you in the Hall of Scholars."

"Your apology will be gratefully accepted if you'll give me a hand up," Ashe said. "The sand is beginning to seep into my trousers."

———

As he followed the two men into the Citadel of Scholarship, Ashe could not help but look in wonder at the exotic architecture of the central building complex in Gaematria.

At the very center of the shining building was a towering obelisk, twisted in much the same way as the shell the guard had used. Ashe recognized it immediately as the White Ivory tower, the only structure that had been present on the island when the members of the Second Fleet crawled upon the shores of the island after the sundering of some of their ships.

The twisting spire had been formed from White Ivory, a type of stone found nowhere else in the Known World. Unlike its cousin, the substance known as Black Ivory, which was utterly dead and inert, and used to hide objects from those instrumentalities that could scry for them, White Ivory was as porous a stone as had ever been seen on land.

The spire had been fashioned by the sea wind itself, whipping for centuries uncounted around and through the mountainous regions of the island. It was said that the obelisk absorbed all of the vibrations carried on the wind across the wide world, bringing news and information to Gaematria, where, until the Cymrians of the Second Fleet came to live there, it was heard only by passing birds and sea lions. The Sea Mages had learned to harness that information, allowing them to keep apprised of the events of the world around them without having to make contact with it.

The obelisk formed the central tower in the Citadel of Scholarship, and the man-made architecture was designed similarly to echo its shell-like form.

Something akin to hope, almost unrecognizable to him, began to pound in Ashe's chest as he followed his escort. The White Ivory tower was the primary reason for his journey to Gaematria; while he would be grateful for the counsel of the Sea Mages themselves, in truth much of their discernment was made possible by this instrumentality.

Finally, he thought. *This is what will provide answers, a new vision. This is the day the tide will begin to turn.*

In spite of having briefly been to Gaematria twice before in his youth, Ashe had never been allowed inside the White Ivory tower, but he had never expected to be; only the very most senior of the Sea Mages, the men and women who were the elders of the academics of Gaematria, were deemed worthy to enter the building. It was the closest thing to a religious sanctuary.

Llauron, his father, had brought him to Gaematria for the first time as a young boy, upon the death of Edwyn Griffyth's spouse, a gentle, thin man named Raeymik, to attend the funeral and commitment to the sea of his ashes. Ashe had met Raeymik before at Days of Convening on the continent, and had always been fond of him; Raeymik alone among the Sea Mages had both an affinity for and an interest in children, attributes that even his own uncle did not possess.

Raeymik had told him stories of the White Ivory tower: how the wind had carved it from the precious porous stone, how the great telescope atop it, through which the Sea Mages could see the faces of the stars and planets in the black night sky above the island, was powered by the tower, and how within it was the power to heal, to see across wide vistas, to know things that were otherwise unknowable. Ashe had remembered the tales long afterward, and when Rhapsody told him of Achmed's plans to rebuild Gwylliam's Lightforge in Canrif, repurposing it as a Lightcatcher, the description of it rang a chime in his memory.

It made him realize that the Sea Mages had their own version of it.

And, in spite of that, they had sent Jal'asee, their ambassador, all the way to the continent to discourage Achmed from pursuing the rebuilding of it.

He shook his head, trying to contain his excitement.

The Lord Cymrian was led rapidly through the Citadel's streets to the Hall of Scholars, a magnificent building beautifully appointed with fulsome libraries, lore collectives, and laboratories, as well as meeting rooms and observatories. He jogged quickly up the stairs that led to the front doors, passing his escort, seized the handles, and dragged the doors open as the men who had found him on the beach stared in shock.

He hurried into the Pathway of Knowledge, an entrance hall lined with academic frescoes and high ceilings, where he almost ran into his uncle, who was waiting impatiently there.

Edwyn Griffyth eyed him suspiciously.

The High Sea Mage appeared exactly as he had the last time Ashe had seen him, at his wedding to Rhapsody. A more portly, softer version of his brother Anborn, Edwyn had the same piercing azure-blue eyes, hooked nose, and solid jawline as could be seen in the paintings of their father, Gwylliam, Ashe's grandfather, that Ashe had seen in the Cymrian museum and in countless other places across the lands of the Alliance. The unmistakable mark of brilliance was evident in his eyes, almost as evident as was his displeasure.

"How did you get here?" he asked, acid in his tone. "Where is your ship?"

"Good day to you as well, Uncle," Ashe replied, a similar edge in his voice. "I came on no ship. I walked."

"Through the *sea?*"

"I had no choice. It was in the way."

"What in the world were you thinking?" Edwyn Griffyth demanded. The High Sea Mage's voice was trembling alternately with rage and alarm. "If you want to speak to me, next time send a diplomat. You've never been shy about using them before, although you seem to be perfectly capable of ignoring the summonses and commands of mine. Jal'asee reported utter failure of his mission last year to convince your confederate, the king of the Firbolg, of the danger of the research he was undertaking."

"Jal'asee also failed at getting Anborn to make use of your gift of the walking machine you designed and had made for him, so his trip was unsuccessful at all levels save for the opportunity for him to attend the investiture of my namesake, Gwydion Navarne, as duke of his ancestral province. I hope at least that undertaking received a favorable report from him, since that new duke is standing in for me as Lord Cymrian while I have undertaken to report personally to Gaematria and Manosse that *we are at war*."

Edwyn's face turned an unhealthy shade of purple.

"What are you babbling about, nephew?"

"Surely you must be well aware, Uncle, that the sea between your lands and mine is blockaded with every possible type of vessel, from armed fishing trawlers to ballistaed warships," Ashe replied mildly, "though apparently that gargantuan military buildup has managed to escape the notice of Manosse."

"What are you *talking about?*" Edwyn Griffyth demanded again, a thunderous tone in his voice that Ashe knew bespoke shock and surprise, two states which he had rarely if ever seen displayed by his uncle before. "I have received nothing but positive messages and reports from you, including the one that was delivered yesterday."

"Then, like Manosse, your vaunted wisdom and unassailable security have both been compromised as well," Ashe answered. "You have received no such happy tidings from me, nor apparently have you received any of my orders and payments for warships or pleas for assistance. Any positive messages you may have received from me have been counterfeit, I assure you. Talquist's grip on all commerce and information is unassailable.

"The blockade actually consists of three layers, stretching across the shipping lanes. While the layer closest to you is a deceptively persistent flotilla of merchant vessels, seemingly plying the sea in their usual commerce, the central layer is in fact a well-organized route of pirate ships, some of which are actually receiving the goods being off-loaded at sea by that merchant fleet for delivery to less savory ports.

"The inner layer closest to the Middle Continent is a formidable blockade of the western continent's entire coastline, from Avonderre in the north to Port Tallono in the southern Lirin realm, by most of Talquist's non-merchant ships, the military vessels he inherited from the empress upon her death, those of the navy of Golgarn, which Beliac apparently has ceded to him, and every captured ship he has taken custody of in his regency year, while he was playing the humble nominee of the Scales to the throne of Sorbold.

"I cannot understand how he was able to deceive the Sea Mages, who I thought made it a point to keep track of all of the comings and goings across the Wide Central Sea at least, not to mention the rest of the Known World. Perhaps if you had been more interested in keeping on top of your own traditional responsibilities and guardianships, rather than insisting that the Bolg king cease production of the one instrumentality that has kept the Alliance apprised of anything nefarious, you might have noticed that the Known World is essentially on fire."

Edwyn's well-defined jaw snapped shut with an audible click. The livid purple of the High Sea Mage's face was replaced by the utter absence of blood as it drained from his cheeks, leaving him pale and shaking.

"How? How is this possible?" he whispered when he could speak again. The arrogant confidence was gone, replaced by what Ashe recognized, with a twinge of sympathy, as the terror of having failed in one's stewardship.

"I have no answers to that question," Ashe said in return. "I came here hoping you could provide me some. Take me into the tower."

Edwyn's brow darkened.

"Is that the command of my sovereign?" he asked testily. "Or the request of my upstart nephew? 'Lord Gwydion the Patient,' as you are occasionally referred to around here—shall I assume it's as much a misnomer as the names the Cymrians gave to your grandparents—Gwylliam the Visionary? Anwyn the Wise?"

"*You* would be wise to refrain from comparing me to Gwylliam and Anwyn," Ashe said quietly, the air growing drier and the multiple tones of the dragon in his words. "You can believe, Uncle, that I would not have crossed the sea to come to this place, its unrivaled reputation for warmth and hospitality notwithstanding, had I not been bringing the direst of news with me. Now *take me to the bloody tower.*"

17

The High Sea Mage stared at the Lord Cymrian for a long moment. Then he took a step closer to his nephew, his dark eyes burning with the fire of rage.

"You clearly do not understand what it is you are requesting," he said softly. "For more than a thousand years, no one has set foot inside the tower except for members of the High Council, the elders, and even then those men and women have undergone purification rituals to prepare them for the experience and to maintain the sacrosanctity of the tower. In all due deference, my lord, you are not prepared to do so.

"Had you chosen to forswear the ways of your father and uncle, putting their military training aside and dedicating yourself from an early age to the pursuit of knowledge, as the residents of this place have, you would still not have achieved enough wisdom or years to even approach the tower, let alone summit it."

"Apparently you have not been hearing me, Edwyn," Ashe said, in a similarly soft voice reeking with the same threat that his uncle's had carried. "I have left behind everything I love, and everything I am sworn to protect, because the forces that are massing against the Middle Continent eventually have their sights set on the domination and destruction of the Known World, of Life as we know it, and the Afterlife beyond that.

"If it were merely a political squabble, if the only thing at issue were a throne, a crown, I would yield my title to any even marginally qualified replacement in a heartbeat, abandon the Lordship, and go build a goat hut in the woods for my wife and son. But given that it is likely a demonic element is involved, that Gaematria has been kept in the dark somehow, most likely Manosse as well, that Talquist's forces have taken Sepulvarta and have begun committing atrocities in sanctuaries for orphans and against nations, enslaving entire populations, I thought perhaps it wise to come to the repository of all ancient knowledge and lore, the place where the most gifted of sages and wielders of nautical magic have been sequestered for centuries, studying the mysteries of the universe for just such a moment as this.

"You have an instrumentality that could reveal the answers to the mysteries, could show us what Talquist has done, is doing, can help me find a way to end this blockade. I need to know how he plans to attack the Bolglands, where his army is going next. So while it never occurred to me that I would have to explain any of this to you, and while your hesitation appalls me to the very core of my being, I apologize most deeply for my impatience and ask you once again to take me to the blasted tower."

He looked back to see Edwyn staring at him blankly.

"Son? You have a son?"

Black rage exploded inside Ashe. He seized the Sea Mage by the shoulders and shook him forcefully.

"For the love of God, the One, the All, take me to the tower! You alone may have knowledge that will make the difference in this war. There isn't time to argue about this. Help me, Edwyn; *help me*. Time is growing short."

Edwyn Griffyth pushed him away angrily.

"Unhand me," he commanded, his tone deadly. "The only reason I do not cause your brain to swell and shatter your skull with a single word is that you by yourself are the last generation of Gwylliam's line. It would be a little bit like killing the last mosquito in the world; while it's tempting to eradicate the annoyance, the task should be left to one who has made a career of death, not scholarship." He smoothed his robes and glared at Ashe again.

"I will in fact go to the tower, but not until you have left this place, *m'lord*. Gaematria may be a party to the Alliance, but we are not under your command when it comes to revealing our secrets or allowing those who do not know those secrets to make use of sacred instrumentalities."

Ashe stood in silence. After a long moment he spoke.

"Then you will not help me? You will give me no aid in this matter?"

Edwyn waited in similar silence. Finally he shook his head.

"No. Not in this. I am genuinely sorry, nephew. But I can put you on a ship to Manosse, to your lands there, to your mother's family—"

The Lord Cymrian waved him into silence. "You haven't been listening. A ship cannot get twelve nautical miles past this place without being blown to bits. Your offer amounts to a suggestion of regicide. But it doesn't matter; the death of my respect for you is sufficiently devastating without allowing you to kill me outright as well. It is a sad day on which one learns that the greatest scholarly minds in the Known World, including one's own uncle, would prefer to sit on their secrets rather than share them in the attempt to save the Known World and the world beyond it. Your ridiculously long life of study, and the lives of those who have shared this place with you, have amounted essentially to nothing."

The High Sea Mage looked suddenly older. When he spoke, his words were measured.

"God, the One, the All, whom you have named in the manner by which *we* address him, unlike those on your continent, has provided our citizens with the appreciation of knowledge for its own sake. His gift to us may be incomprehensible to those in the everyday world you occupy, but I assure you, such study is every bit as holy as anything in your late father's nature faith, or the Patrician religion of Sepulvarta. I'm sorry you didn't come to understand this in the brief time you spent here in study. You can't blame me for the woes of the rest of the world."

"I absolutely do blame you," Ashe said bitterly. "You and every vaunted academic who have lived out your endless lives isolated here, on this island of rare beauty and immense power, in your Citadel of Scholarship. Two thousand years of research and learning, the pursuit of magic as a science, unmolested by the reality of the world, and what have you done with it? What have you done with all that knowledge, what single ounce of good have you achieved?

"My father was a flawed man in his youth, misguided in his support of your mother, but after the War, rather than seizing power or resting on his considerable laurels, he put all the things he learned in his travels and in his conservatories to excellent use, teaching half a continent better planting practices, medicine, and healing for people and the livestock they raised, harvesting techniques that let almost nothing of use go to waste. What have you accomplished with your life, Uncle? Scholarship and academia mean nothing if they are not applied. The Sea Mages have collected in their time one of the greatest treasures of the world—knowledge—what have you done with it?

"You build the finest ships in the world, and you sell them for a pretty price, but what is your contribution to the improvement of the practice of navigation, of shipbuilding in the world at large? You take great pride in your pacifism, in the peace that those who came to live here by accident found two millennia ago. Had it ever occurred to you that you might be able to share that peace with the world at large had you come down from your towers of ivory stone and either welcomed the people you share the world with here to learn it as well, or at least gone out to their lands, bringing the knowledge you acquired with you?

"No; instead you sit, sanctimonious, elevated in your own minds to godlike stature when those of us who live down in the muck, who struggle to end wars, feed populations, and make the world better one seed, one grain of sand at a time, do the *real* work of God, the One, the All. You speak as if you and He are intimate friends. Well, spare me your sanctimony—I sincerely doubt you and He run in the same circles. By your very definition, He would not be allowed into your blasted tower.

"History taught me to believe that you were a man of principle, refusing to be Gwylliam's heir, rejecting the titles, the glory, the riches, the power and stature to make a peaceful and happy life with your spouse, may he rest happily in the Afterlife. Part of me still wants to believe this. But that you could turn a blind eye to the impending disaster that is in part a legacy of our family—your parents, my grandparents—and the death that it will visit on this world, and the *next*, proves to me that you are no hero, no sage. You're just a selfish old man who will design an ingenious machine to allow his own brother to walk again, but sees no need to benefit anyone else with such technology, because, after all, there are no other cripples in the world.

"I am sorry for you, Edwyn. You will never know the true meaning of life, which is that it is a blessing, an honor, to spend the time that you have been given protecting everything that you love, and anyone and anything that needs your strength and wisdom, with everything that you are, until there is no more life left in you. You are far more dragon than I ever imagined, hoarding your knowledge like a wyrm in his rotting lair. May it keep you warm as the world grows cold and dies in the emptiness of the universe you have so carefully mapped and seen through your telescopes."

He turned and strode angrily in the direction of the massive doors. When he reached the threshold, he turned one last time to the High Sea Mage, who appeared to be trembling with fury.

"Oh, by the way," the Lord Cymrian said flatly, "condolences on the death of your mother, which has finally come to pass, permanently this time. And, for the record, the pursuit of knowledge for its own sake is not holy, it's just another form of masturbation. Goodbye, Uncle."

He tore open the doors with such force that the floor of the Hall of Scholars vibrated, sending books and scrolls tumbling from the shelves that lined the rotunda above him.

Slamming them shut with equal force behind him.

Ashe strode out of the Citadel of Scholarship at a pace that increased with each footstep. He broke into a run when he reached the fountains in the gardens at the center of the Academy of Science complex, startling the robed and hooded academicians who scrambled quickly out of his way.

His dragon sense and the memory of his previous visits allowed him to head unerringly to the beach on which he had landed. That same inner sight made note of his uncle watching from the wide arched window on the second floor of the Hall of Scholars, following his departure as he left the Citadel.

Ashe spat on the inlaid stone walkways as he left, desperately seeking to dispel the rampage that was rising within him, by which, if he were to give himself over to the dragon in his blood, he would destroy everything on the island, beginning with his uncle.

When the beach was in sight he drew his sword. Kirsdarke's blade was raging almost as angrily as he was, with searing blue waves rolling savagely from the tang to the tip, where they appeared to vanish into nothingness. As he ran into the tide, he swung the blade above his head, banishing the disappointment from his mind.

And threw himself into the arms of the sea.

Heading west again.

Edwyn Gryffth watched, frozen in his stead at the window of the Hall of Scholars, watching his nephew, the only member of the next generation in the royal line of the Cymrians, making his furious exit from the Citadel of Scholarship, tearing elemental power from the air around him and leaving a barely visible path of residual smoke in his wake.

He was so riven with anger that he could not quell the shaking of his body, even as his Longsight, a skill he had learned a lifetime before, allowed him the view of Gwydion running into the waves of the Gaematrian coast, swinging the elemental blade of water ferociously over his head as he entered the sea.

More like Anborn than his father, he mused as he narrowed his eyes, trying to catch a last glimpse of his nephew's disappearance. *A shame.*

He turned to see his chancellor, the dean of sciences, and Jal'asee, the ambassador of Gaematria, staring at him, wide-eyed. Edwyn sighed deeply and waved them away, almost dismissively.

The High Sea Mage waited for the scholars to depart, then slowly made his way out of the Hall of Scholars and deeper within the Citadel, to the place where the White Ivory tower stood.

The sea wind was high as he exited the lower levels of the Citadel, whipping his hair about him and filling his nose and mouth with salt, a sensation akin to having them bloodied. Edwyn ran a hand through his flying curls, salt-and-pepper tresses that had been the hallmark of his father, which his nephew had inherited, though Gwydion's shone like metallic copper, a gift from his grandmother, Anwyn, Edwyn's mother. He pulled his hair back angrily and shielded his brow with his forearm in the screaming sea wind.

He made his way through the hallways that led to the obelisk, carefully maintained yet rarely visited, and crossed the threshold of the circular mosaic that meticulously graphed the seven seas and landmasses of the world on the near side, and astronomical charts that represented the major constellations on the far side, to the circular building of sand-polished rose stone which was erected around the tower almost two thousand years before. Then he pulled from the massive key ring at his belt a series of almost identical keys and, pushing his flying curls aside one last time, he stepped forward to address the door.

As he stood on the silver square at the threshold, a column of light appeared from below him, wrapping him for a moment in a clear, glorious vortex of spinning illumination, humming with sound.

"Edwyn Griffyth ap Gwylliam ap Rendlar tuatha d'Anwynan o Serendair," the Sea Mage said.

After he had spoken, the spiraling light whirling around him shattered and fell, as if in solid pieces, to the ground around the silver square and vanished like snow. The clear, bell-like sound ceased, and a series of thousands of keyholes appeared in the door.

Quickly and rotely, Edwyn inserted the keys in the pattern he had known for most of his life, since the time he had abandoned his family on the continent and had come to live here, among the Sea Mages, seeking to learn their wisdom, their secrets, as well as to distance himself from the parents he loved but could not appease. After three dozen had been placed in the correct holes, the door disappeared in much the same way the vortex had.

The High Sea Mage hurried inside.

Above him the obelisk towered, its thin rockskin infusing the space beneath it with pale, ivory-colored light. Edwyn made a quick visual check of the doorways that led off of the great round foyer and, seeing nothing amiss, made his way to the circular stairway leading to the top of the tower and began to climb.

Though his Cymrian physiology had granted him an excessive life span, his energy and vitality were no longer what they once were. Edwyn gripped the polished stone handrail as he ascended the stairs, taking his time, measuring his breathing, pausing every now and then, promising himself a respite from the delicious pastries and heavily sauced seafood he had been indulging in of late, until at last the wind of the sea coming in through the open windows rippled through his hair once more.

"Damnation," he snorted as his curls fell across his eyes.

He fought his way through the thickening sea breeze, which was growing stronger with each step, until finally he came to the room atop the tower. It was little more than an enclosed platform, and the largest telescope of the Gaematrian isle stood in the center, pointed at this moment out to sea to the south.

Edwyn stepped carefully across the platform until he came to the enormous ancient spyglass. While the astronomical telescopes were housed within the high towers off the central foyer, this instrument was specifically built to view the welkin of the sky, the horizon, and the expanses of the sea all the way to the Manossian islands.

He sighted the instrument, then looked through the lens.

At first he could see nothing but the vastness of the ocean beyond and around the island. The sea appeared as it always did, neverending, endlessly blue-green, reaching to the horizon. Except for the occasional passing bird and a strong, heavy-hanging mist that sparkled brightly, the vista was unbroken.

Strange, Edwyn mused. *Not even a single vessel within a hundred leagues.*

He shook his head, annoyed and bewildered at his nephew's unfounded hysteria, and had proceeded to move away from the lens when an infinitesimal flash caught his eye.

Had he not been shaking his head in disapproval, it was unlikely he would have seen it, but just in case he positioned his eye on the lens again.

And looked closer, from a different angle.

Allowing his eyes to relax and go unfocused.

At first, he saw nothing but a blurry blue sea.

Until the sparkling mist flattened before his eyes like a card.

Revealing an armada that stretched from the edge of the island's reef into the endless distance.

With serpentine shapes flying above a large number of the vessels.

Exerting an unmistakable and threatening control of the vast sea.

"Sweet God, the One, the All," Edwyn whispered.

18

FIELDSTAFF, PROVINCE OF CANDERRE

The Lord Marshal had been hearing updates all morning of the approaching armored caravan. By the time it finally arrived within the garrison's walls, he had been striding the grounds below the ramparts, impatiently wearing a pathway in the mud left over from the rains of the previous two nights.

He made his way quickly to the carriage, only to see that the person he sought was actually on horseback in the center of the mounted brigade before the coach. He hurried through the other horses and men atop them until he came to a Lirin forest horse shaking the rain from its mane.

"You are looking well," Anborn ap Gwylliam observed, smiling up at the Lady Cymrian on her plaited roan. "I see you have recovered from the arrow you took in Bethany." He reached up without waiting for acknowledgment and gently took hold of her waist, hoisting her from the mare and delivering her easily to the ground. "I trust you are feeling better."

"I am, for the most part," Rhapsody said, kissing his cheek. "Still don't have full range of motion on the left side, but the pain is all but gone."

"I would think Lirin healers would have been able to bring you farther along," the Lord Marshal grumbled as he hoisted her saddlebag off the roan and took her by the elbow. "You are just in time; I was concerned that you might miss the briefing."

"We came as quickly as we could," Rhapsody said, allowing him to steer her around mud puddles and fresh horse droppings that had yet to be cleared. "Tyrian had been enduring and repelling increasing numbers of raids from the southeastern border; it's clear that Sorbold is testing us, gauging our resolve and our military capacity while it sacrifices a few of its seemingly unending supply of soldiers in the hope of escaping with intelligence it cannot get from outside of Tyrian."

"What do your commanders think they are trying to gauge specifically, if anything?"

"They think they are trying to discover the trap system and the natural defenses that were developed within the forest and not built or designed with any components from Talquist's trade stream," Rhapsody replied, nodding pleasantly to the soldiers that bowed as they passed her, staring intently at her until they caught Anborn's glare of displeasure, then quickly returning to military decorum. "I'm not certain I entirely agree."

"Oh? What do you disagree with?"

"Well, I have no doubt they are interested in the forest defenses, but it seems odd to me that they keep taking pieces of trees with them when they retreat."

Anborn's brows drew together. "Please elaborate."

"The incursions that were occurring just before I left had a common pattern—the scouting parties would send a preliminary sortie to just outside the forest, then veer off, whether they had drawn a response or not. Then, shortly thereafter and no fewer than two leagues away, another sortie would actually broach the forest, riding a protective barrier around a swift group on non-barded horseback that would break off limbs of a few trees, then retreat quickly, the rest of the assault force covering them.

"There was enough enemy fire to hide this action in what looked like regular offensives and attacks, but I noticed on my way back from seeing Achmed off at the southern border that certain trees had been sampled, harvested, it seemed, in ways that no Lirin would have done."

Anborn opened the main flap of the conference tent and held it for her.

"And what do you conclude from all that?"

Rhapsody's face was serious as she passed beneath his arm.

"I believe they are testing substance weapons on the wood," she said, nodding politely to Solarrs and Knapp, two of the general's most trusted men-at-arms, who bowed in return. "I am not certain, of course, but I believe they are looking for materials that might be capable of burning the specific trees native to Tyrian. Word has no doubt spread of the sapling of Sagia that is growing, unmolested, in Highmeadow after an attempt was made to set it on fire by a soldier who had deliberately allowed himself to be taken prisoner from a raid in Avonderre. He didn't survive his attempt, of course, but that seems an odd thing to do unless there is a plan of chemical attack in the works."

She came to a stop in front of a table around which traveling chairs had been set.

"Is that the tree in which you put a harp that endlessly plays a protective melody?" Anborn asked.

"It is, so it is a unique situation. The trees of southern Tyrian—white elms, heveralts, and gray gums, along with a unique group of pine species—are well suited to withstand fire attack, some because they shed their drier, older layers, assuring a high moisture content in their leaves or needles, and others because they actually reseed through fire. I imagine that their plan is to systematically burn the forest and establish temporary bases as they continue to move the burn line forward. Sooner or later, if successful, they'll have a foothold in the south that they can connect all the way to the occupied harbor of Port Tallono on the west coast. Then they can off-load troops from the sea and press forward from the south until they meet up with their forces that have already taken and occupied coastal Avonderre in the north."

"Hmm," said Anborn. "Were you able to set anything in place as a deterrent?" He pointed at a chair and took up the pitcher on the table, pouring two glasses of water from it, handing her one.

Rhapsody took the cup and raised it to her lips. "Thank you," she said after taking a sip. "Gavin and I did a universal blessing of the trees and plants of the Great Forest, which should protect them somewhat from damage by fire, though little else. In the Tyrian raids I noticed the heveralt seemed to be of special interest, or at least that is the type of tree which seemed to have the most samples taken from it. It is certainly one of the most plentiful species in the southern forest, so before I left for the Circle, I sang a song of protection in its language, the name of the species, in the hope that it might help specifically."

"I hope so, too," said the Lord Marshal. "Now, take a seat, if you please, m'lady. While you, the young duke of Navarne, Solarrs, and Knapp are about to be assigned to the division command of one of each of the northern cities and basilicae, the other half of the new military forces are about to be deployed under my direct command to the south along the Threshold, which the reserve troops have been holding since our far-too-easy victory in Bethany, north of Sepulvarta. We need to rid the holy city of its occupiers and move the front back into Sorbold proper."

Rhapsody nodded. "Where are you putting me, Lord Marshal?"

"I was going to offer you the choice. Your husband has been recruiting and training these troops I am about to see for the last three years, or so he continuously claims. Those men have been mostly deployed for training in this province, and within the other northern states of Yarim, Bethany, Navarne, and Bethe Corbair. There were mercifully few in Avonderre, owing to that being a naval area, not an army installation, and so at least those new soldiers were spared. So, if there is one place that you think you would prefer to be assigned as the division leader, now is the time to say so. I assume young Navarne will want to be similarly assigned in the encampment of his own province."

"That would make sense."

Anborn's face grew serious.

"I think you might wish to avoid Yarim, and potentially Bethe Corbair, m'lady," he said, a quieter and more direct tone in his voice. "Those are bad places traditionally for women. Now, you will have a whole garrisoned city of men to protect you, but I am only leaving a half contingent in each and moving the rest down to the Threshold of Death in the south.

"Talquist's forces have a history of harming women and children, and rape is an instrument of war where he is concerned. Fhremus Alo'hari, the supreme commander of the Sorbold forces, is a good man, or at least he was when he trained with me long ago, but since the Merchant Emperor has taken the throne, the atrocities that have been reported are inconceivable. I would not want anything to happen to you."

His words ground to a halt.

Rhapsody was staring at him as if his head was sprouting fire.

"Please tell me you are joking," she said flatly.

A smile passed between Solarrs and Knapp as they directed their gaze down at the tabletop.

Anborn drew himself up severely.

"I never joke in the advent of war," he said, equally flatly. "I have only the greatest respect for your abilities with a sword, m'lady—"

"Clearly."

"—but as your sworn knight, I have pledged my life to you for your protection and need. It will be hard to defend you in a place where both the enemy army and the *populace* are known for brutal attacks on women, at least historically."

"Not since the new Cymrian Age has begun," Rhapsody said, trying to keep the amusement that had risen within her out of her voice. "Ashe sent extra divisions to Yarim at the very beginning. Ihrman Karsrick has assisted in the undertaking with his provincial troops. The crime rate has dropped markedly."

"You cannot undo two thousand years of culture overnight, m'lady," Anborn said darkly. "And so, since you asked, I will amend my offer to 'any of those provincial garrisons *except* Yarim.'"

Rhapsody bowed her head humorously.

"I will request Bethany, then," she said. "The basilica of Fire is there, and that is an element I am very comfortable with, given that I bear the sword dedicated to it."

"An excellent choice—a well-fortified citadel and centrally located. Should all else fail you could evacuate the province and flee to the south, to the central garrison of the Threshold of Death just north of Sepulvarta that we defended together a short time ago."

"Thank you," Rhapsody said, a wry smile touching the corners of her mouth. "Now, if you will allow me, Lord Marshal, I should like to show you some precautionary armor that might make you worry less about me and the women of that province."

Anborn nodded agreeably.

She rose and went to the saddlebag Anborn had carried for her and rummaged through it. Finding what she was looking for, she returned with a ring about a knuckle and a half in diameter, forged of thin, flexible metal. Inside the ring were tiny metal wires, similarly thin and forming a fluid, bristly circle that resembled a miniature wire cleaning brush. Anborn touched one of the tiny wires and then withdrew his finger, bleeding slightly.

"What is this?"

Rhapsody smiled. "Protection against rape. Or at least deterrence."

The three men exchanged a blinking glance.

"Please clarify," said the Lord Marshal.

Rhapsody took the ring and held it up to the light.

"Those metal wires are tiny and flexible, but, as you can see, they are sharp, barbed, and easily draw blood. There are about five hundred of them in each ring. This ring is worn internally; if a woman is violated, the rapist's penis goes through the ring, and the wires catch on however much of it goes through the circle, embedding themselves in the skin of his shaft. Or sometimes just the head, depending upon how enthusiastic he felt when he began the undertaking."

The three men, ancient warriors of more than a millennium of epic heroism and valor in battle, blanched white.

"While he can disengage from the woman he has assaulted, he cannot disengage his tarse from the ring itself. The wires dig in, and the tiny barbs at the tips anchor like a fishhook into the shaft or the glans, depending on how far—"

"I believe we understand, m'lady," said Anborn quickly. "Thank you—"

"The man is neither able to walk nor urinate until the ring is removed," Rhapsody continued, nonplussed. "It must be removed by a healer with experience in such things, which most humans have never seen before. The pain is said to be excruciating, and if the ring isn't removed in a timely manner, gangrene can easily set in—"

"For the love of the All-God, Anborn, make her *stop*," Knapp groaned.

"—and oftentimes the man would need to have his penis cut off, lest he succumb to the gangrene. It seemed a better choice to just remove it rather than to die while it rotted off."

Anborn was struggling not to laugh and vomit simultaneously.

"I yield to your point, m'lady. This is a—er, Lirin armament?"

"Yes."

"Well, I am surprised the Lirin have cause for such things."

A moment before, Rhapsody had been struggling to keep a straight face as she rendered her explanation. The humor drained out of her eyes now like water running downhill.

"That is a circumstance dating back to the old world," she said curtly. The hard edge in her voice was as sharp as the wires she had been describing, and all three men fell silent as she spoke.

"In Serendair, there used to be a myth among human men, most often human soldiers, that Lirin women had a sweet taste to them, to their skin and lips."

"'Tis no myth," said Solarrs, who had been married to a First Generation Cymrian woman of Lirin extraction. "You do taste sweet, m'lady." When Anborn and Knapp looked at him, astounded and aghast, he quickly corrected himself. "I mean, Lirin women do."

"Aye," Rhapsody said seriously. "That's not the part of the custom that is mythic; the chemistry of the Lirin body is perceived as sweet to the human tongue. To the Firbolg tongue, as well—Grunthor often tells me that our race was always his favorite of the carnivorous palate, followed distantly by deer. The myth is that if a man, generally a soldier, can drink of a Lirin woman between her legs, imbibe the 'juice of her excitement,' as they used to call it, he gains some sort of invulnerability or strength in battle, or some other hogwash. It is obviously nonsense.

"Lirin women primarily lived in forests and fields, or in small communities with longhouses and barricades that prevented the human world from catching them alone. But when a Lirin woman lived in a city, as some did, it was not uncommon for her to be standing in the street, a basket over her arm, buying bread or potatoes one moment, and to find herself the next moment in an alley, in the grip of three men or more, with her skirt over her head, being harvested for such juice, shall we say, whenever a human regiment happened to be in the city on leave."

Solarrs and Knapp looked down at the tabletop. Anborn's eyes traveled over her face, which was set in a solemn mien.

"And did you live in a city, m'lady?" he asked softly.

"Easton." Rhapsody folded her hands on the tabletop.

The three men fell even further into awkward silence.

"So, that is the reason that this ring was designed and produced," Rhapsody continued. "Because a human man was not always satisfied with a beverage, and sometimes wanted more of a meal."

"Did you design it for use here, in this world?" Anborn's voice was quiet but steady.

She shook her head and smiled slightly. "No. Grunthor did. He was aware of the custom and took great pleasure in doing so. But it works for almost any woman of any race. It comes in multiple sizes, for women of all internal dimensions. It is a very popular item among Bolg women."

"Bolg women?" Anborn asked incredulously. "If anything, I would think the race most needing protecting against rape would be human women, from men of the Firbolg variety."

"Certainly you would," Rhapsody agreed. "Just as the Spring Cleaning exercises that Roland used to engage in against villages in Ylorc were effective deterrents to marauding killers of women and children—oh, wait. My mistake; the only women and children who ever died in those events were Bolg."

Again the three men lapsed into silence.

Rhapsody rose from the table.

"Well, now that I have my assignment, I suggest we go and meet the trained soldiers that Ashe has recruited and brought into professional status," she said, pushing her chair back under the table. "The volunteers and the reserve forces have fought bravely and successfully, but if you plan to hold the northern cities *and* reinforce the, er, Threshold, you will need to get these professionals deployed quickly and efficiently."

"Agreed," said Anborn, following her to his feet. He smiled as he stood, remembering a recent time when he had been unable to do so.

"If I might have a moment, I need to attend to nature's call—it was a very long ride from Tyrian—and check in on my mare. I shall return momentarily."

The other two men rose and bowed as she left the tent.

Once she was gone, Solarrs turned to Anborn. "What in the world has gotten into her?" he asked incredulously. "I've never known her to be even vaguely like that, so coarse and hardbitten. Is it the war?"

Anborn's mind was far away, remembering a beautiful child that Rhapsody herself had all but forgotten.

A child with whom she had left a very significant and lovely piece of herself, her true name.

And that most of the world did not know existed.

"In a way," he said distantly. "But she is your sovereign and mine, lest you forget. Whatever she said, harsh and direct as it might be, was the truth, as any Namer would tell it. And while she has always been humble and without the airs and the insistence on protocol that her position would warrant, do not allow yourself for a heartbeat to believe that I will tolerate any but the most reverent of respect being directed to her face or behind her back. I would happily die for that lady, and even more happily tear the throat out of any man—even an ancient friend and ally—who gainsays her in any way."

"Understood," said Solarrs quickly. Knapp merely nodded silently.

When Rhapsody returned a short time later, she and the three Cymrian soldiers went to the garrisons where the troops were beginning to arrive, eighty thousand in total. The four of them came in through the heavy gate and stopped to watch the muster.

Anborn looked out over Ashe's trained soldiers, who were taking a last opportunity to practice before assembly.

In nearest sight, a rank of archers was toeing the line, nocked and drawn, before a stand of targeted haybutts three hundred yards across the courtyard. At a shouted command, the troops drew back and let fly, their arrows whizzing from a draw point a hand's length past each archer's ear, plummeting into the centerpoint of each target, thudding resoundingly.

Without a single miss of center.

Farther beyond the gate, another rank of soldiers stood before another stand of haybutts, these closer, unleashing upon command round after round of throwing knives, their technique as perfect as Anborn had ever seen.

He stared at them in shock.

A smile crawled over his face. It continued to spread, like a wandering river, until it almost reached the corners of his ears, his teeth gleaming brightly in the light.

Then he opened his mouth and he laughed until he could stand straight no longer, doubling over.

19

The Teeth
(Manteids)

★

● Night Mountain
Earth Basilica

Desert

VIADUCT UNDER THE CITY OF JIERNA'SID

$\mathcal{D}$ranth had visited the palace of Jierna Tal on three occasions before, each time entering through a hidden passageway beneath the city which had at one time been an enormous sewer.

The historic use was clear in the odor that still remained, centuries later.

And while Dranth had cultivated a supremely sensitive sinus system and nasal passages in order to be able to detect infinitesimal traces of poison and other toxic substances, he felt no disgust at such odors, being long accustomed to hiding out in places where they infused themselves into the air.

This fourth occasion was a bit more dicey than the first three, however, for two reasons. The first was the sort that was always a hazard: on all other occasions, he had been specifically invited by the emperor, and so there had been arrangements made for his safe passage into and out of the palace at the highest levels of security. This time, he knew, Talquist was unaware of his impending arrival, and so there might possibly be unexpected difficulties to solve.

Nothing he could not handle.

With any luck, Yabrith would follow his lead and not find himself in harm's way.

Secondly, this was a visit in which he needed to deliver bad tidings. Obviously one never wished to find oneself in such a situation, but Dranth was still comfortable with the trump card he was holding, a piece of information that Talquist was seeking.

And so he felt their chances of coming to a mutually satisfying solution to the unpleasant failure of the first attempt on the Bolg king's life were strong.

As they made their way into the viaduct, Dranth scanned the towering arched ceiling in surprise.

The last time they had come through, a massive breeding program was under way, filling the viaduct tunnels with screaming noise. Dranth had not ventured into the bowels of the vast sewer to see precisely what was going on, but it was clear to him that it involved beasts of some size and considerable power.

Now, while some of the sounds and the stench remained, the noise was greatly reduced.

He skirted that part of the tunnel and kept to the far wall which led inside the palace.

Yabrith traveled silently behind him. Occasionally Dranth checked over his shoulder to make certain he was still there, and on those occasions it seemed to him that Yabrith was holding his breath, more in trepidation than in actual reaction to the stench of the place.

Finally, after many hours of traversing the stinking water and cold, black emptiness, Dranth and Yabrith came to the hidden passageway that led into the library of the emperor. Dranth effortlessly found the handhold that opened the passage.

The doorway was obscured by a moving shelf of books which swung open silently, leaving them in direct sight of the center of the enormous room.

A page, a middle-aged man with short salt-and-pepper hair sitting at a table near the floor-to-ceiling books, blinked upon their entry.

Talquist looked up in surprise from behind his desk. He swallowed and inhaled silently, then gestured for them to step into the room. Dranth did so, scanning the remainder of the room, which was empty.

"Apologies, Majesty. The sentries let us in." It was a lie, but covered their surprise appearance.

"Did they?" the emperor said. "Hmmm. I shall need to get new sentries, it seems, if they are not able to announce my guests better than that. What brings you gentlemen here this evening, from so far away?"

Dranth glanced around, but otherwise did not move. Yabrith followed his lead.

"We bring news you were awaiting."

The emperor raised his hand to the page.

"Will you excuse us for a moment?" he said, addressing the man, his gaze never leaving the two members of the Raven's Guild.

"Of course, m'lord." The page stood and began to assemble his papers and leather portfolios.

"What sort of news?" the emperor asked as the page pushed his chair in at the library table, gathered his materials, and took his leave.

The two men looked at each other.

"The name of the child you were hoping to hear about," Dranth said as the page opened the library door behind him.

A wide smile broke over Talquist's face.

"Oh," he said pleasantly. "No need; I already know it."

He nodded briskly.

The page swiveled around seamlessly and with great precision fired the crossbow hidden in his leather portfolio, sending a bolt into the back of the guild scion's head.

Dranth was mostly dead before he hit the floor, where he proceeded to bleed his remaining life out through his eyes.

Yabrith's own eyes opened wide in shock.

The emperor pointed.

"This man as well, Fhremus."

Another bolt, another member of the Raven's Guild was dead on the heavy silk carpet, the magenta coloring of his blood clashing with the scarlet threads of the rug.

From his chair, Talquist exhaled deeply.

"Thank you, Fhremus. Two assassins, just as my information indicated."

Fhremus inclined his head in the direction of the two bodies on the carpet.

"The first man, his reflexes were prime," he said, pointing to the body of Dranth. "I could see him beginning to coil as I fired; had I not surprised him, he would have taken both of us, m'lord. There are throwing daggers in his boot and at his wrist that I imagine he could have heaved two-handed and in two different directions simultaneously; I can tell by the way he stood, balanced perfectly. The other fellow, however, seems a bit of a sluggard. With the notice of seeing his friend shot through the skull, he should have gotten at least to draw. That was a long bit of notice. He hardly seemed qualified to be in the company of that other assassin."

Talquist waved his hand impatiently.

"Nonetheless, I can assure you, he is a member of the same guild as the first. Two assassins, as predicted." He words ground to a halt and he looked askance at Fhremus.

The supreme commander merely nodded. "Orders now, m'lord?"

Talquist loosed an easier breath. "I assume you are going to want to have them gone over by an expert and stripped of all their weapons and traps and whatnot. Please send that person up. And if you would be so good as to summon the chamberlain and let him know the cleaning staff is also needed, I would be most grateful. Thank you for your vigilance. You are dismissed. Go and find company, libation, or slumber. You deserve a good knob, good drink, or a good sleep—or all three, whatever you desire."

Fhremus nodded again and took his leave. He hurried down the steps to the chamberlain's quarters and then to the barracks, making the arrangements that the emperor had requested.

Then he wandered out into the coming night, where the streetlamps of Jierna'sid were just being lit, and the celebratory commerce and cacophony of the city just beginning to rise.

20

Many hours later, after the light stalks had burned down to the stubs and all but the most stalwart of merrymakers had returned to hearth and home, Fhremus remained in the town square of Jierna'sid, a tankard in one hand, the other hand cupping his own chin.

Even the strongest libation had done nothing to numb the raw ache in his gut, an acidic scorching pain that had been brewing there for months.

As the streetlamps began to wink out, one by one, an enormous shadow began to emerge in the half-light, and it fell upon him as he sat on the rim of the Ovris Fountain, whose water-circulating pumps would continue to send its decorative spinning spray skyward through the dark hours of the night.

Fhremus looked up.

Looming above him on a hilltop many streets away, at the Place of Weight, the great Scales rose in the blackness of the night sky, the faraway streetlamps that shone on them constantly, like the ones on Ovris Fountain, casting shadows around the central district of the city.

There was something painful and proud about that instrumentality, a remnant from the Lost Island of Serendair, which had been carefully disassembled in the exodus and transported across the sea to be reinstalled in the place where Fhremus's ancestors had lived, unaware of its tradition and history. Though he was not descended of Cymrian stock, his whole family had lived for centuries in a land that had once been part of the first Cymrian empire, prior to its dissolving in the Great War and returning to an independent Sorbold ruled by the family dynasty of the Dark Earth.

Fhremus's family had been loyal subjects and military servants of that Dynasty, which itself had been installed long before by the Scales.

It was his understanding that every major decision of state in the First Cymrian Age, and certainly the history of the dynasty of the Dark Earth, had been decided by those scales. Fhremus was a man of normal life span, as was the rest of his family, and while he knew that there were those alive who had seen those Weighings, had in fact sailed on the very ships that had brought the Scales to this land in the first place, he could only place his faith in the history and traditions that validated their wisdom. Being a military man, it was a way of life that applied to everything he knew.

Or thought he knew.

As if summoned by an internal call, Fhremus drained the last of the brew in his tankard and set it down on the rim of the fountain, then rose unsteadily and walked the darkening streets to the city hilltop where the Scales stood.

When he finally arrived at the Place of Weight, as the sacred hill was known, he stood at the foot of the Scales and gazed up, his eyes still partially clouded by drink, at the massive crossbeam that held the chains of the two enormous plates on either side of the towering stanchion. There was something deep and mystical about the instrumentality, as if it was its own entity with a spirit, imbued with wisdom of ages past considered so irrefutable, so complete, as to make it the judge for all decisions of state throughout two separate eras, two different empires.

Fhremus himself was one of the few people to ever mount the stand and place himself in front of one of those enormous plates. When Leitha, the empress of Sorbold, had died the year before, Fhremus, as the supreme commander of her armed forces, stepped forward to represent the military in the choosing of a new leader for the now-headless land.

The Crown Prince Vyshla, Leitha's only child and heir, had by coincidence died an hour or so before she had, and she had reigned for so long, almost three-quarters of a century, that all but the most distant of her family had died out in the meantime. To see if any of those distant family members were considered to be the choice of the Scales, the Ring of State, a symbol of royal conference, was placed in one of the two plates, while the individual aspirant to the throne was offered the opportunity to stand in the other while it was held in place.

Then the plate was released.

Each of those family members had been Weighed and found wanting; in the same atmosphere as an event of bloodsport, a gigantic crowd of observers hooted and catcalled each time a prospective emperor or empress was hurled unceremoniously out of the plate by a violent swing of the arm of the crossbeam. It was universally humbling to aspirants who wished to be granted divine status, and Fhremus could not blame the crowd for the joy it took in watching the mighty humbled.

After no one from the actual family survived being Weighed, at least in the ceremonial sense of the word *survived*, various other factions had stepped forward to be considered. Each group presented a symbol that represented it, and that symbol was placed on one Weighing plate across from the Ring of State of Sorbold.

When it was Fhremus's group's turn to be Weighed, their symbol, the military's shield of state used in the service of the empress, was Weighed quickly and rejected, rather than thrown by the Scale arm, so for that at least he was grateful. His humiliation was much less than that of those who had gone before him, and he was secretly pleased by the decision; he had never believed that the military should rule anything, especially a land as powerful and full of resources as the empire of Sorbold. So he returned to his place, watching the proceedings.

The counts of the large city-states, lesser nobles in the pantheon that Leitha reigned supreme over, mounted the stand next, led by a particularly pompous man named Tryfalian. Their symbol, a dynastic seal for stamping treaties, was Weighed and found unworthy, swung violently off the Place of Weight and tossed into the surrounding streets, again to the delight of the crowd. Fhremus had been vocally opposed to the plans of this group and relieved by this outcome, as he was a believer that the empire should remain united, and it was the spoken intent of the nobility to dissolve the empire into a few groupings of some of the larger city-states.

The Scales weighed against both the idea and the individual aspirants.

Then the Hierarch of the eastern Mercantile, a man named Ihvarr, came forward to be Weighed on behalf of the merchant class. The jest in which he had tossed a gold coin of the realm, a Sorbold sun, indicated how certain he was that the Mercantile, a class of people often viewed with disdain by royalty, nobility, and landed gentry for being of the working class, was not the resource from which the next emperor would come.

His shock was no greater than that of the crown when the Scales balanced the coin against the Ring of State.

He made his way amid the taunts of the nobility to the Weighing plate, carefully stepping into it.

And was thrown violently across the square to the base of the reviewing stand set up for dignitaries, local and foreign, breaking his neck with a sickening *crack*, to Talquist's great shock.

When the bitter members of the rejected nobility began taunting Talquist, who was Ihvarr's counterpart as the western guild Hierarch,

Talquist's response to the nobility's jeering speaker had impressed Fhremus. He recalled some of the words by heart.

Nobility, are you, now, Sitkar? You only know one meaning of the word, apparently. There is far more nobility in the hand of a man who earns his bread, rather than stealing it from the mouths of those who do by a distant scrap of Right of Kings. Perhaps the Mercantile represent something that none in your faction ever could: an understanding that the Earth rewards the man who works it, honors it, respects it—not just feeds off it.

Then he stepped into the plate of the Scales and was lifted high, silently, above the stunned crowd in the square of the Place of Weight.

Fhremus remembered the sensation of his knee touching the ground.

A feeling that justice had been served.

And the indication that the new emperor of Sorbold might bring about needed change that even he, a devoted supporter of the empress, knew was necessary.

The words of Nielash Mousa, the benison of the basilica of the Dark Earth, currently missing from Terreanfor, Sorbold's elemental cathedral, had given the last word on the subject.

Whosoever doubts the wisdom of the Scales, it is as if he is calling into question the integrity of the Earth itself. Let none be so blasphemous as to do so.

And yet, all of that memory notwithstanding, Fhremus was feeling blasphemous.

A beating of heavy wings sounded over his head.

Fhremus looked up as an enormous crow soared above him, seeking a place to land for the night. Fhremus's lip curled; crows were loathsome birds as far as he was concerned, filthy and diseased and dangerous in some places of Sorbold that bordered the grainlands of the Alliance, where they could grow to have a wingspan of seven feet, live a hundred years, and pluck out the eyes of deer and small children.

He watched in disgust as it settled into one of the plates of the Scales.

And sat there, making no impact on the balance whatsoever.

Fhremus's brow furrowed.

He stepped closer. The bird was planted squarely in the center of the plate, but that plate remained in balance with its counterpart.

Fhremus picked up a stone from the street and, feeling disrespectful, hurled it at the crow, which ascended into the sky quickly, cawing loudly, and flew off.

The Scale plate did not move.

Fhremus could not believe it.

Even the stone, which was now lying in the Weighing plate, should have set the Scales off balance.

And yet they remained utterly equal.

Fhremus shook his head violently to clear from it the effects of the drink.

When Nielash Mousa was undertaking the first round of determination of which class should be considered for Weighing, he had put the symbols of each class in the opposing plate. The shield of the empress's regiment, the nobility's seal, and the slight weight of even a single gold coin had unbalanced the Scale enough for a moment.

And yet the weight of a large bird, and a sizable stone, did not register at all.

Like a moth drawn to fire, Fhremus walked forward.

And, ignoring the screaming in his soul of the voice warning of his unworthiness, stepped up into the hanging plate.

Which balanced against its empty counterpart without sinking at all.

Sweet All-God, he thought, the world spinning violently around him. *Sweet All-God. The Scales have been altered—rigged.*

He would have more willingly believed in the possibility that the sun could have been convinced to stop its trek across the sky than what he was witnessing.

Like a man who had drunk far more than he had that night, the supreme commander of the forces of the emperor stumbled out of the plate and onto the street.

Then stood, his hand on his chin, contemplating the benison's words again.

Whosoever doubts the wisdom of the Scales, it is as if he is calling into question the integrity of the Earth itself. Let none be so blasphemous as to do so.

Bitter gall rose up in his throat.

If doubting the wisdom of the Scales is blasphemy, then what would the word be that captures the act of altering them to one's whim? Treachery? Betrayal? Treason?

There were no ample words.

Like a man in a stupor, he made his way from the Place of Weight back to the barracks without remembering how he got there.

He lay down on his cot and stared at the ceiling, contemplating the spinning of the Earth.

Which had just gone off-kilter.

And closed his eyes, unsuccessfully praying for sleep to come.

Before his morning shift of guarding the emperor of Sorbold began again.

21

The Teeth
(Manteids)

★

• Night Mountain
Earth Basilica

Desert

THE INNER TEETH, SORBOLD, ABOVE THE GREAT CANYON

At least getting past the first layer of mountains was easy, Achmed thought to himself.

He had just traversed the last rocky slope at the inner edge of the Outer Teeth, the mountains that bordered Tyrian and served as a barrier between the Middle Continent and western Sorbold. Except for a line of watchtowers that were clearly manned and occupied, this outer layer was sparsely settled and obviously used more by the Sorbolds for observation and reconnaissance than for assault capability.

It had served as the first test of his cloaks, and the skill of the leathermakers of Navarne.

From the time he had abandoned the last of his Wings in Tyrian and had traversed the terrain solely on foot, Achmed had taken to traveling at night and sleeping, covered by whichever of his cloaks most nearly matched the terrain, by day. The lack of habitation, the scarcity of man-controlled light and signal fires, allowed his night eyes, eyes of cave dwellers with sight that did not require light in the tunnels of caves and mountains, to function almost as well as normal vision did in the daytime. As a result he was able to cross the first ring of mountains without notice.

Whereupon he found himself now at the top of the ridge, staring down into the deep, twenty-one-mile-wide chasm and across at the second ridge of mountains beyond it.

At the edge of which stood the gleaming palace of Jierna Tal, its beautiful minarets and its famous guardian tower shining brightly in the distance like a jewel in the daytime, like a beacon at night.

Sprouting from the midst of the immense, heavily populated, and heavily armed city of Jierna'sid.

Achmed sighed in annoyance.

The canyon was far more open than the maps had led him to believe; inwardly he cursed Ashe's reconnaissance. The floor of it was relatively flat, but rocky outcroppings of irregular sizes ran across it, providing some decent cover but not as much as he had expected. Large areas of the floor were also obvious flash-flood plains, which made him wonder if one of the reasons for a minimum of human guardianship was the fact that the weather was an ally of the emperor; it was clear that even the smallest of rainstorms could provide savage flooding in a realm where the ground was baked hard as clay pottery.

He quickly checked his supplies before he descended. The water had held up well, as had the flatbread, but a few of the small fruits he had brought along for energy and fluid had molded, making them unusable. Achmed tossed them aside in disgust.

The day was still young when he reached the canyon bottom, so he found a large rock formation with an overhang and, after doing a quick preliminary scouting for wanderers, and finding nothing but a few snakes, settled into the shady side of the formation, covered himself with the matching cloak, and disappeared from the sight of nothing.

The tedium of the crossing suited Achmed well.

Other people might have found the endless plotting of the course through a vast and dry rocky gulch to be frustrating, but actually it was a harkening back to his past, a time in his life when he was alone, having not met Grunthor yet, and traversing a part of the world that looked almost entirely like this canyon.

In the old world he had discovered people living in caves at the upper edges of the canyon, his first introduction to humans who had a great deal in common with Firbolg. There was enough settlement, enough commerce in that place in the old world for him to occasionally come up from the trails to the ridge and purchase or trade for water or food, and so he did, whenever he felt the need.

He recalled a morning when he noted a small child, a good deal less than two summers old, tottering on the rock rim above a canyon almost as deep as this one. The child was unwatched, his mother busy manufacturing a blanket for possible sale to one of the travelers that came by, few and far between. Achmed had no affinity for children; in fact, his sensitive skin-web, the tracings of nerve ending and veins that scored the surface of his skin, allowing him to sense the vibrations of the world, was often in pain in their presence, particularly if they cried or were in need of changing.

But, even in spite of his dislike of children, he was made nervous by watching the little boy walking endlessly back and forth, balancing on a thin, rocky ridge that ended with a drop of a thousand feet or more.

Finally he attempted to get the attention of the woman he thought was the child's mother, and in his best semi-verbal signaling, indicated his concern for the child's welfare.

Should he—be allowed to walk like that up there?

The woman looked up from her weaving and shrugged. As uncertain as Achmed had been of his own communication, he was utterly positive in her reply.

They only fall once.

For days afterward, Achmed had been simultaneously appalled and impressed.

He was recalling the experience when he almost stepped on a bony hand sticking out from beneath some canyon scrub.

The Bolg king regained his balance and stopped.

Lying in the scrub was a body, broken and desiccated. It had clearly been there for some time, but not more than a year or even a few seasons.

Achmed looked up.

He had traversed the entire canyon; how he had managed to not notice this was a shock to him. The roots of the mountains that were the Inner Teeth had begun subtly, and now he stood directly below the rise to the top of the ridge whereupon the city of Jierna'sid was built.

On the southwestern face.

High above him, the tower loomed, piercing the clouds.

Not knowing if this was a trap, Achmed quickly took cover.

He waited beneath his leather cloak for several hours until sunset, and, having seen no one and nothing, made his way out from under his camouflage and went back to the body again before all light had left the sky.

After draping his cloak across two rock formations to mask his movements, he bent down again and brushed the scrub back.

The bones had belonged to a woman, by the appearance of the clothing that they were wrapped in. There was a familiarity about the clothing that nagged at the back of Achmed's mind, though he could not imagine he had ever seen anything like them before.

On his one foray into Sorbold, for the funeral of the Empress Leitha, he had spent all his free time wooing a Panjeri gypsy who was a sealed master in the art of glassmaking, something he needed desperately to aid him in the reconstruction of the Lightcatcher. He had spent every moment he was not actually at the funeral negotiating with her, and finally succeeded in convincing her to come to Ylorc with him and work on his project.

Which she did.

Until Grunthor discovered she was actually Esten, the mistress of the Raven's Guild.

Achmed cursed silently now, recalling the treachery and his own stupidity in allowing it to happen.

But, in any case, he had not spent any time examining the garb of Sorbold women, so the sense that he had seen this form of dress before puzzled him.

Slowly, so as to not be seen from any of the guard towers in either the Outer or the Inner Teeth, or in the tower itself, he uncovered more of the body.

The woman had been tall, from what he could surmise; the bones that were wrapped in shrunken skin were long and thin. The robes she wore were light, making sense with the desert clime, but old-fashioned, as if they had come from another era in Time. Achmed took the fabric between his thumb and forefinger; it felt silky, but also modest of manufacture. It also appeared to be worn and threadbare, as if the owner were poor or not well looked after.

Around the bony, sun-dried neck, he could see there was a leather cord. Whatever bauble or pendant had hung from that cord around her neck in her lifetime had snagged on the brush and was out of sight, in the shade of a large rock beside her skull.

Achmed opened his second cloak and slowly positioned it over more of the body. Then he crept closer, with agonizing slowness, until he could reach the leather cord. When he did, he gently pulled the strings away from the rock, feeling something metal and sharp rise out from behind it, still attached to its leather tether.

Darkness had come into the sky while he took his time, and now it was night in the canyon.

Within the very last shaft of radiance at the horizon's edge, there was just enough light to see by if he held the object up to it.

He slid his hand over the neck of the corpse and gently pulled the object over the broken shoulder.

And held it up to the fading light.

It was a metal tool, hinged together at the top, with two identical legs like calipers that were attached to the hinge, allowing them to be spread or closed. Between them was a support hinge that ran crosswise, and at the end of the legs were sharp points clad in tiny leather caps, ostensibly to avoid injury.

She's probably not too worried about getting poked at this point, Achmed thought grimly.

He stared at the tool, in the last of the light.

As a sickening realization came over him.

It was a compass.

The sort of tool a mariner used to plot courses on charts and maps. An ancient tool that had, long ago, allowed a seafarer to find this place, or, actually, the western coasts of the continent, its seaside cliffs wrapped in the clouds of mist that had hidden it from human sight for all of history, and helped him to find it again on his way back from the Island of Serendair.

Merithyn's compass.

"Rhonwyn," Achmed whispered.

He knew she couldn't hear him, obviously, had dispensed enough death in his lifetime not to believe in ghosts or spirits or even vibrations clinging to the empty shell of abandoned bodies after life had fled, but there was something sad and necessary about invoking her name.

He had met her twice in life, and seen her thrice, the second time at the Cymrian Council where Ashe and Rhapsody had been chosen as Lord and Lady, the third time at their wedding, where he had not spoken to her.

But the first time he had ever seen her was in an abbey in the holy city of Sepulvarta, where he had traveled with Rhapsody to get some answers about the children of a demonic construct known as the Rakshas.

Rhapsody had been trying to find out where on the continent these children, products of horrific rape, could be found. Rhonwyn's gift as one of the Seers, the three triplet daughters of Merithyn the Explorer and Elynsynos the dragon, was all-encompassing knowledge of the Present. Unfortunately, the realm of the Present to Rhonwyn was a span of approximately seven or eight seconds, after which the Present became the Past, and beyond her sight. She had driven Achmed almost insane with her prattle, until Rhapsody finally determined how to speak to her successfully, so by the time they had left her abbey his head had been throbbing with a headache beyond all proportion.

He could still hear in his mind the last exchange she had shared with Rhapsody, after hour upon hour of insane conversation.

Thank you, Grandmother. Rest now.

The Seer had looked at her dreamily.

You are called Rhapsody, she had said. *What do you ask?*

The same words she had greeted her with, hours before.

Achmed's head hurt with the memory.

And then another memory formed in his mind, painful in a different way.

It was a memory from a meeting that was held in secret, a council of war, really, which took place immediately after he, Grunthor, and Ashe had brought Rhapsody back with her newborn son from Elynsynos's cave in the forest of Gwynwood, where the child had been born. They had descended into a hidden cellar room and spoken in secret with Anborn and Constantin, the Patriarch, as well as Gwydion Navarne, who had just been invested as duke of his province.

The Patriarch had been the one to break the news.

Much is missing—much more than you can even imagine.

Tell us, Ashe had commanded.

Many things are missing, but I will begin with the one closest to your own family. Rhonwyn, your aunt, Lord Marshal, your great-aunt, Lord Cymrian, the Seer of the Present, has been taken from the Abbey of the Sun in Sepulvarta.

While he had always suspected Talquist was responsible or at least complicit in her disappearance, it had never occurred to Achmed that anyone would be foolish enough to murder the most helpless and harmless of the three Seers, known as the Manteids, for which Gwylliam originally named the mountain range known as the Teeth.

Women who had been vested with the deep lore of vision into the Past, Present, and Future.

Epic figures in history.

Gods, he thought as he looked at the body now with new realization. *Gods; he must have thrown her from the tower.*

He looked above him, where the tower stood.

And knew he was right.

As much as Rhonwyn had annoyed him with the necessity of her form of speech, Achmed found himself nauseated at the thought of her death, imagining her last moments and the utter confusion she must have suffered.

One more reason to add to the list, Talquist, he thought bitterly.

He thought back to the morning months before when he had left Ylorc to begin this mission, the first solo assassination he had undertaken since coming to the new world.

He had been in the Great Hall of Ylorc packing in preparation for his journey to Sorbold when Grunthor appeared. The Sergeant-Major had sized up the situation instantly, but had felt the need to ask the question anyway.

Where is it you will be goin', sir?

After Talquist. As soon as she's gone.

Achmed had ordered the Sergeant-Major to activate the Archons, his most trusted advisors after Grunthor himself. The Sergeant had nodded and turned to leave, then looked back at the Bolg king.

I'm never goin' to get that image out of my 'ead, he had said quietly.

Achmed had nodded in silent agreement. He had been thinking the same thing from the moment he had come into the Great Hall.

He shook his head now to try to drive Rhapsody's voice out of his ears, unsuccessfully as always. She had uttered the sentence that was burned in his memory after discovering that Talquist had had dealings with the baron of Argaut, a man the Three had all known in the old world as Michael, the Wind of Death, who had been especially brutal to Rhapsody. Until that moment, however, Achmed had not realized exactly how much.

Occasionally, when I inadvertently crossed him in a way he did not find stimulating, or when he was merely bored, his favorite pastime was to encourage—no, actually, command—his entire regiment to rape me while he watched. Every one of them. Repeatedly.

Given that Michael had been the voluntary host of a F'dor demon, the possibility that Talquist had been compromised, might even be a demonic thrall, was certainly enough of a reason to hasten his decision to go after him. But, in truth, it was really the unwanted picture now in his mind that had been the impetus for him to finally leave the mountain, to narrow his focus to the singular intent of putting an end to the life and plans of the Merchant Emperor of Sorbold.

He had almost spat the explanation at Rath when the Dhracian demon hunter had objected to his targeting of Talquist at the expense of his participation in the Primal Hunt, the tracking and extermination of the loose F'dor in the world that the ancient Brethren practiced to the exclusion of every other priority.

You may not understand this, Rath, but not every evil in this world is conceived and executed by elder races. The F'dor may have brought the forces of destruction and chaos into this world at its beginning, but they no longer are the exclusive owners of the concept. A man wants something: a child, a woman, immortality, sadistic satisfaction—and if he has a crown, he thinks he can have whatever he wishes, and do whatever he wants with them. He doesn't have to be of an elder race. He doesn't have to be part of a larger design, he doesn't have to desire the unraveling of the world. Your lore disregards the wretched sadist, the petty manipulator, the cruel abuser, the power-mad despot—not everyone who needs to die is a demon.

Especially someone who might be carrying on the legacy of the maniac who had degraded one of his only two friends in the world in such a terrible way.

Now he had a concrete image of one of the nightmares that had tormented her constantly, terrors he had witnessed every time the Three had slept on their endless trek through the root of Sagia, along the Axis Mundi, through the depths of the world. More often than not, when his sleep was peppered with dreams, that was what he saw.

It was as if he had inadvertently taken Rhapsody's nightmares on himself.

It was the top entry on his imaginary list of reasons to snuff out Talquist's life.

Now he was looking at another one.

He stroked the woman's mummified hand, then took the compass and held it up before his eyes.

"I wish that you could explain to me one nagging mystery," he said aloud to the corpse, almost absently. "If what your sister Anwyn said to Rhapsody was true, then the prophecy about death in unnatural childbirth has already occurred, in the Past. But, if I'm not mistaken, the Seer that uttered that prophecy was Manwyn, the Seer of the Future. Mayhap when the Past is changed, whatever replaces it is the Future of a sort. I wish you were still alive to explain this to me. Though no doubt you would just stare at me and babble something about the Present."

He brushed a spider off the Seer's mummified forehead that had started to crawl into what was left of her hair.

"I must leave you here, I'm sorry. One day, when this is over, if the continent is still in one piece, I will come back for you and get Rhapsody to do whatever it is she does by way of burial rituals. But I will take your father's compass back to your family. It shouldn't be left here. I'm sure you would agree if you were able."

He thought a moment longer.

"Of course, seven or eight seconds later, you would forget that you had."

The last light left the sky, plunging the world, and the depths of the canyon, into total darkness.

22

PROVINCE OF BETHANY, ON THE WAY TO THE CAPITAL

The column of mounted soldiers thundered down the trans-Orlandan thoroughfare, four abreast, displacing enormous amounts of earth into the hot summer air.

In the center of the front rank rode the Lady Cymrian atop a barded warhorse, her chest similarly armored by a mail shirt of red-gold dragon scales, her green eyes gleaming in the clear wind of the Middle Continent. Upon her head was the smallest helm that the Bolg had ever smithed; the Sergeant-Major had presented it to her solemnly a number of years before, telling her that if it was too big to suitably protect her skull, he could use it as a codpiece to protect his genitals. Then he had shaken his head.

Naw. Would be too tight.

Beside her to the left was Knapp, Anborn's longtime man-at-arms. She was well aware by the vibrations emanating from him that Knapp had resisted being deployed with her, even if she could not hear what he had said when conferring with the Lord Marshal prior to Anborn's leaving

Canderre. Rhapsody did not take offense at such things; she had been short of stature compared to her compatriots in all endeavors since childhood, and had long since learned to ignore being underestimated. The initial resistance had not resolved, as it generally did, but rather baked into a sullen, silent mien set across the face of the First Generation soldier.

It did not bother the Lady Cymrian whatsoever.

They had encountered a cohort of scouts that had breached the Threshold fifteen leagues from the capital of Bethany, and a party of chase had made short work of the men, capturing their horses and taking three of the six prisoner while slicing down the other half in an exchange of bolt fire. A quick conference had found the three commanders and Knapp to be in agreement as to the origination point of the cohort, but the Lady Cymrian had disagreed, citing the false notes she could hear in each of their confessions.

She had dismounted when the men were brought before the front rank, their hands bound behind their backs, and made her way impatiently through the line of guards until she stood directly in front of them.

The sternness of her expression was something Knapp, who had known her since her ascension to the Ladyship, had never seen before; there was a palpable fury in her emerald-green eyes that made it seem almost as if they were on fire. Her golden hair, shorn to the nape of her neck, had a distinctly masculine aspect to it, an effect so unlike how she had always appeared. The sharpness of her features and the coiled musculature in her stance made the ancient soldier unsure as to whether the cold chills sweeping his body, and clearly those of the three surviving members of the sortie, were signs of terror or arousal.

With a ringing sweep she drew Daystar Clarion, pulling it forth from its scabbard in roaring flames. The intent in the grip with which she clutched the hilt was deadly.

She looked at the other two captives, and with a decisive tilt of her head, she silently commanded the guards to remove them from the proximity.

The soldiers quickly obeyed.

"From whence did you deploy?" she demanded in the Sorbold tongue to the remaining soldier when the other two men were out of sight.

"Sepulvarta," the Sorbold said.

The vibration of his words rang false against her ear.

The Lady Cymrian seized the hilt of the sword with both hands and, two-handed, slapped the man square across the face with the burning blade, lighting his beard on fire. When he reared back, wide-eyed, she grabbed his shoulder and slammed him to the dirt of the roadway, face-down in the grit, where she snuffed the flames by rubbing his chin in the dust of the trans-Orlandan thoroughfare.

"Again," she said, her voice calm but her body betraying her rage. "From whence did you deploy?"

She signaled to the nearest guard to flip the man over onto his back.

She stared down into his face; it was striped with tears of terror. Her expression of anger receded, and her aspect became thoughtful. She bent down on one knee and leaned over the supine man, looking directly into his eyes.

"You will tell me the truth," she said softly, the tone of True-Speaking in her voice.

"You are—demon," the man whispered. "Painfully beautiful, but with an evil heart."

A small smile took up residence on the Lady's face.

"Had I been a demon, I would have slashed you across the eyes hor-izontally instead of slapping you with the blunt edge of my blade," she whispered in return. "I would have let your face burn off and enjoyed lis-tening to you scream, rather than snuffing the fire. I would have eaten your soul, but I assure you, if you had one when you crossed the border, you still do. It is you who are trespassing in my lands, not I in yours. *From whence did you deploy?*"

Something in her gaze was so intense, so compelling, that the soldier staring into her eyes felt as if he were looking directly into a roaring in-ferno. Against his will, a word formed on his lips and spilled out.

"Mvekgurn," he said.

Rhapsody blinked. "Mvekgurn?" she demanded. "You came in through the Hintervold?"

The man nodded weakly.

The Lady Cymrian looked up at Knapp and the commanders, whose faces bore all varying degrees of shock. Her stare returned to the Sorbold on the ground at her feet.

"How many? How many are coming?"

"I—I—"

The ancient sword of fire and ether was at his throat. *"How many?"*

"Thirty thousand Icemen," the Sorbold soldier whispered.

"How many men of the Sun?"

"I do not know."

The tiniest hint of a smile came back to the corners of her mouth. The Sorbold soldier's body stiffened on the ground.

"I don't believe you," the Lady Cymrian said softly. "One more time—how many men of the Sun?"

The swarthy man swallowed.

"I—do not know many details," he said in the harsh language of his nation. "But I heard Titactyk say that he was commanding one hundred and twenty thousand men."

For a moment the only sound on the thoroughfare was the ripple of a light wind.

The Lady Cymrian looked at him thoughtfully a moment longer, then nodded. She patted his face gently.

"Sorry about the beard," she said. "I do hope it will grow back quickly."

Knapp cocked his head. The guards seized the Sorbold and took him into the lines of the caravan. The Lady Cymrian returned to her horse and mounted again.

"Well, that's unfortunate," commented Decken, one of the field commanders assigned to her battalion.

"I wonder where Talquist has been quartering them," Knapp said, as if to himself.

"Perhaps he transported them on the blockade ships, and dropped them off in the north on their last seemingly legitimate run before the assaults," Rhapsody suggested. "Let's get on to the capital city; time is even more of the essence than it was a few moments ago."

*W*hen they arrived at the western gate of the city's edge, Rhapsody signaled to Knapp, indicating that she wanted him to follow her off the road a short way from the rest of the regiment. The First Generation Cymrian had not spoken even once during the remainder of the journey, but silently nodded and obeyed.

When the noise had receded enough to hear, she took off her helm and ran her fingers through her short hair, clearing it of sweat and tangles.

"I am not certain what I have done to annoy you, Knapp," she said directly. "You have been very withdrawn and short with me, even more so than usual, since we left Canderre. If you are displeased with Anborn assigning you to serve with me, I'm sorry about that, but—"

The ancient soldier looked suddenly older.

"Not at all, m'lady," he said stiffly. "It is to you that I must apologize."

"For what? I certainly take no offense at my comrades being quiet or short—it's a vast improvement over what I get from my Firbolg friends.

I just want to make certain we are not carrying silent problems around when we are about to be defending our Alliance's capital."

Knapp looked away. Then he sighed and met her gaze again.

"In the old world, being a human soldier, I occasionally took part in that custom you mentioned back in Canderre," he said quietly. "The, er, harvesting of Lirin women's—I am sorry, m'lady. I hope you will forgive me."

Rhapsody did not blink, but absorbed his words.

"Do you remember me? From that time?"

Knapp looked away again. "No, indeed," he said stonily. "If I ever saw—someone's face, I don't remember it; I tend to recall that I never did."

She nodded. "Is that all?"

Knapp looked back at her in surprise. "All?"

"Is there anything else bothering you?"

"No, m'lady—I am, well, have not thought about those days in more than a millennium, I am ashamed to say."

She nodded. "Very well. Let us get back to the regiment." She took the reins in hand and clicked to the warhorse.

Knapp sat up in surprise. "M'lady?"

"Yes?"

"Can—you see fit to forgive me? Whether it was you or not?"

Rhapsody exhaled.

"No," she said shortly. "I've forgotten how. If it consoles you, Knapp, I probably left the Island long before you were born. If it doesn't, ask me again after the war, if we both survive, and if it still matters to you. I will probably need to know how to forgive myself for things I've done as a soldier by then as well."

She clicked to the animal again and made her way back to the first rank of the regiment, Knapp a few heartbeats behind.

As the battalion set off into the capital city, the Third Armored Garrison of what Anborn had named the First Front.

The map shows "The Teeth (Manteids)", "Night Mountain / Earth Basilica", and "Desert".

THE IRON MINES, VORNESSTA, SORBOLD

The monstrous caverns of the volcanic deposit in which countless slaves toiled without ceasing were ringing in the unending cacophony of hammers and diamond-edged trowels, the maddening noise vibrating through Evrit's blood. Evrit had long become accustomed to that cacophony, having been surrounded by it for so long he could not remember what quiet actually felt like.

He was one of those slaves, taken with his family in the wake of a shipwreck into different places of servitude, his older son and he to this place of endless noise, the iron mines of Vornessta.

Talking during work hours, which comprised all but four in each day, was strictly forbidden, so Evrit had learned little of the geography of Sorbold; he had no idea where in the world he was. Sometimes when he was curled up against the wall of the sleeping tunnel, just before he would fall into an unconscious state, the ever-present noise more distant but still vibrating in his skin, he would pray to the God he was no longer certain he believed in to show him, just once, an image of his wife or his younger son, even if it was only in a dream.

Apparently that God could no longer hear his unspoken prayers over the pandemonium in which Evrit existed now.

But, in spite of the inevitability of a bad ending, Evrit had hope.

Sometime before, how long it had been he could not even begin to fathom, a lashman had hovered over him, whip in hand, and had dragged him from his place along the wall of ore up to within a handsbreadth of the man's mouth. While the rest of the slaves on the wall beside him skittered away in fear, the guard had whispered words in the language of Marincaer, his homeland, words that Evrit now repeated in his mind with every waking breath.

Fear not, friend, your liberty is coming. Be ready when the call comes to fight. Tell no one else. For what I must do now, I apologize.

Unconsciously, Evrit's hand went to his neck now, where a thin scar remained that the lashman's whip had drawn in blood.

Ever since that day, Evrit thought he had noticed glances between his fellow slaves and the guards, but having been a gentle tailor and the leader of an even more gentle religious sect called the Blessed in his former life, with no understanding of the practices of war or self-defense, he had no real way to gauge if those exchanges were meaningful or not.

He rose painfully at the foreman's whistle with his scuttle of ore and joined the line of his fellow slaves making their way to the enormous wheeled bins along the track from the smelting fires. The slag from the forges that had been sent up from below had been off-loaded into what could only rightfully be called a mountain of rock waste that towered to the ceiling of the enormous cavern. The bins were now empty again, awaiting the fruit of Evrit and his cave fellows' work.

One by one they tossed their scrapings over the edge into the wheeled bins two levels below and moved hurriedly back to the deposit wall under the eyes of their guards.

On his way back to the wall Evrit cast one last quick glance at the mountain of slag. When he first had been brought to the cave where he and hundreds of other slaves spent their days, one of dozens on that level, with dozens more on levels above and below him, he had heard several of the guards discussing the slag pile, which even then had reached to three-quarters or more of the height of the dome of the vast cavern. The tongue of the Sorbolds was a difficult one to learn, but Evrit had always had a capacity with language, being in the trade, and he felt certain he heard the men make humorous reference to the fact that the only exit doors out of the mine, other than the ones they had entered in at the base of the mountain range, were behind the towering pile of slag.

At least we never have to worry about escape.

In his time working in the mine, the mountain of slag had grown at least ten times thicker and had reached the top of the dome. It was a constant visual reminder of how and where their servitude would end, if anyone had ever thought to believe otherwise.

As he picked up his trowel again, Evrit looked furtively around at the guards and the lashmen. It seemed to him that the men with the whips were largely new, but it was hard to be certain in the dark of the sweat-filled cave. Any direct eye contact was punishable with the lash, so keeping one's eyes averted was a basic survival skill.

He was almost certain, however, that he saw the guard at the opening of the cave in which he was toiling nod to him, then turn away again.

Evrit returned to scratching ore, trying not to let his hope become too entrenched. That was the only thing that could completely crush the fragile resolve he had nurtured to survive long enough to find his family again.

23

THE OPEN SEA, BETWEEN GAEMATRIA
AND MANOSSE

*O*ow many days and nights Ashe had walked the waves between Gaematria and Manosse he no longer knew. He'd found it quicker and easier to travel the depths in the heavier water of the Twilight Realm, where the drift was minimal and the wake of a ship or a particularly large breaker did not drag his vaporous form off course. His mind was still reeling at what he could not help but consider a betrayal, fighting the knowledge that the refusal of the Sea Mages to aid the Alliance might very possibly have been the signing of the Middle Continent's death warrant.

And perhaps that of the Known World.

And the world beyond it. The Afterlife.

He was keeping track, however, of the passage of ships over his head. As he had predicted to his uncle, he was only able to traverse less than a dozen nautical miles before the ship traffic picked up again. By the feel of the pressure in their passage, he could tell that the vessels deployed off the coast of Gaematria were by and large warships, with merchant vessels and pirate ships fewer and farther between.

How in the world could you miss this, Edwyn? he wondered, but the loss once again of his corporeal form, and the return to a vaporous ele-mental state, had dispersed his rage, leaving behind only his fear.

For the first time in many weeks he was unable to beat back the thoughts of Rhapsody and Meridion. Giving voice to his son's existence, unplanned and unwise as it was, had planted the image of them both in what was left of his mind, filling his thoughts with worry for their safety. As a result, he found himself occasionally coming suddenly to awareness as large fish or cetaceans swam past, startlingly close to him, or noticing enormous gatherings of prey fish when he had already floated into their midst.

There is not enough of me left to concentrate on where I am going and what I have left behind at the same time, he thought sadly. Having to put aside thoughts of what gave meaning to his life in favor of concentrating on the duty he resented beyond reason was sheer torture of mind and soul.

He began to allow himself a few moments of the sweet respite of mem-ory whenever the despair threatened to overwhelm him. When he found himself thickening, his bodily form becoming heavier, he would cease his forward movement and hang motionless in the drift, as he had in his in-fant memory, closing his filmy eyes and letting his thoughts travel back to the Middle Continent, back in Time, to the scant moments in which he had held his wife and son in his arms together, cradling the family he loved.

They were the two people in the world who had given him the ability to conceive of family as something to be treasured, rather than the bur-den the one he had been born into had always been. Edwyn's refusal of aid or counsel had reinforced the horrific memories, the betrayal and ma-nipulations of his grandmother and father, so when the image of his wife and baby made their way insistently into his consciousness, he ceased push-ing them away and allowed himself a few moments of time to bask in them.

But only a few moments.

Deep as he was in the dark sea, where everything else was shadow, Ashe knew that should he luxuriate too long in the happiness of the Past, he would inadvertently sacrifice the Future.

So he mentally cut the lifeline those pleasant thoughts had attached to him.

It was a sensation similar to ripping the hand of the F'dor out of his chest and soul a quarter century before, leaving him in surpassing physi-cal and spiritual agony then. Now the agony was only spiritual.

But in some ways it was even more painful.

Finally the water became shallower, causing him to rise into the Sun-lit Realm once more.

I must be approaching Manosse, he thought, seeing more exotic plant life and signs of human existence—the wreckage of ships, empty barrels, and driftwood along the sandy bottom. *Soon, soon I will be home. My mother's home.*

And then, finally, I will have the aid I need to return to the continent.

24

Gwydion Navarne was absolutely terrified.

Having only participated in one battle in his entire life, now being quartered in his province's garrison, without his adopted grandmother or the Lord Marshal for the minimal comfort of familiarity, was difficult enough. But given that Anborn had decided that he was to serve in the First Front as division leader over a garrison of trained soldiers, all of whom Ashe had selected personally and for whom the Lord Cymrian had designed the regimen of training, the young duke was so nervous that he had been unable to sleep and barely able to eat since arriving in camp.

Rhapsody, who had been sent with Anborn's trusted comrade Knapp to defend the capital of Bethany, the largest and most central of the Orlandan provincial capitals, within the Third Armored Garrison, had taken him aside and looked thoughtfully into his eyes before deploying herself. He had expected her to pat his face comfortingly as she had on so many other such occasions, but instead his adopted grandmother had merely stared at him and satisfied her own need for information about him, whatever it was.

Trust the soldiers that are coming, she had advised. *They know what they are doing, even if you don't.*

If her intention had been to reassure him, it had failed.

After much weighing of his options, he had decided to address his concerns to the Lord Marshal before he had left to head south to lead the Second Front in the assault on Sorbold. Gwydion had confessed his doubts about his own fitness to lead, and requested that someone, anyone of higher rank and greater experience than he could be named commander. Anborn's stinging retort was still was ringing painfully in his ears, long after the Lord Marshal had departed.

The bandage roller and the piss boy both are of higher rank and greater experience than you, cur. Stop sniveling. You bear an elemental sword, and you have no right to dishonor that blade with your doubt. Stand up straight, look the men you command in the eye once they get here, and remember your lineage; your father held off an entire brigade of Sorbold soldiers with little more than a roasting fork at the assault on the Winter Carnival four years ago. My father Gwylliam would have thrown himself from the deck of his ship or from the peaks of Canrif on numerous occasions had it not been for the wisdom and strength of your ancient forebear, Hague, for whom this place is named. This is your family's citadel. Defend it. You can do this, whether you believe it or not. And even if you cannot, you will. You have no other choice.

Once the soldiers from Canderre had arrived, his hope had risen somewhat upon seeing how well trained and prepared they were. But not long after their arrival the skies had begun to turn gray in the north, fraught with distant smoke and the faint smell of burning wood and metal, and an ominous rumbling that kept growing ever nearer.

The scouts had reported that the approaching Sorbold army from the northwest numbered approximately twenty-five thousand, with reinforcements from the Hintervold of five to seven thousand more coming from northeast. Gwydion had been shocked at the numbers, given what a major percentage of the enemy forces he knew they comprised.

Then realization came over him like a cold wave, with the understanding that his western province of Navarne was an eastern gateway to the Great Forest, and that if the capital was taken, it would be a perfect outpost from which the Sorbold army could launch offensives east into Bethany, north into Canderre, and west into the forest itself, in close proximity to the Filidic Circle and the Great White Tree there.

His ineptitude might very well be responsible for the loss of the Middle Continent.

He thought of Haguefort, his family's keep and ancestral lands to the west, and wondered dully if it was in the direct line of fire from the advancing Sorbold forces. Anborn had deemed the keep and its surrounding wall insufficient to withstand a siege and had ordered it evacuated, the villages around it left empty in the path of the oncoming enemy.

Gwydion thought of the Cymrian museum, his father's beloved historical repository on its grounds, where Stephen had spent endless hours lovingly polishing and maintaining the relics and remnants of an all-but-forgotten age, patiently recounting stories to Gwydion in his childhood of all the reasons they had to be proud of their lineage, and some of the reasons they had not to be. He thought of the frescoes on the ceilings of Haguefort, the small castle of rosy brown stone that had been his and Melisande's home, the suits of armor and the weapons proudly displayed for only a few eyes to appreciate.

And wondered if it would withstand whatever atrocities might be committed upon it in the war that was rumbling closer with each passing moment.

It occurred to him that his rapid death might in fact be the best possible outcome for the troops that were standing, in a full muster, within the central courtyard of the walled garrison that had once been Navarne City. At least then an experienced soldier would rise from within this muster and take over command, someone who knew what to do, who would not falter in the face of direct combat.

Dear All-God, help me, he prayed silently as the troops broke muster and headed off for duty and their shifts at the wall. *Give me strength, give me wisdom, not for myself, for them. They don't deserve the commander with whom they have been shackled.*

He had no idea that the All-God had placed the answer to his prayers just beyond the gate.

"M'lord, we have need of your attention to a matter at the wall," Lieutenant Lausten, his attaché, said, hurrying across the town square that had been transformed into the central courtyard of the garrison.

"What is the matter?" Gwydion Navarne asked nervously as the man passed him, indicating the direction he should follow.

"The captain has asked for you, m'lord, and says it is urgent," Lausten said as they made their way to the wall. "The scouts are involved; Solarrs has sent his last report before riding east to Bethany. Hurry, please, sir—"

Gwydion broke into a dead run.

A cohort of archers was ascending the north wall as he arrived at the garrison's edge. Gwydion watched them climb, quickly and efficiently, and spread out across the rampart, setting their crossbows and longbows into the wooden stands that had been designed with vertical slats to shield them as they fired.

Before him was a small cadre of archers surrounding a man in a hooded gray robe, the kind often seen on religious pilgrims and men of the Great Forest. The man was kneeling on the ground, his hands behind his head, his hood still up.

Each of the crossbowmen was aiming at his head.

"What is going on here?" Gwydion demanded.

"M'lord, this man was found beyond the gates and the trenches, in the same position you see him now, bearing a scrap of parchment with Solarrs's imprimatur," the captain, a man named Filius, said quietly as he handed the scrap to Gwydion. "As we needed to set the final seal of the gates, I deliberated and decided it was best to bring him inside, rather than delay the closing of the gates."

"Good," said Gwydion Navarne. "Maintain your stance, archers."

He walked to the man, whose face was still shielded by his wide hood, and stopped before him. "What are you doing here, friend?" he asked, trying as hard as he could to evoke the voice of his father. "And with the signature of Anborn's chief scout?"

"I have come to your aid, at the request of the Lord Marshal," said a deep voice from within the hood. "Solarrs recognized me on the road, or rather I recognized him. He was in a hurry, but he gave me his imprimatur that you would know I am a friend. As you have just named me."

Gwydion blinked. The deep voice was familiar, but he struggled to recall where he had heard it before.

"By all means, stand, please," he said, "and lower your arms."

He did not tell the archers to stand down.

The man obeyed, shaking the dust from his robes.

"Where do I know you from, friend?" Gwydion asked.

"From a meeting in the depths of your own domicile," the man said, his tone indicating annoyance. "Or perhaps from your attendance at High Holy Day ceremonies in mine."

The young duke of Navarne dropped to one knee.

"Your Grace," he said, his voice choking with emotion.

The broad-shouldered man exhaled, then took down his hood.

As recognition swept throughout the garrison, the archers lowered their bows and dropped to their knees as well.

Constantin, the exiled Patriarch of Sepulvarta.

"Get up, you young fool," he thundered at the duke. "I told you that when we met before. You are a child of the All-God, as am I, as are they." He gestured impatiently at the soldiers, who hurried to a stand as well. "The enemy is coming; it does not suit for them to find you on your knees, lest they bring you to them against your will. Here, in this place, we shall stand!"

A roar rose from within the streets of the barricaded capital.

"Back to your posts," the Patriarch commanded. "If your commander wills it, that is." He looked markedly at the young duke, who signaled his agreement. Then, as the soldiers returned to their posts with renewed vigor, Constantin came to him and looked down at him seriously.

"Your task here is a mammoth one, young Navarne," he said quietly. "It is likely that those of us within these walls have seen our last sunrise. But I have finished all but the last of my tasks reconnecting the Chain of Prayer, and if we live through the stand we are about to make, and I am successful in Avonderre, I will need your assistance to help free Sepulvarta from her captors. So today, I will help you in your fight; then, when I am ready, you will assist me in mine. Are we agreed?"

"Absolutely."

For the first time since taking down his hood, Constantin smiled.

"Good. Then let us set to defending your province."

25

The morning shadows of the Teeth were serving to hide the invasion force well for the moment, Hrarfa noted.

The longest shadow other than that cast by the sun through the towering, fanglike peaks of the mountains was her own, or, rather, that of the titanic stone body that she shared with the Faorina spirit, Faron. She had been unable to sense his presence for all of the night and the better part of the day before, when she had felt a glimpse of his simmering anger, a flash of resentful rage, or something like it. The caustic burn that rippled briefly over her consciousness had caused her nagging worry; Hrarfa knew that if they were to assault the Bolg mountains together in one stone body, the potential that the demonic child might balk, resist, or outright refuse at a time when his cooperation was critical could bring about disaster.

Faron, she whispered in the empty darkness of the Living Stone sepulchre. *Faron, please speak to me. We need to be of one mind again before we go forth.*

We have never been of one mind.

The words, spoken harshly, in close proximity to her conscious mind, startled Hrarfa, sending waves of shock through her amorphous being.

Thudding silence followed.

Faron, Hrarfa whispered, trying to keep her thoughts from angering the Faorina further, *tell me what has you distressed. Please.*

For what seemed like forever, the silence remained unbroken. Finally, she heard the voice of the Faorina, distinct and calm.

What you want is not what I want.

The F'dor spirit went cold.

How can that be? Hrarfa whispered when she recovered her ability to do so. *You are one of us, Faron, one of the firstborn race of this world, the Children of Fire. We* all *want the same thing—to shatter the Vault of the Underworld, to set the Earth to flame as we dance upon its surface, free.*

No. The rejection was so intense that it made Hrarfa's consciousness vibrate. *No. That is not what I want.*

What—what do you want, then, Faron?

An image formed in Hrarfa's awareness almost immediately. It was that of a man, the long-lived escapee from the Island of Serendair that had been known as the Seneschal, the human host of the demon that had fathered the Faorina child. In the image, the man was sitting beside a pool of gleaming green water, feeding eels to a misshapen monster that Hrarfa assumed was Faron's true form. There was, for a fleeting moment, a re-membrance of the comfort of the water, a fondness beyond her under-standing, a tenderness in the thoughts that she found disturbing. When it abated, and the image faded, she spoke in careful thoughts again.

I know that you wish to be reunited with him, Faron, and in order for that to happen—

I saw him pass through to the depths through the green Death scale, the Faorina spirit spat in return. *You can do* nothing *to reunite us, your prom-ises to the contrary.*

He is in the Vault with all the others of our race, our family, Hrarfa thought insistently. *As are all the others who have gone back there from this world before him. All we need is the key to the Vault, the rib of the Sleeping Child—*

Have you ever returned to the Vault since your escape?

This time silence reigned from Hrarfa's locale.

I thought not, Faron said bitterly. *So you have never seen for yourself if those spirits that die upon the Earth are sent back there for Eternity. For all you know, when we open it, it will be empty.*

No, Faron, no, Hrarfa thought desperately. *I can* hear *them. I can hear their dark voices, chanting, gleeful. Our kind can never die—we can but be contained. Your father awaits you. Come—let us go to the Bolglands, take the rib from the Earthchild, and go to the Vault. You will see.*

The silence that followed did not surprise her.

Finally, when she did not sense a reply forthcoming, Hrarfa began to chant softly, whispering the incantations of elemental fire. She wove into them the lust of battle, the glee at the smell of carnage, the excitement of the energy of fear that had always raised gooseflesh on her human bodies when she had inhabited them. She spoke ancient words, sounds more of crackling flames and howling wind than those that were uttered by worldly tongues, countersigns in the evilest of speech, dire words of prehistoric power.

A lullabye she suspected the demonic half of his father had whispered to him at one time or another.

Now spiced with the buildup to the glorious fornication of assault, of battle, of savage destruction.

Of war.

With each new phrase, she could feel the stone body of the titanic soldier stiffen, a tumescence akin to that of sexual desire, as the lore of the element reached into the thoughts of the child who was half born of it. She spoke the poetry of beheadings, chanted the rhymes of savage rape and disembowelment, whispered the percussive noise of crunching bone and slithering brain as it escaped the casing of the skull. She crooned the paths of blood rivers, intoned the thump of organs being exploded by the stomping boot, hummed the timber of agonized wailing and the gasping of fear.

And smiled to herself as she felt the Faorina spirit respond, at first unwilling, though aroused, then more excited as she intoned her symphony of death, her serenade of widescale brutal murder.

She could all but feel him panting.

She had knobbed enough men in human form to recognize the point after which she was in utter control of his thoughts, and chuckled to herself in the knowledge that her abilities of seduction had not left her even when she had been evicted from her flesh host. When the bloodlust was all but orgiastic, she allowed her song to rise to a resounding crescendo, then urged the stone body to turn to the assembled armies, its eyes gleaming a ferocious blue, the sign of Faron's utter mania.

Let us go now, Faron, she whispered. *We will destroy everything in our path—none will keep us separated from your father any longer.*

The statue obeyed, its Living Stone genitalia erect, tumescent with bloodlust.

Hrarfa was almost as excited.

Come! she shouted in the shrill voice that had become that of the titan upon Faron's acceptance of her. The screech rippled up the mountains to their summits and shouted angrily at the cloud-strewn sky. *To Canrif—leave nothing in one piece. Adorn yourselves with their gore.*

A war scream that shook the roots of the mountains answered her.

The titan turned again, at the phalanx of a valley of moving soldiers and matériel.

Heading east into the rising sun.

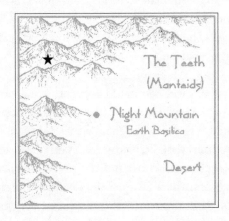

THE IRON MINES, VORNESSTA, SORBOLD

*A*nd then it was the day.

Or the night—Evrit had no concept of time in the depths of the mine, but it didn't matter; he only knew that in this one moment everything was different from the endless torture that had been each waking moment of his existence prior to it.

It took more than a few heartbeats for him to realize what was happening. He was hunched over, scraping the bottom rank of the wall section he had been assigned, when a strange wave of motion swept through his cave.

The four lashmen who patrolled his workspace, the muscle-bound men who had been walking their regular beat up and down the aisle that bisected the line of scratchers on either side of the cave, suddenly turned to the guards also on patrol.

With a coordinated attack of lightning-fast whiplashes, they encircled the guards' necks with the falls of their whips and, with teeth gritted, pulled tight, lifting the men off the ground as they strangled or broke their necks outright.

"Come!" one of the lashmen shouted to the petrified slaves as he dragged back on the whip. "Here's your chance!"

Evrit remained frozen, trembling, as several of his fellow slaves leapt from their crouches and charged the compromised guard, swinging their diamond-edged trowels with a vicious vengeance. He rose to a stand as they began to gouge the man's eyes and guts from his body, ripping open his leather armor and screaming in glee as the guard's entrails were exposed. They continued to hack at him, joined seconds later by more of their fellow captives, until the lashman swung the mutilated corpse from side to side, shaking them off.

"Back away!" he commanded. "Plenty more to be done!"

Then, with the newly empowered slaves jumping and dragging the others up from the floor behind him, he carried the body to the edge of the cave and hurled it perfunctorily over the side to the track on the floor below, then spat down over the ridge.

A roar of ferocious delight bellowed through the cave, building to a feverish howl of joy as similar bodies began to rain down from the levels above and across from them. Evrit felt his blood inflame at the sight of the falling guards, often torn limb from limb, from each of the caves across the great cavern from them.

From the highest level of the cavern, the crossbowmen moved hurriedly into defensive posture, falling to a prone position with their weapons, taking aim at the caves across the cavern from them.

As if bursting forth from cocoons or hives, the slaves flooded out of the caves, scrambling up the ladders and swarming the ridge. Evrit saw blood behind his eyes as his heart leapt in rage; he bolted forward, pushing aside the bodies of slaves that had been struck with bolts, and clambered up with those who had led the charge, screaming in fury as they climbed.

A number of those who had been first fell from the ladders above, shot in the face or throat, but within moments the climbers swelled over the tops and into the ranks of the archers. They fell on the bowmen, hacking and gouging; Evrit joined them, rage blinding him to anything but the thought of freeing his son and himself, and finding the rest of his family.

With a savage swipe, he put all of the muscle he had built since his captivity began into a roundhouse swing of his trowel, slashing the throat of the bowman in front of him open, releasing a wellspring of blood, and sending the man's eyes spinning back in his head as he fell at Evrit's feet. With his bare heel, the former pacifist leader of the Blessed stamped the rest of the man's life out, breaking his nose and eye sockets, then assisted his fellow slaves in tossing the man's body over the edge, watching it fall four levels into the growing stack of corpses on the stone floor below.

Out of the corner of his eye he could see the lashmen, who were stripping the guard bodies of their weapons and armor, leading a cohort of former slaves to the front doors of the mine, in a great river of roaring voices and slashing arms, pushing the reinforcements back, and barricading the entrance against the onslaught of army troops. Every bin, crate, lift, wagon, tool, and broken body was hoisted and tossed into a growing mountain reinforcing the enormous doors.

For a moment his rational mind resurfaced out of the darkness of his rage, wondering what would happen now that the slaves and lashmen controlled the mine that they were barricaded within. The mountain of slag would defend the back entrance; the massive doors beyond it were hewn into the side of the peaks, hovering well above the ground below, even if the towering pile could be broached, which was impossible.

But long-term survival beyond their revolution seemed in doubt to him; foodstuffs and fresh water had never been in great store, and the army of Sorbold, for the moment sealed out of the ironworks, would surely bring far greater force than the tens of thousands of slaves could muster when they regrouped.

But then the realization that, whatever was to come, he and his fellow captives had just thrown off their servitude, if only for a short time, had broken the will of the emperor of Sorbold, and would live, or die, free once more banished any doubt or concern from his mind.

He threw his head back and joined the swelling cry that was echoing throughout the iron mine, rattling the rock dome of the ceiling far above, laughing as the grit rained down on free men.

Free men, entombed by choice, within a molten mountain.

26

VLANE, MANOSSE

 $\mathcal{T}$ he streets of Vlane, the capital city of Manosse, looked almost exactly as they had the last time Ashe had walked them.

Vlane was a city on the water, one of the earliest built on the continent that ringed the western edge of the Wide Central Sea. It was sometimes also called the City of Sunrise for its eastern exposure and breathtaking morning views. Vlane had chosen to preserve its historic architecture of stone homes with neatly thatched roofs and a beautifully appointed waterfront where glistening white docks reached eagerly out into the thriving harbor toward the coming day. It was an amazing sight each morning as thousands of vessels, primarily fishing and crabbing boats, set off simultaneously into the rising sun, gathering the riches of the golden seacoast a few miles from shore.

Ashe stood for a moment, shedding the water from his clothes and allowing his lungs to adjust to the air of the world again after his long trek through the sea. He had arrived just as the fishing fleet set out as it always did, to the sound of joyful bells ringing tidings of wishes for good luck, fine weather, and plentiful catches.

The glistening sound caught in his throat; he could almost see

Rhapsody standing before him, exactly as she had a little over two years before, watching the sunrise ceremony with a look of wonder so encompassing on her face that he thought his own heart had stopped at the sight of it. The sky had been reflecting the morning light very much as it was today, causing her golden hair to outshine the sun in its rising, making her smooth cheeks glow and her green eyes sparkle with life.

Ashe closed his own eyes for a moment, bidding the image in his memory to remain as long as it could. Over the last few years he had thought back to that moment many times, especially in times of great despair, because of the power it had to banish any sadness from his heart.

Rhapsody had always dreamt of going to sea; she had first told him so on the night they had met in their youth, the eve of her fourteenth birthday, outside a foreharvest dance in her hometown of Merryfield in the old world of Serendair. He still did not know to this day, almost two thousand years later, how he had come to be plucked from his own time, from the road to town he had been walking, a fourteen-year-old himself, and thrown back in Time to meet her in that place, that innocent farming village full of unknowing souls who could not have foreseen the tragedies of war and cataclysm that were to come upon them.

But nonetheless they had met, had instantly recognized in each other the other half of each of their souls, had decided to marry and had consummated that marriage beneath the lacy shadows cast by the willow tree near the stream that wound through the pasturelands of her family's farm. In those few sweet hours together, before he was ripped back in Time to what for him had been the Present, she had confided to him the desire she had always felt for leaving her little village, studying music, traveling the wide world, and, most of all, seeing the sea which her grandfather had plied as a sailor.

With his eyes closed, he could still hear the excitement in her young voice at the thought of being able to go there with him, calling him by the name he had been given by the people of her village, a name commonly used for an unknown stranger, and which she had continued to use when they met up on the other side of time and had fallen in love again.

Sam?

Yes?

Do you think we might see the ocean? Someday, I mean.

Of course. We can even live there if you want. Haven't you ever seen it?

I've never left the farmlands, Sam, never in my whole life. I've always longed to see the ocean, though. My grandfather is a sailor, and all my life he

has promised me that he would take me to sea one day. Until recently I be-
lieved it. But I've seen his ship.

How can that be, if you've never seen the sea?

Well, when he's in port, it's actually very tiny—about as big as my hand.
And he keeps it on his mantel, in a bottle.

The screech of the ropes from the vessels in the harbor now, the cry
of the gulls, the smell of the salt air stung his ears and nose as tears stung
the corners of his eyes.

Generally, when he recalled her voice speaking those words to him, it
was the sweetest of recollections. But now, in a more recent memory of
the last time they had seen each other, just before he departed into this
same sea but half a world away, the woman whose face graced his dreams
had been entirely different than the one in his sight.

She had come to him through the power of the blue element of the
light spectrum that was the central power source of the instrumentality
Achmed had rebuilt from Gwylliam's Lightforge, designed and manufactured by the Nain of Canrif a millennium and a half before. The blue light,
in concert with a musical note and the sounding of his true name, had
given them a few moments together before she went off to war and he
went into the sea to summon aid for that war.

He had barely recognized her, not because her face had lost any of its
seraphic beauty, but because the name she had been given at birth, a name
no one living beside himself had heard sounded, Amelia Turner, as well
as the nicknames by which he, her friends, and her family had called her
in the old world, Emily and Emmy, had been stripped away from her. She
had given to their infant son, Meridion, to keep him safe, to keep him
company, to comfort him in her loss when she left him with the beloved
women who were her friends and adopted family in the Deep Kingdom,
the place known as Undervale, tucked away in the northeastern mountains of the Nain of the continent, the safest place she knew to leave
him, to hide him from Talquist, who sought to eat the baby's beating heart
in a quest for immortality.

A wave of nausea, loss, and wrath so violent and all-consuming swept
over him then, leaving him shaking as he stood, the clothing that clung
tightly to the heavy muscles of his chest, arms, and legs all but dry now
in the morning sun and the sea wind.

The woman he had last beheld before he went into the sea looked a
good deal like his wife, whose aspect the dragon in his blood had mem-
orized down to the tiniest detail. He had carried the picture of her in his

heart across two lifetimes, and so when he saw the filmy image, the wyrm within him had panicked.

She was sharper of feature than he remembered; the softness of her face, which had been burnished to perfection in the cleansing fires that raged within the heart of the Earth itself, through which she had passed on her way to the new world, gone, replaced by an aspect of severity that he did not recognize. And her glorious hair, a part of her he had cherished greatly, had been sawed off, shorn to the nape of her neck, leaving her with the face of a warrior.

She had warned him in an earlier visit through the Lightcatcher of her intention to separate her soul out this way, to wrap it around Meridion so that her love would remain with him as he was hidden away in the Nain kingdom. Her forewarning was a blessing, given that if he had not been alerted ahead of time, the wyrm within him would have rampaged at the sight of her now—stern, emotionless, and distant.

Hollow.

More than anything else, this image haunted him to the point where he had to push it from his consciousness and refill his thoughts with sweeter, older memories, lest the reality of the Present—and possibly the Future— drive him insane.

Ashe reached back again now, lighting on the memory he had been enjoying a moment before, from the trip they had made in the second year of their marriage to visit his family and holdings in Manosse. He opened his eyes again and took in the sight of the docks, now mostly empty of their vessels but brimming with foot traffic, and settled the nagging voice of the dragon again, a voice that had been largely silent during his time in the waves.

He found her easily, glowing in the light of a Manosse morning, smiling at him, laughing in the wind as it blew her long golden hair around her.

And, with that picture firmly fixed in his mind, he ignored the stares of townspeople at his odd clothing as he turned from the docks and made his way as quickly as he could to the city center, where the Council Hall stood.

The Magisterium of Manosse, the interprovincial body that was made up of representatives from each of the provinces within the vast nation of Manosse, held all of its meetings in the large columned building at the city center of Vlane.

Manosse was, in large part, a rural nation, with many country estates, forests, and conservatories of plants for both agricultural and ceremonial use in the Filidic religion, the faith in which Ashe's father, Llauron ap Gwylliam, had served in the position of Invoker back on the Middle Continent.

Ashe himself was Chief of the House of Newland, one of the largest and oldest of Cymrian houses, and therefore had many holdings in several of the different provinces that comprised the nation of Manosse. The variety of representation was interestingly diverse, and the numerous consulates that housed the diplomats from those provinces reflected that diversity in their architecture.

Ashe ran past small, tidy houses of one or two stories with blooming gardens that he knew housed Gwadd from the farthest reaches of the nation, small, gentle people who were very often of or descended from the First Generation of Cymrians, that stood next to the towering edifices of the consulates of Seren diplomats, an even older, rarer, and vastly taller race, as well as buildings of every shape and size in between.

His presence was gaining attention, he noted, as he sped by the citizens of Manosse on the carefully cobbled streets of their capital city. Whether it was his speed that caught their attention, his strange attire, or his red-gold hair that shone in metallic tones owing to his dragon ancestry and its dominance in his blood, Ashe neither knew or cared. He was mounting the wide marble stairs of the Council Hall when the interest finally caught up with him in the form of a coterie of armed sentries that appeared at the gated doorways of the Hall.

Armed and drawn.

Ashe stopped mid-stair and put his hands up, elbows bent in a non-aggressive stance.

"I am Gwydion of Manosse, Chief of the House of Newland and Lord Cymrian," he said quickly, forestalling a demand for the information from the head of the contingent. "I have urgent business with the council."

The first guard blinked. He turned to a soldier behind him and gave a quick incline of his head; the man ran off through the doorway behind him.

"Well, while I do not doubt your word, sir, and you certainly have the bearing that gives credence to your statement, I have to ask you to wait here until I can confirm your business."

"I am come from the Wyrmlands, from the Middle Continent—from Traeg," Ashe said, trying to keep the impatience that was threatening to explode in rage out of his voice. "No one knows that I am here, but if you summon Vincent de Malier o Serendair, he will vouch for me."

The guards exchanged a glance among themselves.

"Please be so kind as to wait a few moments more," said the head guard. Ashe nodded curtly, and the soldiers lowered their weapons, though they remained drawn.

After a maddening wait, the doors opened wider, and a man in the red- and gold-banded robes of the consulate stepped through them. Ashe had known he was coming, and so had allowed his rage to cool as it was someone within his acquaintance, a distant relative.

"Lord Ellsworth," he said. "I must speak with the consulate."

"Lord Gwydion?" the man asked, shaken. "We—we had no notice of your arrival, m'lord."

Ashe gestured impatiently at the guards; Ellsworth nodded quickly in agreement, and they dispersed, looking relieved.

Ellsworth started down the stairs as Ashe hurried up them.

"What brings you here, m'lord?" he asked, still shaky. "Is all well with the continent?"

"By no means," Ashe said, passing him on the stairs. "Please, I don't mean to be rude, but you must take me before the consulate immediately."

Ellsworth nodded, struggling to catch up.

"This way," he called after the hurrying Lord Cymrian, then gave up and ran behind him to the meeting room of the Manossian consulate.

27

The members of the consulate sat up uniformly in alarm as Ashe burst through the double doors of their chamber.

"What—what—" stammered the woman officiating the meeting, a half-Lirin landowner of considerable wealth he recognized as Cecelia Montagne.

"Pardon, Madam Chair," he said hastily. "I beg pardon for this intrusion, but I bring news of the direst nature."

Lady Montagne stared at him blankly, then rose in her place, quivering slightly.

"Lord Gwydion?"

"Yes, yes," Ashe said impatiently.

"Who exactly is this rude oaf?" demanded a whippet-thin, silver-haired gentleman in the livery of Adelhoston, a manufacturing province deep inland. "How dare you, sir—"

"Silence!" thundered another silver-haired gentleman, this one with resplendent muttonchops and a chain of gold around his neck from which dangled a five-pointed star. "Rise, one and all, for we are now in the presence of the Lord Cymrian. I would think you might recognize him; his portrait hangs in the center of the Great Hall of Manosse, and his face is on every coin in this realm."

Immediately a large portion of the inhabitants of the room rose to their feet, while a few who were clearly not of Cymrian lineage stared at one another in confusion, then stood as well.

The second gentleman came out from behind the table at which the consulate was sitting. Ashe recognized him immediately as the gentleman he had requested to see, Vincent de Malier. He was an elder member of the consulate, and a First Generation Cymrian who had sailed with the

Second Fleet, coming to Manosse as a child, where he grew up to establish a well-regarded commerce in furnishings, clothing, and durable goods that were traded around the globe.

And the husband of Rhapsody's closest friend, Analise, also a First Generation Cymrian, who was now sequestered with their child, hidden away from the sight of the world in the Nain kingdom.

Vincent hurried quickly to Ashe and knelt before him. Ashe took him by the shoulder and brought him to a stand again.

"What are you doing here, m'lord?" Vincent asked nervously. "I was under the impression you were playing host to my wife at Highmeadow."

Ashe's hand remained on the man's shoulder to steady him. "I'm sorry to have to tell you this, Vincent, to tell all of you this, but the Middle Continent is at war, and has been for some time."

"What—" De Malier turned back to the table as the other members of the consulate began speaking to each other in a cacophony of voices. "Be silent! Decorum must be observed immediately; we are in the presence of our sovereign and a visiting head of state."

From the very end of the table a quiet cough was heard.

Everyone in the room turned in the direction of the sound.

Sitting at the table's end was a middle-aged man, clearly of Liringlas origin, with long white hair woven into a braid that hung down his back. His eyes were unfocused, cloudy, and Ashe's dragon sense noted that they were without the capacity for sight. He wore robes of simple gray wool, without ornament, cinched at the waist with a rope of braided flax, a garment Ashe was familiar with. He had seen such robes adorning his wife when she was in attendance at meetings of state in the Lirin realm of Tyrian on the continent, where she ruled as titular queen, but often acted in her other capacity.

As a Namer of Lirin lore.

The woman who was chairing the consulate's meeting addressed the man. "Yes, Frantius? Do you have a point of order?"

"I do," said the blind Namer in a soft, clear voice, deep and beautiful of tone. "With respect, a falsehood has been perpetrated in speech, possibly unintentionally."

"What falsehood?" demanded Vincent testily. "Nothing has even been stated yet."

"Please elucidate," said the chair of the consulate to the Namer. "Are you saying that the Middle Continent is not at war?"

Frantia shook his head. "No," he said. "I'm saying that the man who has just come into your presence is in fact not the Lord Cymrian."

The councillors began to mutter among themselves again.

Vincent de Malier flushed with anger. "Nonsense!" he sputtered, turning in the direction of the Namer. "What you're saying—"

Ashe squeezed his arm to silence him. "Actually, he's right, Vincent," he said quietly. "If you'll allow me a moment's grace, I believe I can set everything to rights."

He released Vincent's arm and walked slowly over to the end of the table, not wishing to unintentionally intimidate the blind man, coming to a stop at a respectful distance away.

"I am Gwydion ap Llauron ap Gwylliam tuatha d'Anwynan o Manosse," he said. "By election and coronation I am, in fact, the Lord Cymrian, but I have transferred and left my Right of Command with my namesake back in Roland so that he might continue to prosecute the war in my absence. I have come to make the Second Fleet aware of the atrocities that have been visited upon us by the newly crowned emperor of Sorbold, Talquist Rev-Penthor, and to summon all maritime aid immediately that is not necessary in the defense of your own coastline, which, by the way, has been left far more vulnerable than you can imagine."

"Wait, wait," began the thin, silver-haired man that Ashe did not know.

"Hold, please," said Cecelia Montagne. "We must return to order. Frantius, are you satisfied that this man speaks the truth as to who he is?" The Namer nodded. "Well, that's a good start. Now, Lord Gwydion, please take a seat. We will get you some refreshment and—"

"There is no time," Ashe interrupted, struggling to keep the multi-toned voice of the dragon at bay. "I'm not here on a visit of state as I was when I met you, Lady Cecelia. I am here to summon the fleets of Manosse in defense of the continent, and to set you to your own defense. Between your lands and the lands of the First and Third fleets, the Wide Central Sea is alive with ships, slavers, merchants, pirates, and warships, all pledged to the same admiral, the emperor of Sorbold. He has been assaulting nations across the globe from Argaut to the distant shores of Myc'lamur beyond the eastern nation of Golgarn, enslaving entire populations to work in his mines, producing arms and armor for a campaign of conquest the like of which the Known World has never seen before. We are at the tip of the spear now, but you will be next."

"Are you telling us that you wish us to deploy the fleet? To the Middle Continent, half a world away?" demanded the thin, silver-haired man, one of only two in the room who were not of Cymrian lineage. "To engage in battle at open sea and along the coast of the Wyrmlands?"

"Yes—yes." As the heaviness of the air in the room descended on him, Ashe bent over at the waist, suddenly exhausted.

"Against the newly crowned emperor of Sorbold?"

"Again, yes. And the fleets he has conscripted, either by right or by deception."

"You must be out of your mind."

"Lord Lynfalt, you are out of order," said Lady Montagne reproachfully. "Courtesy is the rule in this consulate."

"And you must be out of yours, Lynfalt, to speak to the Lord Cymrian in that manner." Vincent's eyes were blazing.

"What you have clearly missed, Vincent, is that, in fact, he is *not* the Lord Cymrian," said Lynfalt contemptuously. "Did you not hear the Namer or, in fact, the man himself? He has passed his Right of Command on to another. You, sir, are therefore not the sovereign of the Cymrian Alliance, and have no international standing as a head of state. You do not even have the right to enter this council, let alone make demands of it."

"You are of a younger Manossian House, Lynfalt, and can almost be forgiven for not knowing your Cymrian history, but you would have to be willfully ignorant to not know who Lord Gwydion is just in terms of his Manossian heritage. He is also the Chief of the House of Newland, the Speaker of the Second Fleet, and descended of both Merithyn the Explorer and MacQuieth Monodiere Nagall," said Vincent de Malier angrily. "And, Madam Chair, if you do not silence this fool I will personally gut him with my teeth, your demand for protocol and courtesy notwithstanding. Lord Gwydion, where is my wife? Is she safe?"

"When I left the continent, she was well out of harm's way," said Ashe as calmly as he could. The dragon was rising within his blood, leaving him struggling to maintain the human side of his nature in control. "Until we are back in a place where our words cannot be overheard, I can tell you no more." Vincent nodded, looking suddenly older.

Ashe turned to address the consulate again.

"I ask you again to hear me," he said, his voice steady. "Over the past eight seasons, I have sent orders and payment to Manosse and Gaematria for warships that have never arrived. Everything that has been sent from our shores has probably been interdicted, certainly diverted, stolen outright, or compromised in some hideous way. You know none of this, because a great barrier of vessels has been patrolling the central sea, destroying communication between the coasts as well. The man who has just been crowned emperor was, prior to his ascendance to the throne of

Sorbold, the Hierarch of the western Mercantile guild, and thereby had immense reach across the world."

"Indeed," said Lynfalt. "Manosse has been privileged to do business with Talquist both through the Mercantile of Sorbold, and as a transportation magnate for our goods and services, Lord Gwydion. My province is one of manufacturers, and our goods are transported all over the world through the shipping network Talquist has put together, maintained, and run over the last three decades. We have no complaint with him, and I personally have met him, as have many of the members of this consulate." He cast a glance at de Malier. "You, in fact, Vincent, have had him as a guest in your home, have you not?"

Ashe looked at the First Generation Cymrian. The man's eyes were wide and his face stricken.

"Indeed," he murmured as beads of sweat appeared on his brow. "I have indeed been his host."

At the utterance of the word *host*, something in Ashe's memory turned over suddenly.

"His host? What do you mean by that, Vincent?"

The First Generationer shook his head slightly. "You know my business, Lord Gwydion," he said softly. "I entertain merchants and manufacturers from all over the world, and quite often that entails having them as guests in my home. You and your lovely wife have slept beneath my roof; Analise and I were honored to have you visit in that manner also, though it was not for business but because our wives are old friends."

"Yes, yes." Ashe's brain was on fire, trying to make sense of the information that was scattering about in it like pieces to a puzzle, but the solution was eluding him. "Do you remember what his business was when you were his host?"

"I—I don't rightly recall," said the elderly Cymrian. "I actually hosted him on a number of occasions. Most of the time he was traveling by himself, but once I remember him bringing along an associate, a seneschal or judge of some sort. An unpleasant fellow; we were glad to be rid of him. His friend, not Talquist. Talquist was always a pleasant guest."

The word *seneschal* made the blood in Ashe's veins run cold.

The last time he had heard it uttered, it was by the mouth of a dead man, his blood wrung from him by Constantin, the Patriarch of Sepulvarta.

A dead man who had been in the employ of the beast that had taken his wife hostage.

A First Generation Cymrian himself, the host of a F'dor demon.

Known in the old world as Michael, the Wind of Death.

"Seneschal—do you remember where he was from?"

Vincent was beginning to shake. "I—I—"

Another man, this one with the characteristic auburn hair of some of the noble families of the Middle Continent, and of clear Cymrian lineage, spoke up.

"Wasn't that the baron of Argaut, Vincent?" he asked. "I remember dining with you that evening as well, if that is the occasion you are referring to. I try to make it a point not to judge, especially those from cultures other than our own, but I found him quite terrifying, if I recall correctly. There was a—fragrance to him I found unsettling, as well as other characteristics that made me glad when supper was over and I was on my way home again. In particular, I found the attention he gave your wife, Lady Analise, to be most inappropriate and overbearing." He glanced over at the Lord Cymrian.

Ashe had gone white.

"M'lord?"

"The baron of Argaut spent time in your home with your wife? With Analise?" His voice was so soft as to almost be inaudible.

"Only on one occasion, m'lord," said Vincent.

Ashe did not hear him. His brain was full of other voices, other memories.

The memory of Analise, Rhapsody's friend from the old world, sitting at his table, when she had come to aid Rhapsody with the birth of their child, only to find that she was already gone.

M'lord, I came from Manosse because, until six months or so ago, Rhapsody and I were in regular contact, exchanging letters on each Alliance flagship that sailed between Manosse and the Middle Continent. She had written to me in great excitement and joy of her pregnancy; as you know, I be, by profession, a midwife and healer specializing in young children. But then, suddenly, the letters stopped coming, and I thought perhaps, feared really, that something had happened to Rhapsody or the baby, that she was grieving, or ill—

No, no, he had assured her. *Rhapsody has had quite a hard time of it in the last six months. First, she was kidnapped by a maniac from the old world when I was away at the funeral of the empress of Sorbold—*

A maniac, you say? From the old land? Not—not—Michael?

You knew of him?

The elderly woman had nodded. *Not of him; I knew him, in the most horrible of ways. Rhapsody did not tell you how we met? Not even before you came to visit my family in Manosse?*

No, Ashe had said. *She does not speak of those days to me.*

It is because of what she did for me in those days that I be alive and here this day, Analise had said quietly. *Michael killed my family before my eyes, set our longhouse on fire, and took me, wrapped in my mother's bloody shawl, away with him to the city of Easton where he used me as leverage to gain her attention. My memories of that time be those of a child, because I was spared the details, as Rhapsody made sure to shield me as much as she could as well, m'lord. But I know that Michael's intentions for me were brutal, and that Rhapsody's intervention spared me from them.*

Michael, the Wind of Death.

Who, sometime around the Cataclysm that had taken the Island of Serendair to the depths of the sea, had found new life and immortality as the baron of Argaut.

The seneschal.

And the host of a fire demon from the Before-Time.

A F'dor.

An entity that had the power to subjugate an unknowing person as a thrall, or take a host.

Just like the one that now walked the continent in a body of Living Stone.

Harvested and brought to life by Talquist, the emperor of Sorbold.

Who, long before his ascension to the Sun Throne, had brought the baron to Manosse to meet with Vincent de Malier.

And de Malier's wife, Analise o Serendair.

Rhapsody's friend from the old world.

The Liringlas child that, in another life, she had saved from Michael's cruelty.

Who had undoubtedly recognized him upon meeting him again, even in his new guise.

And who now was tending to and guarding his son in the Nain mountains.

Beyond any communication or reach he might have.

Ashe's conscious mind exploded.

The dragon roared forth, swallowing his will and preparing to rampage.

The outward signs were subtle at first; the vertical pupils in Ashe's eyes expanded, his muscles began to thicken, but the councillors were busy arguing among themselves again, and did not notice.

Lord Ellsworth, who had come to the front steps to meet him, had begun to speak.

"It seems to me, Lord Gwydion, that Lord Lynfalt has a valid point; while you make a serious charge against Sorbold's new emperor, he and even Lord Vincent have had peaceful commerce with Talquist, commerce that did not result in any damaging action on the emperor's initiative that we know of. Your claim of a wide blockade seems, well, somewhat fatuous in comparison to what our experience has been; our fishing vessels ply the sea on a daily basis and have reported no sign of such a blockade, even if, admittedly, they do not venture very far from shore—and so to commit the naval forces of Manosse to war with Sorbold, with no evidence to speak of—"

His speech came to a halt as the table of the councillors began to shake, sending charts and papers flying.

The large windows, fired in blocks of heavy crystal and bound in brass, shattered pane by pane, spraying glass into the air and out into the streets.

The members of the consulate dove to the floor in terror.

"I suppose I—neglected to remind you, Lord—Ellsworth, Lord Lynfalt—that in addition to his—other bloodlines—the Lord Cymrian is—descended of the—dragon Elynsynos as well?" Vincent de Malier puffed from beneath the council table. He pulled his legs in closer as chairs, books, and goblets were thrown about the room and into walls. Suddenly the room was bathed in intense blue light, rippling in waves.

Ashe stood in the center of the room, running one hand rapidly through the shining curls of his hair. In the other hand, Kirsdarke was roiling, tumescent, angry, like the sea in the grip of a hurricane.

Or a tidal wave.

The Lord Cymrian's eyes were smoking in the same blue color as the elemental sword of water.

He inhaled deeply, and the spinning currents of air in the room flashed with ancient power. The members of the consulate felt the slap of air like an assault, and curled against whatever walls or objects they could, seeking shelter.

A moment later, the rampaging winds and violent tremors that had shaken the room ceased.

The consulate members slowly unfolded themselves from beneath or behind their places of hiding, and stood shakily.

The door was open.

The room, save for them and the detritus of their meeting, was empty.

The Lord Cymrian was gone.

28

IN THE HIDDEN KINGDOM OF THE NAIN,
UNDERVALE, NORTHEASTERN MOUNTAINS

Someone had left the window open, or so it seemed to Melisande.

She had been fast asleep in her bed, after a long and entertaining day of traveling the Nain kingdom with the crown princess, Gyllian, joined for a part of the walkabout by Faedryth, the Nain king himself. Gyllian had understood how cramped and boring Melisande's vigil entertaining Meridion could be, and so occasionally arranged for the little girl to have outings under the guise of being a foreign dignitary and the princess's young friend.

They had dined in splendor at a café near the artists' district, located near some beautiful crystal formations that had reminded Melisande vaguely of the sky. The colors were glorious, blues and purples and yellows that glowed softly in the artificial cold light of the radiant globes that hung from every lamppost, much like the ones in her father's keep, Haguefort, the ancestral home of rosy brown stone she had grown up in.

The thought had made her melancholy and reflective, and so she had hurried off to bed, planning to get as much rest in as possible before her early-morning shift of feeding, changing, and entertaining Meridion.

I wonder how long we will be down here, under the mountain, she had mused as sleep took her. *Maybe the war will never end, at least not in my lifetime. Maybe I will be here forever. At least they won't have to bury me; in a way I'm already buried.*

She awoke from a roster of disturbing dreams, shivering with cold.

From the smell of the room, the fireplace in the central part of their apartments had gone out. Melisande was surprised at this; the three women were very careful to make certain it had been well stocked and stoked before putting the baby down and retiring for the night. One of them stood watch at all times, but it was a drowsy duty. Faedryth's soldiers stood watch in so many layers, and had installed so many warning bells, that it seemed impossible that an intruder might make his way in without their knowledge, so as the months passed, the women took turns sleeping upright in the soft, padded chair in which the baby was always fed the clarified goat's milk that was still the staple of his diet.

No alarm ever rang.

Fully awake now, but not wanting to disturb the baby or whoever was on guard, Melisande slipped out of bed, put her freezing feet into her cold slippers, and made her way to the fireplace.

In front of it, to her surprise, she found Analise, closer than she had expected.

The Liringlas woman was cradling Meridion's head in her hands, his tiny feet up against her breasts, looking down into his face. Melisande swallowed; it was a position in which she herself had been forbidden from holding him, because his head was over the floor and vulnerable should he start unexpectedly or squirm suddenly.

Analise, whom she could see in profile, seemed to be studying the baby's face. She turned him absently in small degrees, inclining her head as if to get a better angle, then shifted him into another position, gently and slowly.

Meridion, oblivious, slept on.

"He be beautiful, be he not?"

Melisande blinked. Until Analise spoke, the little girl had no indication that she had known Melisande was there.

"Yes," she said uncertainly. "Yes, he is."

"Of course he be," Analise said. "The Child of Time, born of a woman from the old world, nurtured in the magic of Serendair, and sired by a man from the new one, both graceful of face. Steeped in the lore of fire, of water, of wind, as all Lirin children are, of earth, as all dragonlings be. A truly special child."

"Why did you let the fire go out?" The words came from her own mouth, but they sounded hollow to Melisande.

At first Analise did not answer, but rather continued rocking Meridion slowly with his head pointed toward the hearth. Finally, when she spoke, her voice was soft.

"To make the voice go silent."

"What voice?"

The elderly woman sighed, her silver eyes full of memory.

"The voice that has been speaking to me for more than two years now, his voice."

"His?"

A smile spread slowly across the ancient face.

"Michael's voice. For all that he was a terrible man, his voice was sweet, and his eyes were blue, blue as the pinnacle of the sky. Rhapsody said that to me once, after he had gone."

"I'm sorry, I don't know what you are talking about." Melisande hated how young and frightened she sounded.

Finally, the elderly woman turned to her and looked at her thoughtfully.

"That was in the old world, of course. In the old world, Michael, the Wind of Death, was an evil man, a brutal man—a merciless killer with the voice of a sweetmeat vendor, and eyes as blue as the pinnacle of the sky. After he killed my family and took me away to the human city with him, I never again trusted another man with blue eyes."

Melisande lapsed into silence. She felt a sense of calm descend, a steadying of her will that came upon her in moments of danger. With the amount of threat she had experienced even before turning ten, she had come to rely on the gift of calm.

There really was no alternative to it that would end in anything but death, she knew.

"I never saw the death of the Island—did you know that, Melisande? I be sure you must; your dear father was a great student of history, and the curator of the Cymrian museum, so I'm sure he told you all the tales, did he not?"

The little girl nodded.

"I sailed with the Second Fleet. Our ship sundered at the Prime Meridian, in the backwash of the great wave that had broken the First Fleet, had drowned Merithyn. I opted to go to live in Manosse, a place I was certain Michael, if he had survived the Cataclysm, would never find me."

In her hands, the baby stretched, his tiny arms reaching out of his swaddling blankets and over his head, then settled down again.

"Imagine my horror when he came into my house as a guest, with no warning," Analise continued quietly, billing the side of Meridion's head gently with her forefinger, caressing his golden curls. "I have no idea how he found me; it be vain to think it was anything but a chance of Fate, an accident. He did not recognize me. He had never bothered to learn my name in the time when I was in his clutches; he had given me an insulting name, a human name—Petunia. He was calling himself by another name as well—the baron of Argaut. The blue eyes were tinged with red at the edges now, and he carried the stench of the demon."

"Let me take Meridion, please, Analise," Melisande said softly. "Please, give him to me."

The Liringlas midwife's face went slack. She turned and looked at Melisande for only the second time that night.

"He will wake—let him sleep," she said, then shook her head and went back to studying the baby.

Melisande fell back into silence.

"Michael never knew about Meridion," Analise said after a long moment. "Unlike the Merchant Emperor, who is ceaselessly seeking the Child of Time, Michael was only looking for Rhapsody. After all those centuries, millennia, really, he had heard her name on the wind somewhere, and came to my house, because he had heard she had been a guest there with Lord Gwydion. Sailors are bigger gossips than fishwives, you know."

"I know," Melisande whispered, but she didn't; she only knew that she feared what would happen when Analise went silent.

"He wanted to know how to identify her, what sign he would have that she was the same Rhapsody he had known. I—I told him that the woman who had visited my home wore a locket of gold, and his eyes lit up like bonfires of leaves in autumn. The woman he was seeking had also worn such a locket; it seemed to be the clue that he needed."

Melisande's heart was pounding so hard that it was almost drowning out Analise's words.

Analise exhaled.

"I believe that's how he found her, ultimately," she said. "But until recently, everything he said to me had left my mind; if I had been able to remember, I would have warned her.

"But the voice—that only began speaking to me once we came here," Analise continued. "It is very distant, very far away—as if it is coming from the Vault of the Underworld itself."

"What does it say? This voice?"

Analise kissed the child's belly.

"It tells me I must put the baby in the fire." When Melisande gasped in horror, the midwife turned and looked at her. "Oh, do not fear, child—Meridion is his mother's son. The fire would never harm him."

"Then why would the demon command you to do that?"

The question seemed to perplex Analise.

"Why, so that the demon can have him, of course. Fire be the element from which those demons sprang. They be the masters of it. On occasion, they can reach through fire itself and take what they wish."

Tears began to roll down Melisande's cheeks.

"Please," she whispered, prepared to lunge if she needed to. "Please don't do that."

Analise blinked.

"Well, of course not. Of course I would not do that."

Melisande's tears stanched suddenly at the look of shock in the elderly woman's eyes.

"Do you not see the fireplace, child?" When Melisande nodded, Analise turned Meridion into the crook of her arm and kissed his forehead softly. "I told you from the beginning, I let the fire go out to make the voice go away."

"How—how can you do that, if you are—in thrall to a demon?" the little girl stammered.

The look of shock became one of quiet outrage.

"*In thrall to a demon?* What be you talking about, Lady Melisande Navarne? I could never be in thrall to such a thing."

"I—I thought anyone could be made a thrall—unless they were stronger than the demon—"

Analise's face wore equal expressions of amusement and annoyance.

"Now see here, Miss Melly—no demon can take a soul that already belongs to another, if the bond be old and strong enough. And while there be no doubt that my soul be shared with my husband, I had sworn my soul and my life to your grandmother long before I met him. I can never repay what she did for me in Serendair all those years ago; my life and soul are hers.

"There was nothing within me for the demon to latch on to, nothing to take; it had been given away in the old world, on the day she put me atop a horse in front of the leader of the Lirin of the fields outside of the city where she had met me. She had bargained with Michael for my life; I do not know what she paid, but I know it was dear. She saved me; I would never harm her or her child at the command of a voice from wherever this be coming from. Instead I just let the coals burn out. Fornicate him."

Melisande released a sigh of relief so loud that Meridion twitched in Analise's arms and turned on his side away from her.

Both women, young and old, chuckled quietly.

"Back to bed," Analise commanded as Melisande came to her side and bent to kiss Meridion's head. "You be on duty in the morning, and he be bound to be hungry after the depth of his slumber tonight. Make certain you leave time to rekindle the fire. And make it a big one—I want to be able to feel it in my room with the door closed."

The little girl nodded and hurried back to her bedchamber.

29

THE PENINSULA OF SITHGRAID, VLANE, MANOSSE

Ashe was running so hard that it almost seemed his pounding heart might cease to beat.

To the end of the peninsula of Sithgraid, the place where his ancestor had stood to hold vigil for the Island and the son he had unwillingly left behind there.

Ashe, having left his own son behind in the mountains, finally understood what MacQuieth had felt.

The fragmenting of his sanity settled within him; the wyrm in his blood was in control now, but focused.

Ashe closed his eyes.

He imagined the distant shore of the land he stewarded half a world away, imagined the harbors smoldering from the northern tip of Traeg, the windswept fishing village where he had once met MacQuieth, and where he had stepped into the ocean to come to this continent so many months before.

He imagined Avonderre Harbor, the jewel of the Cymrian Alliance, where guardian towers topped with light had once welcomed thousands of ships from around the world into the safe haven of its docks and the men who crewed them into the warmth of its hospitality, now riddled and broken by assault from the air, its harbor now a graveyard of those ships and the men who crewed them.

His mind, overridden by the ire of the wyrm now in control of him, imagined the gentle harbor of Port Tallono in the southern kingdom of the Lirin, a place his own grandmother had once helped build, when her wisdom was used for good rather than for destruction, decimated in blood and fire as Avonderre had been.

He pushed the picture of his wife out of his mind, knowing that she would be fighting with everything that was in her to spare her realm from invaders from Sorbold who doubtless were engaging her on two flanks, from the sea and from the south, assaulting the forest that had not seen invasion since the Cymrian War four hundred years before.

And all the way to the east past the coastline of Sorbold, he imagined the coast of Windswere in the Nonaligned States, where helpless orphans, children, and babies and the female acolytes who had cared for them lovingly had been butchered or catapulted, alive, into the sea, all by the order of the man who now called himself emperor.

He did not even feel his last vestige of restraint as it cracked within him.

Ashe raised the ancient sword of elemental water over his head.

The surf around his legs spun in churning waves.

The blade of Kirsdarke spun with them, sending blasts of spray skyward.

In the distance he could hear someone shouting his name, but it echoed, inert, deflected by his concentration. His dragon sense did not register anything except the mammoth power swelling within him, the element of water drawn into the air by the sword that was born of it.

Beneath his feet, planted in the sand, he sensed a cracking within the Earth, a trembling that changed the currents around him, sending them into a spinning vortex.

The dragon within his blood sensed an overwhelming increase in the power of the waves around him.

With everything he had, Ashe returned to the picture in his mind of the coast of the lands on the other side of the Wide Central Sea, half a world away.

Pockmarked by wanton destruction.

Occupied by the forces of the enemy.

Blockaded from the rest of the world.

And, with every thought, every sense, every intent he was able to summon, he channeled all his strength through the elemental sword of water.

Directing the wave homeward.

*L*ord Gwydion! Lord Gwydion!"

Atop the swiftest horse he had been able to seize from the seaside livery at the harbor, Vincent de Malier was thundering in approach, holding on to the reins for dear life. The elderly Cymrian's face was set in a grim mask of concentration, his eyes blazing, as he rode down the peninsula of Sithgraid, shouting Ashe's name into the wind.

In the distance he could see the Lord Cymrian standing in the surf, and he tried not to choke at the sight. He had been one of the people who had witnessed the vigil of MacQuieth a millennium and a half before, had seen the captain of his vessel and the commander of the Second Fleet toss the sword the Lord Cymrian now held above his head into the waves and wade out into the surf, his eyes locked on the southwest, where the Island of Serendair had been, half a world away.

Where he stood, up to his thighs in the surf, staring southwest, refusing the company or sustenance of anyone but his daughter-in-law, Talthea, his grandson, Aidan, and his newborn granddaughter, Elsynore, who held vigil with him from the shore.

Awaiting the death of the Island of Serendair.

And that of the son who had stayed behind to guard it.

It was a sight that had broken the collective heart of the Second Fleet.

The Lord Cymrian's seeming repetition of the event now terrified Vincent even more.

He urged his mount forward mercilessly, the hoofbeats thundering a terrible tattoo along the sandbar that was the peninsula of Sithgraid.

Vincent ceased his shouting, knowing that it was lost in the wind that was beginning to pick up markedly. He bent his head down over the horse's neck and held on tightly, in a full gallop, down the peninsula.

Before him, he could see a marked withdrawal of the waves that had been pounding the coastline a few moments before. With each new wave breaking toward the shore, the water in the seabed seemed to pull back a good deal more, until even the demarcation of the lowest of tides had been exceeded. Fish flapped on the sand, suddenly exposed, amid swales dotted with shells and seaweed, driftwood and pebbles.

With each withdrawal, the water seemed to rise higher.

Finally Vincent arrived at the end of the penisula. He dragged his horse to a halt and shouted into the sea wind.

"Lord Gwydion! *Lord Gwydion!* Please!"

The Lord Cymrian didn't seem to hear him.

Rather, he watched water beyond the naked sea bottom rise and turn in its direction, then head out to sea.

Slowly he lowered the sword as he stood in the dry air of the seabed. As the taller wave withdrew, heading east, new water flooded back in, incrementally, quickly covering Ashe's feet, the next wave his calves, the next his knees, and finally his thighs until the waves were crashing as they customarily did.

Vincent shielded his eyes and looked farther out to sea. The elevated ridge of water was still there, moving beyond his sight.

Still heading east.

Vincent opened his mouth to speak, but could force no sound out. He swallowed and tried again.

"Lord Gwydion!"

Finally Ashe turned around. His red-gold hair, which had caught the sun a few moments before and reflected back like copper melting in a forge, had cooled in the coming of evening. His face was pale, and his eyes seemed focused once again.

"Lord Gwydion, come, please," Vincent urged from atop his mount. "If we hurry, we can sail before dusk."

The Lord Cymrian just stared at him.

"M'lord?"

"Sail? Dusk?"

Vincent sat up a little straighter in the saddle.

"Indeed, m'lord. Can you not hear the bells?"

The world around Ashe was moving more slowly than he was accustomed to, the sea winds buffeting his face. He shook his head and concentrated.

On the wind were the vibrations of bells: carillon and church bells, harbor bells and bells on fishing boats.

All clanging in a random tintinnabulation, filling the air with frantic music.

"What is happening?" The three words took more effort than he ever remembered expending in speech.

Vincent exhaled deeply.

"The fleet, m'lord. The fleet is preparing to deploy, under your command—all of it, every warship, even those that are not yet commissioned. Everything but the fishing boats; they would never stand the voyage to the continent."

He waved his hand to the Lord Cymrian.

"Come, m'lord! The consulate voted unanimously, and the harbor-master has summoned all the captains to sail. We leave as soon as you return."

"The—wave," Ashe stammered. "We will be following a wave—"

Vincent's face took on a serious mien.

"Aye, that might be a complication," he said. "We have dealt with such waves at sea before, and it was not a pleasant experience. But at least this time it is heading in the other direction. And we will once again have the Kirsdarkenvar to lead us. Come; let us be on our way."

30

THE THRESHOLD OF DEATH, SOUTH OF BETHANY

The line of soldiers stretched into the west as far as Anborn could see.

The Lord Marshal was seated atop his warhorse, riding the line as he did each morning, inspecting the recruits and the arriving enlisted soldiers as well.

Only this day, instead of the makeup of the line consisting mostly of volunteers, adolescent children, and those who had survived previous conflicts when the remainders of their families hadn't, and so were serving for lack of anything better to do now that life had lost all meaning, the defense barricade was largely peopled by soldiers who had been recruited and trained by his nephew for the last several years, who had followed him from Canderre after his meeting with Solarrs, Knapp, and Rhapsody.

An experienced, well-trained fighting force, admittedly outnumbered by the vast Sorbold army, but one to be reckoned with.

Anborn looked out over them with an unmistakable fondness. While the men-at-arms who had served with him, some from the Cymrian War itself, rode the line in sections, taking battalion leaderships along it from the western sector to the eastern encampment, he was assessing his new troops, soldiers who had chosen in peacetime to take up arms and train to defend the Alliance when no apparent need to do so had presented itself yet.

Even though they were new in his command, he felt immensely akin to them.

He, like they, had taken up arms cheerfully and with the belief that to do so was a noble way to spend one's life.

Or to lose it.

As he looked out over their faces now, most of them youthful but occasionally some in middle age, still in fighter's trim, still excited in the anticipation of battle, he remembered how it felt to be one of them, in days far gone by. As peaceful and secure as days may have been when they first took up arms, there was no misunderstanding now that the war they were about to enter would be brutal, that they were facing an enemy that had long trained, had long planned this destruction, and that outnumbered them seven times over.

And still there was glow to their cheeks, shine to their eyes.

They were looking to him with the same loyalty and vigor that he had felt for his original commanders, the men who had taught him all that he had known, not just about swordsmanship and defensive maneuvers, horsemanship and battlefield configurations, but camaraderie, valor, and endurance. He had trained with them, fought beside them, bled beside them, carried their corpses out from the desolate grounds of battles lost, and buried them with honor.

He remembered them, when all of history had forgotten their names.

The field commanders were counting off their muster now.

Anborn rode to the eastern battalion and stopped before them, standing in a seemingly endless assembly.

"Men of the Alliance," he said solemnly, his voice booming over the encampment, "today we begin the purge that will return the holy city of Sepulvarta, the City of Reason, to its religious leadership, will drive the aggressors from our homelands, and will take back control of the Middle Continent. The nation of Sorbold, under the leash of its new emperor, has committed atrocities not only on the religious city-state, but across the Known World. It is time he and his armies are brought to heel."

A roar of approbation echoed across the plain.

Anborn hid a smile of delight at the sound.

"Rules of engagement," he continued briskly. "Any Sorbold soldier who surrenders on the battlefield or off it is to be captured when possible, though never at the risk of your lives or those of your comrades. No wanton or needless destruction is to be visited upon their towns and villages, though, of course, those towns and villages must be subdued first in any manner necessary within your training and your oath. No women are to be defiled—"

A mass snort of amusement rumbled across the plain; Anborn smiled.

"No *civilian* women," he corrected. "In short, you are to comport yourselves in a manner that will not reduce your own humanity, but that will at the same time ensure victory of our cause. Because the cause you take up this day is not just a noble one, it is an essential and necessary one, the driving out of a monstrous invader, the protection of your own homeland. It is the righteous defense of the Known World, Life, and the Afterlife. When you are contemplating your objectives, do not lose sight of the urgency and importance of your mission—for failure will cost this world far more than I can put into words. Are you ready?"

The answering call of *yes sir!* rolled over the fields of grass and all the way to the foothills of the Teeth.

"The first wave will ride with me to the aid of Sepulvarta; the second will defend the Threshold," Anborn commanded. "Your comrades who remained behind while you advanced to this place are at this moment defending the northern city-states of Roland; our prayers go with them. Divide and come with me, First Wave; Second Wave, may the All-God guide your swords and arrows, and mind your horses, cavalry. Mount up!"

The shout of acclaim that answered him sent a thrill through Anborn's blood and reinvigorated his battle-aged bones. He nodded to the field commanders of this division, then set off westward, to repeat the call to arms to each of the factions that would follow him south this day.

THE HARBOR OF VIENEZ, GOLGARN

$\mathcal{F}$ar past the Firbolg mountains to the south, a thousand leagues away from where the Lord Marshal was addressing his troops, a ship was docking in the quiet port of Vienez in the seaside kingdom of Golgarn. It was a royal ship, but that notwithstanding, its arrival was unheralded, its flag the standard not of its own kingdom, but that of the new Emperor of the Sun in the neighboring land of Sorbold.

The ship, after a drawn-out dispute with the harbormaster's vessel, was finally allowed to land in the royal dock, much to the outrage of its sole passenger.

Beliac, Golgarn's king.

He waited, silently and impatiently, as the various documents of passage, harbor certificates, and logbooks were examined, inspected, and eventually approved, allowing the ship to off-load its single passenger and copious cargo, then strode down the gangplank to the pier and eventually to the street, where a royal coach had been summoned but had not arrived yet.

"We had no notice of your return, sire," the minister of the harbor said sheepishly, trying to keep his eyes from meeting the furious gaze of his king. "You departed six and a half months ago; we did not know what had happened to you."

"I've been at *war*, you imbecile," the king growled. Then he coughed, somewhat abashed at the overreach of his statement. "Or at the edges of it."

"Yes, Majesty." The minister turned at the sound of horses' hooves approaching, clattering against the cobblestones of the street. "Do you wish to return immediately to the palace, or will you be stopping at the Sea Duchess, as you did before you sailed?"

"To the palace, of course," Beliac said, climbing into the coach as the minister held the door. "The royal family members are no doubt beside themselves with worry."

The royal family clearly was beside itself, Beliac discovered upon returning home, but worry was not the emotion that had them in its grip.

Upon being greeted by the palace servants, the king was escorted into the dining room, where he discovered his wife, Queen Eunice, and his eldest son, Prince Hariton, at supper. The crown prince rose immediately to his feet at his father's arrival, wiping his mouth with his napkin, while the queen remained seated, a look of unmistakable displeasure wreathing her face as she chewed and swallowed the bite of food she had taken in as he entered the room.

"Father! Welcome home."

Beliac nodded to his son. "Hariton, good to be with you again. Dearest, you are looking well."

The queen said nothing, but dabbed her mouth and folded her napkin decidedly.

The servant-at-table looked around awkwardly, as the queen was occupying the king's customary seat.

"Never mind," Beliac said, gesturing toward the empty chair at the other end of the table. The servant-at-table quickly pulled it out, and the king sat down.

All the waitstaff disappeared in the direction of the buttery.

The queen and the crown prince returned to their meal, while the king of Golgarn stared in amazement.

"Have you all gone quite mad?" he demanded as his wife and son looked up again. "What happened to decorum?"

"Sorry, Father," Hariton said nervously. "How was the coronation?"

"Did you meet the Lady Cymrian?" his wife asked, laying down her spoon again.

"*Lady*—no! I didn't come within a thousand miles of her. What is the matter with the two of you? Where are the other children?"

"To bed," said the queen, taking up her spoon again. "What kept you, then?"

"Are you unaware that the Known World is *at war*, dearest?" Beliac demanded.

The queen and the crown prince exchanged a glance.

"I am aware that Golgarn is without its navy," Queen Eunice said finally. "Much of the palace guard has been redeployed to help protect the harbor from an undesirable element that has sprung up since you gave the emperor of Sorbold our warships, but of late they have also recently been fired upon by incoming vessels, as has the harbormaster."

"You must be joking," Beliac said as the servants-at-table returned, bearing a simple repast, which they set before him.

"I assure you, Father, 'tis no joke," said Prince Hariton seriously. "The Spider's Clutch is running rampant on the waterfront now. And we have had to repel several attacks just outside the palace walls."

"This is *insane!*" Beliac sputtered. "Attacks? Was it the Bolg?"

The queen and the crown prince exchanged another glance.

"What?" the king demanded. "Why are you behaving so oddly? Has that encampment of Bolg been the instigating force behind all this insanity?"

"The good news, Father, is that there are no Bolg," Hariton said after a long moment.

"What do you mean, *no Bolg*? An entire outpost of them was discovered not long before I made my alliance with Talquist, the emperor of Sorbold. Up in the hills, not three leagues from here! It was grisly, I tell you—you were here, Eunice, when the scouts came with the reports—human skulls on guard posts, partially eaten body parts strewn everywhere—"

"It was a fraud," said the queen steadily. "There were never any Bolg within three hundred leagues of this land."

The king stared at his wife and son as if they had lost their minds.

"I—I am at a loss as to what to say to the two of you," he said at last, putting his fork down beside his untouched plate.

The queen rose in her place at the table.

"Well, my dear, perhaps that is so, but believe me, I am at no such loss. The palace soldiers went, at your instructions, on a regular guard route to make certain that the encampment of Bolg did not grow larger, or begin to come nearer to the border. Each week there seemed to be less and less movement, fewer heads appearing on posts and the like. Finally the sortie of soldiers screwed up their collective courage and approached the lair of the Bolg, only to find it empty."

"Empty?"

"Perhaps that is incorrect. It was uninhabited by anything living, and apparently had been so uninhabited for several weeks. What was left behind, besides the realistic-looking human heads—some of those actually *were* real, in fact—was nothing more than litter, dice, a few decks of playing cards, and a pig's head atop a scarecrow of a body dressed in furs and armor. Other than that, there was no sign of anyone, human or Bolg."

"It's true, Father," Prince Hariton said quickly as a look of dismay beyond measure took up residence on the king's face. "I went to the encampment myself—under heavy guard, of course—and toured the place. It was exactly as Mother has described it."

"So while you have been away these last seven months, playing court fool to the new emperor of Sorbold, our kingdom has been beggared, our citizens are living in fear, and our trade has fallen to almost nonexistent—"

"There is a *war* on, dearest!" the king all but shouted. "The entire Known World is at war! The Patriarch of Sepulvarta was an apostate, a purveyor of atrocities you cannot begin to imagine. The Lord and Lady Cymrian, while fair of face, are apparently rotten and evil at heart, were starving and poisoning the citizenry of the Hintervold! And the Bolg have been massing all along, waiting to overrun—"

Queen Eunice pushed in her chair impatiently.

"Excuse us, please, Hariton," she said.

The crown prince's glance went from his mother to his father, then back to the queen again. Quickly he rose and pushed his chair in, then left the room in all due haste.

The queen walked around until she was standing beside Beliac.

"Your childish obession with being eaten alive by Firbolg has cost all of us dearly, Majesty," she said curtly. "I have spared the children the truth, but I know it; I endured your flailing about in your sleep during the years we occupied the same marriage bed as you groaned and whimpered and wept about it. Apparently you must have confided it at some time or another to an untrustworthy friend or ally outside the family, or perhaps a palace servant overheard you when you were tossing in your sleep after we began to maintain separate chambers. Who knows? All I can surmise is that you were manipulated because of it, led to believe that the monsters you fear were stalking you, when in reality, it was all a lie.

"But it doesn't matter now. Even if you wished to wreak vengeance on whomever has had such amusement at your expense, you are in no position to do so. Our treasury is empty, our reputation as a world power is soiled, denatured, our military might belongs to Sorbold now, and you are the laughingstock of your own people. Welcome home. I hope your journey west was worth it."

She bowed slightly and stormed out of the dining room, leaving Beliac staring at his untouched supper.

The Battles of the Citadels

31

BETHANY

℃he Sorbold commander to whom the challenge of sacking Bethany, the capital seat of Roland, fell was an infantryman by the name of Georgis Dantre, a man who, though well schooled in military practice and capable of great logistical planning, had a reputation for brilliant leadership tempered with occasional rashness.

Gwydion of Manosse, the Lord Cymrian, had been known throughout the duration of his reign for his remarkable patience and careful approach to diplomacy as well as military strategy; it had never ceased to impress the First Generation Cymrians in his service that the grandson of two of the most mercurial rulers ever known on the continent and even on the Island of Serendair was able to be so thoughtful and considered in his undertakings.

He had shown great wisdom by giving his uncle, Anborn ap Gwylliam, a wide berth in helping to reestablish the armies of the Alliance, had followed Anborn's somewhat paranoid warnings about the need for a buildup of armaments. As a result, when the Lord Marshal of the Cymrian War had been proven correct about Talquist's secret buildup and the

Merchant Emperor's plans for domination of the Known World through its shipping routes, Ashe had been ready.

Or, at least, almost ready.

In the months leading up to Talquist's coronation, it would have been completely possible for any leader of nations over which he was only the titular head to miss the increase in the hidden slave trade, the destruction of small seaside cities and taking of their citizens captive. Talquist had, quite brilliantly, insisted on remaining as regent of the empire of Sorbold rather than taking the throne immediately, as he could have, making the rest of the world see him as a humble leader, one who understood trade and manufacture, but who needed a year's time to become familiar with the more violent and harsh realities of running a nation.

It was a strategy that caught his dearest allies, Hjorst, the Diviner of the Hintervold, and Beliac, the king of Golgarn, completely off guard and enabled Talquist to draw them into his war without them understanding how grievously they had been manipulated.

But, thanks to the paranoia of his uncle, Gwydion of Manosse had been ready to defend against Talquist's aggression nonetheless.

He was just several months behind Talquist's plan.

As a result, his wife had an army of only one-third the size of Georgis Dantre's to defend the citadel she had chosen to hold.

And Anborn had taken all but a few of its men to follow him in the First Wave, which was marching to free the occupied city of Sepulvarta.

Leaving those few behind to guard a population of women, children, the old, and the infirm.

The spies had passed this information quickly to their commander, who had thrown his head back and laughed upon hearing it.

Georgis Dantre had been a friendly rival to the supreme commander of the Empress Leitha's forces, Fhremus Alo'hari, and so upon being assigned the command of the unit that was ordered to commence the occupation of Bethany, he had been happy to discover that one of the young lieutenants assigned to his command was Kymel Alo'hari, Fhremus's gifted young nephew.

The Alo'hari family possessed the most impressive name of any military dynasty in the land. Fhremus had served the Empress Leitha bravely, as had his father and grandfather before him, and Kymel was said to be carrying on the tradition admirably when Dantre had come by ship with his battalion to the outpost outside Avonderre Harbor.

The harbor had once been the pride of the Known World, an immense commercial facility capable of off-loading over a thousand ships in a single day, as well as being a military base for the Cymrian Alliance.

It had only taken one strike to bring it to its knees, admittedly, a strike making use of almost magically modified creatures known as iacxsis, great hybrid beasts with the wings of bats and the serpentine bodies of dragon-like lizards possessing the jaws of the plague locust, as well as the fragility and enormous, unquenchable appetite of those insects. The sailors and merchants plying Avonderre Harbor on that bloody day had been incapable of a response, being outnumbered, outweaponed, and unable to take on the iacxsis, whose stonelike hide and fierce jaws had burned the coastline and rendered the fleet useless before even a single retaliatory weapon returned fire.

Thus it fell to Dantre to train and lead the invasion force that would be expected to take the capital.

And he decided his right hand in that task would be the nephew of his great rival and hero, Fhremus Alo'hari.

The first thing Dantre undertook to do was to make certain the whispers about Kymel were unfounded.

"Are you all right, Alo'hari?" he had demanded in a private meeting with the young lieutenant in the barracks at Mvekgurn, the hidden cavern in a snowy world in the northern province of the Hintervold. "I have heard rumors that you are slow to recover from your last deployment."

"I am well," the young lieutenant whispered. "Thank you for your concern, however, sir."

"They say you were slow to participate in whatever was assigned in your mission in Windswere."

Kymel had shaken his head; Dantre had noted that his objection was not listless, but neither was it vigorous.

"I believe the emperor would say that I accomplished my task to his satisfaction," he said. "No one but I was assigned the task that the emperor gave me. It is reasonable, if petty, of my comrades to be critical of my undertaking due to jealousy."

"Hmmm." Dantre examined the scroll that had been given to him upon taking the supreme commander's nephew into his command. "We are likely to encounter women and children, as well as civilian men, in the course of our duty. Does that disturb you in any way?"

Alo'hari had shaken his head, though Dantre was uncertain as to whether there was resistance in his doing so.

"I assume we will use the traditional rules of engagement when encountering them, will we not, sir?" he had asked.

Dantre had exhaled.

"We will," he said gravely. "But I must remind you, Alo'hari, we are at intercontinental war at this point. The depravity and criminality with which the Lord and Lady Cymrian are conducting this conflict is well known. The depth of their wickedness is legendary; the Lord is a man born of the line of dragons, the Lady a sorceress of primal beauty and even more fundamental perversion. Lord Gwydion has not been seen since the beginning of the war; it is said that he is dead or in hiding. The Lady Cymrian's whereabouts were largely unknown until recently, when she rained dark fire from the sky down upon the liberators of Sepulvarta.

"Of the two of them, the far more dangerous is the Lady," he continued, noting Kymel's mien remaining stoic while his coloring sallowed considerably. "So, therefore, we must take no chances. If she is encountered, she needs to be contained and dealt with using the harshest terms of military justice; it is highly likely she will be executed even before standing trial because of the power of her wiles."

"But—that would merely be the rules of engagement concerning the Lady Cymrian, would it not, sir?" Kymel asked quietly. "The—other women, the children—"

"By standard R.O.E., they will not be harmed," Dantre said reassuringly. "The law of comfort will be observed, of course—the battles of the citadels are to result in occupation, not sacking or destruction, so that undoubtedly will be necessary for everyone's sake. But no harm will come to anyone, Alo'hari."

Kymel had gone even more ashen, but merely nodded, Dantre had noted.

The practice of Comfort Law was a long-held system of occupation. Under Comfort Law, the civilian men captured in a citadel or province under occupation were taken into work camps, almost always in another occupied area, to prevent their knowledge of the region and its hiding places or secret stores of weapons from being used against the occupiers. The children were impressed into similar work camps, though generally in the occupied area they had been born in, so that their own mothers were present in the place they were working, often overseeing their behavior and to keep them compliant.

And the women of the occupied area, save for the crones and the hags, were subject to the law of comfort, which required them to provide sexual services and other amenities to the occupying forces to prevent what was known in military terms as "deprivation rage."

It was systematic and legalized rape, something the military minds of Sorbold had long ago deemed necessary for the welfare of their troops. The scrolls on which the Comfort Law had been codified and recorded noted the value of the "contribution to the war effort" such women provided, and as such, it was expected they were to be treated humanely and only beaten or injured if they refused to participate willingly in the service of the troops.

Dantre had continued to observe Kymel throughout their interview, and at the end he determined that, while the young man seemed to have been traumatized by whatever had occurred in the conduct of his previous mission, he was nonetheless fit to serve, and decided to elevate him to battlefield commander status.

It was a decision that led to a moment of agony that could not have been anticipated.

The eleventh division, the Sorbold contingent that had been assigned to overtake and occupy the citadel of Bethany, had been comprised of three smaller units, each the size of the invasion force of those for the other Orlandan provinces.

Bethany was the capital, and the intelligence in Georgis Dantre's possession had indicated that the circular walls that protected the citadel were of prohibitive height and depth to be taken by anything but a simultaneous four-front assault. Additionally, the elemental basilica of Fire was known to be in the center of the capital city, and while the Lady Cymrian's whereabouts had not been determined by reliable intelligence, it was assumed that her presence might be highly possible in a place where such power existed, given that she was the bearer of the ancient sword dedicated to that element.

For that reason, he had appealed to the supreme commander for additional troops and matériel. Under normal circumstances, that commander would have been Fhremus Alo'hari, whose military wisdom was beyond question.

But Fhremus Alo'hari had been temporarily relieved of command, it was said, to serve as the personal guardian of the emperor, and his temporary replacement was a young man named Titactyk. Dantre had been unimpressed in his interactions with Titactyk, but the emperor's sudden elevation of him to a post that was generally earned in decades of faithful service and a reputation for extraordinary military wisdom and unquestioned character made Dantre, and all the other division commanders, assume that they had misjudged the young soldier and, in most cases, seek to gain his good favor.

So Dantre had sought his counsel prior to being deployed with the eleventh, asking for additional troops and supplies so that, in his words, "a devastating blow can be struck from the outset, an unquestioned occupation of Bethany can be swiftly undertaken, and, given the citadel's geographic placement in between the currently occupied city-state of Sepulvarta and the other targeted northern provinces, an occupied Bethany could allow that former capital seat to serve as a source of supply and support for all the other occupation undertakings."

Titactyk had contemplated his words and seen wisdom in them.

He had granted Dantre a force of sixty thousand men, a little less than half of his entire army.

But, he had noted, given that the intelligence provided by the spies from the area of Bethany indicated that most of the trained men had accompanied Anborn on his misguided journey to liberate Sepulvarta, Titactyk felt comfortable that he could assign the lesser-trained regiments and those soldiers who were considered to be, as he told Dantre, "in the second half of the rankings." Dantre had protested, reminding Titactyk again of the importance of the objective in question, but the newly appointed supreme commander would not be moved in his decision.

So Dantre had exhaled angrily but quietly retrenched, returning to the sixty thousand soldiers he had been assigned, many of whom were reasonably trained and in good standing.

While many of them were also thugs, brigands, bullies, and abusers of anyone weaker than they were.

"It can't be helped," he had told a horrified Kymel, who had protested even more vehemently than Dantre had to Titactyk. "The supreme commander is unmoved by our words. We will have to try and make the best of this. There is nothing more to be done."

And thus Kymel set forth on the road to Bethany, riding with Georgis Dantre in the same ranks as many of the coarse ruffians who had accompanied Titactyk on his drunken revels the day before he had deployed as the new supreme commander.

32

The citadel of Bethany had first been sighted by a lookout with sharp vision, but it was only a momentary accomplishment; seconds afterward, all the forces in Dantre's regiment had seen the thin wisp of steam that signaled the presence of the flamewell in the center of the elemental basilica of Fire, said to be a direct vent to the fire at the heart of the Earth.

The division had traveled by means of the trans-Orlandan thoroughfare, the great road that bisected the continent, built in the ancient times known as the Illuminaria, the era of Gwylliam's greatest architectural undertakings. It was often overlooked as one of his most important such undertakings, traveled a millennium later by most of the foot and commercial traffic that crossed the continent.

Now, Dantre had determined, it was necessary for the division to divide itself even more and approach each of the four gates, each built at one of the cardinal direction points, all set on major roadways, rather than approaching the citadel in one solid force of sixty thousand.

"It might lose some of the effect to divide so," Dantre said to Kymel. "Admittedly, I have never been in the position either to approach or be approached by an enemy numbering even close to sixty thousand, but I cannot even begin to imagine what the enemy will do when they realize they are so surrounded."

Kymel merely nodded. He sat atop his warhorse as he heard the orders pass up and down the travel line, closing his eyes at the vulgar commentary and the hideous undertone to the reactions the news engendered in the "second half of the rankings."

"You take the far side of the thoroughfare," Dantre said as the division began to split as ordered. "Approach the city from the east; I will take the western side of the thoroughfare. Levis and Skraw will lead the northern and southern attacks."

Kymel swallowed. Both of the men named as division leaders were among the most repugnant of the enlisted soldiers.

There was no question in his mind what sort of damage would occur once the northern and southern gates were opened.

$\mathcal{I}$t took more than two hours before his division of the regiment was at the eastern gate.

From the distance they were maintaining, Kymel could see a few archers up on the inside wall, a pathetically small contingent that was spread far too thin for the defense of any walled city, especially the capital of Roland.

The sight saddened him immensely, knowing how weak the defense would be behind that wall.

He turned atop his warhorse to the soldiers behind him.

"Remember the rules of engagement," he cautioned them seriously. "If Comfort Law is to be enacted, it will be undertaken at Dantre's orders *only*."

A widespread snicker and low laughter answered him, as did the sarcastic voice of one of the men in his division.

"Oh, yes, *sir*, of course, *sir*. Wouldn't have it any other way."

Kymel sat straighter in his saddle.

"Do you wish to come closer and repeat that to me, soldier?" he said in a deadly tone, one that he had heard his uncle employ on very rare occasions of misconduct.

The mutterings and amusement reduced to a somewhat quieter level.

"I thought not. Be careful, the rest of you—if a man's too much of a coward to stand by his own words when he is with his own regiment, imagine how quickly he will desert his comrades when in the fray."

The mutterings fell to a sullen silence.

"The archers are positioned only on every third crenellation. Keep to the outside of their range."

Kymel turned back to the gate, feeling the hatred boring into his back as he did.

Or not, he thought as he took up the reins.

He signaled to the wagoneers whose dray horses were carrying the battering ram, one of the four that had been harvested and had its tip cased in metal the night before.

He could hear in the distance shouts from the wall; the archers had made note of their arrival.

By now, the entirety of the citadel knew that it was surrounded.

Kymel signaled to the brawny soldiers who would carry the battering ram.

"Set to," he ordered, hearing the trumpet blast from the western gate.

He waited until he heard the other two trumpet calls, indicating that each of the other three divisions was set, then waved his arm at his own trumpeter.

A silvery blast rent the air.

"*Charge!*" Kymel shouted.

The soldiers bearing the battering ram stormed the enormous gate under a hail of arrow fire, while the archers with the Sorbold regiment returned fire. Kymel directed the advancement of the foot soldiers, watching detachedly as they assaulted the gates, some spinning to the ground, impaled with well-shot missiles, others returning short-range missile shots, toppling the occasional archer from the wall.

It's only a matter of time, he thought as he watched the assault. *Skilled as their archers might be, our numbers will win out eventually. It's inevitable.*

And he was right.

The northern gate was the first to give way.

With a resounding trumpet signal, the gate beyond Kymel's sight tore open.

A wide chorus of gleeful screaming sounded at the northern quadrant of the wall. It was almost as if the initial opening was the bellwether; little more than a moment later, the eastern gate ripped open as well.

Kymel's division blasted in, screeching with orgiastic fury.

It was all he could do to keep ahead of them on his warhorse, galloping full out.

They rode and ran over the bodies of the fallen, their fellow soldiers and the enemy archers alike, pushing and charging through the splintered gate of what at one time Kymel knew to have been one of the most heavily defended cities on the continent.

He rode forward into the central streets that surrounded the basilica of Fire, his division immediately behind him, and the rest of the regiment riding and stampeding into view.

He pulled his warhorse to an abrupt stop and held up his hand for the rest of his division to do likewise.

Standing in the streets of the city was an enormous number of wild-eyed women, some with children sheltered behind them, but most alone, thousands of them, Kymel noted, perhaps ten, even fifteen thousand, spread across the city in a circle, staring at each directional point where the gates had been broken through.

Attired in common clothing, holding bread baskets and small looms, trays of fruit and baskets of laundry.

Caught in the midst of their daily chores and life.

From the back of his own division, a familiar voice began to chuckle.

It was a sound that made his blood run cold as it was picked up, almost immediately, by many others standing behind him, then by the other three divisions of the eleventh regiment behind their commanders.

The eleventh division of the Sorbold army, having just taken the citadel of Bethany almost without wielding a single weapon, began to laugh uproariously.

Across the city central square, Georgis Dantre held up his hand, accompanied by a stand-down call from his trumpeter.

The women of Bethany, abandoned by their men, it seemed, continued to stare at their captors in terror.

Georgis Dantre nudged his mount forward, his hand still aloft to hold back the troops from charging.

"Surrender," he said kindly in the Orlandan tongue. "Put whatever you are holding down in the street before you, kneel where you stand, and put your hands behind your head. You will not die, and you will not be abused under the Comfort Law."

The women, stunned, looked at each other in dismay.

They stood, frozen, for a long moment.

With evident impatience, Dantre signaled to them again.

"Kneel if you want to live," he said, annoyance creeping into his voice.

Once again, the ranks of women looked at each other, then turned back to face their captors.

And began to kneel, putting their baskets and trays down into the streets before them.

"Hands behind your heads," Dantre instructed as the voices of the men behind him were starting to rumble again.

Reluctantly, the women obeyed, their eyes glistening.

Kymel, fighting a wave of nausea, was moved to pity at the sight of their tears.

"Easier to see and judge the orbs when they's arms is up like that," shouted an oaf in the ranks. "I see a few that look tasty."

"Don't cry, darlin'—I don' want any salt on me bodkin when you're suckin' on it," yelled another.

"Stay down like that; I'm gonna shove my broadhead up your arse!"

Over the rising laughter, a single flat voice could be heard.

"Don't be jealous, ladies—we're going to knob you *all*."

A deafening chorus of hooting and gleeful screaming arose, filling the air of the city.

Georgis Dantre signaled angrily for silence. He rode forward slowly until he was almost to the center of the city square.

Then, it seemed as if in a dream to Kymel, the dark-haired woman at the front of the arc of the circle on the western side snatched the cloth from the top of her laundry basket, raised a crossbow that was lying beneath it, and fired a bolt into Dantre's forehead, neatly parting his hair.

The commander of the regiment fell to the cobblestones, his split head making a resounding crack as it impacted the street.

As the invading force stood for a moment in utter shock, from every basket and tray, out from behind every linen apron came weapon after weapon, mostly crossbows but also some throwing knives and longbows, which were fired seconds later in great sheets of arrows and bolts by women soldiers who had taken on an immediate battle formation that gave them ranks of height, each one behind or above another.

Another flight of arrows screamed through the air and stung into the eyes of the invading force.

Leveling the entire front line.

"Fall back!" Kymel shouted as the stunned invaders recovered their wits, swung their crossbows forward and fired, or charged the line furiously, raving in rage. It was of no use; the men, laughing the moment before, had regained their anger and turned it on the ranks of women they outnumbered more than four to one.

Their efforts were of no use, either.

The fifteen thousand defenders of Bethany had been part of the force that Anborn had observed before he went off with the men of Roland to fight along the Threshold of Death and set up to begin to break the occupation of Sepulvarta.

He had broken into raucous, full-bellied laughter a few moments after observing them training, noting their skill, delighted in his nephew's decision that had not been specifically communicated to him to enlist an equal, possibly greater-numbered cohort of female soldiers, as well trained and talented as their male counterparts, skilled in missile weapons, into the army of the Alliance.

And, by the look of what was coming out of their bread baskets and linen trays now, swords and cudgels as well.

They're not crying, Kymel observed distantly, remembering the gleam in their eyes upon first being confronted by the occupation force. *They are furious, and rightly so.*

In the center of the southern division, a blond woman with a dowdy kerchief in her hair was standing at the fore now, a long whip of some sort in her left hand, drawing a sword with her right.

Her face, fair with skin like a rose petal, was set in grim determination as she stepped even farther forward into the line of fire, her white apron bib scarcely concealing a scale breastplate of gleaming armor.

She wound back and struck with her whip, a clean, terrifyingly long blow eliciting a snap that sounded like a crack of thunder. The whip encircled the neck of Skraw, who clutched his throat, dropping his crossbow as she dragged him off his horse and pulled him nearer to her.

She drew her sword from its scabbard; it roared forth with thick flames whispering up the blade.

Dear All-God, Kymel thought. *The Lady Cymrian.*

With the cleanest sword stroke he had ever seen, she sliced off Skraw's head and kicked it away from her as the neck began to spurt blood.

"We surrender!" shouted one of the women bawdily from within the ranks of the archers.

A roar of higher-pitched laughter went up from the center of the city.

Then the women charged, some with crossbows, others with short swords or knives; they engaged their invaders, fighting hand-to-hand in the street, some falling back, some falling, but holding their own.

From the ramparts above a new rain of arrows sailed down; Fhremus looked up to the raised ramparts to see a soldier he thought he recognized giving the commands. *Who is that?* he thought hazily. He racked his brain until a name came to the front of his head.

Knapp. *One of Anborn's men.*

Whom the Lord Marshal had obviously felt confident enough to leave behind.

He was musing about the irony when a crossbow bolt caught him in the throat.

The world spun in color interlaced with seconds of black as Kymel pitched sideways off his horse, falling to the ground with a resounding thump that he did not feel.

He looked up, the sky askew above him, to see a woman with steel-gray hair approaching him; he watched her boots as they came to a halt next to his eyes.

In the distance he heard a distinctive voice shout over the roar of the battle.

"Elsa! Don't—he hasn't moved since he came in here with them. Wait—"

The gray-haired woman looked down at him flatly, sizing him up. Then she crouched down next to his shoulder.

"You assaulted our gate, came into our city, our home," she said. Her voice had a wobbling tone, as if the words were being spoken in a distant cave. "If for only that alone, your life is forfeit. My apologies."

He could only hear, not see, the knife being drawn, felt it dragged cleanly across his neck, saw the life gushing out of him.

And, with the last of his energy, smiled a trembling smile.

How I wish I could have told you I respect you all, he thought as his consciousness dissipated on the wind. *My only sadness is that I am dying without you knowing I was cheering for you.*

*L*ater that night, Knapp descended from the wall where he and the other archers atop the rampart, a combination of Anborn's experienced forces and some of the new recruits selected and trained by the Lord Cymrian, had been needlessly awaiting the arrival of support troops and reinforcements.

He came over to the Lady Cymrian, who, with dozens of other women charged with the cleanup duty of bodies and sorting the supplies stripped from them, was making her way systematically through weapons and arrows, bolts and armor.

"All is well, then?" he asked.

Rhapsody nodded, continuing to count.

"In due deference to the soldiers we lost, I don't believe that could have gone much better."

"Agreed." The Lady Cymrian finally seemed satisfied with her tally, and looked up into Knapp's face. "Quite a haul; they were well armed, even if they weren't well trained."

"It's hard to say whether they were or not," said Knapp, uncorking a flask and offering it to Rhapsody, who accepted gratefully and took a sip. "We had the element of utter surprise. It would not have come out so beneficially if we hadn't."

Rhapsody nodded, took another sip, and returned the flask. "Again, agreed, and thank you."

"How many did we lose?"

"Eleven hundred seventy-four. All but one hundred eighteen women."

"Remarkable. And on their side?"

"We have roughly eleven thousand prisoners. Tallies disagree, but it is upward of forty-five thousand dead." She wiped her hands off onto her apron. "Bethany is a large and well-appointed city with many places to hide. It will take a while to ferret out all the deserters. But Luisa is charged with that, and she is relentless."

"Indeed. So what are your plans now? Do you intend to remain here and await a second assault?"

Rhapsody shook her head. "If that prisoner we met on the road is to be believed, they just lost over a third, close to a half, of that one commander's forces—what was his name? Titactyk? I am absolutely certain that our new forces, men and women, have the citadel secured. I have been awaiting word from Gwydion Navarne and from the leadership in Yarim, Bethe Corbair, and Canderre, but so far no bird has arrived. Once I know how they are faring I will make a decision as to where to deploy next. But unless there is a serious need of more arms, I suspect Ashe's new trainees have things well in hand."

Knapp nodded agreeably.

"So if that be the case, I believe I will head off to join Anborn and the First Wave." She chuckled as the ancient scout's left eyebrow arched, but he said nothing. "Just in case there are any more iacxsis out there, Knapp; I do have a decent weapon for use against them." She patted the dragon's tongue whip she had used to pull Skraw from his mount, curled at her side.

"I know."

"Thank you again for the cover. Well, unless there's something else you need of me, I think I will go bed down. My tent is looking very comfortable in my mind's eye."

"Get some sleep—you well deserve it."

"As do we all. Good night, Knapp."

"Good night, m'lady." The scout looked away, suddenly tired.

Rhapsody stepped closer and looked up into his face. "Are you all right?"

Knapp exhaled. "Yes—I'm just struggling with old demons, having witnessed what I did this day."

"I can imagine," Rhapsody said simply. "Good night."

———

$\mathcal{L}$ater that night, in the depths of her small regulation tent, Rhapsody was beset by old demons herself.

She had long been blessed, or cursed, with the gift of prescience, the ability to see the Past and often the Future, and even occasionally the Present, in dreams and visions that occasionally left her exhausted, drained, and terrified. Though she did not remember, those dreams had been held at bay for years by the men in her life, her husband and son, neither of whom she currently thought of, as a family member, in Ashe's case, or at all, as it regarded her son. The dragon blood in their veins allowed them to wrap the protection of their lore around the images in her mind and guard her from them.

This night she had a glimpse of a tiny child, with enormous blue eyes, the irises scored by vertical pupils, as Ashe's were. In her mind she saw him quite distinctly for a moment, lying on a pillow beside her, waving his tiny arms in the air.

Then the vision vanished.

Rhapsody groaned and rolled over onto her other side.

After a few moments' respite from the visions, her dream changed.

She was back in the Past, on a summer's day nearly two years before, back when Anborn had still been lame.

She had come to bid him goodbye before she and Ashe had set off to the province of Yarim to meet up with Achmed and the Bolg artisans who would undertake, successfully as it turned out, to rejuvenate the dead, ancient relic of Entudenin, a rock obelisk that had once been a fountain of life-giving water in the middle of the arid red clay desert city that was the capital of the province.

She had found the Lord Marshal staring out over the fields of waving golden highgrass, a contemplative look in his azure eyes.

She could see him, could hear him speak the words again he had spoken to her in that field what seemed like a lifetime ago.

It's coming from the west, I believe.

In the depths of her dream, Rhapsody felt the same queasy feeling in her stomach that she had experienced then.

Anborn, a Kinsman like she was, though far more familiar with the brotherhood of soldiers sworn to the wind, was referring to the Kinsman call, the summons spoken into the wind by those who had been welcomed into the fraternity for a lifetime of selfless service bearing arms, or for a heroic gesture, risking one's life for an innocent.

He had been granted his Kinsman status long ago, she recently, he for the first reason, she for the second.

And, like him, she had been hearing, or rather feeling, something strange on the wind.

What is it? she whispered in her sleep, as she had into his ear then.

The Lord Marshal, almost as real to her in her dream as he had been in the grassy field, shook his head.

I don't know. But I thought I heard the Kinsman call the other night. On the Skeleton Coast.

What neither of them could have known was that what she was feeling was the eyes of Michael, the Wind of Death, her hated adversary and pursuer in the old world, gazing at her through the scrying scale that his child could read.

The Faorina Michael had called Faron.

The demon host that was, in fact, coming for her.

From the west.

The dream shifted again, and Rhapsody sighed painfully.

She was now atop a rocky promontory that lunged out into the sea, a large jagged structure beside other such structures that rose from the sand like fingers, as if a giant hand had landed from the sky, palm down, at the ocean's edge. The sea crashed violently to the shore below her.

Around her was violence and devastation too grisly for her mind to comprehend, a purge for sheer sport with soldiers ravaging young mothers as well as their children, the brutal sodomizing of an elderly woman in the vestments of a member of the clergy.

And, worst of all, a line of soldiers carrying screaming infants to a catapult positioned at the end of the promontory, which they used to fling the babies, still screaming, into the sea.

All the while a young soldier with dark hair and a neatly trimmed beard, whose face was hidden in the night shadows, laughed uproariously as he directed the mayhem.

With a scream of her own, Rhapsody bolted upright in her bedroll, trembling.

The next several minutes were spent apologizing to the various soldiers who had come rushing to her aid, bringing her hot cider and sympathetic glances, but who were clearly confused by whatever it was that bedeviled her.

How can they possibly understand this sensitivity? she asked the bottom of her mug of cider as the shaking of her hand subsided. *Even I don't understand it.*

Eventually she was able to calm herself again and climbed back into her bedroll, brushing the rocks out from under her head first.

Trying to remember, as sleep came for her, what she had first seen in her vision before it had turned to a nightmare.

And failing.

*T*he next morning, when a message had come from Navarne that their attack had been repelled and that Gwydion and Constantin were making their way to Sepulvarta, she packed her meager possessions, requested and received a mount, and left quietly before most of the city had awakened.

On her way to meet the two men that, long ago, she had adopted as grandsons, one still young, one now very old, one to heal his broken young heart.

And one to save his soul.

33

NAVARNE

In the smoldering aftermath of the attack launched against the citadel that carried his father's name, and his own, Gwydion Navarne left the walled capital city that had been successfully defended, but at a horrific cost in human lives and structural damage, and made his way north to the keep that had been his family's home.

Once the walled city had been declared safe after the onslaught, a rout that had left the streets behind its wall running red with blood, Gwydion had quietly sought the Patriarch's blessing to return to Haguefort, where some of the most wonderful and hideous memories of his young life had been made.

When at first he had approached and spoken to Constantin, the Patriarch had been attending to the wounded, applying the power of the Ring of Wisdom that he had been given upon his investiture and his own deep knowledge of healing he had gained, it was said, beyond the Veil of Hoen, the place between life and death. His back had been to Gwydion as the young duke had quietly put forth the request that the Patriarch assume responsibility for the citadel in his stead for a few days while he went to check on Haguefort.

At first the Patriarch had turned, fury in his blue eyes, in angry astonishment to confront Gwydion, vituperative words struggling to break out of his mouth. The casualties of the battle had been enormous, and the work of rebuilding and sustaining the citadel was a heavy burden, expected to be borne by all present.

But upon beholding the young man, his rage had tempered, and the former gladiatorial arena slave had reverted to being the compassionate man of faith he had been since his return from the Veil of Hoen.

He had nodded his assent.

"Do what you must do, young Navarne," he had said simply. "You have well earned the leave; I will pray that, whatever you find, the All-God will give you the strength to accept it with the gratitude that your province has been largely spared."

He cast a glance around the streets of the city, broken and blackened, with bodies being stacked in neat rows, and shook his head.

"Perhaps not largely."

"My thanks," the duke had said, turning away.

"Remember, m'lord," said the Patriarch as Gwydion began to take his leave, "that you owe me your time in return for mine. I will await your return three days hence, whereupon I will go and finish the reconnection of the Chain of Prayer. And then I will come and collect you to ride to Sepulvarta, where you have agreed to help me retake *my* citadel."

Gwydion had merely nodded.

He had ridden the forest road alone. It was more difficult a passage than he had imagined it would be; the road was the same thoroughfare his mother and aunt had traveled ten years before on their way to purchase a pair of shoes for his baby sister Melisande. It was on this road she had met a grisly death, one of the many acts of random violence perpetrated by the thralls of a demon that had held the continent in terror and disarray.

He had not realized, until he had ridden her final path, how much more had ended that day than he had ever realized.

Perhaps that was because, by traveling from the city to which she had been heading when her carriage was assaulted, to the place from which she had departed, he was quite literally traveling back in Time.

His father, Stephen Navarne, had been a man of almost unquenchable optimism, in Gwydion's recollection from that hazy time in childhood. He had done his grieving in private at the death of his wife, choosing to focus instead on helping his young children recover from it.

How did he manage that, I wonder? Gwydion thought as he cantered past the bodies on the roadside, or beneath the trees of the forest, riding a bloodstained pathway back into the past on his way to a home he was not certain was still standing.

But it was.

As he rode past the guardian towers that had long welcomed visitors to Haguefort, he was relieved to find them still standing, but he had only gone a few hundred paces before the edifice of the rosy brown stone keep had come into sight.

Blackened with soot, its windows broken, great sparkling piles of glass glittering across the grounds.

For as much as he had expected it to be the case, the sight still made Gwydion want to vomit.

He tied his horse to the blackened trunk of what had once been the tree he and his mother had planted in the gardens of the courtyard when Melly was born. His throat tightened as he thought of his sister, hidden away with Rhapsody and Ashe's son in the shelter of the Deep Kingdom of the Nain, or at least as he thought they were.

And then he realized there was literally nothing about which he was certain anymore, no one he loved that he actually knew was safe.

Walking what had once been the hallways of his childhood home was both bitter and strangely reassuring; everything of any value was gone, as he expected, but many things that had mattered greatly to his father, suits of armor and family crests, relics and antiques from bygone eras and renderings of historic buildings that no longer existed, had been wantonly destroyed and left as garbage in the rooms he had been born in, had played and been schooled in.

It matters little, he told himself as he walked through thousands of shredded books and manuscripts that his historian father had collected so meticulously. *I had never realized victory could be so painful.*

The sight of his family's historical treasures in ruins within the keep made him think in horror of what must have happened to the Cymrian museum, the squat, plain two-story stone building not far from the keep in which his father had lovingly kept and restored artifacts of the Cymrian Age. That repository had even more valuable treasures than the family home; unlike the libraries of the keep, which stored scholarly works, the museum was the depository of historic swords and other weapons that doubtless had made their way into enemy hands and had been used, in sickening irony, against the innocents of the continent yet again, much as they had in the Great War.

He made his way out of the gutted keep, heartsick, and across the courtyard to the museum, only to find it unmolested. The single window of thick glass above the doorway was still intact; hurriedly Gwydion located the key and went inside, only to find it exactly as he had left it when he had moved himself, Melly, their household servants, and their late beloved chamberlain Gerald Owen to Highmeadow almost a year before.

He quickly climbed the stairs to the second floor, which, like the first, had been left untouched. Gratefully he ran his hands over the items in the collection; it was almost as if the items his father had guarded and treasured had been of no interest whatsoever to the invading armies.

Much as his father had once told him they were to even the descendants of those whose memories were enshrined there.

For a man of seventeen summers, I am far too old and weary of the world, he thought as he closed up the place and locked it carefully again.

He felt a sudden chill on his cheek and looked up.

A fine, light snow was falling, a dusting merely, but unmistakable. Utterly unseasonable, but meaningful to Gwydion beyond measure.

Snow had often been the harbinger of his birthday, the last day of autumn, an upcoming anniversary that he had utterly forgotten. That day was frequently the Gathering Day for the Winter Carnival that his father had so loved and had made an unbreakable tradition while he had been alive.

That tradition had been sullied four years before when a cohort of soldiers from Sorbold, demonic thralls, had assaulted the celebration, leaving it in ruins and smoldering ash. Gwydion winced at the memory of his father's face as he boosted him, then only thirteen years old, over the keep wall and handed a wailing six-year-old Melly up to him.

The expression in his eyes had long haunted Gwydion's dreams; it was an extraordinary mixture of terror and relief, the realization of danger at the same moment he was sending his children out of the fray.

Just as his godfather and namesake, Gwydion of Manosse, had done with his wife and child.

It was at just such a carnival a year before that he had been invested as duke, had inherited all his father's lands and titles, had become a man, really. Ashe and Rhapsody had proposed the idea of reinstituting the tradition three years after the bloodbath, telling him that it was time to go back to living.

Looking around Haguefort and remembering the sights he had seen on the way to it, Gwydion was not ready for that yet.

But the soft falling snow, as it dusted his eyelashes, felt gentle and almost warm on his face, like a reminder from afar that life would go on.

Like an early birthday greeting.

Gwydion raised his face to the sky and allowed the snow to fall on it.

"I'm doing the best I can, Father," he whispered. "Thank you for guiding me, as always. Kiss Mother for me."

Then, when remaining thus began to feel self-indulgent, he retrieved his mount and made his way back to the capital seat, Navarne City, where a nightmare of destruction required his attention.

34

YARIM

℈n spite of the fact that his journey with his troops to the far eastern province of Yarim had been the longest that any of the divisions of Icemen had traveled on their way to attack one of Roland's northern provinces, it didn't take long for Hjorst, the Diviner of the Hintervold, to come to the conclusion that something was very wrong.

In the many late-night strategy sessions that he, Beliac, and Talquist had undertaken after the new emperor's coronation, the necessity for the Hintervold to strike in a preemptive manner had been clearly reinforced time and again as intelligence came in indicating that the Alliance forces were leaving the northern citadels to mass along the Threshold of Death, as the pompous leaders of that alliance had chosen to call it.

Of the three nations affected by the aggression of the Alliance, Hjorst felt that his had by far the most to lose. While Golgarn had discovered an encampment of Bolg a mere three leagues away from its capital in the mountains to the north, and Talquist had expressed concern about manipulation of crops and other trade goods, the Diviner was facing the prospect that his lands would be beggared and starved.

Given that his people were by far the most threatened, Hjorst had invested as much as he could fairly put on the table. The Hintervold, though it comprised an enormous landmass that lay across almost the entirety of the northern border of the lands of the Alliance, had managed, by fate and the hands of ancient gods that resided in the land and water, according to the belief system of the Diviner, to inherit a terribly hostile climate. The weather regularly ran the gamut from brutal winters to scorching summers with a heavy canopy of clouds in either season, leaving little growing season to provide food for the people who were intrepid or foolish enough to brave its elements and live there.

And since starvation seemed to trump Talquist's loss of income and Beliac's fear of monsters who had not yet attacked his cities, Hjorst felt that he had the obligation to hold the line, as he had been requested to do, by providing support troops to an invasion force that would conquer and occupy the northern citadels that Talquist had assured him were all but empty with a sincerity that all his instruments of divination had confirmed was genuine.

So it was with great surprise that when his forces, in league with a commander named Rasnike from Sorbold, consistently seemed to come upon walled garrisons and highly reinforced barricaded encampments where the once-pleasant capital cities of Canderre and Yarim, Bethe Corbair, Bethany, and Navarne had stood, there was no word from Jierna Tal as to how the army of Sorbold, massive as it was, could not spare more troops to counter the buildup that had apparently gone unnoticed.

Still, he had committed but thirty thousand troops, while Talquist's forces numbered in the hundreds of thousands. It didn't seem to matter that his contingent represented a larger portion of his overall forces; the requests for donations of valuable supplies and troops seemed to have no end.

Hjorst tried not to think about what the men he had left behind along the way from Navarne to Bethe Corbair had encountered.

But if it was anything like what he had found in Yarim, he ran the possibility of being recorded by history as the worst leader the Iceworld had ever known.

Given his family history and lineage, that was an enormous accomplishment of the worst possible kind.

So when he was summarily captured and imprisoned at the battle of Yarim, he knew that something had gone terribly wrong with the world, or with his decision making.

But by then the losses were so grievous that it didn't really matter.

As he trudged along, silent and stunned, in chains like the other prisoners of the Alliance, behind wagons drawn by horses that seemed to have eaten their weights in prunes each morning, Hjorst was trying to make sense of it all.

Has any nation on this side of the Wide Central Sea ever had a sovereign taken prisoner before? he wondered dully as he marked time and the pathway to wherever it was that he and the other troops were being herded.

He was trying not to think of Elivan, his second-youngest son, who had been reported killed in the battle for Bethany. Word had spread almost silently that the rout in the citadel had been led by the Lady Cymrian; Hjorst did not know what to believe; the battle tales about her behavior were so outlandish that he had begun to think it possible that perhaps he had been misled.

Each new step on the road seemed to uncover a new level to which that may have happened.

Your quest for immortality may have undone us all, Talquist, he thought ruefully. *Who could have known that your seeking to cheat death would bring so much of it on all of us?*

But he couldn't brood about it for too long.

Because after a few moments' rest, a whip was cracked.

And he, with the other prisoners of war, were on the road back to Bethany again.

35

*H*rarfa could barely contain her excitement.

It had been more than a thousand years since she had last visited the place that had been known at the time as Canrif, the Cymrian word for *century*. It had been so named because a First Generationer named Hague, Gwylliam the Visionary's best friend and confidant, had famously told the first Lord Cymrian that within a century the citadel in the mountains he was designing would be the greatest civilization the world had ever seen.

Fool, she thought now as she had then. *What did you know of what the world has seen? I, and those like me, who were around at the* beginning *of this world, know of secrets and civilizations that you could never even imagine.*

Her excitement was diminished somewhat by the memory of what had driven her out of the place long ago. She had been in male form at that time, occupying the body of a low-level soldier in Gwylliam's standing army; she had still been weak, even after the millennia that had passed since her escape from the Vault when it was ruptured by the impact of

Melita, the Sleeping Child, a piece of a dead star that had fallen out of the sky and into the depths of the sea.

Her host body had been owned by a young man of human blood who had traveled on one of the ships of the Third Fleet, the Cymrian faction loyal to Gwylliam, long before it was discovered that the First Fleet had survived the storm at sea as well, and had elected Anwyn as their leader. The soldier whose soul she had eaten was of insignificant rank and standing in the world, so it had not been too difficult to take him as a host. His greatest flaw had been his inability to control his red, easily excitable tarse, and he had made copious use of it whenever possible as if it had enslaved him.

He had been enthusiastically knobbing a less-than-enthusiastic camp-following whore when another soldier, drunk on spirits and the misconception that his own tarse was the only one that should ever reside up her skirts, had come upon them and had beaten her soldier-host body to death on the spot, not even having the grace to allow him to disengage from what he was doing first. As a result, the only option to spare Hrarfa's true spirit form from an ugly death and disappearance from the world was to take on the prostitute as her new host, fleeing Canrif.

And thus a new means of rising to power had come into her awareness.

So the demon's memories of Canrif were both reminiscent and horrifying.

It seemed to her that it had taken a great deal more time to come to the place than it should have, however.

The journey from the mountain edge of Sorbold into the no-man's-land that was the southern edge of the Krevensfield Plain should have taken less than a sennight. Yet almost three weeks had passed since the army had moved away from the southern Teeth toward where she remembered Canrif being, and still they seemed to be wandering aimlessly, with no view in sight of the eastern mountains that were home to the Firbolg.

Faron, she whispered cautiously. *I think we are lost.*

As usual, there was no immediate reply.

The stone titan came to a halt in the middle of the endless plain, the horizon visible from every side. It turned slowly, its enormous head making a careful sweep of the vista around it.

Behind it, the invasion force of almost seventy thousand soldiers, twenty thousand on horseback, dragging with them the matériel and supplies for an assault on a mountain fortress, slowed to a halt as well. The field commanders were becoming used to the lack of any sort of forewarning or instruction from their massive leader and had put in place a system of largely silent communication to keep from crossing him.

So, amid a minimum of squeaking from the wheels of battlewagons and the screeching of horse leather, the three divisions of the Sorbold army that Faron had commandeered rolled to a stop.

Hrarfa was growing frantic and angry.

Faron, she whispered. *Where are we?*

The stone eyes of the titan turned blue and piercing as once again it surveyed the open landscape, searching for a massive mountainous kingdom that had all but disappeared.

You are the one who has been here, the sullen thoughts of the Faorina said finally. *You are the one who has brought us here. Why do you ask me? How could you lose a mountain range?*

In an explosive burst of fury, the mind of the F'dor spirit screamed in rage.

The body it had commandeered froze, the Living Stone from which it had been formed utterly rigid.

After a long moment of silence, Hrarfa heard Faron's voice, as deadly and serious as she had ever perceived it.

If you ever do that again I will kill you. Even if I have to kill both of us to accomplish it.

The intent could not be misconstrued.

Quickly the demon set about making soothing thoughts, gentle vibrations she hoped would lull the primitive spirit back into calm compliance. After a few moments of attempting it, she realized her ministrations were having little effect. Finally a thought occurred to her.

Do you remember how Talquist had you obscure the trade routes with your blue scale, Faron? Is it possible the Bolg have one, too?

The stone titan stood deathly still, contemplating.

In the fields around them, Hrarfa could feel the army factions growing uneasy.

Peace, she said aloud to the battlefield commanders, keeping her screeching voice as low and palatable to the ear as she could. *I am assessing.*

She thought she could hear relief in their silent response.

She held her silence as Faron's hand reached into the groove in the stone at his waist where his scales were kept. She could barely quell her building excitement as he withdrew his own blue scrying scale and held it up to his unnaturally blue eyes, making a slow circle around him.

For the longest time she perceived nothing. Then she heard the titan's thought.

Green.

I don't understand, Faron—

I can see nothing with the blue scale. But hanging, mostly invisible, in the air of this plain, just above the highgrass, is a mist of green. That I can see with my eyes if I look closely enough.

Hrarfa's excitement exploded. *It may work the same way the blue clouds do, only on Earth, through grass, rather than water, obscuring the mountains the way you obscured the sea for Talquist.*

If such a thing is possible, we will be fighting blind.

Hrarfa silently signaled agreement. *We don't need to see the Bolg armies,* she whispered soothingly. *We can find the Earthchild without using our eyes. We will wait until morning, and then we will follow the song of the Living Stone through the mountains.*

And them? Faron's intention was crystal clear.

He was referring to the Sorbold columns behind them.

A wicked chuckle arose from the depths of the statue, a snide vibration that no one other than Faron could perceive.

We never really needed them anyway, Faron. They are here to serve as a distraction, nothing more.

Everything we need to accomplish our aim we have had all along.

36

Constantin stood outside the soot-stained doors of the enormous cathedral in the rain, thinking.

There was devastation all around Abbat Mythlinis, the elemental basilica of Water. The cathedral had been built during the Illuminaria, the shining age in the first Cymrian era when the great buildings of the empire were being constructed—the five elemental basilicas, the buildings of state in the Orlandan provinces and Sorbold.

And Gwylliam's great masterpiece, the mountainous realm of Canrif at the eastern edge of the empire.

Abbat Mythlinis, like the other basilicas, had been constructed on blessed ground, making it a sanctuary for a storm-tossed people, erected on the site of the landing of the First Fleet from the wreckage of some of the ships that had carried the refugees from Serendair to safety in a new world. It had been fashioned to evoke the shape of an immense vessel, broken and grounded, jutting forth from the sand of the beach north of Avonderre Harbor. The wood of the trees of Earthwood, a forest that yielded a harvest of Living Stone, had been used in the construction both of ships and of Abbat Mythlinis, and even after the passage of Time and the wars that had been waged they had never rotted or crumbled.

Nor had they burned.

Looking around him at the destruction the attack on Avonderre Harbor and the western coastline had delivered, the Patriarch felt sickened to an even deeper level of his soul than he had felt up to this point.

The manse of the priests who served and tended the basilica had been burned to the ground. Constantin could see a number of skeletons in the rubble, some beneath the timbers of the building, meaning they had been inside when the fire erupted. There were also the remains of bodies clogging the roof joists, as if swept there from the sea.

All of Avonderre Harbor was exactly the same, buildings and quays, docks and ships in ruins. There were certainly enough soldiers and invading wastrels occupying what was once the jewel of the shipping lanes to have disposed of the corpses, which were beginning to stink in summer's approach. Apparently the occupation force did not have immediate designs on rebuilding or reusing the harbor of Avonderre or the city around it, which had once been home to more than one hundred thousand adherents of the Patrician faith of Sepulvarta.

Constantin closed his eyes, imagining the ruins of that city as well.

Then he shook off the thought and opened his eyes again.

Looking around him, he saw no soldiers approaching. The rain had begun softly enough but had grown into a full-blown pounding storm, making the normally placid harbor froth, as if with anger.

Constantin seized one of the heavy basilica doors and hurried inside, closing it carefully behind him.

The towering ceilings of the cavernous basilica rose over his head, out of his range of sight. He had conducted services in this place on several occasions, the first time being the rites he offered just after being invested as Patriarch in each of the elemental basilicas.

He had begun in Avonderre, because that was the place where the Cymrian colonization of the continent had begun.

He had completed a circuit with each of the other elemental basilicas, ending, of course, in Lianta'ar, the basilica of the Star, in Sepulvarta, having offered humble prayers in supplication before the All-God that he be a worthy advocate for the people of the continent, adherents to the Patrician faith or not. He had felt a surge of power in reply upon offering his last prayer in Sepulvarta, a beam of light shining down upon him at the altar from the Spire itself, and a sense that each of the five basilicas had been resanctified, cleansing each of them from whatever taint had touched them by the hand of the F'dor demon killed in Ryles Cedelian by the Three.

Making all five of them blessed ground again, something that a demon could not broach.

Until a mortal man did.

Talquist. The Merchant Emperor, whose atrocities dwarfed even some of those of demons.

Constantin's tired eyes now took in the sight of the great fractured timbers that had been the structure of numerous ships, repurposed into a different sort of building. Rhapsody had once said it looked to her like the fragmented skeleton of a giant beast, lying on its back, its spine the long aisle that led up forward, ancient ribs reaching brokenly, helplessly upward into the darkness above.

The round porthole windows that sat in a line high on the walls let in little light; the rain pounded against them, much, Constantin imagined, as it had at sea.

The long line of thick translucent glass blocks inlaid into the walls at knee height was allowing the blue-green radiance of the sea to gleam into the dark church, filling it with an eerie light, the only illumination present. That light, which customarily illuminated the entirety of the basilica to the point of daylight, even at night, had dimmed to the palest of glows, a sign of the diminution of the blessing that normally sanctified the now-vulnerable ground on which the basilica was built.

The Patriarch made his way over the rough surface of the floor to the center of the building.

At the midpoint of the aisle the ceiling opened into a tall shaft, a broad tunnel of blackness with small slits cut into the distant top of it. The wind and salt spray whistled through the slits and down the shaft, their howl echoing within the temple.

Constantin stopped and looked above.

The mast, or what had been formed to look like it, towered above the ceiling in the open wind.

On the floor directly below the mast was a small, round fountain carved of blue-veined marble in the center of circular stone benches made of the same stone, and a series of larger basins opening into ever-wider circles specifically designed to catch the overflow.

A stream of water, pulsing inconsistently, was bubbling in the font, spraying occasionally into the air and then subsiding in time with the rhythm of the waves pounding against the basilica walls outside in the part of the building that was partially submerged in the sea.

This is it, the Patriarch thought as a violent jet sprayed forth, almost to the ring of seats around the fountain. *This is the last of the places of elemental power, the last of the towers that will allow the Chain of Prayer to be reconnected, restored, to the Spire in Sepulvarta.*

He had been to each of the other places that had been built in celebration of the elements and was still accessible—the great brazier lifted high atop a pedestal above the well of Fire in Vrackna, the basilica in Bethany, and the bell tower of the winds that stood in the center of Ryles Cedelian in Bethe Corbair—to offer supplication and chant the invocation that would allow a rung on the invisible ladder by which prayers were channeled, together, to the All-God.

The earthen cathedral, Terreanfor, had been sundered in a great earthquake and was not able to be broached, even if he could reach it within the borders of Sorbold, so instead he had made use of the Bolg king's Lightcatcher to bring the element of earth into the mix. He had begun the effort in that place; now, in this last place, he would end it.

Restoring the connection between All-God and man again.

And resanctifying the ground beneath the Spire in the City of Reason. Sepulvarta.

Braving the wind and rain that was sheering down from the thin openings in the mast above him, Constantin waded into the fountain. He stepped easily into the center, astride the bubbling fountain base, arranging his stance to allow for the occasional blast of sea spray, and looked above.

Then he raised his hand on which the Ring of Wisdom rested, skyward, to the mast.

And began to chant his supplication.

Slowly, as if building the scaffolding that a workman would use to erect a building, the exiled Patriarch reached his chant out into the night air whistling around the mast above him, searching for any uttered prayer that an individual was offering up at that time, aimed at, by name, the local priest of that person's province.

At first he heard nothing in response to his uttered call but the silence of the basilica and the howling of the wind beyond the mast.

Then, like bubbles of air as if from the fountain below him, songs and words, spoken ever so softly, began to whisper in the air around him.

Tears stung the weary eyes of the Patriarch, who had heard no such utterances since the night the holy city had been taken.

He increased the volume of his call, like a shepherd summoning sheep from hillsides around him. The prayers of the faithful grew louder, and higher above the ground, floating in the air around his waist. These were prayers from the priests of all the regions, pastors of villages and clerics in small towns, raised with somewhat more skill to their regional abbots, the men who sat in chancery, offering services at holy days and blessings at funerals and births.

When Constantin could hear the priests' intentions as solidly as a confident choir, he increased his volume again, and raised the pitch of his chant once more.

At this level, gathering the offerings of the abbots was easier to do, as if they had been carefully prepared, like wheat that was lovingly threshed and cleared of all of its chaff. The song of the abbots wrapped warmly around his shoulders, invigorating the Patriarch and reinforcing his strength. For the first time since the night Sepulvarta fell, Constantin felt the underpinnings of joy, and they manifested in a small smile that spread across the dried leather of his wrinkled face.

Finally, with the abbotsong firmly in place, he opened his arms wide and raised the tone once more, his chant resounding off the walls of Abbat Mythlinis, calling for the prayers that the living benisons of the continent and those across the sea in Manosse and in small missions around the world had gathered from their faithful.

That song returned to him wholeheartedly, the singing of a glorious oratorio of millions of combined voices. It was a sound that never failed to bring the fragments of tears in the corners of his eyes to his cheeks, this man who had been raised in youth in the brutal battleground of the gladiatorial arenas of Sorbold, weeping openly as had been his custom each night when he had been serving the All-God at the altar of sacrifice in Lianta'ar.

The song settled around his neck like the stole he had worn in those days, wrapping his throat in protection and making the utterances he was singing one with it.

He was too enthralled, too transported with rapture, too wrapped in the light that had begun to shine brightly through the glass panes in the floor and from the mast above him, to hear the door of the basilica opening.

37

Nince and Jirunt, two members of the second landing party to deploy from Avonderre Harbor into the ruins of the city, were on the loneliest of security details, known comically as Checking on the Dead or Dead Check, which reminded the soldiers of Bed Check.

While the parts of the city of Avonderre farther away from the harbor required serious policing and virulent shows of strength against a populace that was cut off from the rest of the Alliance, whose garrison had fallen back in the rain of fire from the sky in the iacxsis attack, the landing party that was assigned to harbor detail was essentially monitoring a front in which none of the original populace was still alive.

It was considered to be a duty that could be undertaken while one was essentially asleep, and therefore assigned to men whose limited capabilities were not needed somewhere essential.

So it was surprising to Nince and Jirunt to come into what had been the harbor proper, on the street where the harbormaster's office had once stood, to see through the black rain and wind an unmissable beam of light, radiating diffusely in the storm that was raging, pointed skyward.

"What—what do you think is goin' on here?" Nince said, squinting into the gloom.

Jirunt, a man of fewer words, raised his crossbow and gave a curt nod of his head in the direction of the harborfront.

They hurried through the empty streets, giving a cursory glance in each direction, but following the beacon in the foggy air. Finally they arrived at the basilica, which was north on the beachfront outside the harbor limits.

The light was emanating from the spire of the cathedral, up through the mast on the roof.

"Should we get others?" Nince whispered nervously.

Jirunt shook his head. "Take too long," he said curtly. "C'me."

The two soldiers hurried to the double doors, and while Jirunt covered the entry, Nince opened one.

Constantin, arms still spread wide, raised his hands high in the last stage of the Chain of Prayer, offering the combined praise and entreaties into the depth of the living universe, what the people of his faith called the All-God.

The light that was beginning to form around the base of the mast solidified and descended in a gleaming column, encircling the Patriarch.

In one final step of the chant, Constantin raised the pitch and intensity one last time.

From across the continent, where the spires of the other four basilicas dedicated to the three elements that had been born in this world—earth, air, and fire—had been realigned, beams of similar radiance shot through the sky, connecting to the ray that was emanating forth from the mast atop Abbat Mythlinis.

The four rays of light converged over the central southern point of the continent, the enormous Spire that stood on the hilltop across from the basilica dedicated to the element of ether, starlight, the only element to be born before the world itself was born, according to the Creation myth of the faithful.

Too distant to see, the Patriarch could nonetheless feel and hear the song of the Spire as the piece of the star atop it joined in the chorus of praise.

Uniting the five elements from elevations across the Middle Continent.

Light of intense radiance began to pour forth from the Patriarch's eyes.

In the harbor, the sea waves roared.

The flames in the few torches that had been kept lit leapt and crackled.

The packed sand on the harbor beach trembled and split, leaving great fissures in the ground.

The winds picked up, whipping even more furiously than they had been in the course of the rainstorm.

And, for the briefest of moments, the cloud-riven sky cleared, and the stars shone down on the embattled and ash-covered land.

As the ground of each of the basilicas was resanctified, returned to its Blessed state.

From the doorway of the basilica, one of the soldiers fired a crossbow bolt into the column of light at the Patriarch.

It passed through the light and fell to the floor on the other end of the basilica, clinking impotently.

The Sorbold soldiers froze.

In the center of the basilica, a tall robed and hooded figure was standing astride the fountain beneath a cone of light that filled the dark, cavernous cathedral with intense blue radiance. Its robes were blowing about it in a spinning wind that was whipping down from the spire atop the building.

"Wha—what is happening in here?" Nince murmured.

Jirunt raised his crossbow and pointed. "Step out of there and get on the ground," he demanded in the harsh Sorbold tongue.

The figure said nothing, but the light that had been shining from its eyes dimmed gradually until it winked out.

Around them, the light blazing in the long, thick blocks of glass and in through the portholes atop the walls faded as well, leaving only the pale, blue-green glow of the churning sea beyond.

The wind that had been circling in cyclonic ferocity a moment before diminished down to a gentle circling breeze beneath the mast. It flapped the robes of the figure, snapping the material of its cloak around it.

On the ground!" Jirunt screamed.

The figure did not move.

Jirunt fired the crossbow again.

The bolt did not fall to the ground, but seemed to disappear into the figure's robes.

Jirunt drew his sword and strode up the aisle to the fountain at the center of the basilica and the figure standing behind it. Nince drew as well and trotted in step behind him.

"Orlandan scum—" the Sorbold soldier snarled as he charged.

When the connection to the Chain of Prayer was complete, the light diminished and winked out, leaving the Patriarch empty and bereft.

Just in time to absorb a crossbow bolt in the forearm.

The power of all of the prayers on the continent channeled up through the mast and tied to the other elemental basilicas had made him ethereal, formless while he was sending the power of the supplications up the Chain, so when the first bolt soared through him, it passed through and fell, harmless, to the ground.

The second, however, pierced his forearm.

Constantin blinked; otherwise he did not react.

But there was something about the injury, something reminiscent of his days, long ago, in the gladiatorial arenas of Sorbold, that made his blood run differently than it had since his time in the realm of the Rowans, the place where he had learned to let go of his past sins and the life he had known.

The sting of the bolt was minimal; though he had lived the equivalent of six hundred years behind the Veil of Hoen, there was enough Cymrian blood in his veins from his unknown mother to have maintained the muscle tone, the strong constitution that had been both his birthright and the result of his gladiatorial training. In his day, he had been a champion in the arena exactly for those reasons, had been able to press on when injured even to the point of death, so nothing as minuscule as the muscle damage and blood loss from a bolt injury even threw off his balance.

The sky-blue eyes narrowed.

Constantin inhaled.

The air that came into his lungs felt different from what he had been breathing in the throes of religious ecstasy a moment before: the sweet, rich air of spiritual renewal, of unconditional acceptance, not just of him, but of every one of the faithful.

This next breath of air was thinner, and had the smell of the arena in his sinuses, perhaps also in his imagination, but the next breath carried with it the smell of blood and sand, the constant scent and feel of the arena floor.

His eyes beneath his pilgrim's hood sighted keenly on the men charging down the aisle at him, armed with swords, and his muscles tensed, as they had so many times in combat.

He did not move.

The first opponent was slightly ahead and heavier, his age-old battle sense told him. The fire of anger was in the man's eyes and muscles, while the one behind him was a follower, more than a little afraid.

Constantin waited.

Then, when the two Sorbold soldiers were within two body lengths of him, the Patriarch's muscle memory of his years in the arena snapped to life.

With the graceful movement of a discus thrower, the former gladiator bent to the ground and swept up two armfuls of sand and pebbles, detritus from the fountainbed where the spewing stream of ocean water had deposited it over time. Like the sand of the arena floor, it was good material for blinding, and with a long horizontal sweep of his arm he hurled it directly into the faces of the Sorbolds, stunning them and throwing them off balance.

With molten anger rising up inside him from a place of memory he had long buried, Constantin seized the first man's sword arm that was swinging wildly in the air above him and dragged the weapon deeply across his throat, tossing his bleeding corpse to the ground like parchment paper.

The second man, having been behind a few steps, had just enough time to see the arm of the Patriarch, a crossbow bolt embedded in the forearm, cross his throat as he was seized and twisted in one flipping motion like a rag doll. He heard the crunching snap of his own neck as he fell to the floor, broken and paralyzed, choking on his own blood.

The world dimmed quickly in the darkness of the temple into the black of oblivion, leaving only one last thought in his vanishing consciousness—*what just happened?*

Constantin stood, suddenly winded.

The rage that had caused his teeth to clench to the point of soreness drained out of him like water off a slanted roof; it ran across his burning shoulders to his arms and down off of them, rushing off his hands and dissipating into the night air of the cavernous building.

He looked around; save for the broken bodies on the floor at his feet and the sound of the churning of the waves, there was no sound or sight other than heavy darkness.

He took the shaft of the bolt in his arm in his fist and, bracing his foot against the fountain edge, pulled it from his forearm, tearing a vast hole in the muscle. Then he tossed the bolt aside and wrapped the fingers of his hand with the Ring of Wisdom around the gushing wound and willed it to heal, a test of his connection to the All-God.

The ring, its positive and negative markings within a clear stone, gleamed in the darkness of the basilica.

Beneath his fingers, the bleeding wound glowed warm, then cooled again.

Then the ring returned to its normal state.

Constantin examined his forearm; it was whole.

He exhaled deeply, then put the broken bolt in the folds of the jerkin the second man wore and hoisted both bodies over his shoulders, carrying them out into the streets of the basilica.

As he passed through the door with the dead men slung over his shoulders, he turned one last time and looked up at the mast of the basilica of Abbat Mythlinis.

Salt spray and wind were spinning down into the cathedral from the slits in the spire, just as they had been when he had entered.

But now, the ground was warm and solid, and the light of the waves of the sea battering the glass blocks gleamed blue, brightening the floor of the place.

Blessed ground.

He allowed a small smile to cross his lips, then walked steadily through the entry doors with his burden, closed them behind him, and carried the bodies to the wreckage of the manse, where he dumped them unceremoniously in the ash amid the skeletons.

Then he turned and made his way in the direction of Sepulvarta, the City of Reason, through the battering wind of the rainy night.

NAVARNE CITY

Gwydion Navarne drew his camp blanket up closer to his neck, covering his up-ear. He had spent each night since the battle's end after his return from Haguefort encamped with the soldiers of his regiment, billeting in a tent of the same modest manufacture as those his lowest-rank soldiers occupied. He was grateful for the privacy of his solitude, because the moaning and shuddering groans from the wounded that continued, unsated by day's end and uncomforted with night's arrival, left him shuddering in a most unregal manner.

Constantin had departed for Avonderre a sennight before, leaving the young duke in charge of a dying city. Or, more accurately, it was a city of dying men and women, Orlandan and Sorbold, some of Cymrian descent, more not, tended to by the injured and those that had escaped injury of the body, all of whom were moving among their suffering fellow humans, ghostlike and hollow-eyed from lack of sleep.

The images that haunted Gwydion's dreams now were no longer the memories of what he had seen in his family's keep. Rather, they were the recollections of the battle for Navarne, the pitting of Ashe's forces of the Cymrian Alliance against the invading tide of desert dwellers and Icemen from the Hintervold, all grimly intent on taking or holding the citadel on the eastern edge of the Great Forest.

And for all that Gwydion had been struck with a terror that had not consumed him in his first experience with warfare in the farming settlement Anborn had converted into an armored garrison, what had really terrified him was watching the man who had stood in Anborn's stead in Navarne.

The Patriarch of Sepulvarta.

Disturbing as the seventeen-year-old found war in general, the sight of Constantin in battle was so unsettling that he could hardly bring himself to close his eyes at night.

The Patriarch, whom Gwydion had met on a few occasions prior to his "surrender" at the gate of Navarne's encampment, had always been a man of religious bearing, often garbed in the robes of a simple pilgrim, with a sense of peace in his aspect.

So the sight of him, armored in nothing more than a mail shirt and armed with a spear and a sword, fighting in brutal hand-to-hand combat, had shaken the youth to his core.

There was something almost obscene in the beauty of Constantin's battle movements, his thunderous strides as he approached the enemy, sweeping men from their feet with the spear and stepping on their throats as he dispatched them rapidly. Gwydion, alone among both the defenders of the Alliance and the attackers from the north and south, was aware of the Patriarch's past in the gladiatorial arenas of Sorbold, had understood his insistence that he would lead the fighting on the ground while others manned the walls or the ramparts with missile weapons, arms that he had never used.

The sight of the holy man, his teeth bared in hatred, tearing men limb from limb in the blood-splashed streets was something Gwydion feared would never leave his mind.

So when the aide-de-camp arrived to wake him, informing him that the Patriarch had returned to the capital, Gwydion had come forth from his tent shaking and covered with sweat, having been woken from a nightmare in which the Patriarch had been putting everyone in the city to the sword.

He swallowed his terror and followed the soldier to the citadel's central courtyard.

Gwydion was relieved to see the religious leader in the dim light of the campfires and torch stalks; Constantin's face was visible, his hood down, and the serenity that had been the hallmark of his aspect before the war had returned. His eyes, searing blue in the colors of the Cymrian dynasties, sighted on Gwydion, and he walked away from the captain who had been addressing him before the man was even finished with his report.

"Young Navarne," he said, approaching Gwydion, "come with me."

"Yes sir," Gwydion said eagerly. "Where are we going?"

"To wrest Sepulvarta from her kidnappers."

Return from Across the Sea

38

VLANE, MANOSSE

By the time Ashe returned to the harbor in Vlane, the fleet had indeed assembled, every magnificent warship, each merchant and passenger vessel equipped with ballistae and catapults, the great smoking braziers amidships being stoked with the makings of a substance called Rancid Fire, a type of coal that was almost impossible to put out. The sailors and soldiers of Manosse had received the harbormaster's summons and had responded with surprising alacrity; now the wharf, which routinely docked over a thousand ships in a day's time, was crackling with excitement, anger, and energy.

Ashe was amazed.

He followed the harbormaster, who was waiting for him at the pier, to the ship that had been selected for him to captain, a two-masted brigantine sailing under the flag of Manosse, but with a secondary banner in his own colors and with the symbol of the Cymrian Alliance proudly displayed.

On the stern, the name *Valiant* was proudly displayed.

"A good thought," he had said to the harbormaster, who smiled.

"We're keeping a secondary billet here for defense, but everything else is going with you, m'lord," the man said pleasantly, though there were obvious signs of concern in the wrinkles around his eyes.

He piped Ashe aboard and saluted him, then disappeared into the noise of the growing crowd on the docks.

Ashe greeted the first mate, a Manossian man of mixed human and Lirin blood named Stavos, and was quickly briefed on the crew and the headings. Then, while the crew finished loading and running the rope check, he went to the prow of the ship and looked off into the distance, at the eastern edge of the harbor and the open sea beyond.

And, for the briefest of moments, allowed himself to revel in the memory from two years back again, an earlier moment from the same trip he had recalled upon arriving in Manosse that morning.

He thought back to the elaborate surprise he had contrived for Rhapsody upon realizing that, in spite of trekking across the world inside its depths and through its heart, she had still never seen the sea. He had arranged for a visit to Avonderre, her first, and had taken her out to the harbor to the quay, where a beautiful ship was moored, and had offered her a tour of the vessel, which she eagerly accepted.

He closed his eyes again, remembering the joy on her face, her hands over her mouth, as she stood at the prow trying to quell her excitement as she looked west, just as he was now looking east out of the harbor that had been their destination. That joy had exploded into a palpable thrill when he told her they were sailing to Manosse, all packed and ready; her reaction had been so effervescent that he had felt it physically, from the roots of his hair to the heels of his feet.

He had taken her aloft on the mast once they were out on the open sea, the dragon cherishing her excitement as if it were the greatest wonder in the world. After holding her, cradling her against his chest in the crow's nest, pointing out pods of accompanying dolphins and breaching whales, the ocean spilling over the horizon under the welkin of a sky more full of stars than she had ever seen, and the aurora borealis coloring the northern heavens, she had turned and given him a lingering kiss of grateful joy tinged with the salt of tears that he could still taste if he recalled it.

That night, he had held her tenderly again in the beautifully outfitted cabin belowdecks, steadying her in the rocking of the ship, luxuriating in the afterglow of passionate lovemaking that was still sparkling from her exhilaration. With his eyes closed now, he could still hear the words she had whispered to him then when their lips had finally parted.

Sam?

Yes, my love?

Now I can see you even more clearly.

He had smiled at her in the dark of the cabin. *Really?*

Abovedeck, I mean. With the ocean all around you, I can more fully see the power of the element of water in you; your steadiness, your consistency, but also your ever-changing mood; your strength, your depth. I understand you so much more deeply now that I've seen the sea. Thank you for showing it to me.

He had sighed in her arms and rested his lips on her cheek, his forehead against her temple. Wrapping his body and his life around her, for her sole protection, the desire and commitment to keep her safe ringing happily through his heart.

Will you bring me here again? When we are ready to have children, can you bring me here, for at least one of their conceptions? Make love with me as we just did, so that the sea will always be part of him or her?

Anything, he had whispered. *Anything you ever want. Anything.*

The memory faded as he choked on the fear that rose to take its place.

Because she was not safe. For all he knew, she was not even alive.

He grasped the rail, steadying himself against the ire of the wyrm churning within him.

Trying to force back the picture of her he had seen through the Lightcatcher's radiance, staring at him as if she barely knew him.

And didn't love him.

The ire turning to nausea when he thought of their child, possibly in the hands of a thrall of the demon. Or those of the demon itself.

Or the Merchant Emperor, with his terrible intentions.

Nausea turning to the poison of terror.

The wyrm's rage rang out through his throat, sending ripples of waves in the otherwise calm water of the harbor.

It roared across the docks, and throughout the harbor, which, moments before, had been ringing with the excitement of a sea adventure.

Turning the mood of the entire assemblage to one of grim resolve.

As it should be.

"Are we ready, Mr. Stavos?" The tone was not a question, but a threat.

"Aye, m'lord captain," the first mate shouted in reply.

Ashe turned to face the crew, spread across the deck and aloft in the ropes. "Are you ready, men and women, to take to the sea to save your fellows on the Middle Continent?" he shouted, his voice full-throated with the ring of the wyrm.

"Aye! Aye, sir!" The answer rolled back like thunder, not just from the *Valiant*, but from all the ships within earshot. It spread to other ships, farther out, until the reply had echoed through the entire harbor.

"Set sail, then," he commanded. "Let nothing intervene, nothing keep us from taking back our lands and driving the Merchant Emperor's forces from the place our ancestors claimed."

A chorus of excited babble rose in answer along with sails, one by one, climbing masts across Vlane Harbor.

The *Valiant*'s sheets caught the wind and she launched, eager, her sailors shouting joyfully as she broke from the moorings.

Followed, every few seconds thereafter, with ship upon ship, hastening to follow.

Into the coming night, growing thick with clouds of dark rain.

Following a growing wave.

39

IN THE LORITORIUM, DEEP WITHIN YLORC

Generally when sitting watch, Grunthor made it a practice not to imbibe potent spirits.

But this watch had lasted so long, and threatened to be so malignant when it finally came to a head, that he had made an exception in this case.

Many exceptions, actually.

He was cracking open a cask of one just such exception now.

"Ya know, Rath, yer only the third Dhracian Oi've ever known. And Oi can't say there's much in common between you and the Grandmother 'oo used to be the Child's guardian, compared to 'Is Majesty, at least from my perspective."

The Dhracian's smile was wry.

"'Tis true. Your king is unlike any our race has ever known. The fact that he would see himself in the role of king is evidence of his unique stature."

Grunthor took a sip from his tankard and nodded.

"Not a race o' kings, are Dhracians, then?"

Rath stared up into the dark vault, as if lost in memory.

"Not in the least. The Brethren, the *Zhereditck*, are of one mind, like a hive of bees or a kingdom of ants—we can feel each other's thoughts on the wind; we have no leaders. All are of equal worth. Your king is not the only Dhracian among the *Dhisrik*, the Uncounted, those who choose to remain outside the Collective Mind, but he is the most significant of the outliers. More than that, I cannot say, except that he is very important to our people."

The Sergeant nodded thoughtfully.

"'E's fairly important to the Bolg as well. They was a bastard race before we came 'ere, put upon by ev'ry conquerin' culture what subdued 'em. The king was the first to make 'em see themselves as worthy o' bein' alive, bein' 'ere. *Firbolg* may mean something fancy in your ancient languages—"

"'Wind of the Earth,'" said Rath softly.

"Yeah, the Grandmother said. But to us, the word *Bolg* means *'ard, unyieldin',*" the Sergeant continued, taking another slug from the tankard. "These folks, related distantly to my father's people, live by their wits, and rule 'allways or tunnels or clans, if they're lucky, for as long as somebody bigger don't come 'long and push 'em out. But to rule a nation—to bring this 'ole civilization to 'eel—'e didn't get that from his father's side o' the family, if ya take my meaning."

"So your father was Bolg, like his?"

"Yeah."

The Dhracian exhaled. "The rape and captivity of the king's mother, and his birth that killed her, was one of the most horrifying events the Brethren ever lived through. She had been trapped, alone, when a colony of Dhracians known as the Gaol on Serendair was overrun by the Bolg, and abused by every one of the men in that brutish clan."

Grunthor winced. He recalled Rhapsody, devoid of the gentleness that had been such an endearing part of her now that she had given her name away to Meridion, blandly describing the same horror being visited upon her.

And the Bolg king's reaction to hearing it.

Summon the Archons.

Now, or in the mornin'?

Now. I want to be ready to leave at daybreak, right after Rhapsody departs for Bethany. I need them activated and in place before I go.

An' where is it you will be goin', sir?

After Talquist. As soon as she's gone.

Rath had just provided him with another explanation of his friend and sovereign's extreme action. Grunthor would have wagered a considerable sum that Achmed would not have left the mountains for any reason short of an invasion of Ylorc.

Now, upon hearing the explanation of what had happened to the Bolg king's own mother, he would have withdrawn that bet.

The Dhracian did not seem to notice his contemplation.

"Because our minds are inextricably linked, we felt and bore witness to everything that happened to her, until her terrible death in childbirth. It was a nightmare that lasted for almost two years, a short time in our life span as a race, but exceedingly painful, as you can imagine, given the sensitive network of nerves and veins we share by physiology and the mindlink we have."

Grunthor shook his head. "That musta been rough."

"We have been seeking him ever since that day; we did not know what happened to him after she died, because he is Uncounted, not part of the Collective Mind. In his youth, he registered on our senses briefly when he was taken in by another of the Uncounted, so we caught fragments of his trail again. Finding him was as much a primordial mission as the tracking of the F'dor." Rath finally looked away from the ceiling of the vault above, focusing what the Sergeant guessed was a sympathetic look at him. "I am sorry to know your mother met such a fate as well."

The Sergeant-Major laughed aloud.

"Well, thank you, but ya couldn't be more wrong about that."

Rath blinked his liquid black eyes that had no scleras.

"My mum was a Bengard fighter in the gladiatorial arena, an undefeated champion o' bloodsport, sonny," Grunthor went on, still chuckling. "She was almost as tall as me, and almost as wide, I reckon. Champion of the pickax, and the four-prong fork, and the 'eadbasher.

"She took my dad as tribute in a surrender agreement with the Bloody 'And clan, one o' the most fearsome gangs in Grangnorn, in the southeast caves of the 'Igh Reaches o' Serendair. And while she only intended to knob the *hrekin* out o' 'im and, most likely, eat 'is eyes and brain, as was Bengard custom, apparently 'e was cute, or good in the sack, or somethin', because she kept 'im on and they raised me together. 'Ad a right proper upbringin' and family life, a lovely child'ood, Oi did. So save yer sympathy."

An uncharacteristic smile took up residence on the Dhracian's face.

"I'm glad to hear that," he said. "Children are the greatest asset of any ancient race, like mine. Born or conjured, they are equally precious to the Brethren. It is not sentimental; it is key to the survival of our traditions and our mission, which is deeply entwined with that of the world."

Grunthor drained the rest of his libation and wiped his mouth with his forearm. "Conjured?" he said after a proper belch.

The Dhracian nodded slightly.

"When your race's life span is seemingly endless, after a time producing new children becomes difficult, because even marginally immortal bodies become aged—something you may have to contend with one day, given you come from Serendair and those who made that voyage across the world seem to have cheated Time somewhat.

"One of the most ancient of all lores is the conjuring of a child, the magical joining of the pieces of two willing souls into a unique being, a lore ritual I plan to pass along to the Lady Cymrian for safekeeping, assuming we both survive what is coming. It is the very process that produced the Earthchild."

He glanced over his shoulder at the Sleeping Child, then stood abruptly, as did Grunthor.

She was shaking like an autumn leaf in a high wind.

Grunthor was on his feet, his pick hammer in hand. He looked around, scanning the tunnel and the Loritorium around them.

"'E must be comin'."

40

AT THE EASTERN EDGE OF THE
KREVENSFIELD PLAIN, ON THE STEPPES

It is said that when an army relies on its skill, its intelligence, and its bravery, what it does not need to rely on is the senses.

The titan was addressing the divisions of the Sorbold army he had brought all the way across the continent for the purpose of assaulting the Firbolg mountains, an undertaking that literally no one in the ranks was looking forward to.

A few years prior, before Achmed the Snake had taken the mountains, turning the land of brainless cannibalistic beasts into a powerful producer of goods for sale and an even more powerful military threat, a raiding party into the former Canrif would have been an interesting expedition, good training grounds for young soldiers, the way it had been before the Bolg king had arrived.

But now, given the brutality and precision with which those demi-human monsters had repelled a raiding party of two thousand men of Roland, as well as conquered animated corpses called back from the dead by the dragon Anwyn, no man in his right mind would ever seek to venture to that place, rife with tribalistic magic and monstrous might.

Yet here they were, supposedly at the doorstep of the Teeth, apparently about to sacrifice themselves in what could be the worst possible manner of death in war.

Under the command of an animated stone statue with disturbingly blue eyes.

Who seemed to be telling them they were going in blind.

A moment later, the titan confirmed their fears by giving a few more orders and then turning and stepping back into his eight-horse chariot.

And driving off into a seemingly endless green field.

Grunthor had left Rath to guard the Earthchild long enough to get to the speaking tube that allowed him contact with his military commanders and the Archons, who were assembled in the two war rooms, one deep in the bowels of and the other atop Grivven Peak, the highest tower in Ylorc.

"Report—whaddaya see?" the Sergeant demanded. "Grar?"

"Browns look lost, sir," the lieutenant replied, referring to the color of Sorbold eyes, skin, and hair. "Going sideways."

"That's odd. How many, Kubila?"

"From ground, a hand and half of finger, sir."

"Same from Tower, sir," said Grar.

Grunthor whistled, causing the two Firbolg aides beside him to flinch. "Seventy thousan'? No kiddin.' Well, it looks like ol' Talquist isn' playin' with all 'is cards. And like our weapon're workin'. All right, then. Commanders, step to! 'Ave a little fun, and remember, they prolly can't see ya 'til yer on 'em. Loot, but don' eat. We're big boys now."

A decided sound of disappointment whistled back down the speaking tube, causing the Sergeant-Major to chuckle with delight.

C*an you feel the song of the Living Stone?* the F'dor spirit whispered excitedly in the darkness of the moving statue. *Is it calling to you?*

Not yet. The answer came surprisingly quickly.

Keep going, Hrarfa urged. *You will hear it when we draw close enough.*

The enormous statue came to a blistering stop in its tracks, causing an aftermath of cavalrymen dragging horses to heel, wagons and foot soldiers frantically trying to avoid one another as seventy thousand soldiers were pulled up short in an endless field of green.

Faron's thoughts still contained very few actual words, very little verbiage, only thoughts and emotions, but the message in his response was remarkably clear.

And blistering.

How would you know? the internal voice demanded furiously. *You are a formless spirit, utterly without substance. A child of Fire; what would you know about being buried in a body of Earth?*

Hrarfa, usually the source of communication within the titan, said nothing in reply.

Stop talking to me, Faron said. *Leave me alone; I need to concentrate. There is old magic everywhere here, magic that speaks to the scales and speaks to me. And it is trying to lead me away from this place.*

The titan spun around and screamed at the army behind it.

Now, forward! Leave none alive.

Then continued across the hazy green field toward the east, following the sun's rising.

Until an army of well-provisioned Bolg appeared as if out of the very air, seeded entirely within the very ranks of the Sorbold fighting forces.

The titan heard the screams of shock from men and horses, the crashing of blunt weapons against wood and steel, could almost see the ghoulish faces with the element of surprise tearing into the army it had conscripted and brought with it to a valley of unseen death.

And whipped its chariot horses into a frenzy, reining them forward until it could actually feel the mountains rise up out of the misty green grass before them.

Following the lead of the blue scale.

Leaving the army to fend for itself.

As the titan made its way, first by the direction of the sun and then, when the mountains eventually loomed before it, following the lead of the blue scale, it began to feel a sense of ventilation.

Or, more correctly, a sense that ventilation might be the key to entering Ylorc.

The mountainous fortification was, to be certain, all but unassailable. The massive statue had battered its way almost with impunity through the fluid battle lines of the Firbolg army as it systematically destroyed the troops of the fifth, eighth, and twelfth divisions, which kept the Bolg busy, at least.

One difficulty that the two demonic spirits residing with the titan had not anticipated, however, was the foresight the Bolg had used in preparing for its arrival.

Any weapons that were turned on the statue were not the sharp bladed ones it had been anticipating, but rather sling pellets and rocks hurled as projectiles from catapults, hammers, and pickaxes. Having been accustomed to being able to repel any attack by any weapon, it was caught up short, not only because of the splitting and shattering of small areas of its body, but also because the knowledge that the Bolg had been awaiting its arrival was more than a little unsettling to both Faron and Hrarfa.

But the sheer mass of will that had fermented in the course of their journey to Canrif made any minor wound to the ten-foot Living Stone body encasing their spirits of small consequence.

The battle of wills that had begun not long after the primitive consciousness that was Faron had agreed to host the long-lived, calculating F'dor demon that was Hrarfa had cooled to a silent détente.

The burning desire to be rid of his guest and able to be reunited with his father was all that was driving Faron now; deep within his prison of Living Stone, he had shut off the shrieking voice that was gleeful now, concentrating instead on the memory of being lovingly fed eels and blackfish in a pool of gleaming green water, of being useful as his father's scryer and tended to kindly most of the time.

Even the fits of rage that his parent had had with his own demonic parasite that had occasionally led to outlash and cruelty did not cloud the strong sense of love and loss in the one time Faron had ever known it.

The ability to understand those emotions was something he clearly must have obtained through birth from his Seren mother, as it never could have originated with something as twisted and vicious as the race of his father.

Hrarfa, on the other hand, was singing a silent, orgiastic song. The nearness of the Earthchild, and her invulnerability within the body of Living Stone, had not only been felt by her but by every other one of the Unspoken, the F'dor spirits still living upworld, still chanting dark curses and fomenting the building rise of chaos and death.

She had come to realize that her particular sexual proclivities during the time she had been climbing her way through a ladder of human hosts had really been nothing more than the bodily representation of the utter abandon, the fierce and ferocious joy in the coming destruction that all F'dor sought and craved.

Even consciously knowing that, in the end, their successful achievement of it would exterminate their race as well.

So the slings and thrown hammers made little or no impact on the titan as it blasted through the breastworks at the foot of Grivven Peak, tore through the battle wagons, and snapped the backs of horses and Bolg alike.

Charging onward toward the systems of air intake and the venting of forge-fire smoke that were the infrastructure of a civilization carved from an unforgiving mountain range. Places that were too high for a humanoid to climb, too deep for one to survive a fall from, too hot to keep flesh from melting.

But to which a stone statue was impervious.

After more than a night's span of hours, Faron found it.

A winding tunnel in the back of the mountain: an air return, from the look of it.

Faron had made the climb without much effort; his body of Living Stone felt traces of life in the stone in places of earth that had not seen the light, leaving it still fresh, still humming with at least a little animation. The element of earth welcomed him, so it had not taken much effort to follow a twisting and confusing series of tunnels down to a mysterious central corridor, a circular meeting room with the image of a dark hand pressed into the wall.

Hrarfa was overjoyed at the freshness of the stone, still humming with a little of the fire left over from the world's creation.

The statue put its hand, far and away bigger than the image of the hand, on the image and pressed.

Where is the Earthchild? the titan asked.

The image of the hand began to glow, like coals of a fire that had been refreshed with a touch of breath blown across them.

And finally almost reluctantly illuminated the fourth finger.

One that represented a tunnel pointing toward the south.

Overjoyed, both demonic presences inside the Living Stone body hurried forthwith down the corridor.

41

Almost running smack into Grunthor.

The Bolg Sergeant-Major, newly minted pick hammer in hand, was leaning casually on his elbow against the tunnel wall.

The titan came to an abrupt halt before the soldier, uncertain what to do next.

Grunthor threw back his head and laughed.

"'Ow disappointin'. Now, 'ere Oi've been told you was really tall an' brawny, but actually yer nothin' special. Crushed by the truth, Oi am."

The titan snickered in return.

Oh, you will indeed be crushed, but not by the truth.

"Well, that certainly remains to be seen. But before we set to blows, Oi thought you deserved to 'ear one of yer favorite songs to 'elp make the occasion of our long-awaited meetin' special. Thought it might be yer birthday or somethin'."

The titan's eyes narrowed. Without another word it started to stride down the stone hallway, a look of murder unmistakable even on features that did not move.

Only to be dragged to an inadvertent halt by a high-pitched humming note.

A note that expanded, a moment later, into a four-note pattern, like a net of invisible vibrating threads woven from the four winds.

Because they, in fact, were.

Faron almost fell forward in the stone hallway tunnel.

Like a knife to the brain, the sound set the frame of the stone statue abuzz with a shrill vibration that instantly took the power out of its stride.

It tried to step but found itself frozen in place.

The sudden lack of control over the body of Living Stone made the Faorina spirit panic, but not with the hysteria that had suddenly seized the F'dor.

An explosion of foul cursing and ancient oaths of violence and anger ripped through the statue, stinging Faron's spirit with its invectives.

Hrarfa, unlike Faron, had heard this song before.

And knew what the lyrics meant.

The Thrall ritual! she screamed virulently, heedless of Faron's warning regarding what would happen if she ever did again. *How can that be? The—Dhracian—the Bolg king—he is with Talquist! I saw him in the scale, the second assassin—that's why we left when we did—*

From the depths of the stone statue, a nonverbal attack of caustic thought silenced her.

The titan's two demonic sides struggled with as much strength as either of them could summon to break the bonds of the net of vibration and the wind of the Earth that were wrapping around their essences, but the Dhracian who was chanting the ritual older than Time was one of the original Brethren, the *Zhereditck,* and had been searching for Hrarfa ceaselessly for millennia with a blood rage unsurpassed by any destructive impulse the F'dor could summon.

Rath, who had combed the pockets of air across the wide world since the fall of the Sleeping Child had torn the Vault open.

Looking for this demon and all her like.

By sheer will, he was relentlessly crushing their life forces.

Grunthor broke into a wide grin. He picked up his enormous pick hammer and stepped closer.

"Cast 'er off, sonny," he said softly to the Faorina spirit inside the stone titan. "Yer not like 'er; Oi know all about you. You took 'er on outta pity, but is she worth dyin' for? 'Cause that's what's about to 'appen. Not an easy death, a return to the earth, but an eternal one in a Vaultful of screamin' bitches like the one inside ya. You decide."

The statue remained rigid. Only the disturbing blue eyes darted furiously in the stone head, growing more distended and shot with cracks by the moment.

The expression on the giant Sergeant-Major's grinning face was resolving rapidly into a ferocious mien, his amber eyes taking on the glow of righteous rage.

He brought the pick hammer forward and tapped its perfectly balanced handle menacingly into his palm.

"You pathetic bitch," he said softly to Hrarfa, venom dripping from his words. "All this time you've been suckin' the tarse of weak men, whorin' yer way across the world, across Time. The body you occupy once belonged to a real soldier, somebody 'oo lived and fought and died and was buried with honor. You got no right to be in there, darlin'. Time ta go."

An unpronounceable curse blended with a scream of rage that shook the tunnel walls echoed forth from the titan.

Rath's hand, which had been winding in the air as if wrapping each of the four winds around his palm, rose up before him. He emerged from the shadows, a glittering in his scleraless black eyes, glaring at the titan with a look so hateful that it drew blood to the surface of his own skin.

"Last chance, my friend," Grunthor said to Faron.

*G*et out.

The thought, whispered in actual words inside the titan's body, thudded against the inside of the prison of Living Stone that Faron had been occupying since Talquist had placed him on the Weighing plate of the Scales.

A burning rage as filled with hate as the F'dor's screams was rolled up in Faron's consciousness. He let the formless essence of his mind wrap around the alien vibration that had been sharing his host body all this time and, not knowing what else to do, squeezed it violently with his own mind.

Hrarfa's screams of rage became even more scathing, even more dire.

Faron, no! What are you doing—

Get out!

You can't live without me, Faron, Hrarfa's thoughts said in a tone that was equal parts wheedling and dark loathing. *He will kill you in a moment, and then where will you be? Do you think our kin in the Vault will forgive your treachery?*

I think they will celebrate it. The titan's thoughts dripped with disdain and ferocious hate. *I may be sired by one of your kind, but I choose not to be your kin. Get out!*

Your father was—

My father was the host of a F'dor, just as I have been. Neither of us have enjoyed the experience. Get out!

The third command finally shattered the existential link that Hrarfa had formed with the body of Living Stone back in the forest of Haguefort when she had begged for shelter, and had gotten it, from Faron.

The air in the underground tunnel filled with acrid smoke so caustic that both men's eyelids shriveled.

A howling cry echoed throughout the tunnels of the Hand. The sound was so horrific that, even miles below, the Earthchild heard it and trembled violently.

The formless spirit of Hrarfa, ejected from her host, was trapped in the subterranean tunnels, fading into oblivion.

That notwithstanding, her desperate will to live was still strong.

She weighed her choices.

She could try to run, try to find something in the immediate vicinity, a thought that she immediately discarded.

Any Bolg weak enough for her to subsume, especially in her compromised state, was outside, tearing apart the fifth, eighth, and twelfth regiments at that moment.

Most likely.

The Dhracian who stood behind the Firbolg soldier before her was not an option, of course. Even if she had the presence of mind and strength of purpose to undertake an attempt to forcibly take him as a host, the sheer diametrical opposition would rend her spirit like a wolf with a bird in its teeth and toss its scraps to the four winds over which he had control.

Mastering the will of a Dhracian, especially a member of the *Zhereditck,* was something that could not even be contemplated.

But the Firbolg commander who stood before her dissipating spirit now might have some weakness, some way inside him much like the ventilation tunnels that had allowed the titan to broach Ylorc.

In her fading consciousness she sought to assess him and was immediately overwhelmed with the vibrational signature that slapped her in return.

The grinning fool was in possession of a physicality that radiated life, health, strength, and muscularity. Despite the taste of the old world that hung in the air around him, there was a conflicting impression of youth and a surprising lack of scarring or injury to him. His skin, green-gray like the color of healing bruises, was supple, his teeth were amazingly without pits, his tusks polished and bright, and his hair was mossy and thick like that of a man of two decades, not the more likely age counted in at least two millennia.

It would be a challenge in which she was unlikely to be victorious. She had no other choice.

$\mathcal{A}$ split second after the burning cloud of poisonous smoke had sublimated into the air of the underground tunnel, it shot forth as if on a stiff breeze and wrapped itself around Grunthor.

Rath, witnessing the attack, let go of the vocal chant.

"Hold your breath!" he shouted.

Feeling the Thrall ritual shatter as he did.

Grunthor looked around and above him.

He was wrapped in a caustic fog, falling on him like heavy rain.

His pick hammer trembled in his grip.

Before his eyes an image formed. It was a hollow face, much like a flattened skull with eye sockets and a toothless mouth, a vertical oval hole where a nose would have been. And as the mist wrapped around him, the vaporous face seemed to open its mouth and soar straight toward his eyes.

Grunthor was having none of it.

"BUGGER OFF!" he roared.

Then he swung back and delivered a shattering roundhouse blow, leading with his claws, cutting through the stinking cloud of vapor like an ax blade through a sapling tree.

Tearing the face to formless shreds.

Dissipating the mist.

And summarily ending the existence of one of the most relentless and powerful F'dor spirits to walk the Earth since the opening of the Vault.

And, regrettably and inadvertently, releasing the body of Living Stone, still occupied by the Faorina spirit Faron, from the Thrall ritual.

And any hold that Rath had held over it.

42

$\mathcal{D}$odge. Now."

The distinct voice of the Dhracian cut through the tunnel commandingly.

Grunthor, long used to following commands without even a second's hesitation, stepped aside as the titan lumbered past, its arms outstretched for Grunthor's throat.

And, with a mighty swing, struck the titan's extended right arm with his newly crafted pick hammer.

Shattering it utterly and smashing it off.

It fell to the earthen tunnel floor and broke into five pieces and an impressive quantity of dust.

The Sergeant-Major stepped back, panting, waiting for the titan to attack.

But instead it stood in the center of the tunnel, its gleaming blue eyes staring wildly at the stump below its shoulder.

The place that had connected to the missing arm was open to the dank air of the tunnel and to the sight of the Bolg and the Dhracian.

At the place where the lower arm had been attached, instead of the healthy glow of Living Stone was a wet, claylike substance that smelled of the healthy green of forests and caves, rich brown with striations of vermillion and purple, blue and gold.

But the broken area was dry and brittle inside, the only part of it still living was the very core of the limb, a red-brown center around which was nothing but dry, dead clay.

Grunthor waited for a return charge.

But instead, the titan continued to stare at its upper arm in what seemed like shock.

Then it looked up at the Sergeant-Major in what most closely resembled the emotion of terror.

And, without a backward glance, it dashed back up the corridor through which it had entered the Bolglands faster than any living man of flesh could run, and lumbered out into the night.

Running south through the remains of the battle of the steppes where the army it had led lay bleeding and dying, a few of them crying out to the sky for water or their mothers.

Grunthor and Rath stared at each other in astonishment.

After a long moment, the Sergeant-Major turned to his fellow guardian of the Earthchild and shrugged.

"Can we follow 'im on the wind? Never really understood 'ow ya do that."

"It works more favorably when you are either willing to appear randomly to wherever the wind is willing to take you, or if you are going to a static place rather than following a moving target. But I see no other choice than to try."

"Damnation," Grunthor grumbled. "Oi expected 'im to fight me, to put 'is all into finding the Earthchild. Can't believe after all the bloody F'dor initiatives to get to 'er, the bloody coward turns granite tail and runs! Oi was so very ready—"

"What you fail to understand is that once the F'dor spirit you were taunting died, it left the titan with nothing but the Faorina inside it," Rath said. "It may or may not be a threat to the Earthchild any longer, but the damage it may leave in its wake is immeasurable."

"Could be, and that would certainly be a shame," Grunthor grumbled. "But fer my money, if it's not lookin' for the Child, that's better than any other thing that could come out of this. That titan made its way, alone, for goodness' sake, into and through the tunnels of Ylorc. This could 'ave ended way diffr'int. Any day you don't 'ave to fight a demon is a good one. One o' my favorite sayin's. Shall we go?"

"I will do my best," said the Dhracian. "After all, I *am* a hunter dedicated to the extinction of that species. And, for once, we are in luck."

"'Ow's that?"

The Dhracian smiled. "I have his trail."

Grunthor's brow furrowed, then relaxed.

Then a massive smile spread across his wide face, revealing gleaming tusks.

He threw his head back and laughed aloud.

"So, what's keepin' us, then?" he asked.

"I want to check the weather patterns across the Krevensfield Plain one more time," said Rath. "When one is riding the wind, as my race and kinsmen can, and you arrive where you meant to, it is an even better day than the one you mentioned. Let us go."

Rath made his way down the same tunnel the titan had fled through, Grunthor grumbling quietly behind him all the way.

43

LIANTA'AR, THE CITADEL OF
THE STAR, SEPULVARTA

The victories in Yarim, Navarne, and Bethany were substantial enough to convince Anborn that the skeletal armies housed in those cities were sufficient to maintain the Threshold of Death, allowing the bulk of the Alliance troops to move southward to recapture the holy citadel of Sepulvarta.

By the time Constantin and Gwydion Navarne arrived in the late afternoon, Rhapsody was already there, with Knapp, who was pleased to be reunited with Solarrs and Anborn.

"Glad your defenses were successful," the Lord Marshal said within the canvas walls of the officers' tent outside the fringes of the city. "These next few days are critical—the scouts have relayed information that the largest and most bloodthirsty units of the Sorbold army are advancing from the south, or have been recalled from the western front. At least we know where we're likely to make our last stand."

He saw Rhapsody exhale silently and smiled, though worry was also present in his expression.

"You are right to assume that this will take some pressure off of Tyrian, m'lady, but the fight here may prove to be far fiercer than it would normally have been."

The Lady Cymrian shrugged.

"I am armed with an elemental sword, as is Gwydion, in the presence of three ancient Cymrian soldiers, and the tongue of Mylinmacr, surrounded by the elite forces of the Cymrian army. If I can't be useful here, I am of no use anywhere."

"Having served with you in Bethany, m'lady, I can attest to the untruth in that," said Knapp pleasantly.

The hollow queen did not smile, saying nothing.

"Very well," said the Lord Marshal, "let's have at it. The soldiers have been itching to free the holy city, as I'm sure you are, Your Grace."

The wordless snort from the Patriarch set the leaders to laughing at the understatement before they headed out of the tent and back to the Threshold again.

The army of the Alliance had set up positions inside the walled city in preparation for laying siege to Lianta'ar, the only remaining occupied stronghold, when Rhapsody straightened up sharply, glancing around at the foothills in the distance to the south, and the Teeth beyond them.

Gwydion and Anborn, who had been conferring, both looked in her direction.

"What—what is that sound, Anborn?" she asked.

The Lord Marshal inclined his ear, then shook his head.

"I hear nothing, m'lady," he said.

She listened again, then shook her head as well.

Only to see, behind where her loved ones were standing, an astonishing sight.

The air of the city outside Lianta'ar was spinning vertically, almost like a waterspout. There was an aura of power, ancient and elemental.

The wind picked up suddenly, spinning in much the same way as the cyclonic vortex seemed to be doing. It rattled the flags on the crumbling ramparts, shaking and rattling the stained-glass windows of the basilica.

"Look," she said to the Lord Marshal again.

He turned behind him.

Just as he did, the sound she had heard vibrated through the spinning vortex again. As it did, she heard a voice she thought sounded familiar, but that she did not recognize.

By the Star, Oi shall call—Oi—shall wait, Oi shall watch, and shall be 'eard.

The Lady Cymrian's blood ran cold, and her face turned pale in the setting Sorbold sun.

"No," she whispered. "Is that—is that the Kinsman call?"

Anborn's brows drew together, and he looked over his shoulder, his black hair streaked with silver catching the wind as he did.

"I didn't hear it."

"I must be imagining things, then," Rhapsody said, dabbing her sweating forehead with her sleeve. "It spoke in the same manner that Grunthor does, but not in his voice—or certainly not as *I* have ever heard his voice."

The Lord Marshal's eyes narrowed immediately.

"You heard the call? Where? From where was it coming?"

Rhapsody pointed behind him. "From that pattern of swirling wind in the almost dry fountainbed in the courtyard."

Anborn's face went slack with shock.

"Go! Go!" he shouted, grabbing her arm and drawing her away from their astonished companions. "Get out of here! You must never delay when you hear the wind call!"

Rhapsody turned and fled toward the swirling pathway in the wind that apparently only she could see.

She never turned back, but had she done so, she would have witnessed astonishment on the faces of the Patriarch and her godson.

And something much darker, much more fearful, on that of the Lord Marshal.

44

The Teeth
(Manteids)

Night Mountain
Earth Basilica

Desert

THE CANYON BELOW JIERNA TAL, SORBOLD

The closer he came to the wall of the chasm, the more slowly Achmed moved.

The cloaks of stone-colored leather had served well, it seemed, to keep him from sight as he made his way by late afternoon into night crossing the canyon floor. No one and nothing had taken notice of him save for the occasional bird or jurillas, small rodents similar to prairie dogs that prowled the canyon floor by day, searching for vegetation, specifically cacti.

On more than one occasion Achmed had been come upon by the large-eyed animals, startled to discover him beneath his leather sanctuary, sending them screeching in their unnatural voices as they darted away again, leaving his sensitive skin stinging from the vibrations.

His body, normally thin and wraithlike, had dried out considerably in the heat and the dust. He rationed his precious water and food supplies carefully, so his daytime slumber and nighttime movement were timed to make the best use of his resources.

The journey felt like it was taking forever.

Especially once he came within sight of the tower, within eyeshot of the Seer's withered body. Achmed had decided upon taking the time to cover her with scrub, rather than risking her shredding at the beaks of carrion or loathsome creatures like jackals or coyotes, but after he had undertaken to gather the scrub and bury her in it, it occurred to him that there was almost nothing left that resembled meat on her desiccated bones to lure that sort of predator, anyway.

At long last he found himself at the seam of the canyon, where the vertical wall met the floor. The agonizing climb, undertaken only during the evening and night hours, and requiring him to find a large enough shelf on the vertical wall to sleep on when the sun came up, racked up even more days in his journey.

Finally, toward dusk, he had risen to the lip of the canyon, atop which the smooth tower of Sorbold marble rose skyward, an arrogance evident in the very stone of it.

Achmed stretched out beneath his cloaks and allowed sleep to wash lightly over him.

He awoke in the near-dark, a few hours later. The light had left the sky, and on the other side of the palace the moon had risen, waxing. Between the moon and the palace lampposts on the other side of the tower, a faint wash of bland radiance hung in the air, impotent.

Quickly he rifled through his pack, discarding anything that was not utterly necessary to shed weight. His body had done so in the course of his journey as well, as he had intended.

He did not expect to need as much heft to accomplish what he had to do as he needed lankiness and the ability to hide that came with it.

Finally, with no weapons but his cwellan slung over his back and the small pick hammer Grunthor had made as a model for the new outfitting of the Bolglands, he fished out the last objects in his pack, the two folded cloth lanterns that Rhapsody had given him in the forest of Tyrian.

He opened them slowly, careful not to damage the coated canvas fabric, and stretched them out to their odd honeycomb shape. Inside was a small frame fashioned of thin wires; Achmed assembled it quickly, then attached the solid wax fuel that had been formed into a square. It fit perfectly into the center of each wire frame, coated with a slightly oily veneer.

Achmed wiped his fingers off on the rocks around him.

He quickly attached the lanterns to his belt with his last lengths of the white tensile braided rope he had brought with him from the Bolglands. One of their best-selling products in the international trade stream, the Bolg had developed the material from tunnelfuls of spiderwebs that had been discovered in the deepest parts of Ylorc when he, Grunthor, Rhapsody, and the orphan girl named Jo had first come to the mountain.

It had become a favorite of sailors and shipbuilders for its impressive strength in combination with its lightness; its weight was a mere fraction of that of the heavy ropes that those who plied the seas were forced to contend with regularly.

Its shiny softness also made it a popular material in the beautiful and scandalous undergarments Rhapsody had designed out of the same material, products whose sales rivaled those of the rope.

Achmed chuckled silently at the thought.

He tucked his head down, still under the cape, and allowed himself to ruminate on his friends. Jo, of course, had been dead for more than four years, the victim of one of the minions of the F'dor he and the other two of the Three had slain beneath the bell tower in Ryles Cedelian, the basilica of Air in Bethe Corbair. It was the first time he had thought of her in years.

But Rhapsody and Grunthor were never far from his thoughts. He raised the cloak slightly and felt the air for their heartbeats; he could feel them pounding in the distance, as if they were traveling rapidly; though they were nowhere near each other, they seemed to be converging.

Good, he thought. *At least, wherever they are, whatever they are facing, they will be together.*

He swept the thought from his mind and concentrated now on the tool he had devised to help him ascend the tower.

He took the last piece of flint he had saved and struck it against the rock ledge until it sparked a flame, then held it quickly to the edges of the wax fuel squares.

The edges of the squares caught fire quickly and began to burn to the center. As they burned, the heat from the cell filled the open fabric lantern and began to cause it to expand a moment later.

And ascend slightly into the air.

Had he been a man who gave any thought whatsoever to his appearance, Achmed might have been uncomfortable at the sight of himself, attached to floating festival toys, crawling over the rock ledge at the base of the tower and making his way hurriedly to the stone obelisk. The Assassin King was incapable on a conscious, subconscious, and unconscious level of worrying about what anyone thought of him, however, so he took the pick hammer out and, with as much of a running start as he was able to make, held on to the cloak with his other hand and ran for the tower.

And, upon approaching it, leapt for it.

The lift of the lanterns surprised him; Achmed himself was capable of achieving a decent height in climbing on the initial approach, but with the assistance of the hot air and the cloth, he was tugged up one and a half times higher than he could have reached on his own.

The success caught him a bit off guard, so he dug the pick hammer into the mortar between a row of stones in the tower and clung there a moment, catching his breath.

The lanterns tugged insistently at his sides.

Achmed dug his fingers into a handhold, then pulled the pick hammer out of the mortar.

And tentatively let go.

The lanterns lifted him skyward slightly. The Bolg king kicked with his feet and achieved a good deal more altitude, wobbling only slightly under the hooded cloak. He grasped the tower wall again, affixing himself with the pick hammer.

Then, slowly, hand over hand and with the aid of the lift provided by the lanterns, he made his way up the exterior of the tower toward the open aperture he could see from below.

Hoping that no one would see him—or, more correctly, see the ridiculous floating lanterns that were lifting him up the side of one of the tallest structures in the Known World.

As he suspected, his ascent only caught the attention of nightbirds and spiders, none of whom made comment about it.

*I*t was past midnight when he finally reached the tower window, Achmed guessed.

He wrapped an arm around the lower ledge of the opening, a window that was much bigger up close than it had seemed from below, and, after ascertaining that there was no one in the dark tower room or on the stairs inside it, cut the floating lanterns with the sharp edge of the pick hammer, allowing them to float up into the eaves of the tower's roof.

Then, as silently and with as little motion as he could arrange, he slid carefully over the ledge and into the tower room.

He held deathly still to make certain that he had not set off any traps. When after a moment he could perceive no changes in the floor or the air around him, he acknowledged that the ridiculous height of the tower and depth of the chasm below had undoubtedly left the planners and architects convinced that no additional security arrangements were necessary save for the mirrors he could see at the tops of each turn in the stairs, set up for the purpose of seeing attacking troops coming up them.

As he caught his breath and acclimated to the height and thinness of the air in the tower, Achmed leaned up against the wall beneath the tower window.

The leather cord around his neck pulled uncomfortably; absently, he rearranged it with his finger, then ran his hand down to the pendant that hung from it.

Rhonwyn's compass.

Or, rather, that of Merithyn the Explorer, her father, who had used it and its compatriots, Anwyn's spyglass and Manwyn's sextant, to find his way across the world to the lands of their mother, Elynsynos the dragon.

Her compass had the power to show the Seer what was occurring in the evanescent moment of the Present. Achmed gripped the instrument in his hand and concentrated, opening his brain to the question of what was occurring in the world around him at that very moment in Time.

Almost immediately, the compass began to glow in his hand.

Startled, the Bolg king took a breath and closed his eyes.

At first he saw a darkness blacker than pitch.

Then, from out of that blank panorama, a skyline appeared, the peaks of familiar mountains pressed against the sky. It was an image of the Teeth, a place he knew innately, almost as if he himself had been Gwylliam, the man who had built the impressive city-state out of unforgiving rock and started a new civilization and a new era in history there.

Achmed concentrated.

And gritted his teeth as the image formed more completely in his mind, then vanished.

Hrekin, he thought. *At this very moment, the titan is battling Grunthor.*

45

ON THE SKELETON COAST

$\mathcal{G}$runthor and Rath had followed the titan, night into day into night again.

They sought its trail across the empty Krevensfield Plain, whose fields still bore the ruts of the wheels of the wagons that not long ago had carried the soldiers and armaments of Sorbold to the Bolglands, only to be destroyed in a useless rout.

While Sorbold had annexed the sea and managed to amass an enormous number of slaves in their factories, their crop of military victories was beginning to grow thin. The western coast of the Middle Continent was still securely in their control, but the attempts to annex Alliance strongholds had been repelled, first by a skilled army largely comprised of women, then by a boy of seventeen summers with an elemental sword of air and an aged man who reports said fought as ferociously as an arena fighter, then by the sheer bad luck of bad intelligence that resulted in the capture of a sovereign.

Had the conflict been Weighed on the Scales of Jierna Tal, it might have been found to be balanced completely.

But none of the military matters had made their way into the ears of the Sergeant-Major or his Dhracian shadow as they traveled the continent on the occasional current of air when they could find one, or on foot when they could not.

Time was becoming suspended, Grunthor thought one late evening as they followed the scent of human flesh in fire that was inexorably wrapped around Rath's viscera.

The trail he had joked about having obtained.

Chasing this towering statue, fragile yet deadly, had become the sole focus of the Sergeant's awareness.

There's nothing left, he thought when one day of running had turned into yet another day of running. *This is all Oi can think of—all Oi can do.*

Until the day they came upon Faron on the Skeleton Coast.

46

WIDE CENTRAL SEA, EAST OF MANOSSE

$\mathcal{I}$t did not take long for the ships of the Second Fleet to develop a battle pattern.

Once they were outside of the fishing zone and the inner shipping lanes, which Talquist's armada of sporadically appearing pirate ships and armed merchant vessels had scrupulously avoided, the outer fringes of his merchant vessels began to appear.

From the bridge of the *Valiant*, Ashe watched them come, turning in to the wind.

"Come, then," he said under his breath. "Let us hope that you enjoy the ride."

He turned astern and shouted to his first mate.

"Stavos—prepare the braziers, the catapults, ballistae and archers!"

The orders were shouted excitedly from stem to stern. The rumble of the heavy ballistae moving into place beside the affixed catapults, the hauling and setting of the projectiles for the catapults, a heavy spear being set into each ballista ahead of its windlass being drawn back, the sheer sound of war being prepared caused a frenzy among the crew, eager to avenge their allies, friends, and families on the continent.

The wind following the ridge wave was high, so while Ashe could not hear it, he could tell by the spilling of sails and the appearance of crew scattering about the decks of nearby vessels that they were under similar orders from their captains.

As the first rank of ships in the Second Fleet came within sight of the privateers and pirates, the stronger, better-armed ships took to circling with others in the armada, trying to form a battle group, while the singletons broke and fled. So focused on the approaching ranks of battleships was the emperor's flotilla that the captains scarcely noticed the rising ridge of water that bisected the sea from north to south.

Until sight of the Second Fleet was suddenly lost, replaced by a wave that rose twelve feet, blotting out the view of the approaching ships and replacing it with a blue-gray wall moving quickly toward them, in many cases as tall as their masts.

Panic broke out, with captains on Talquist's payroll struggling to turn about in the unforgiving wind, hoisting their sails madly, doing everything they could to outrun the approaching rift in the sea.

In helpless futility.

*H*ang back!" Ashe called as the flotilla of Talquist's ships vanished in front of the ridge of water that the Second Fleet was following.

The vast fleet spilled their sails, slowing their course, waiting for the wave to move beyond them, biding their time to see how the flotilla had fared.

The rising wall of water swept through, relentless, unremarkable in any aspect but height, and continued east, its undertow dragging the ships of the Second Fleet more rapidly with it.

As it moved away, still heading eastward past the place where the flotilla had appeared, in its wake the ships of the pirates and merchants were floating in disarray, some sundered, some capsized, all spun from their courses and struggling to get back aright.

Ashe's eyes narrowed. He turned to the crew, who seemed stunned by the terrifying maritime episode they had witnessed and that was still moving across the open sea.

"All right, let's have at it," he commanded, signaling to the ballistae. "Spare no one. Take no one aboard, unless it happens to be a child."

Lieutenant Stavos swallowed hard. He, like his crew, was still in shock from the sight of the wave and the devastation it had left among ships very much like the merchant vessels in their own port. And the Lord Cymrian, their sovereign and liege, whose face appeared on the coinage of the realm, had a reputation throughout the Known World as a patient, just leader, unlike his mythic grandparents, who had torn the Middle Continent apart over a simple marital spat.

The man who stood before them was giving orders against the Code of Rescue, hate of unmistakable intensity burning in his cerulean-blue eyes.

"M'lord captain, might—might we—"

The gleam in Ashe's eyes grew hotter.

"These men have broken the law of the sea," he stated, his voice ringing in the tones of the dragon within him. "They are not Talquist's innocent dupes. They are no mere pirates and merchant privateers; they have aided in the enslavement of entire nations, in the brutalizing of tens, perhaps hundreds of thousands of people, in poisoning and starving unsuspecting friends and allies of this Alliance, and in the all-out destruction of the western coast of the continent, from Traeg to Windswere, razing the harbors of Avonderre and Tallono to ashes. Unless you see a captive in the waves, his hands tied, a woman who is with child, or an actual child, you are to scuttle each and every one of these ships and *send them to the bottom.*

"They seem helpless because, unlike the warships we will engage next, their weapons are hidden, their intent to profit off the misery of innocents. And they have, growing rich on the blood of those innocents, who, if they survived, occupy slave mines and factories building more armaments for Talquist's global conquest. No mercy, just as they have shown no mercy. Now *set to.* Those ships in the back rank of one hundred fifty, take care of this and follow us. The rest, we will proceed. Is that clear?"

Lieutenant Stavos shook off his shock. "Aye, sir."

Ashe's head dropped as the orders were called up the ropes and aft of the deck, then signaled by flag to the ships around him.

He gripped the rail as the sails were raised again.

As the fleet set out, following the wave.

*J*ust as when he had walked the sea, Ashe at the helm of the armada of ships of the Second Fleet had become little more than the element of water from which his sword was comprised. The sailors aboard his vessel had come to address him as little as possible as he stood, day into night into day again, at the prow of the *Valiant,* staring east, only taking nourishment on occasion and refusing all sleep.

Being the Kirsdarkenvar on the deck of a ship had much the same effect as a waterspout on the sea.

Across the shipping lanes, past cadres of pirate ships, the Second Fleet fought its way, acting in many ways like its own tidal wave.

Until finally, two hundred leagues south of Gaematria, they came upon a vast flotilla awaiting them.

There, in the First-light of the eastern morning, spread against the sky at the horizon, was a flotilla of ships, great vessels shaped to slide through the wind, two towering masts amid each, the fore bearing the crest of a dragon, the aft shaped and colored in the image of a tall tower of White Ivory.

Their sails spilling wind, white of background, on which the symbol of the Cymrian Alliance was emblazoned in glorious color.

"The Sea Mages! Lord Gwydion, look! It's Edwyn! He has answered your summons!"

Ashe blinked in astonishment.

The Sea Mages had skirted the wave, having known of its coming and timing their launch to coincide with its passing.

On the deck of the lead ship stood Edwyn Griffyth, resplendent in his sailing robes.

"Can we ride with you, then?" he called through a speaking horn to Ashe, who was standing amidships on the *Valiant*. "I understand you may have some need of eviction services for rats and mice along the western coast of the continent. We have a good number of special tools to help you. What do you say?"

For the first time in as long as Ashe could remember, he grinned.

"I say come along, if you can behave yourself."

Edwyn's initial reply was a laugh, but it choked off rapidly. He stared behind Ashe's shoulder.

Over which something was rising from the sea.

47

From the deepest part of the sea the tremor began, raising currents from the depths until they crested the surface, tossing ships around like corks on the waves.

After drawing the water from the shallows into itself, leaving exposed and dry the sand beds several thousand feet from the shore, it towered in the air off the coastlands, a giant wall of water, frothing at the top like a madman's mouth.

At first the captains of the ships were too busy shouting orders to notice the form the wave was taking.

But Ashe recognized it immediately.

"Great-Grandmother!" he shouted.

In the center of the rally of ships, a great sparkling form appeared from the depths. It was wyrm-shaped and towered, gleaming in translucent hues of copper and blue.

"Elynsynos?" Edwyn asked reverently.

"Well, hello, my grandson," the wyrm's voice replied, sending ripples across every wave, causing the ships of the Second Fleet and those of the Sea Mages to dance precariously in the waves. "It is lovely to finally meet you, since you have never undertaken to make my acquaintance." She chuckled, a thunderous sound, as Edwyn's face turned scarlet. "I understand you are headed to spare the continent from those who are slaughtering the Cymrian Alliance."

"Yes!" Ashe shouted. "Will you help us, Great-Grandmother?"

"Yes, I believe I will," said the wyrm.

"Forgive me for asking, but what made you change your mind?"

The enormous ethereal beast smiled, revealing gleaming teeth as big as swords.

"Well, for all these centuries, Singers and bards and Cymrian school-children have been reading that tripe, *The Rampage of the Wyrm*. For the record, I am very offended.

"But since it's part of the lore now, I feel I should make the lies into the truth. So, if you are willing to have me—I am ready to rampage.

"Let us go and aid your wife, and your people, in their battle."

48

So at the specific request of the dragon, the Second Fleet remained back at the Prime Meridian while the ridge wave was transformed, by the power of a raging dragon beneath the surface, into a thunderous wall of traveling water, slipping across the sea and rising to a peak taller than that of the light towers that had stood in the harbors of Avonderre and Port Tallono.

The wave could be seen several miles inland, though it missed the coast of Traeg and began its assault on the shoreline of the continent at the northernmost point of Avonderre Harbor, turning over ships, docks, and naval settlements and blasting them inland as far as the edge of the Great Forest, where mountainous ruins were left in its wake.

By some coincidence of nature, it stopped just short of flooding the forest, however.

Further south it roared through the occupied edge towns all the way down to the captive Lirin harbor of Port Tallono, sweeping along the edge of Windswere and the Nonaligned states.

Heading for the eastern harbors of Golgarn.

Taking with it, in a slurry of froth wrapped in a bitter storm of rain and lightning, the recently-built bulwarks of the occupying forces that had been strangling the continent for the better part of a year.

Later, when the history of the tidal wave was written and retold, many firsthand accounts of the rampage were passed along.

Witnesses, too numerous to have their testimony explained away by tricks of the mind or insanity, insisted that in the sky above the raging wave, set against the blackened clouds and the flashing lightning, the image of a evanescent wyrm, sparking in the hues of copper and gold, lashed about in the air, as if it were directing the assault of seawater.

Roaring in a voice that shrieked over the screaming wind and the horrific noise of the tidal wave.

While the armada of ships flying the colors of the Alliance and those of the Sea Mages hovered behind the wave, seemingly undisturbed.

It was said that some sharp-eyed observers noted that, at the prow of the lead ship, believed by some to be the *Valiant*, stood the shadow of what appeared to be a human man, dark against the sky, colorless save for what appeared to be a shining crown of copper-colored hair and cerulean-blue eyes.

Who seemed to be holding the sea beyond the blasting waves calm for the flotilla of ships.

As was another shadow of another man on the deck of the lead ship of those flying the colors of the Sea Mages, without the gleaming hair, but with the same blue eyes.

Who seemed to be doing the same.

Once the all-clear was given, Ashe led the soldiers and sailors of the Second Fleet through the streets of the harbor towns, first Avonderre in the northwest, then the Lirin-sheltered harbor of Port Tallono. As difficult as it had been to muster a willingness to aid the continent in the first place, now it was difficult restraining the fury of the Alliance forces in combat with those occupiers who had survived the storm.

What few there actually were.

Edwyn's walking machines were deployed quickly and sent into enemy encampments that had relied heavily on arrow fire. Ashe later commented that, regardless of Anborn's unwillingness to make use of the machines for himself, their invasion of the two harbors and any surviving encampments of the forces of Sorbold spared the lives of thousands of men.

"Proof that sometimes intention is not always best for the outcome," the High Sea Mage said to the liberating troops.

49

THE SEA DUCHESS EATING HOUSE,
PORT OF GOLGARN

Beliac, Golgarn's king and sovereign, had a fondness for dining out-of-doors.

Particularly now that his palatial home had become less of a welcoming place since he had traveled, seven months prior, to Sorbold for the coronation of Talquist.

He had been properly served, at least, greeted respectfully and led, with full decorum, to the most elegant table on the seaside balcony of the Sea Duchess eating house, an expensive and well-appointed facility at the end of the slanted street leading down to the wharf, with a breathtaking view of the harbor that had a royal balcony reserved for his use alone.

The inn's finest libations had been swiftly delivered, and each dish he requested had been spectacularly produced and presented to him, amid a good deal of bowing and scraping and protocol followed properly. His guards took their places by the door from the inn to the balcony, allowing only the table servants and the owners to pass to and from the eating house proper to the royal balcony.

Beliac sighed. The Sea Duchess was one of his favorite places to eat.

He glanced around the inn as his *pe'detroi* was served, a regional delight made from local nautical ingredients—tiny scallops, quail, and crab—lightly sauced, carefully spiced, and served in a pastry shell that never was heavy or dense and topped, decoratively so, with the tiniest tip of a shark fin. Beliac had dug in with relish; then, upon realizing that a number of well-heeled nobility had chosen to dine at the eating house that night to be nearer to their sovereign, he sat back in his chair and carefully attended to his mouth and chin with his heavy linen napkin.

The expressions in the eyes of the spectating diners and the deferential table servants soaked through him like a freshening stream; Beliac could palpably sense their admiration, and it warmed his heart, which had been so intensely exposed to the cold recently.

He lifted his snifter toward the nobility watching him from behind the thick glass of a long window and saluted them, bringing him an excited round of polite applause and murmurs of *Bless you, Your Majesty.*

He was too busy enjoying the favorable attention to notice that the noise of the street below him, the clopping of carriage horses' hooves, the bickering of street vendors, the sounds of argument and flirtation, sales pitches and conversation, had died away utterly.

Beliac took a long and luxuriant sip, allowing the bouquet to fill his slightly open mouth and sinuses. He swallowed, feeling the pleasant burn as the liquid went down his throat, and sighed happily, anticipating the relief the potable would bring to his injured pride.

He looked back up, smiling brightly at his subjects of all classes, both on the balcony and behind the window.

Only to see them staring past him, their eyes open wide, their faces set in shock.

Beliac's brows drew together quizzically.

He turned to the headwaiter, who had been standing politely at his shoulder, the bottle of brandy in his hand, awaiting the king's order to refill or step away.

And found that the man was drizzling expensive alcohol onto Beliac's shoes and trousers, the bottle hanging limply from his hand.

Aghast, the king pushed his own chair backward, slapping angrily at the stream of wasted brandy with his napkin.

"You graceless *idiot!* What are you doing? What are you—"

He caught sight of the waiter's face, and those of the other diners and servants, still staring over his shoulder, but the shock on their faces, which he had assumed was in response to the damfool who had been pouring fine brandy into his lap, had melted into a richtus of terror.

He turned around, following their gaze.

Only to see that the water in the harbor had drawn back half a league or more, revealing the seabed. Flapping fish and grounded ships were lying in the naked sand where the tide had been a few moments before.

Approaching the harbor was a towering wave, roiling with gray fury, sweeping ships and bricks from the decimated lighthouse that had been standing, moments before, at the end of the quay, toward the shore.

And the town that lined that shore.

The king scrambled back, his ears finally opening to the sounds of screaming and panic, as table servants and noblemen alike scrambled for the door, pushing tables over and shoving their way to the stairs inside the eating house.

"Hurry, Your Majesty," urged the captain of his guard regiment. "Down the exterior staircase—"

Beliac was unable to respond in words, but let out a harsh, back-of-the-throat gurgle as the captain seized his arm and dragged him away from the table and his *pe'detroi*.

Together the two men followed the rest of the guard down the staircase off the balcony and into the street that had been all but empty a few moments before. The guardsmen had their longpoles drawn and were slapping the frightened villagers out of the way, clearing a path for the king.

Beliac was shaking so hard that it took a moment for him to notice the drops of water that were raining down above him, lightly at first, then harder, like an insistently pelting rain. He looked above him and saw the cloud-riven sky, rolling and gray with angry clouds, then glanced out to the harbor again.

With a thunderous roar, the monster wave smashed down on the pier, shattering the docks and the remaining ships that had been moored there a moment before, bouncing on the forewave like dogs leashed to a fence post. Then it rushed up over the sand and the harborfront, filling the streets systematically with water that seemed to bleed forth.

Swallowing everything in its path.

"Run, Majesty!" the guard gasped, holding out his longpole futilely, as if doing so could hold back the rushing tidal surge.

Blindly, the king obeyed, turning to the slanted street and dashing up it as fast as he could.

He had only managed to progress a few steps, pushing futilely at the crowd of fleeing citizenry, when the air around him turned gray-black and the most sickening sound he had ever heard filled his ears.

A moment later, smashing water taller than his head engulfed him, drowning out the screaming all around him and sucking him, with an intensity far greater than his body had ever withstood before, first forward, dragging him up the slanted street, blind to anything but the overwhelming gray, and then rapidly back toward the harbor.

At least his terrified mind thought that was what was happening as he tumbled in the grip of the surf, arse over elbow, gasping and choking on water with no access to air whatsoever.

This cannot be happening, he thought as the drawback dragged him down the street and into the harbor proper, pulling him as fast as a team of racing horses. *A moment ago, I was enjoying a fine brandy—*

His head broke the surface.

Beliac's eyes had been pounded in the surf, strafing them with salt, so there was little he could see, even now that, for a moment at least, he was head-up in the light of day.

If he could have focused on the distance before him, he would have seen the wave continuing across the city, engulfing carts and horses and humans with ease, climbing hills as if they were not even there. But instead he was forced to take in the sight with his diminished eyes of the carnage around him, the bodies and barrels, horses and haycarts floating in the sea all about, a few living creatures still struggling, but most broken and dead, whatever eyes they had once possessed reflecting the glare of the blackened sun overhead.

The scene turned red a moment later; Beliac realized that his head was bleeding down into his eye.

And at the same moment understood that he had, in fact, survived the wave.

He set to righting himself in the calming surf, pushing wildly and unsuccessfully away from the flotsam and jetsam banging into him with each undertow, slapping back dead flesh and shattering wood.

I'm all right, he thought. *I have been a mariner all my life; I can stay afloat, can make my way back to shore—*

Something heavy slammed into him from behind.

Beliac lost his balance, floating in the surf, and was dragged momentarily under the surface again.

He curled up into a ball in the drift, struggling to save his arms and legs from being broken by the piece of the ship that had nicked him. Beliac held his breath for as long as he could; then, his lungs screaming, he uncurled and swam rapidly toward the surface and the light he saw there.

He took an immense gasp of air when he broke through, and kept reminding himself the rule that sailors used to chant when their ships were compromised.

Do not panic. Panic will kill you, even when nothing else wants to.

If this is not proof of my Right of Command, I don't know what is, he thought woozily. *All about me is death; everything floating around me in the sea is dead, except for me. And yet, from this maelstrom I have been saved. It appears that I alone have survived.*

Because I am king.

Again, something slammed him in the back.

Beliac curled up again, anticipating another contact with a broken ship that had been docked before the wave hit.

And, to his shock, felt a dragging on his leg, then a terrible ripping as it was torn off at the foot.

Numbness swept through him.

What is happening? he wondered.

As a large oblong creature moved past him, a familiar triangle on its back pointed at the forbidding sky.

His lower leg in its teeth.

Beliac flinched, then began to shudder.

He looked around him.

In the swirling red water, he was surrounded by more of the triangles, circling menacingly, as the sharks that had been displaced by the wave righted themselves.

And sought nourishment.

As his lifeblood began to pulse from his leg, his darkening consciousness fought to remain alert.

No, he thought desperately. *No—this isn't happening—*

As another shark sank its teeth into his side, his wife's words from the night he had returned home to Golgarn rang in the shrinking consciousness.

Your childish obsession with being eaten alive by Firbolg has cost all of us dearly, Majesty. Welcome home. I hope your journey west was worth it.

In spite of being the king of a nation proudly known for not having a state religion, Beliac began to pray, thoughts that made no sense offered in supplication to a deity or deities he had never believed in.

Just before the last shark seized his flailing arm and dragged him down to the depths in pieces, a final irony occurred to him.

The last picture in his dissolving mind was that of the tiny tip of the shark fin that had topped his *pe'detroi.*

And now was being torn out of the stomach into which he had swallowed it.

50

ON THE SKELETON COAST

Faron was growing frantic.

Day by day the place where his arm had broken off was crumbling more, leaving him off balance and weak. The dry, sandlike interior of his formerly smooth flesh of Living Stone chipped away with the slightest of contact, making the former freak-show exhibit feel as if he was dissolving.

Largely because he was.

In the first few moments of shock after the greenish beast had struck him with the rock on a stick, shattering his arm, it occurred to Faron that once he was free of Hrarfa, nothing was preventing him from going where he wanted and getting away from the demands of the demon that had rent his brain, day and night, with the endless call for more destruction, more fire, more blood.

And more speed in the achievement of her overall goal, the finding of the Earthchild in the mountains of Canrif and, in turn, the key to the Vault of the Underworld.

The overwhelming and relentless demands of the demon had made Faron long even more for the days he had spent in the company of his father. There had been comfort in the warm green water, comfort that his almost boneless body had craved. As each day passed and he became more and more brittle, all he wanted, above everything else, was to return to that time, and if not that time, at least to that sensation.

Which is why, for the first time in his life, Faron craved the sea.

When he first had come to awareness on the Scales, encased in this new, unwieldy, and uncomfortable body of Living Stone, he had panicked, had run from Jierna Tal down the forbidding mountainside, all the way to the shore, where he could feel some of the dragon scales his father had given him in a stranger's hands, a stranger who had stolen them from him when he was compromised, weak and dying after the destruction of his tank of green water on his father's ship. He had come to the water's edge, but had balked at going in it, terrified of the massive blue monster that had taken his father from him.

But now the sea no longer made him fear.

Now it was, perhaps, the only place where he might find the comfort he had experienced with his father.

He was able to run day and night, because his stone body required neither rest nor sustenance. All he knew was that he could hear his father's voice, calling to him lovingly from somewhere far away, all that he wanted in the entire world.

And, when he finally reached the Skeleton Coast, the fog and the water, the cool mist and the breeze that gently buffeted his missing arm all managed to obscure the giant and the shadow that were waiting for him there.

$\mathcal{G}$runthor waited in the shadows of the broken ships, partially buried in sand for a millennium and a half.

Rath had been tracking the titan from the moment they left the Bolglands, had kept silent while he was following the flickering fire of the demon's essence. It had been more difficult to track than even the most elusive of the F'dor he had followed in the past, largely because the creature that the Sergeant called Faron was so largely dilute, so clouded with other bodily legacies that the part which was dark fire was evanescent, hard to keep a mental grasp on.

And yet he did.

So when the titan was within a league or so, he turned from the silence of his meditative position.

"He's coming."

"Yer certain?"

"Yes."

"All right, then. Oi'll be ready."

By the time Faron's shadow appeared, long and thin in the morning light, they both were.

$\mathcal{F}$aron came to the shore, alone in all the world, it seemed.

For as far as he could see up and down both sides of the beach and everywhere behind him, he was the only moving object.

Gingerly he waded out into the water, feeling the soothing sting of the cold salt. It seemed to him that something was strange about the water; it was very far away from the shore, farther than he ever could imagine. On the wet sand of the beach, revealed when it pulled back, fish and crustaceans were flapping and moving awkwardly, struggling with their sudden lack of cover.

For a short while, the seabirds had a feast.

But then the world became quiet.

Disturbingly quiet.

$\mathcal{A}$nd then Grunthor struck.

Hiding below the crest of the waves in the shallow water, he had been waiting.

Faron was caught unaware.

The Sergeant-Major lunged forward, throwing his arms around the titan's knees and slamming it onto its back in the surf.

Almost immediately the counterpunch broke his nose as his body was hurled into the air above the froth by the hardest impact he ever remembered sustaining from anyone. As the surface of the sea was streaked with his blood, Grunthor looked up to find the titan towering over him, the hand on the end of his remaining arm clenched into a fist that came down on his head, causing the world to go black for a moment.

Grunthor, woozy, felt around in the surf until he located his pick hammer. When the titan reared up again before him, he swung with all his might, nicking the statue's chin and breaking the area around its eye.

Blinded, Faron rose and slammed himself down onto Grunthor's head, flattening him into the beach.

His one good arm shot out and grasped the Sergeant's throat.

He squeezed, crushing the windpipe.

Until another swing of the pick hammer broke his remaining elbow.

Armless, Faron fell back, struggling to rise.

Grunthor, clutching his throat, rose shakily to his feet and readied the hammer again.

When off in the distance, something caught his eye.

At the horizon, the water from the sea had shifted, it seemed. Blood was gushing from a gash across his brow, but Grunthor was fairly certain he could tell what was coming.

He glanced around, but could find no trace of Rath.

The wall of water was moving quickly, sweeping broken ships and houses from the other side of the world in front of it.

The Sergeant-Major looked at the statue, panting furiously in the sand at his feet.

Then back at the coming tidal wave.

And, given the odds, decided to go for the kill.

He raised the hammer one final time and brought it down on the statue's head.

Shattering it.

Then, with the last of his breath before the towering wave swept in, he began to chant.

By the Star, Oi will watch, Oi will wait, Oi will call an' be 'eard.

He could see no sign of Rath.

He was waiting, standing vigil, when the wave crashed down, taking everything in its path away with it.

51

The Teeth
(Manteids)

★

• Night Mountain
Earth Basilica

Desert

THE TOWER OF JIERNA TAL

The first indication Achmed had that the Merchant Emperor of Sorbold was on his way up the stairs was the slightest repugnant stench of human flesh in fire.

The trace odor was extraordinarily faint, a mere whisper of the fetid smell of demonic spirits, the F'dor specifically, but even just a hint of it was enough to fill his Dhracian sinus cavities with the stinging indication of the presence of ancient evil that his blood screamed to stamp out.

The long journey across the massive canyon followed by the extraordinary climb he had undertaken had stripped him of more of his strength than he had expected. The life he had lived prior to coming to the new world had kept him fit and wiry; while he still kept himself in trim, there was no denying the softening of his hardness, the diminution of his ironlike grip. The hard vitality that he had always counted on, while still mostly present, was not something to take for granted, he had learned.

So he pressed himself up against the corner behind the stairs in the tower room overlooking the vast vista, much of which he had traveled through, and waited, willing his heartbeat to slow and his breath to be silent. He held Rhonwyn's compass in his right hand and, with caution that surpassed extreme, waited for the emperor to come into sight.

And it almost worked.

Calquist was humming as he climbed those stairs, drying his hair, wet from the scented bath he had just taken, with a thick, small towel.

The routs of Avonderre and Tallono had established an impressive foothold along the eastern coast of the Middle Continent; the international network of slave traders and armed merchant vessels, cleverly hidden for so long by the blue scale that Faron had employed, still seemed to be maintaining control of the seas, even now that the magical occlusion was no longer present; armaments of all kinds were being produced at record speeds by his slave factories; and, by far his favorite bellwether, word had come from Navarne that the Lord Cymrian was, in the words of the scouts, "dead or fled."

He could not be happier.

Granted, there had been losses as well. The Great Forest to the north and Tyrian to the south had proven thus far impervious to the tests for widespread burning with the long-smoldering ores the slaves had accidentally discovered in the mines of Jakar, where seven hundred of them had inhaled the toxins, only to breathe out increasingly heated blood with each exhalation. By now he had anticipated occupying the western forests from his own borders to those of the Hintervold in the north.

But it was coming, he knew.

All in good time.

He was almost at the top of the stairs leading to the tower room when the mirror placed unobtrusively in the corner caught a flash of movement, ever so slight, behind the tower staircase.

Talquist froze on the stair.

Hrekin, Achmed thought. *He's seen me.*

He glanced out the stairway door to the place where the string of an alarm bell hung.

He had not yet caught sight of Talquist himself; the emperor had come to a halt just beyond the range of his vision from beneath the staircase above him. But he had been a student of human behavior long enough to recognize the signs of being seen, had been able to detect a change of heart, plan, or mind, knew the sound of the quick intake of breath or the expulsion of similar air that indicated an unseen person knew of his presence.

One thing that cheered him somewhat was the fact that the odor of F'dor did not grow stronger as the emperor stopped. Achmed had been around enough targets with whom the ancient demonic race had interacted that, while he could not always catch a trail of a demon, he could usually gauge the level of its connection to the human host. Whether a person had come into the most distant of contacts and was therefore only under the slightest of suggestions, or the full-fledged host of the demon itself, Achmed could never be certain, but he had come to be able to often weigh the density of a demonic presence.

And, though he silently acknowledged that he could be wrong, he decided the likelihood that Talquist had either been taken against his will or, a little more nerve-racking, had offered himself as the demon's actual host, was minimal.

Or at least he prayed it was.

Come on, you demonic knob, he thought. *Come out and play.*

Exhaling quietly, Talquist drew the violet scale of the New Beginning from the folds of his robes of state, garments of the finest bleached white Sorbold linen, trimmed with gold.

And held it up in the moonlight streaming through the window.

He watched as it cleared to almost an outline of itself, the violet hide and primitive scratching of the image of a throne inscribed on its surface fading until nothing but the outline remained.

Talquist waited patiently, listening for sound from beneath the stairs, but hearing none. He glanced without moving his head into the stairway mirror again and saw nothing.

Much the way he had as a child in the orphanage when he had heard footsteps or a sudden bump on the stairway, potentially indicating the approach of the despicable bastard caretaker who gleefully used the penniless children in his care for his own nefarious purposes, he suppressed the urge to scream threats or issue commands—*Leave here now! Leave us alone! I have a knife*—and waited until his own hand and forearm went clear as the scale did.

The moonlight being as strong as it was that night, it only took a moment.

As Talquist felt the density of his body change, he smiled with the irony of what he had just undertaken. It was this scale, this precious object he had found in the sand of the Skeleton Coast a lifetime ago, that had allowed him to walk through the streets of Jierna'sid in the dark of night, to enter both Crown Prince Vyshla's bedchamber and the royal suite of the Empress Leitha and absorb into the carapace of the scale all of their Right of Command, all but dissolving the prince and desiccating the empress almost immediately.

And, with the removal of the Ring of State from the dead empress's hand, giving him the object he needed, drizzled with a few drops of his blood and placed on the Weighing plate of the great Scales of Jierna Tal, to take the throne for himself.

Just one more time, he thought as he watched the rest of his body turn clear and vanish. *Please, please. I will never leave the tower window open again if you just assist me in this, please.*

And smiled, knowing that he, one of the true disbelievers in the world, who had chosen to publicly worship the old animist gods that he didn't believe in rather than acknowledge the Cymrian deities he didn't acknowledge either, he, the Royal Cynic, had just uttered a bartering prayer.

If it wouldn't lead his predator to him, he would have laughed aloud.

If there is anyone there, it must be the second assassin that Faron's augury spoke of, he mused. *Fhremus was right; that second fellow with Dranth could hardly have been mistaken for an actual assassin.*

Fortunately, the moonlight was bright that night.

He tucked the violet scale into the pocket in the folds of his robe.

𝒜chmed did not know why he was certain, but somehow he knew that Talquist had stepped off the stair.

One of the reasons he knew was that when he leaned incrementally farther out from behind the corner of the staircase, he could no longer see the emperor's stout belly as he had a few moments before.

Hrekin, he thought to himself. *He's got something that hides him from sight.*

He set about moving the cwellan forward with motions that were agonizingly slow, tasting the air in front of him to see if the flavor changed.

And in a moment, it did.

𝒯alquist stepped off the stair.

He came around the corner as slowly as he could, holding the dragon scale in front of him.

And silently drew the blade that he always kept in a sheath on his lower leg, even now that he was the emperor of the Known World, with the greatest soldiers on the continent protecting his every breath.

I will have to discipline Fhremus for allowing this breach in security, he thought, highly displeased.

He stopped and took a breath.

Crouched behind the stair was a man in black garments, simple trousers and a shirt, with a hooded scarf that covered his neck.

Talquist's blood ran cold.

He had seen this man before, at the funeral of the empress and her son, as well as his own coronation.

He thought of curses vile and vulgar that had been part of the world he had inhabited for most of his life and decided that none of them were even vaguely sufficient.

Well, he thought ruefully, *if someone is going to try and take the emperor of the Known World down, at least it's appropriate that it's the king of assassins.*

He stood, not breathing, for the span of eighty heartbeats, then gingerly stepped forward.

Only to have the man beneath his staircase swing his strange, crossbow-like weapon around and point it squarely in his direction.

Talquist's throat ran dry.

And yet, even as his heart pounded heavily and his blood ran faster, he had the innate understanding, though he was not certain why, that the gifted killer did not see him.

At least not yet.

He's following his nose, the emperor thought, judging by the angles at which the veiled man aimed his weapon, and glanced about. He regretted immediately the salt bath he had enjoyed that morning, perfumed with sacred oils and ambergris from across the sea that was now plied by ships flying his colors.

The assassin's eyes were not aligned with him.

He lifted his dagger and positioned it for a killing strike.

Achmed knew that he could only take one cwellan shot, and if he missed, it would give the invisible emperor a clean shot with his blade at him.

When the thought occurred to him he couldn't decide if he was amused by it or horrified.

Indeed, were the tales of his life to be written, it would be embarrassing beyond belief to have met his end at the hands of such an utter imbecile.

At the same time, the potential of that happening was far stronger than he was comfortable acknowledging.

His sinus cavities stung slightly, and Achmed put his finger to the side of his nose.

And, in doing so, felt the compass that he had placed in his sleeve shift slightly.

Rhonwyn's compass.

Or, more correctly, Merithyn's.

With some effort he slid the ancient artifact from his forearm into his hand without moving otherwise. The tool felt warm, probably from being up against his bare skin, but once it was in his hand he saw a vision ripple through his mind.

It was the quick, evanescent picture of himself in the tower stairway room.

As if it were reporting to him about his own whereabouts.

Where is Talquist? he thought quickly.

The image changed to a picture of himself from a much closer angle.

Achmed turned to align himself with the space that he had seen a few seconds before.

And felt the odor he had identified move rapidly to his right.

Achmed fired his cwellan.

To his shock, the three sequential disks went wide, all except the first one, which cleanly bisected a small, thick towel that lay on the ground at his feet.

His reflexes, reputed to be some of the quickest in the Known World, noted the absence of the familiar scent.

Talquist was gone.

*T*he Merchant Emperor had made a decision at the very last moment that made use of good common sense, an attribute he had relied on all of his life, particularly during his days plying the trade.

While the dagger in his hand might work once he got around behind the Assassin King, there was no possible way that he could make a successful strike against Achmed from the front.

Unless he wanted to be shot at point-blank range before he drew his next breath.

So he tossed the towel and bolted.

He had managed to get almost to the door of the tower room when a hail of disks whirled past him in an arc, whistling through the air and spinning out into the stairway beyond, where they clinked upon falling to the floor.

"Coward," murmured the Bolg king.

Talquist felt his face go hot.

Perhaps, he thought grudgingly. *But we will see who lives to hurl the next insult.*

He remained, still as death and as invisible as the Afterlife, exactly where he had landed.

Where is Talquist? Achmed silently asked the compass again.

This time, he saw himself from a completely different angle and distance, far closer than he had imagined.

Too close for a cwellan shot.

He dropped his weapon and lunged.

And connected with Talquist's soft stomach, driving his shoulder into the Merchant Emperor's chest.

Taking Talquist's breath from him.

The moment the connection was made, the emperor appeared on the floor beneath him.

A blade hovering in his hand, close to Achmed's throat.

The Bolg king seized the emperor's wrist and squeezed with as much crushing force as he could manage, shocking himself at how weak he had become in his travels across the twenty-one-mile-wide canyon and the tower climb.

Talquist, a man of many streetfights and tussels in the course of building an empire of merchants, gasped and twisted, managing to pull his shoulder around but not to free himself. He struggled to shout for help, but the pressure of the Bolg king's shoulder against his chest just below the heart was beginning to interrupt his breathing, making him woozy.

"Help," he gasped quietly, not even loud enough for the word to leave through the tower window where high-flying birds might hear it. "Help me."

"Oh, please," the Bolg king said disdainfully. "Surely you can do better than that."

"You will—never—get out of—here—alive—"

"Perhaps not," Achmed said, wedging his feet at an angle on the floor and driving more pressure from his shoulder into Talquist's chest. "But we will be traveling companions in any case. Unless you make an unfortunate dive out the window."

"Halt, or you shall both go over."

52

The emperor, sweating and pale, looked up to see his supreme commander, crouched menacingly, his crossbow pointed. He was too close to the tower window to be relieved yet, but his hopes rose.

"Fhremus," he whispered. "Help me." He tried to pull free of the Bolg king's grip, but it was like iron, as unforgiving as death.

The muscles of Fhremus's shoulders tightened visibly as he gripped and sighted his weapon. They were the only muscles in his body to make any movement.

"Do not move, Majesty—I am here."

He looked at the Assassin King without turning his head. "Release him and step back from the window."

The Bolg king neither moved nor obeyed, merely tightened his grip and dragged the emperor's upper body more fully in front of himself.

Fhremus took one deliberate step closer.

"I know you have no qualms about your own death," he said in a toneless voice to the Bolg king. "But if you do not obey me, you will not be able to attend to your appointed task. Release the emperor."

Talquist's brows drew together.

"His appointed task?" he demanded, choking as the unforgiving grip tightened even more. "Fhremus, his—task *is to murder me*. This—is the second—assassin the augury warned—of—"

"No, Majesty, no." Fhremus's voice had the ring of false comfort. "I killed both assassins that came here, on your orders, before your eyes. This man is no assassin. He is merely a workman, a leavener. The sort of man you represented in the Mercantile when you were guild Hierarch—the 'noble man who works with his hands,' as you called people like him."

When Talquist squinted even more deeply in confusion, Fhremus's eyes blackened and bored into his.

"He has come to repair the Great Scales, Majesty. It seems that someone unbalanced them deliberately last year and they have been weighing falsely since. This workman is a skilled craftsman who has come all the way from Ylorc to rebalance the Scales. It is the duty of every true Sorbold to assist him in his task." He spoke to Achmed again. "Release him."

The Bolg king stared at him a moment longer.

Then let go and stepped away.

The trembling emperor lunged forward.

Only to be caught full-force in the throat and driven back to the window by the supreme commander's crossbow bolt.

Fhremus fired again, and Talquist fell onto the opening of the aperture, twitching and gagging.

He reaimed his weapon.

"Wait," Achmed said, holding up his hand to the supreme commander. Fhremus paused.

The Bolg king stepped rapidly to the window and plucked the violet scale of the New Beginning from Talquist's robes, then leaned over the emperor, who was drowning in his own gore.

"For a short while you lived in the guise of a king," he said in his sandy voice that scratched the dying man's eardrums. "In death, you are, for all time, still only a man, and not much of one at that. Greet Rhonwyn nicely when you hit the bottom; without her help I never would have found you."

He held up the compass with his left hand before Talquist's glassy eyes.

"Look well at this," he said. "For the Present, you are still alive. Six to eight seconds from now, that will be in the Past."

Then he shoved the Emperor of the Sun out the tower window.

A moaning gargle fell as Talquist did, disappearing quickly in the sound of the wind around the high tower.

Achmed turned to the supreme commander and opened his arms benignly.

"Shoot me if you will," he said seriously. "I have done what I needed to do—completed my 'appointed task,' as you said."

Fhremus watched him for a long moment, then lowered his weapon.

"So have I," he said.

He walked over to the window and stared down at the broken corpse of the emperor, tiny in the canyon below, only discernable by its bright white robes of fine Sorbold linen.

Then he spat out the aperture.

"For Kymel," he said to the wind howling around the tower. "And each man like him you betrayed."

He looked in surprise at the floating lantern wedged in the tower roof, then turned to Achmed, thin and wraithlike before him.

"You climbed?"

The Bolg king nodded slightly.

Fhremus nodded in return.

"I assume you would prefer to leave by the stairs."

"That would be a vast improvement, but not a necessity," said the Bolg king. "It can only be easier climbing back down."

The supreme commander beckoned to him, and Achmed followed him down the tower staircase. Fhremus led the Bolg king into the library and opened the hidden passageway.

"Go down and out through the viaduct, taking the northern tunnel when you come to the main vein. No one will see you—by then we will all be mourning the disappearance of our emperor."

The Bolg king gave the supreme commander of the armies of Sorbold a considered look.

"We are still at war, are we not?"

Fhremus met his gaze. "Yes. Until a halt to hostilities is called. That is more your area than mine, Majesty."

"I thought so. Well, if we both survive until that time, come for a visit and I will favor you with a splendid single malt. If we don't, thank you for the use of your stairway."

Fhremus smiled slightly and nodded.

Achmed bowed and stepped through the passage.

He followed the hidden passageway for a great distance, into the underground sewer where the stench of centuries stung his sinuses, breathing easier in spite of it, until he finally found himself at the buried gate. He crawled out into the blinding desert sun, into a free wind, and expelled the smell from his nose.

Then he closed his eyes and tasted the sand in the air.

Only to be slapped by a wind from the southeast, carrying Rhapsody's voice.

Screaming his name.

Achmed! Achmed the Snake! Come to me—oh gods—

He felt quickly around for a favorable breeze and, concentrating as Rath had shown him, caught it and was taken aloft by the wind.

53

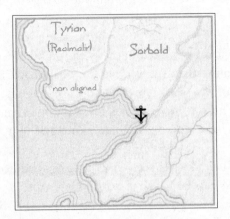

ON THE SKELETON COAST

Grunthor!" Rhapsody shouted into the sea wind. "Grunthor, where are you?"

Only to hear her voice drowned out in its call.

Frantically she slapped at the swells that threatened to pull her feet out from under her. The drawback from the tidal wave had receded, and now the waves of the sea were crashing on the shore as if nothing had ever happened.

All evidence of catastrophic destruction to the contrary.

Glancing all around her, she scanned the broken bones of the old Cymrian vessels, usually wedged in the sand and the fog, but now partially submerged in the surf that swirled and rushed around the new shoreline. The wind whistled through again, whipping her hair into her eyes, making it impossible to see clearly.

Fighting to keep from being swallowed by her terror, she was suddenly struck with the memory of her first of only two previous visits to this haunted place. The second time she had traveled here she had been with Ashe; the memory of that journey was as foggy as the coast itself, as most of her memories of him were. But the first time she had come with Achmed and Grunthor, seeking to study the shattered timbers of the ships, which had been made from the trees of Living Stone known as Earthwood that had been harvested in the buildup to the Cymrian exodus from their homeland.

Achmed had been seeking information about the blue-tinged wood of trees that they had discovered in the deep forests of Canrif, far beyond the engineering and artistic marvel that Gwylliam had carved into the edifice at the front of the mountain range. His research had suggested that they might be related to the trees of Living Stone that had grown outside the castle Elysian where Serendair's king and family had resided in their day.

Rhapsody, who had never seen that castle but had been aware enough of its legends, had chosen to name her hidden grotto, the cavern full of stalagmites where a small cottage stood on an island in the middle of the underground lake in the Bolglands, after that palace.

As the thundering sea and the piercing wind rattled the bones of the ships all around her now, she thought back to that journey with her two dearest friends in the world, remembering how their presence had been the only thing that allowed her to keep from succumbing to the nightmarish gloom that kept most every other traveler away.

After they finished investigating the graveyard of ships, a bottle of fine rum had been passed around, far more potent than any of them had expected. The resulting merriment had been uncharacteristic, even for the Three, who had traveled the entirety of the Earth together and by that time considered each other the only family they had left in the world. Great merriment and hilarity had occurred, including an impromptu belching contest in which Rhapsody had enthusiastically been named the winner by the two Firbolg, an event that in itself had resulted in even greater tomfoolery.

Grunthor had been moved to offer a solemn toast.

'Ere's to the Three, he had intoned, lifting the empty rum bottle high. *As long as we's togetha, the rest of the world can go get knobbed.*

Rhapsody had sworn later that even Achmed had giggled, but in the sober light of the next morning, she realized that it must have been a mistake of her alcohol-infused memory.

The recollection came and went in the passing of a single heartbeat, leaving her with nothing in her memory but the visage and name of the man she needed, the only one in the world that could help her find their friend.

Even as diminished as she was from the loss of her name, she could still feel the importance of both of those men in her life.

She raised her head to the angry gray sky above her, heavy clouds racing past above.

"Achmed!" she screamed into the battering wind. "Achmed the Snake! Come to me—oh gods—"

Her voice choked off as her mouth was filled with water by a passing high wave.

Rhapsody struggled to stand and angrily spat out the brine, trying to keep from swallowing the seawater, and shouted again, and again.

The wind around her moaned and screamed in return.

"Achmed—"

"Peace," the Bolg king said from behind her, his voice all but drowned in the tempest. "I am here. Save your voice and your breath."

Rhapsody turned quickly and stared, wide-eyed, at her dearest friend in the world, the other side of her coin.

The Bolg king opened his arms to her.

"Achmed," she said, trembling violently, "I can't find him. I can't find Grunthor. Please, help me, please help me find him." She came, exhausted, into the Bolg king's embrace and clung to him, finding a stronger anchoring in the sand with his weight.

"Where's Rath?" he asked quietly.

"I don't know."

I am here, Bolg king.

Achmed heard the words in his mind. He turned in a full circle, looking for the Dhracian, but all he saw were the crashing waves threatening his balance and the rolling gray sky.

"Where?"

From atop one of the fragmented wrecks that littered the coast, the detritus of history from which the shoreline gained its name, stuck unceremoniously in the crow's nest, the ancient Dhracian hunter held up his hand shakily.

"Where is he? Where's Grunthor?"

Rath shook his head. "I know not. He was out past the first sandbar when he took the titan beneath the waves."

Rhapsody and Achmed looked out to sea.

"Can you feel his heartbeat?" Rhapsody asked. "As you did when you found MacQuieth?"

Beating back his hatred of the element of water, Achmed let go of Rhapsody except for one hand, tore back the hood of his veils, and, taking a deep breath, closed his eyes and plunged his head into the surf.

The howling of the wind and the noise of the gale disappeared, replaced by the bellowing, churning sound of the furious sea.

The Bolg king listened intently. At first he could discern nothing in the mayhem.

But after a moment, he thought he heard something familiar, though vastly changed, in the near distance beyond the first dropoff of the sea bottom.

His head broke the surface and he shook the watery hair out of his eyes, then looked at Rhapsody.

"Come."

She nodded and followed him out past the pounding surf, where the water was deeper.

Achmed closed his eyes, following the tremulous sound of Grunthor's heart. The Sergeant's pulse was a rhythm he had known almost as long as he had known his own.

Fortunately, as with all things having to do with Grunthor, his heartbeat had very little subtlety.

Unfortunately, it also had very little vigor.

Achmed dragged Rhapsody in the direction of the sound, through the relentless waves.

"I could never—imagine—I would ever say this," he gasped, "but I wish—your loathsome husband was here. He, at least, has some power over this disgusting element. This—is the worst—possible situation I can imagine."

Rhapsody, barely able to breathe, merely nodded.

Finally Achmed stopped in water just above his waist.

"Here," he said, indicating the sand on the ocean floor.

"He's—what? He's buried in the sand?"

"So it would seem."

Rhapsody, shaking violently, crouched down and dragged her hands across the bottom.

"We—we have to dig—him—out—"

"I don't know if we can," the Bolg king said, gasping in between words as he scratched at the ocean floor. "Every handful of sand only gets replaced each time—another—wave comes in—"

"How—is he even—still alive?"

Achmed shook his head, his hair soaked with seawater.

"No idea—but I can still—feel his heartbeat. It's getting weaker, of course. He's failing rapidly."

"This is the—curse of power," Rhapsody said, digging as fast as she could, trying to sink her fingers deeply into the sand but getting nowhere. "All our weapons, all our titles—all our lore—and in the end we are left to helplessly digging in the sand of the sea—"

"I share—your frustration a thousand times over—believe me," Achmed said in return, furiously gouging as much of the sand out of the ocean floor as he could, taking a breaker full in the face as he dug.

"Is there nothing—do you not have *anything* we can use?"

Achmed looked up at her seriously.

"Perhaps," he said.

He felt inside his garments for a moment, struggling not to lose the contents of his pockets to the whipping tide.

And then held up a piece of violet oval carapace.

Which, had it been examined in gentler circumstances, had an etching of a throne on its convex side.

"What is that?" Rhapsody ceased digging for an instant.

"I believe it's one of those—scales from Sharra's deck," Achmed said. "I took it from Talquist's miserable hide before I—flung his arse from—his bloody—tower."

Even in the gray light of coming dusk and the rolling cloud cover, a prismatic flicker of light skittered across its surface, making it shine with a violet cast.

Rhapsody went back to digging furiously.

"Do you have any idea how to use it?"

"Not even a guess. I tried to get instructions—from him as he—was falling into the canyon, but he—refused to speak up."

"Well," Rhapsody said, "if it's violet, it would be attuned to the lore of the New Beginning."

"What does that mean?"

"Practically, I haven't the slightest idea."

Achmed grunted as another wave slapped him in the face. "You really are useless, you know—that? I—offer you a piece of the—most ancient elemental lore—and you don't know how to—use it?"

The afterwave to the one that had slapped Achmed swept over Rhapsody and dragged her under for a moment. She emerged a moment later, still digging furiously.

"Violet, on the color spectrum, stands for *the New Beginning*."

"That sounds promising. Do you know how to use it now?"

"I just told you, no."

They stared at each other, soaked to the skin in the waves.

"Then I suppose we—will just have to keep digging, like anyone else would."

Rhapsody gasped for air, then nodded, fighting panic.

"I can be of assistance." The strange, sandy voice spoke next to Achmed's ear.

Rhapsody moved aside slightly as the slippery sand gave out beneath her feet.

"Do you know how—to use a—violet scale, Rath?"

"No idea. But I can dig."

Achmed nodded briskly and moved aside. "Did you travel down from the mast—on the wind?" he asked, his fingers bleeding through his leather gloves, now shredded from the effort.

"I did."

"Is it going out to sea, or coming in off of it?"

The ancient Dhracian hunter blinked his large, scleraless eyes.

"It's a mix, probably confused by the wave. Right now it is going out."

The Bolg king nodded.

"Well, if you can anchor to a breeze and direct it down to—where we are digging—that might help somewhat—"

The Dhracian nodded and returned to his digging in the sea.

"I think—I feel the titan," Rhapsody said nervously. "There is something harder than—the sand—" She stopped and held up an object retrieved from the seabed.

It was a green scale.

She handed the scale to Achmed and returned, with Rath, to digging furiously.

The Bolg king secured the scale within his garments and returned to the task.

"His heartbeat is fading."

"He seems to have—fallen beneath the statue," Rhapsody said, pulling a blue scale out as well and passing it, again, to Achmed. "Ugh. The Living Stone body seems to be dissolving."

"Good. Rath, give me a—hand with him. I have located his arm. Rhapsody, take hold of his neck and—try to keep his head, or at least his nose, out of the water as much as you—can."

The Lady Cymrian nodded and seized hold of the Sergeant's neck.

Gingerly they stood, or at least attempted to plant their feet in the shifting sands. One mercy was that in the water Grunthor was far lighter, but nonetheless it was like attemping to lift an oxcart. Eventually they were able to raise him sufficiently to let the waves assist in bringing their friend's body to shallower water, where their arms gave out once his nose was above all but the tallest waves.

"Perhaps now your lore would be useful," Achmed said sourly, wringing his clothes free from the heaviest of the water.

Rhapsody had already begun to sing her Naming note.

Quickly and carefully she sang Grunthor's Bengard name, an appellation full of clicking sounds and glottal stops. Her voice, harsh and ragged from the sea, struggled, as it always did, with the pronunciation, but within a few moments the giant Bolg began breathing more easily, his closed eyelids less bloodshot.

With each repetition of his name, Grunthor seemed to regain the flesh and color he had had a moment before. He winced in pain and coughed, expelling a great deal of the sea as he did.

Rhapsody watched him, stoic, as the water from the sea was banished.

By the Star—I will watch—I will wait—

Rhapsody spun around behind her.

The wind was spinning violently at the edge of the sea, forming a tunnel in the air.

"How—how can this be?" she whispered. "I hear the Kinsman call—*again.* In the years since the wind first—spoke to me I—have never heard it until this—afternoon, and it is here once again?"

Achmed looked up from the broken body of his oldest friend, who was breathing raggedly in the shallow surf.

"Do you recognize the voice?"

Rhapsody turned in the direction of the tunnel of air and listened intently.

"I think it might be Anborn," she said.

"Go to him, then. You've done all you can here."

"I can't leave you—leave him—"

"If Anborn needs you, to the point where he—is calling you as a Kinsman, you must go," Achmed said. He examined Grunthor's face, put his head down on his chest and listened to the sound of his friend's heartbeat, stronger now. "We can get him home—can we not, Rath?"

The Dhracian hunter inclined his head into the wind for a moment, then nodded.

"Go," Achmed said again.

Rhapsody leaned over her friend, her protector and comforter. His face was pale, with blue, dark circles of pooling blood under his eyes.

But he was breathing.

She sang his name one last time, weaving into it every incantation, every melody of healing that she knew.

Then she struggled, her clothes heavy with saltwater, out of the surf and made her way to where the wind was waiting for her.

She turned back one last time and looked over her shoulder at the two Dhracians and her beloved Sergeant-Major, and raised her hand in salute.

Beneath his sodden veils, she thought she could see the Bolg king smile in return.

Then she stepped into the wind tunnel and was gone.

54

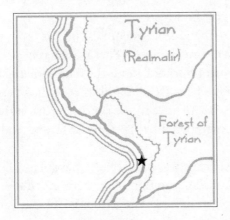

EASTERN COAST OF TYRIAN

The Lord Cymrian stood, breathing shallowly to bring the pain of the injuries he had sustained under control, looking around him in the bloody light of midday.

The southern forest of Tyrian was littered with bodies, mostly of Sorbolds but also a heavy number of Lirin casualties as well. Soldiers and commanders of the Alliance and the Lirin kingdom passed quickly between the treepaths, hauling away the corpses and sorting through the armaments, an air of quiet jubilation about them.

Rial, the viceroy of Tyrian and Rhapsody's most trusted advisor, was giving soft-spoken direction to a contingent of young soldiers, who were listening thoughtfully to his commands; upon the completion of his instructions they turned, leaving in all the cardinal directions as if shot from the numbers of a clock. Rial observed them depart, then made his way over to Ashe.

"You be all right, m'lord?" he asked as he approached.

Ashe waved his expression of concern away, bending over from the waist. "Yes, I'm fine. Any word from the eastern lines of the Lirin army?"

"Aye. The fire assault was attempted against the forest outside the fortifications, and quelled, just as it was here. It was as if the trees of the greenwood refused to burn."

Ashe nodded again. "If only her children could have refused to bleed." He sighed heavily and looked around him. "Is there any word from the field commanders of the Alliance?"

Rial's weathered face grew solemn. "There is little, m'lord, but what has been reported is dire. Anborn's First Wave has been clashing with the southern regiments of Sorbold along the Threshold of Death. The holy city of Sepulvarta has been freed, but to the south, a mass attack is brewing in the Teeth. The Alliance in the southern part of the Middle Continent is gravely outnumbered by the Sorbold forces. And those forces are gathering."

"How much damage was done by the wave? How far did it impact?"

"The geological configuration of the harbor of Tallono helped a great deal in offsetting that, m'lord. The harbor is oblong, and deep; the wave hit it broadside, which swallowed everything but the tallest light tower, including all of the enemy ships and the temporary fortifications they had installed, but everything that had surrounded Tallono was never made to be inhabited, at least by Lirin citizens. Anything that had been there was a construct of the Sorbold navy, and has been eradicated."

"Good. And the forest?"

"The bastions and barricades that were installed after the Sorbolds took the port have been washed away, along with the beachheads, and any that were established closer to Tyrian. The wave did encroach on the forest edge, and while the tree damage is extensive, our breastworks and the heavier defenses are only minimally impacted."

Ashe clenched his teeth in preparation for the answer to his next question.

"And my wife? Has there been any word of Rhapsody?"

The viceroy exhaled deeply.

"She is said to have been heading south from Bethany, where she and the forces of the Alliance repelled the Sorbold attack from the north, and apparently Daystar Clarion and her whip were put to good use in Sepulvarta, but there was no word of her other than that, m'lord. I have tried to keep track of her whereabouts, but communication has been spotty, especially of late."

Ashe blinked. "Her whip?"

A slight smiled crossed Rial's face.

"Apparently she was made the loan of a whip formed from the tongue of an ancient dragon, a lorekeeper like herself, by a wyrm that makes its lair in Faedryth's lands, when she left there to join the fray, m'lord. She showed it to me when she was here before joining up with Anborn. She apparently found it useful in taking iacxsis from the sky, having practiced plentifully in her travels on crows, making them explode, at least before she was injured. That activity seemed to provide her with immense pleasure."

Ashe's tired face took on the hint of a smile as well. "And how was she physically? How was she injured?"

"She had taken a bolt to the shoulder, at the hinge of her upper arm and chest, in the first battle of the Threshold," Rial said, watching the Lord Cymrian wince, "but she was healing well and had the attention of Yltha, the best healer in Realmalir. She seemed in good spirits and health on her way to meet up with the Invoker and your uncle, m'lord, in the waning days of spring and summer's approach when I saw her last."

"And her—state of mind? Did she seem well, and focused?"

Rial's face grew solemn. "Focused, yes, m'lord. She was intensely pragmatic, and seemed to be in little to no distress of body or mind."

"But not well?"

"She seemed well, m'lord."

Ashe gritted his teeth, trying to remain calm. "What are you not telling me, Rial?"

The tinge of amusement left the viceroy's eyes.

"If I had not come to know her as well as I have these past five years, I would have said she was extremely well, m'lord."

"So what does your informed understanding tell you otherwise?"

Rial examined the ground.

"She was not herself when she was here, in my estimation. She was fine, but there was something missing. I asked her upon her arrival why she had been in the Deep Mountains, something she had confided under strictest secrecy to me, and she didn't seem to know. I do not believe she was telling me that I had no business with the information—it was as if she was unable to remember why she had gone there."

Ashe's stomach turned and his throat tightened, but he merely nodded. "Is that all?"

"Perhaps it was her injury, or the seriousness of the coming conflict, but she seemed to have lost, well, much of her spirit, her essence. She was stouthearted and resolved, as ever, but that—that warmth, that energy that be unique to her, I felt it was diminished, gone, even. No one else has commented on it, however, so perhaps I am just overanalyzing the situation."

"Perhaps. Thank you for the report. Now, unless you have further need of my presence, I am off. The sailors of Manosse and her naval forces are ready to assist in any of the retrenching, rebuilding, guard duties, whatever you have need of; put them to good use. They came quite a distance to aid the continent; do not allow them to let the tidal wave and the dragon to have done all the work."

Rial smiled. "Yes, m'lord. So you be heading east?"

"I am," said Ashe, gathering his belongings and checking his gear.

"I would suggest you begin in Sepulvarta," said Rial, signaling to one of the nearby Lirin soldiers. "Be so kind as to obtain the finest available mount for the Lord Cymrian," he ordered.

"It need not be fine, just swift and stalwart," said Ashe. "Thank you, again, for the report, and for your steadfastness in holding Tyrian safe."

"Of course. Travel safely, m'lord. And give my fond best wishes to your wife, when you should come upon her."

Ashe nodded, but the cheer of civility had left his eyes.

He glanced back up at Rial.

Only to see that it was missing from those of the viceroy as well.

55

The Teeth
(Manteids)

★

● Night Mountain
Earth Basilica

Desert

SOUTH OF SEPULVARTA
IN THE SORBOLD MOUNTAINS,
AT THE RADASHAJN PASS, VORNESSTA

ℜhapsody waited until the screaming wind had settled before leaning out of the swirling vortex, then stepped cautiously forward.

She squinted, disoriented, in the blazingly bright light beyond the
wind's door; a moment before, in the surf of the Skeleton Coast, the heavy
mist and the racing clouds had made the day seem as if it was almost
dusk.

Upon looking around, she was slapped almost immediately by a sandy
breeze, a dry wind heavy with the odor of battle, of pitch and bitumen,
and of blood.

Daystar Clarion's blade was roaring with wind-whipped flame, spilling erratic flashes of light around her. Rhapsody stopped and drew a breath;
the wild dance of the fire was owing to how violently her arm was shaking. She steadied herself and glanced about her.

She was standing on the rim of a vast canyon in the mountains, most
likely in the southern Teeth, she guessed by the position of the sun, which

was descending the welkin of the sky, glowing ominously over her right shoulder.

All around her was the detritus of battle, broken wagons and bodies, pools of blood and urine staining the sandy ground, fingers of smoke hanging heavily in the air, and an endless number of arrow shafts and shattered crossbow bolts. The litter of lives and matériel went on for as far as she could see.

And rising across the canyon before her was a mountain peak towering menacingly toward the sky, jutting partway over the canyon so that the ground beneath it was in shadow, its face marred by what looked like an enormous door, small by scale to the mountain face.

The door seemed to be vibrating, a distant thudding sound reverberating from it.

Behind her, almost near enough to touch, stood Solarrs, her recent fellow military commander and Anborn's prized scout, bruised of face with his armor bloodied, one of his vambraces slashed open on his forearm.

He was staring past her, down into the canyon.

Anborn's bastard sword at his feet.

"Solarrs," Rhapsody whispered. "Where is he? Where is—"

The saliva in her mouth dried like a stream in a rocky desert riverbed.

Standing at the base of the jutting mountain cliff in the canyon was the small figure of the Lord Marshal, his arms at his sides, his hand clenched into fists, or so it seemed to her.

He was gazing, his back to her, at the coming onslaught of soldiers of Sorbold, too many to count, just beginning to ride down from over the far rim of the canyon.

Weaponless, shielded only by a stack of sandy rocks, which were deflecting the arrows and bolts being fired at him from above.

Behind her she could hear the noise of distress rising from the soldiers of the Alliance, outnumbered easily ten to one by the advancing Sorbolds. Behind the enemy cavalry, foot soldiers were beginning to swarm over the far rim, blackening the sand-colored rockwalls with their numbers.

"No," she whispered. "He's—he's trapped—Solarrs—we have to get him out of there—"

Solarrs's non-answer was a guttural sound of anguish.

"Anborn!" she shouted, her voice ringing in Namer's tones and therefore unable to mask her terror. "Anborn—get out of there!"

Her words echoed across the rock valley, even over the cacophony of the approaching army.

The Lord Marshal spun around and shielded his eyes with his hand, searching the rim of the canyon until he sighted her. Even as far away from him as she was, the Lady Cymrian could see his smile upon beholding her on the cliff rim.

"Rhapsody!" he shouted. "Open the door!"

She froze, staring at the coming avalanche of soldiers.

"The door!" Anborn screamed, gesturing behind him at the mountain cliff that hung over the valley behind where he stood. *"Open the bloody door!"*

Time seemed to slow as Rhapsody followed the line of his arm back to the throbbing doors in the mountainside. All sound was now washed out in the thudding of her own heartbeat, the overwhelming clamor of death approaching on horseback and foot.

The words reverberated against her skull, the command of the Lord Marshal.

Open the door!

Then, though she could reckon no reason for the order, she felt her body answer her leader's call without questioning it. Understanding took root in her nonresponsive brain; she turned her attention to the burgeoning door and fixed her mind on it.

She closed her eyes, so as not to see the tidal wave of galloping horses and running enemy soldiers bearing down upon her sworn knight, turned in the direction of the door, and pointed Daystar Clarion at it from across the canyon.

Then she loosed a tone from the back of her throat, her Naming note, *ela,* the same note to which the sword, named itself for the star Seren, had been attuned, and raised the volume of her voice until she was all but screaming the note.

In response, the clarion call for which the sword was also named came forth angrily, righteously, winded like a great battle horn. It blasted across the canyon, the ripples of sound skittering over the top, avoiding the valley altogether, and redounded off the mountain peak and its vibrating door.

In the back of her mind she could hear Solarrs shouting orders to the soldiers behind them, positioning them for the onslaught that was coming, a wall of enemies that dwarfed their numbers and threatened to swallow the whole of the army in the backwash of the tidal wave they were now visiting upon the valley in the canyon. Rhapsody shook her head, pushing the competing sounds from her mind, and, having successfully connected the Naming note through the sword, she changed the pitch and spoke the word in Ancient Lirin.

Evit. Open.

She felt, rather than heard, the sickening *crack*, the rumble of rock and steel, the screaming of old hinges.

Then a roar the like of which she had never heard before, as if the Earth itself was bellowing.

Her eyes snapped open.

The gigantic stone doors slammed open at the same instant, up against the mountain face. From behind them a massive flood of rock and slag was vomiting forth, forming a massive wave of stone death, burying the infantrymen that were charging beneath the mountainous outcropping, and rolling forward, chasing those who had outrun it initially.

"Rhapsody!"

The joyful shout echoed in her brain, as if it had been spoken by another Namer.

She looked down into the valley and saw the source of the call.

Anborn stood before the coming tide of horses, soldiers, and sliding slag, his arms open, dwarfed by the oncoming flood, his hands pointed at the ground.

His grin was as wide and unabashed as she had ever seen it, even from as far away as she was. He raised a hand in her direction in a final salute.

"*Goodbye,* my Lady!" he shouted merrily from the bottom of the canyon. His hand went to his face, where he pressed his lips against his fingers, and threw the kiss at her across the canyon.

Then, as the Sorbold army bore down on him from beyond the barricade of rocks, he looked westward, inclining his head and shielding his eyes in the setting sun that was bathing his face in an ethereal light. His final words were spoken more softly, far more reverently.

"Hello, my Lady."

They had scarcely passed his lips when the momentum of the charging onslaught of men, horses, and slag behind him, spilling over and around his rock shield, snapped him from the ground and hurled his body skyward, where it pitched, feet over head, and then was swallowed into the tumult of pounding violence and thrashing rage, disappearing beneath the trampling hooves, the blows of cudgels and swords, and then, moments later, a hellacious rain of rock waste pouring down from the open doors of the mine in the mountain above. It seemed to her that a severed helmed head that spun around in the fray might have been his, seeing where he had fallen, but it was impossible to tell.

Rhapsody's scream of anguish was lost in the roar.

In the noise that swallowed the valley and spilled up the canyon wall to the top of the ridge where she stood, she could not hear her own voice, nor that of Solarrs, who stood beside her in the agony of twitching futility, his sword shaking in his hand, his mouth open in its own scream, every muscle in his body clenched in hatred.

She screamed again, this time in rage, her voice blending with that of Anborn's ancient comrade. As if of one mind, they stepped angrily to the canyon's rim and braced for the onslaught of soldiers who were scurrying up the rock face, hate in their own eyes.

The cavalry, more of which had survived the flood of slag than had the infantry, reined their mounts to a halt and swung their crossbows forward, unleashing a hail of bolts now that they were within range of the southern rim.

"Here!"

Rhapsody felt the clang of metal resonate through her body as one of the field commanders shoved an enormous shield in front of her. A moment later the pinging sound of bolts impacting the steel rang in front of her, and the commander fell back, his forearm pierced with a bolt.

Still in shock from watching Anborn's gruesome death, she clenched her teeth until she tasted blood in the back of her mouth and glared down the Sorbold soldiers climbing beneath the rim. Before the one closest to her was even in reach, she slid down over the rim and grabbed on to a rocky outcropping, leaning almost completely upside down and, with a grim hatred in her swing, slashed Daystar Clarion across his hands, separating one of them from his body and opening the back of the other; then she swung back and slapped him with the blade, causing him to fall, screaming, into the line of soldiers climbing below him, taking three more of them down to the canyon floor with him.

"What are you *doing*?"

A firm grip, bound with a leather glove, seized her by the upper arm and dragged her unceremoniously back up over the rim, tossing her to the ground. Rhapsody looked up in rage to find herself staring into the face of Solarrs, whose visage was even angrier than hers.

"M'lady, don't let your fury make you foolish," he said, clearly struggling to keep from saying something harsher and fouler as he positioned himself between her and the ridge. The other soldiers of the Alliance were engaged now, firing down into the canyon, beating back the Sorbolds scaling the wall. "You would dishonor the Lord Marshal if you fell to your death or died rashly at the hands of a Sorbold dog, given what he has sacrificed to protect you. If you are meant to die in this battle, make it count and take as many of the bastards with you as come your way."

The thrum of battle was all around her, stinging her skin. Rhapsody took several panting breaths and then forced her mouth to close. She nodded briskly at Solarrs, who returned to the front amid the arrows coming from below, and stood shakily.

As she did, she looked behind the forces of the Alliance.

And choked.

Another, larger battalion of Sorbolds was riding, full-bore, at them from the rear flank.

Drawn and screaming.

56

The remaining leadership of the armies of the Cymrian Alliance turned to look behind them as well.

"Bloody fucking hell," Solarrs whispered.

"Well, I guess this is how one dies as a First Generationer," said Cavanur, a field commander who was one himself, who had served with the Lord Marshal and sailed with his father. "Anborn just went first."

Trapped between the swarm of fury rising up from the canyon floor before them and its like bearing down on them on horseback from behind, the soldiers of the Alliance stared miserably at the death race that would claim victory over them one way or another.

Rhapsody was still trying to get air. She was calculating the use of Daystar Clarion in calling starfire down upon them, knowing the Sorbolds were too close to spare her own soldiers from the flames should she do so.

I am the only one of us who would survive, she thought. *My fire lore would spare me, but I would be left here, alone, to face the wrath of the Sorbold survivors from ahead and behind.*

There was no way the Iliachenva'ar could do such a thing.

"I don't suppose there is any point in uttering the Kinsman call," she muttered to herself. "The only other two I have known have either just died before my eyes or called me himself at the point of death immediately afore."

Solarrs returned his attention to the valley below him, where the remains of the army of the Alliance was struggling to keep the southern Sorbold forces from cresting the rim of the canyon.

His face went slack.

"M'lady," he said quietly. "What did the Lord Marshal tell you about this place?"

Rhapsody, whose head barely crested his shoulder, was beside him, staring in the other direction at the approaching division coming from the north.

"Nothing," she said, the elemental sword of fire twitching in her hand. "He considered all of Sorbold a dry latrine, 'godforsaken and smelling endlessly of piss and bad libation, no matter where one goes,' I think that is what he said."

"Think harder," the ancient Cymrian scout said. "What did he tell you about the Radashajn Pass, or Vornessta specifically?"

The Sorbold cavalry was close enough for them to feel the trembling of the ground beneath the hooves of their mounts now.

Rhapsody could not tear her eyes away from them, even knowing the battle that was raging just behind her.

"'An ash-pit,' I think he said. Nothing of use, not even the flax for their linen mills will grow in the northern regions, just—just—"

She glanced up to her right to see Solarrs looking back down at her.

"Just the iron ore of the mountains," she finished.

"Ore mined by slaves," Solarrs said. "M'lady—look."

She turned her back on the approaching mounted death and raised her eyes to the jutting mountain crag across the valley.

From the great yawning mouth revealed by the opening of the enormous stone doors, men were spilling, men pale of skin from their long loss of the sun, hard of muscle, long of hair and beard, gaunt and scrawny from the meanness of their lives and the thinness of food their captors had provided.

From every corner of the Earth, the human spoils of scores, if not hundreds, of brutal invasions, they erupted from their mountain prison and charged down the sides of its fangline face, swinging picks and chisels, the tools of their indentured labor, hardened and ridged in diamond to allow for blades sharp enough to harvest the ore that had, no doubt, been manufactured into the very weapons the southern Sorbold soldiers were wielding against the Alliance atop the canyon rim.

Wanton murder in their eyes.

With speed born of musculature formed by ceaseless drudgery and lives that had existed solely for enforced labor, the slaves of the iron mines of Vornessta dashed as one endless mind bent on vengeance across the Radashajn Pass.

Heading for what was left of the Sorbold army division.

The Sorbolds, bent as they were on engagement, had not yet noticed them.

Three crested the rise together. One engaged two of the soldiers holding the line, only to be heaved back into the canyon into his comrades, but the other two savagely sliced through one of Solarrs's men and stumbled, sweating and panting, aiming for the First Generation scout and the Lady Cymrian.

"He said he had been—planting the seeds—of a rebellion," Rhapsody said, bracing for the charge as she glanced behind her again at the approaching cavalry of the northern Sorbold division. She dodged the soldier's sword thrust by going low, then slashed him across the knees and drove her blade into his abdomen.

Solarrs, who had already dispensed with his own attacker, kicked hers, bleeding profusely, back over the rim and down into the canyon again.

"Not surprising," he muttered, wiping the sweat from his brow with the back of his forearm, his sword at his side. "Anborn was a born revolutionary. Nothing—galled him more than a sedate and presumptuous—ruling class, even if he was one of them."

Rhapsody peered over the rim.

The tide of newly freed slaves was attacking the Sorbold forces from behind, tearing them from their perches or the handholds to which they clung and ripping through their armor with their chisels and trowels.

The blast of a horn, low and foreign, rent the air.

The soldiers of the Alliance turned behind them once again, into the fury of the assault from the north.

And stared in shock.

Behind the charging Sorbold force was another cavalry, outnumbering them three times over, just as the Sorbolds outnumbered the remains of the division of the Alliance. But these were not new Alliance divisions, at least not as Anborn would have counted them.

Stout men on stout horses, thirty thousand or more, with rich-colored banners flying, a shining gold standard rippling in the wind at the head of their column.

Solarrs began to tremble.

"Impossible," he whispered.

"Sweet One-God," Rhapsody murmured. "Is that—is that—?"

"It's the Nain," Cavanur said, almost reverently. "My God—I haven't seen them thus since the Cymrian War."

"I don't understand," Rhapsody said as the massive division, armed with lance and crossbow, unleashed a rainstorm of bolts into the backs of the charging Sorbold cavalry. "Faedryth swore he would never commit forces to this conflict."

"Believe me, Lady, war on this scale can shake even the most sincere and deeply held oaths," Solarrs said, looking back over to the canyon where, between the Alliance forces above them and the slaves behind him, the Sorbold division was beginning to crumble into the slag pile that had been spread across the canyon floor. "There's not much point to being the only one left alive when an enemy has all the other cards."

From deep within her numb soul, Rhapsody felt a new spirit rise, one that was part valor, and a bigger part hatred.

"I tire of this," she said, wiping her blade on her trousers and surveying the mayhem that the Nain were visiting upon what a moment before had been their oncoming attackers. "Let's put an end to it. Having never heard the call before, I have been summoned by wind as a Kinsman not once but twice this day, and have been only marginally successful in either case."

She glanced from horizon to horizon. All around her, on every side, it appeared that the entirety of the world was at war.

"Gentlemen, it's been an honor to serve with you," she said to the remains of the Cymrian division and its leaders. "Let us cast our lot with our allies, whether they be reluctant Nain or manic slaves, and do the best we can to have some part of a world worth saving when it's over, whether we live through the tribulation or not."

All around her, voices answered in the language of the long-dead Island of Serendair in a glad shout.

Vid, Liacor.

Aye, m'lady.

57

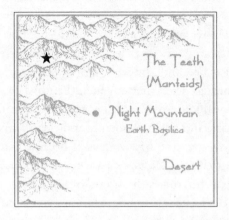

The Teeth
(Manteids)

Night Mountain
Earth Basilica

Desert

THE NOW-QUIET RIM OF THE CANYON, RADASHAJN PASS, VORNESSTA, SORBOLD

When there is not abject surrender, there can be resolution, but not peace.

And there is only very rarely abject surrender.

The words of her beloved late mentor, Oelendra Andaris, came back to Rhapsody, unbidden, as she paced angrily back and forth on the canyon rim.

Early into the afternoon of the next day, the War of the Known World seemed to finally be over.

Or at least its end was beginning.

There was no way the Lady Cymrian or any of the participants could have known that at the time. The scope of the conflict was so vast, so international, that until they were told that Talquist had yielded or died, there could be no sense of completion, no safety.

No peace.

But at least the largest of the skirmishes was finally over.

It had been a brutal battle, one that incurred great loss on all sides. The slaves of Vornessta had displayed the greatest rage, without question, and their oppression and the burning desire for revenge added momentum to their brawling combat, but even the stoutest heart needs armor, another of the Lirin sayings Rhapsody had learned from her mentor.

After initial success brought about by the unfettered element of surprise, the starving men from the iron-ore mines were brutally sliced down, losing a quarter of their number within the first half hour.

The Nain had fared far better by the numbers, she thought, continuing to pace. Well armed and armored, well horsed, and well trained, they were fresh and spirited when they engaged the northern Sorbold division, and their addition to the melee was a welcome one for the exhausted troops of the Alliance. They had quickly and cleanly dispatched a goodly number of the enemy in the first volleys of bolts, the first series of lance attacks, but after the initial release of battle rage and the good spirit of rescue, particularly of the troops the friend of their king, Anborn ap Gwylliam, had loved, the inevitable ugliness of war descended, war that most of them had never seen, even in the battle of the Fallen that had taken place four years before at the council that had named Ashe and Rhapsody to the titles of Lord and Lady Cymrian.

They seemed to be rebounding now, she noted as she cast a bitter glance in the direction of their encampment. *A single battle claims over one hundred thousand lives, and they are most concerned about arranging for their victory feast.* Entitled as they were to their celebrations, Rhapsody could not help but be disenchanted by them.

Her own forces were making their way, like ghosts, to the medic tents that were being set up away from the canyon's rim on the bloodstained ground where so many Sorbolds, Nain, and Alliance soldiers had fallen. Signal fires fought for fuel with the need for the massive pyres the aftermath of a battle of this scope required, and though the support troops were doing everything they could to address the wounded, a few had still died, wandering aimlessly until they succumbed, in spite of aid being within their reach.

While the healing supplies were being gathered and distributed, Solarrs caught up with her. He seemed puzzled at her pacing, and, finding the conversation in which he remained stationary while she paced angrily back and forth to be awkward, he began accompanying her on her futile trek.

"Knapp has arrived from Bethany," he said, trying to match her pace and route.

"Did he bring the medical supplies?"

"Yes, m'lady."

"Good. What news of Navarne? Of Yarim?"

"Both assaults were turned back, as you know. Peace is still holding."

"Also good."

"Word by avian messanger implies that the Merchant Emperor may be missing, presumed dead."

"Even better."

"Forgive me, m'lady," Solarrs said haltingly as they continued to stride the same ground back and forth in a seemingly endless pattern. "Can you stop long enough to explain what has you so—so—"

"So—what?"

"So off center," the First Generation Cymrian said with the gentlest tone of respect he could summon. "So—so—*beside yourself.* We prevailed, Rhapsody—the cost was atrocious, but we were the defenders here, not the aggressors. Stop pacing, m'lady, I beg you, and tell me what, atop of the shock and horror of battle, has you so rattled."

Rhapsody's trek stopped in midstride.

"This—this is not how it is supposed—to happen," she panted, savagely unbuckling her sword belt and hurling it to the ground. "Each time I—know of, when the Kinsman call is answered—aid is able to be—given. Why—why did the wind bring me—here to just stand—and *witness this?* If I could be—of no help whatsoever—"

"Perhaps the Lord Marshal needed to see you before—before—"

"Before he died, Solarrs? Before he threw his life away? Before he was crushed to death, torn asunder, before both of our eyes? Before the life was stamped out of him by every bloody Sorbold in the valley? They *tore his head off and ground it to dust*—"

Solarrs looked down at the sandy heath and sighed dismally. He turned away and walked back toward the rim, searching the ground, until he came upon what he was seeking.

He bent and retrieved it, then returned to where Rhapsody was standing, running her hands violently through her hair as if she sought to pull it out by the roots.

And held it up before her eyes.

It was a bastard sword, one of modest manufacture, unadorned, battle-battered, bloodied.

Anborn's sword.

Rhapsody's frenzy abated. She stopped clutching her hair and stared at the weapon, breathing heavily.

She recalled it from the time she had met the Lord Marshal, unaware of who he was, thinking him merely an arrogant rogue with a large weapon atop a beautiful horse on the forest path, callously coming close to riding down children who were playing in a spring warm spell. The mud from the road had ended up across his face, at her hand, and from that moment had begun one of the warmest, dearest, and most convoluted relationships in her life from the time she had come to the new world.

She stood still and continued to stare at the sword.

She recalled it sheathed across Anborn's back as he appeared in response to her Kinsman call in a bitter winter wind, his black shadow atop the distant image of a black horse in the snow of the southern forest, rescuing her from freezing to death; remembered the sight of him, laying low the armies of the Fallen with it in the Battle of the Moot; and, though lame, riding down Michael's henchmen who had come to kidnap her from atop his horse in the specially devised saddle, taking out a captain's share of them before his mount was shot out from under him.

And how she had left him in the burning forest, having spoken words of sleep and healing, knowing she was about to be taken.

Anborn ap Gwylliam, live; live for me.

In the farthest reaches of her mind, she could picture him still, bending down on one knee before her in the darkness beyond the celebration of her ascension to the Ladyship at the Cymrian Council.

You have my allegiance, Rhapsody—my sworn allegiance—whether as the Lady Cymrian, the Lady of the Lirin, or just as a lady. My sword and my life are yours, for your protection and need.

"I am well and truly honored," she whispered, now as she had when he had sworn himself to her.

Solarrs saw the look in her eyes change, and turned the sword over in his hands, examining it idly.

"He threw it to the ground just before he charged down into the valley," he mused, holding it up in the light of the campfires. "It was not a significant weapon, and Anborn was not a sentimental man; I suppose he just didn't want to give the enemy the pleasure of taking it from him."

"No," Rhapsody said. "No, he knew what would happen. He didn't want to enter the Afterlife as a soldier, just as a man."

She thought back to the last discussion they had undertaken before the outbreak of war, on a rocky ledge in Ylorc.

He had confided a secret that he said no one alive knew—that he had a wife long before, a woman named Damynia, and though he would tell her nothing more of the story, he made it clear that the loss of her had been what transformed him from the idealistic young soldier whom his

First Generation friends remembered to the terror of the battlefield he had become in the Cymrian War.

It was a memory so scarring that he had refused to ever say goodbye to Rhapsody without getting a kiss in return, a strange custom for a man who scoffed at the concept of marriage in the current day.

Your undeserved faith in me has awakened something in me I thought long dead; I am remembering again a time when life's ideals and aspirations actually meant something to me, when camaraderie and valor and love of land and kin were the reasons to pick up arms, not wanton violence and the rage of revenge. It's sparking in me a rebirth of a sorts, a hope of absolution, making whatever sacrifices, whatever efforts in the coming war worth something meaningful; you cannot imagine how important this is to me, after a life as long as mine, time which I have passed, dead inside, until I met you. I have sworn allegiance to no one since Gwylliam, and when I did that I was unrecognizable as a human being. I am not understating this, Rhapsody; you are right that it is a good thing we did not meet in earlier days, because you would have hated me, as the entire empire did. You are well aware that my freedom is what I prize above most other things, but I am not certain you made the connection that my sworn allegiance to you was a voluntary surrender, a limitation on that freedom, that wherever you are, your safety, your need, is my happiest priority now. It is because of that allegiance, and because of you, that I wade back into this fray as the man, the leader I was born to be—unlike the villain I was because of Damynia.

"If only I could cry, perhaps I would feel less—less—"

Solarrs waited quietly.

"Lost," she finally said.

The ancient scout exhaled deeply.

"We will all be trying to find our ways out of this loss for the rest of our lives," he said simply. "A man like Anborn comes along but once in a lifetime; it will be a long time before we will heal. The best advice I can give you is to take comfort in your memories; in the end, they are all that any of us who share an unwieldy longevity have left to comfort us."

He put the sword down gently on the ground and walked away.

Rhapsody waited until she could no longer see his shadow, then reached out and touched the weapon. She heard Anborn's voice on the wind in the distance, speaking the words he had uttered just before he had gone off into the teeth of the war.

Buck up, m'lady; there's no need to be weepy. You are the mother of a fine, strong son who lives and thrives, all predictions to the contrary, even mine. It's a bright morning, with fair weather, and it turns out your husband was heeding my warnings after all, so a worthy fighting force with Right on its side is gathering as we speak, coming to the rescue of an Alliance well worth saving. It's quite a glorious day to be alive. Keep out of harm's way as much as you can, and call me on the wind, Kinsman to Kinsman, if you are ever in need.

His eyes had twinkled; he turned away and started down the mountain pass to the steppes of the Krevensfield Plain below. He had gone a score of paces when he stopped and looked back over his shoulder.

Goodbye, Rhapsody.

Just as he had called to her before the Sorbold army swallowed him.

Rhapsody hung her head for a moment longer.

Then she rose, brushed the sand and the grit from her dragonscale armor and trousers, and went back into the encampment where the wounded awaited her ministrations.

58

The Teeth
(Manteids)

★

• Night Mountain
Earth Basilica

Desert

MOUNTAIN HEATH ABOVE THE
RADASHAJN PASS, VORNESSTA, SORBOLD

The line of injured soldiers stretched into the darkness, beyond the radiance of the torchlight that surrounded the encampment.

The Lady Cymrian, attired in the same black full-body apron and blue headscarf that the other medics wore, was in the open air tending to the walking wounded, having sung songs of extreme healing to those most critically injured to varying degrees of success. She was bandaging a young man from Anborn's regiment when Solarrs and Knapp appeared, one almost immediately after the other, looking for her.

"M'lady, they are bringing in a high-level prisoner," Knapp said, signaling to several soldiers to light additional torches that were propped around the encampment and gesturing to other guards to fall into formation in front of the Lady Cymrian.

Rhapsody exhaled and finished tying up the arm of the bleeding soldier in front of her.

"He or she will have to wait until I am finished with the wounded, Knapp," she said crossly, "unless there is some urgency that you—"

Her words ground to a halt.

Standing in the flickering radiance of the torches just coming to light was a man she recognized, an older man with a fulsome beard and the heavy furs and primitive armor of the cold lands beyond the northern border of the Alliance. He was surrounded by a party of guards with their weapons trained on him.

Hjorst, the Diviner of the Hintervold.

She stared at him in utter silence, with only the crackling of the campfires and torches joining the howl of the night wind. Finally she spoke.

"You came with your men? Fought alongside them?"

The Diviner nodded silently.

"Which citadel did you attack?"

The bearded leader remained silent.

"He and his forces were defeated and taken in Yarim, m'lady," said Solarrs.

"I see." She turned her attention back to the Diviner. "I cannot tell you how surprised and disappointed I was to discover your Icemen in Bethany and the other citadels of Roland alongside the forces of Sorbold. I had been under the grave misconception that you were a friend to the Alliance, Your Grace. The Lord Cymrian gave you a tariff-free grain treaty that could only be described as generous; I gave you plantings, helped you with your agriculture. Did you not write to me and tell me that your harvest two years ago had all but doubled in volume?"

When the shaman finally spoke, his voice was terse and raspy. "I did."

"This is an interesting way of expressing thanks and friendship in return."

"That was before I became aware of your husband's plans to invade and occupy the Riverlands."

The Lady Cymrian's eyes narrowed. "What are you talking about? There have never been any such plans."

"I saw them with my own eyes."

"I have no doubt that your eyes were not deceiving you. That, unfortunately, is exactly what Talquist has been doing—deceiving you."

The Diviner's heavy brows drew together as he lapsed into silence again.

"Does it not seem odd to you, Your Grace, that you and your soldiers have all been captured within the provincial capitals of the Alliance, defeated by armies of women and children left behind to defend those cities, if we were in fact planning to attack and absorb your southern Riverlands? Have you, on the other hand, seen any of our forces north of the Tar'afel or the Erim Rus? In your lands? Half of our soldiers are deployed in the southern part of the Middle Continent, along the Threshold of Death, defending our own breadbasket lands—"

"You have been starving my people for more than a year now." The Diviner's voice was shaky with a combination of bravado and creeping realization. "The grain promised in your husband's treaty either never arrived, or was poisoned with rat droppings and mold."

Rhapsody eyed him sharply.

"And, while I'm sure that was infuriating to the point of wanted vengeance, perhaps did it occur to you that the responsibility for that may have been in the hands of the one who was in charge of *transporting* that grain to you—or interdicting it, so that it never arrived?"

"I—I wrote to you—I demanded an explanation, and was met with silence—"

"Did you send those missives by ship?" She swallowed as Hjorst's face went slack. "Do not blame yourself, Your Grace—the deception with which Talquist manipulated the Known World into a war that could win him the continent and the lands beyond it is true artistry, if you admire that sort of thing. It was a long-planned conquest, making use of a lifetime's work, connections and trade alliances built over decades, like his association with you, and an impressive control of the seas which gave him dominion over a good deal of the ability to communicate between nations.

"The natural tendency of the rulers of lands to demean the merchant class is what allowed it to happen; when the Scales of Jierna Tal named him emperor, it never occurred to anyone that merchants have had their thumbs subtly on scales from the beginning of Time. The only one who saw it coming was the Patriarch, because he knew well what sort of merchandise Talquist regularly traded in—human lives. That is why Talquist attacked Sepulvarta first; because Constantin knew that he was a slave trader, who used his armies to decimate towns, villages, and nations and drag their citizens back as captives to work in his iron mines and linen factories and other foundries and sweatshops that provided the weapons and armaments for his war."

Even in the dim light of the torches, Rhapsody and the soldiers could see the Diviner's frost-browned face pale noticeably.

He had been given a tour of the occupied holy city by Talquist himself after the emperor's coronation.

Rhapsody's aspect hardened. "Anborn knew it would happen, too, I suppose—he always felt war in the air, though even he could not have foreseen the extent of Talquist's ruthlessness. On the day he learned of the deaths of the empress and the crown prince, he told the Lord Cymrian what would come to pass."

She closed her eyes, remembering his words, which had floated into the cool darkness of the carriage in which she had lain, roiling in the throes of the nausea of what must have been early pregnancy.

Mark this moment in your mind, nephew; this is the day when the war that is to come began.

When the emerald-green eyes opened again, they were full of rage.

"And now he is dead, ground to dust and buried in a mountain of slag and the bodies of men and horses—my sworn knight, the Lord Marshal of the Alliance, whom a thousand years of battle could not take down. Part of the cost of you deciding not to at least *ask* what was happening with your grain is too great to be borne, Your Grace. Talquist may have controlled all contact by sea, but a simple messenger sent to Haguefort or Highmeadow might have averted the War of the Known World. It is a shame that a man blessed with foresight, who divines the Future, missed such blatant manipulation."

"I have paid dearly for it," the Diviner whispered, suddenly gray. "I have lost my second-eldest son."

The Lady Cymrian eyed him without sympathy.

"That is unfortunate," she said. "You and tens of thousands of other fathers. Highly unfortunate."

Solarrs and Knapp, standing by as she spoke, looked at each other in surprise. There was not even a hint of gentleness in her voice, so unlike the comfort they had always heard there. They watched as she continued to stare at the prisoner, no mercy or forgiveness apparent in her face.

And were cheered by that absence.

"I am at a loss for words," the Diviner said finally. "Anything I would say now would be woefully meager, incommensurate with what I have done. Do unto me what you will."

The Lady Cymrian nodded curtly. She turned to the Lord Marshal's men-at-arms.

"Knapp," she said, her tone brusque, "bring me Anborn's bastard sword."

The First Generation soldiers exchanged a glance; then Knapp nodded and ran to retrieve the weapon.

"Kneel, Your Grace," Rhapsody said as she saw Anborn's man returning, the long battered blade in his hand.

The Diviner sighed silently and removed the enormous war helm on which the lifelike image of an arctic tiger was engraved. He slowly got down on one knee and bent his head.

Rhapsody took the hilt of the weapon as Knapp outstretched his arm and ran her fingers over the blade, stained with gore and clotted blood that had not been let in battle, but clearly come from bodies that had fallen atop it.

"This will not do," she said aloud, more to herself than to the others. "It should be clean, at least. That's only proper." She pulled her water-skin from her leather baldric, doused the blade, and wiped it off with her cloak. Then she pointed the blade, tip down, to the ground before the averted eyes of the Diviner at an angle where he could see it.

"This was the sword of the Lord Marshal," she said solemnly. "A common blade, one of dozens, perhaps scores that he wielded over time—"

From the edge of the encampment an uproar broke out.

In response to Rhapsody's surprise, the flames in the torches roared with life, then settled down into a seething burn again.

From outside the encampment a din was growing, and a swell of humanity was moving forth to where the leaders were standing with their prisoner. There was hooting and cheering as a man in chains was shoved along at the head of the processional, with arms trained on him at all times.

Dysmore, a lieutenant in Anborn's elite force, was shepherding the prisoner along.

"M'lady!" he shouted. "M'lady, by your leave, look!"

The Lady Cymrian stood straighter and gestured for Knapp and So-larrs to help the Diviner rise.

Amid a veritable thunderstorm of cursing and spittle from the soldiers accompanying the captive, a tattered soldier could be intermittently seen, shielding his head and face from the blows and shouting that were aimed at it as best he could with his shoulders. The man seemed young, though Rhapsody could see very little more in the twisting and inconstant firelight of the torches.

When Dysmore and his prisoner reached the center of the encampment, the lieutenant shoved the chained captive forward, into the presence of the Lady Cymrian. The guards who had been assigned by Knapp to protect her closed ranks around her, aiming their missile weapons at the prisoner so that he was surrounded on four sides.

Now that he was nearer, Rhapsody was certain that she had never seen him before, but there was a familiarity to him that she could not discern. It was apparent that he was a Sorbold, dark of hair, eye, and skin, with a neatly trimmed beard and a tall, broad-shouldered frame. She signaled to the guards before her to step aside and came forward, Anborn's blade in her hand, her face set in a studied look.

"Who is this?"

"Titactyk, m'lady," said Dysmore, breathing heavily and struggling to settle the crowd of soldiers behind him. "Leader of the Sorbold assault force, second-in-command to Fhremus Alo'hari. He was caught fleeing with what was left of the second cohort after the rout here in Vornessta."

Suddenly an image formed in her mind, one she had seen in her nightmares, and the Lady Cymrian nodded. "Are you the man who led the raid on the Abbey of Nikkid'sar?" she asked.

The captive said nothing. He glanced around nervously, his eyes glittering.

"He was apparently heard boasting about it in brothels and some of the taverns in the border towns, m'lady," said Dysmore. "This has been repeatedly verified by the scouts."

"That's not true—" the man blurted. "Please—"

"What do you have to say for yourself?" Rhapsody asked. "This is your chance. Be honest."

"I am innocent," the man said quickly. "Please, m'lady—mercy—"

The Lady Cymrian nodded again. "You are actually a liar, not an innocent," she said. "I can hear it in your voice, in the frequency of your tone; there is no truth in it. That was a grave mistake."

She turned on her heel and strode back to the Diviner, who was standing, frozen in silence, his eyes the only moving part of him. She stopped in front of him and, with one smooth overhead arc of her arm, drove the tip of the bastard sword into the ground at his feet.

"That is for you," she said to the Diviner. "I would not soil Anborn's blade with the blood of his like."

She looked back at Titactyk as she pulled forth the coiled tongue whip from her side.

Both men's eyes widened.

The Lady Cymrian left the weapon wedged in the ground and walked purposefully back to the chained captive.

"Kneel," she commanded.

"M'lady—"

Rhapsody nodded; Dysmore and three of the soldiers behind him stepped forward rapidly and seized the man by the shoulders and head, slamming him to the ground on his knees.

"Please, m'lady, do not put me to the lash," the Sorbold soldier whispered. "You are dressed as a medic, well known for your mercy—"

"That must have been before I read the field report from Nikkid'sar," Rhapsody interrupted harshly. "Long before, actually. I do not remember a time when I felt sufficient mercy to pardon anyone, let alone a man who would sanction, commit, and lead the rape and murder of powerless women, the gang-sodomizing of a woman of the cloth, and the flinging of infants, live, into the sea by catapult in a game of sport. You are no soldier; you are a criminal, an animal. Your atrocities have violated my dreams; I have seen your perversions in visions that have left me shaking."

"Please—"

"Spare me your whining and your family the embarrassment. Until the Lord Cymrian returns, and with the death of the Lord Marshal, I am, unfortunately for both of us, your judge. For that raid, and any other crimes you have committed, I sentence you to death."

"*M'lady—*"

"*Silence.* You gave no heed to the pleas of innocents; I do not wish to hear another word from you." In a vicious sweep, Rhapsody drew Daystar Clarion; the blade roared forth from its scabbard, its flames rippling angrily, its call ringing clearly. "Move back," she said to Dysmore and the three other soldiers; they stood and stepped away quickly as she advanced.

In one last desperate move, Titactyk lurched, trying to rise.

Just as he did, Rhapsody snapped the tongue whip with her left hand, encircling Titactyk's neck and dragging him to her feet. Then she leapt into the air, swinging the sword over her head, and brought it down solidly on his neck, the blade of elemental fire and ether slipping like a hot knife through the butter of his skin and skeleton, severing his head cleanly from his shoulders. It spun to the ground, where it landed with a thud, its eyes still wide, the jugular vein pulsing as it gushed blood onto the dirt behind it for a moment until the wound sealed, cauterized by the flames of the sword.

A gasp rose from the group of soldiers, then resolved into a raucous cheer.

"Silence," the Lady Cymrian commanded quietly again; her tone rang through the air of the encampment, bringing the celebration to an abrupt end. "Bind up the body and remove it as you would any other enemy soldier, with respect in death."

Dysmore bowed slightly and signaled to specific troops as she sheathed her sword, re-coiled the whip, and turned back to the Diviner, whose heavily browed and bearded face was white in the shadows of the torches.

"I will not beg, nor will I resist," the Diviner said. "His sniveling was appalling. I will not dishonor my people in that way." He knelt before her.

Rhapsody's eyes kindled to a deeper green in the light of the torches.

"I was telling you of Anborn's sword," she said, equally quietly, looking down at the ruler of the Hintervold. "While he was a man of fastidious taste when it came to horseflesh, he did not aspire to carry an elemental weapon, or even a particularly fine one. He felt the advantage in battle was in the skill of the soldier, not the superiority of the blade, though he did have a standard beneath which he generally did not choose to go in selecting a sword. I know he carried this one for at least a century."

She lapsed into silence.

"So you are telling me that you will execute me with a common blade, in spite of my office?" said the Diviner dully. "I do not object—it is no more than I deserve."

Rhapsody crouched down until she was balanced, on the balls of her feet, at eye level with him.

"I am not going to execute you at all," she said. "You are going to help me find him."

The Diviner blinked.

"Find him? Who?"

"Anborn—the Lord Marshal." She glanced in the direction of the valley below the encampment, where the body of her friend was buried in the mountainous detritus of battle along with those of Sorbolds, slaves, horses, and soldiers of the Alliance, human, Lirin, Bolg, and Nain alike.

"How—how do you expect me to do that?"

"You will begin by rising now."

The Diviner complied slowly as the Lady Cymrian rose with him. She exhaled when she was standing erect again.

"Did you not tell me when I came to visit you in the Hintervold several years ago, every time you were in your cups, if I recall correctly, the story of how you found Jurun's grave in Cariproth?"

The cloud of nerves and worry in the old man's eyes cleared.

"I may have," he said grudgingly. "I had accomplished that a year or so before."

"You used a silver willow branch that King Jurun had held—I believe it was thought to be the last thing he had so held, yes?"

"Yes."

"Well, this sword is the last object that Anborn held—he threw it to the ground before he charged down into the valley. That's what I meant when I said it was for you—I ask that you help find whatever—whatever *part* of him you can, if anything can be recovered, so that I might properly mourn and bury him. I am a Namer, Your Grace; burial rituals are a major part of my training, my earliest training. He was sworn to me; if there is any link between the two of us that you can divine, or between him and his bastard sword, I ask you to find it, and locate whatever remains you can. I will commit them through the funeral pyre to the wind that he served as a Kinsman."

The Diviner stared at her for a long moment. Then he bowed his head.

"I would be honored to be allowed to attempt it," he said. "But there is likely little, if anything, left to find. And, unlike Titactyk, I will not lie to you, deceive you. If I am not certain the remains are his, I will not pretend that they are, even if it would save my life."

"That is all I ask. Your life is not forfeit at this time; all of us have been unfortunate enough to experience Talquist's deceit and manipulation to our own loss. Come, and I will escort you into the valley, unless you need to wait until sunrise."

"Actually, no," said the Diviner. "The echoes, if any remain, will be easier to divine in the dark."

The Lady Cymrian signaled to the soldier who held Hjorst's tiger helm, and the man hurried over, returning it.

"Very well," she said, dismissing the solider and handing the Diviner Anborn's sword. "Let us go down into that valley of death together, Your Grace. We will be silent; eventually, when you have done what you can, I need you to explain to me how Talquist tricked you into believing that your neighbors sought to invade your realm."

The Diviner's eyes began to shine.

"I fear I must also confess to you, m'lady, that I performed a divination for him about your child," he said, his face colored in shame. "I may have given him the means to find your baby."

Rhapsody nodded. "I know."

"You—you *know?*"

"Yes; I watched you."

"How—how—"

"Come, Your Grace," she said impatiently. "There will be time to speak later, of things I do and do not remember, as well as those things that I wish to always be able to recall. This task is one of those last things."

The old man straightened the helm on his head, then nodded as the Lady Cymrian drew her sword again.

Together he and Rhapsody made their way down into the valley, past the distressed eyes of her guards, lighted only by the flames of Daystar Clarion, pulsing like a beating heart of fire.

As darkness approached the following night, the army of the Alliance began to gather in the valley of the canyon and on the heath above the Radashajn Pass in the glow of the newly lighted battlefield fires. In the light of day the wounded had been attended to, the destruction was beginning to be cleared away, burial and assessment of prisoners took place efficiently and quickly. Solarrs had commented that it was always a shame when such tasks became routine.

But when the sun began to set, the restoration ceased suddenly and silently. A separate unit of soldiers had been working on each of the neighboring peaks, and had signaled the completion of their duties as Rhapsody and Hjorst stood at the rim of the canyon overlooking the site of the flood of mine slag once more.

The towering pile of waste still stood, a new hill at the bottom of the canyon, the bodies of horses and of men being slowly recovered and committed to simple graves. The newly freed slaves and Faedryth's Nain army had joined in the recovery efforts and gathered now with the soldiers of the Alliance, spread across the floor of the canyon, looking up at the barrow of sticks, brambles, and sagebrush that had been carefully built at the rim above.

On the barrow was a rolled cloth, the Lady Cymrian's own cloak, carefully wrapped in a tight cylinder with a small distension in the center. It stretched across the kindling in military fashion, crossing another rectangle of cloth, the flag of the Cymrian Alliance.

Rhapsody stood, the Diviner at her left shoulder and behind, her face set in a serious but calm mien, pale in the light of the setting sun, whispering rites and chants of passage, of loss, of completion. Finally, when she had finished the rituals and liturgies taught to her long ago by her Naming mentor, she raised her eyes to the west, looking beyond the sunset in silence.

Then she drew Daystar Clarion and held it aloft.

The wind itself, whistling through the canyon, seemed to pause for a moment in respect.

The flames of the sword burned quietly, almost as if in respect as well.

Rhapsody leaned a little closer to the pyre.

"I will watch, I will wait," she said softly. "I will call and will be heard."

As if in assent, the wind picked up, blowing the tresses of her hair around her face.

The Lady Cymrian smiled. "Goodbye, Anborn," she whispered in the tongue of her childhood. "May you rest this night in Damynia's arms. Thank you for everything."

Then she stood erect once more and brought the tip of the burning blade to the barrow of sticks and sagebrush.

The pyre caught fire immediately, the brush and brambles gleaming along the lines of their stems, lacy for a moment, then exploding, ripping into flame.

From atop each of the peaks across the canyon fire answered, roaring to life, lighting the mountaintops with glorious radiance, crackling skyward.

From the depths of the canyon floor a shout of gladness arose, rumbling in the voices of men and women, soldiers and former slaves, a salute of fondness and respect that rang across the heath and up to the peaks beyond.

Distantly Rhapsody could hear the voices of the Nain of the Deep Kingdom begin the Chant of Honor, their highest salute to a fallen leader or comrade, but the music faded almost immediately into the wind that was sweeping around her now, rustling her garments and billowing through her hair.

Leaving her numb.

On the canyon floor, Evrit stood, a few paces apart from his fellow former slaves, watching the flames of Anborn's funeral pyre, and the signal fires on the surrounding mountaintops, burning down.

Numb.

A gentle tap on his shoulder nudged him from his reverie.

Evrit turned amid the leaping shadows to see what looked like his own eyes staring back at him.

Jarzben, his elder son, stood before him. Little more than a boy when they had been taken, he had grown into a lean and muscular man with the darkness of enslavement in his expression, which his face was struggling to cast off.

Smiling slightly, something he had not done since the night their gentle religious sect's ship, the *Freedom*, had sundered off the coast of Sorbold.

"Father." It was the only word the young man could form.

Evrit stared at him a moment longer.

Then collapsed in his son's arms, weeping.

When, after a long time, he was finally able to gather himself, he pulled away and looked into Jarzben's face again.

"Selac and your mother?" he whispered. "Do you know anything of them?"

Jarzben shook his head.

"I've been advised to search the streets near the palace chimneys for him, and the linen factories for her," he said, his speech hesitant from lack of use.

Evrit smiled wanly.

"Tomorrow we will set forth to those places and search until we know what has become of them," he said.

And looked up again to the mountaintops, watching the smoke ascend.

Thankful.

59

$\mathscr{A}$she, who had finally arrived, could see her. She was almost close enough to touch.

Her vibrational signature, the unique pitch that his dragon sense could identify innately, was a beacon, like the great light tower of Tallono Harbor.

"Aria?" he whispered.

Rhapsody turned.

She was standing at the crest of a mountain swale surrounded and lit by pools of spattered torchlight. Her face was bruised, and the mail shirt of dragon scales Elynsynos had given her long ago was striped with blood, casting red-gold shadows onto the ground at her feet. Ashe's eyes stung at the sight of her golden hair gleaming in that light, his dragon sense making note of the missing fall of glistening blond tresses that had hung to her knees when he had last been with her. Her cropped locks had stripped some of the feminine aspect from her, making her appear the warrior he always knew her to have been. Daystar Clarion burned steadily in her hand; when she saw him, she gazed at him for a moment, her face solemn; then she sheathed the sword, causing the light around her to dim substantially.

He climbed the swale slowly, struggling to keep from seizing her and dragging her into his arms. Even from a distance, in the dark, he could tell that something was missing; he had known all along that this reunion would be painful, but until he was face-to-face with her, he had no idea how much his dual nature would be horrified by the change in her.

Her emerald eyes, gleaming in the firelight but absent much of their familiar warmth, met his own. When she spoke, her voice, at least, was as he remembered it.

"Are you all right? Are you injured?"

"Only slightly—it's nothing." His own voice broke, and he reached out his hands to her. "Come to me—I love you; gods, I love you. Please come here."

She stepped closer; Ashe sensed that she was uncertain, uncomfortable even. He struggled to keep his need in check.

"I love you," he said again.

His arms remained empty.

The warrior in front of him looked down at the shadowlit ground and sighed.

Ashe's throat went dry, and his blood ran cold. "Can you not respond to me? Do you—do you still love me, Rhapsody?"

The woman slowly raised her eyes to meet his gaze, almost reluctantly.

"I'm sorry," she said quietly. "I don't really know how to answer you."

Ashe choked, and words he had wanted to restrain burst forth from his strangling throat. "The way you have unfailingly before. You have told me 'always' whenever I asked it of you."

"I—I am sorry. I barely know you. I have flashes of memory, of our travels together, most of which took place when you were cloaked in mist, hiding from the world—"

"You are my wife," Ashe whispered. "The mother of my son. The other half of my soul. You gave our child a large part of your true name before you left him in the care of the Nain—"

"I believe you—I do. I can sense in your voice that you are speaking the truth—"

"But you do not remember?"

"No. I do not remember. I am sorry."

Ashe turned suddenly away, overcome with pain.

"Are you all right?" Rhapsody's voice carried the sound of concern, but nothing more.

"No," he said. "The only thing you have ever asked of me is honesty; I have honored that request each day, with each heartbeat, as best as I have been able. I am unwilling to lie to you; your answer breaks my heart. I know you cannot help that; I have understood from the day you told me of your plan to leave your name with our son that it might be painful to come back to you, only to find that you do not love me anymore. But until I heard the words from your mouth, with the ring of True-Speaking,

I had no idea how much I would wish to die upon hearing them. I am by no means 'all right.' I am sorry."

Rhapsody stood silently, absorbing his words. Finally she spoke.

"If I cannot yet be the woman who loves you until we are reunited with our son, and I with my name, I can at least be the woman who wants you."

Ashe exhaled, finally turning to look at her again. "That latter part sounds promising; it takes a bit of the sting away. Can you be more specific?"

"While I may not be able to feel love yet, I can still feel need. And I do—yours, as well as my own."

"And how do you wish to meet this need?"

"Come with me behind the barracks and I'll show you."

With a savage movement, she grasped the dragonscale mail shirt, bloody and brushed with soot, that shielded her chest and dragged it off over her head, tossing it to the ground at her feet, then nodded to the place she had indicated. When he just stared at her, she extended an impatient hand.

Ashe swallowed dryly.

"You—you're not proposing we—make love, are you? Now—here?"

"Love? No. To call it such would be untrue. But you have the right idea." Her gaze hardened. "Are you coming?"

"Rhapsody, from its beginning, without exception, love of incredible depth has been present in our lovemaking—it's never been anything less than that. It has been, at its very least, a communion of hearts as well as of bodies. Since we wed, it has been one of souls as well. Much as I would dearly love to meet your need, and my own, if that love won't be present, I'd rather wait until my wife returns, if you don't mind."

Rhapsody's eyes darkened, but her expression didn't change.

"As you wish," she said evenly. "I feel pained to remind you, however, that there was, in fact, an exception—one night of nothing but need, in a howling wind, in the darkness of the Teeth, up against just such a mountain wall. Tonight, at least, I remember that pounding need being satisfied, and in my memory the man who granted me that release was you, I think. It wasn't what either of us really wanted, but it was enough at that moment."

Ashe shuddered, remembering the incident she referenced.

"And, if you recall, that one exception led you to unspeakable pain, grief, and terror," he said, "since afterwards you didn't know for certain that it had been me in the darkness. The demon manipulated you mercilessly because of it."

"Maybe—I really don't remember that part, I'm sorry. It's not that dark. I can see you clearly now." She shrugged. "But suit yourself. Take care of your injuries and those of your troops. I'll find other ways to sate my need." She turned, snatched up her armor, and started back down the side of the swale.

Ashe's throat tightened as the dragon rose, avaricious, stripping the moisture from the air, making it hum with dryness.

"And with whom do you plan to sate this need, my love, if not with me?"

Rhapsody stopped and turned back to him.

"The quartermaster," she said flatly. She paused, feeling the static filling the wind around her.

Unconsciously Ashe gripped the hilt of his sword.

"The *quartermaster*?" he demanded, the multiple tones of the wyrm rising in his voice. "Who is this soon-to-be-dead man—"

"I've no idea," she interrupted, her Namer's tone slicing through the wind, causing his words to crumble and falter, "other than the soldier who will be responsible for helping me work to the point of exhaustion throughout this night and into morning, packing and provisioning for our journey to retrieve our child and, hopefully, my name—which is *how* I will sate my need. I said 'in other ways,' not 'with other men.' Spare the quartermaster; to kill him would truly be unwarranted, unless he refuses to move fast enough in bringing me the provisions. Then by all means, cut his head off."

She climbed back to the top of the swale and gazed into his face, her eyes narrow and unblinking.

Ashe exhaled shortly.

"Sorry," he said, the draconic tones fading from his voice. "My other nature is beside itself at the change in you; I don't know how to behave around you when you are like this. To avoid drowning in loss, the dragon reverts to jealousy."

Rhapsody's eyes broke with his, and she looked at the ground.

"That part of me which thinks this aspect of you is endearing must still reside in the Nain kingdom," she said after a moment. "What's left of me at the moment finds it annoying and peevish. But no doubt you are feeling the same way about the diminished me. I will take my leave from you now, then, so that we will not damage what we hold sacred when we are our true selves again. But understand this, Ashe; just because I cannot feel my love for you now does not mean that I have ever forgotten the vow I apparently made to you—*ever*." She raised the back of her left hand to his eyes. "I did not even need this wedding band to remind me, at least most of the time. Your suspicion and lack of trust insults me. It's probably a good thing I can feel nothing; if I could, I would doubtless be hurt by your lack of faith in me. Go look in on your men and get your wounds dressed, even if they are minor. I will see you in the morning." She turned and strode back down the swale.

"Wait, please." Ashe noted the fury that swam through the muscles of her back as she came to a halt once more. He followed her down the swale and stopped behind her.

"Please," he said softly. "May I touch you? I need to hold you."

Rhapsody's back straightened. "Not tonight." At the utter absence of sound that followed, she turned and looked levelly at him, and winced at the pain in his eyes. She exhaled and dropped her gaze again.

"You did not understand what I meant by my need, and yours," she said quietly, without emotion. "You forget, Ashe, there is a part of your soul in me, though it is tied to my old name, and even if I cannot feel the love I know I have for you, I *can* feel the loss I share with you through that connection. And it has nothing to do with my missing name, or even being separated from our child this night."

Ashe exhaled. "Then what is it, Aria?"

Her brow blackened, and Rhapsody's face twisted into an expression of devouring pain mixed with anger.

"What I am feeling, and you should be as well, is the loss of *Anborn*," she all but spat. "The death of your uncle—my sworn knight. Your kinsman, and, in a completely different way, my own. The man who rescued me, naked and dying, in a black storm in the forest edge of Sorbold five years ago, who caught me from the sky as I fell from Anwyn's grip in the Moot—who would have saved me from Michael's kidnapping last year had I not lamed him in that fall. Forgive me if I cannot remember the feeling of love in being reunited with my husband—I am mourning the death of my *friend*."

Ashe reached for her but she pulled away from him, struggling to keep from striking out in the growing wind.

"There was barely anything left of him to bury, Ashe. Though the pyre for his remains lighted the whole of the mountaintops, if we had been inclined to only use enough kindling to immolate what survived the onslaught, the blaze could have been small enough to barely warm a pot of campfire soup. He left behind little more than a river of blood staining the ground, his broken weapons, and a few scraps of metal and cloth, his bones ground utterly to dust save for a piece of his jaw and the wrist of his sword arm, which were a hundred paces apart from one another.

"After all the times he saved me, after all he sacrificed in my service, I was unable to come to his aid the one time he needed me. He summoned me to this place, called me as a Kinsman on the wind, only to have me *fail* him; I stood, impotent, as nothing more than a witness to his death. He died grinning, laughing at the sky, in the advent of being stamped out in one of the most gruesome, horrific endings I've ever heard tell of— me, the Lirin Namer, Singer of endless battlefield dirges and historic tales of brutal death. And I cannot even bring a single tear to bear for that loss, because I'm missing the piece of me that knows how to cry.

"So forgive me if I tried to give vent to the rage that is burning what is left of my soul alive. Forgive me for reaching out to you in anger, in *hate*, instead of in love. Forgive me for craving the sweet oblivion of ruthlessly knobbing you in the muddy darkness in back of the broken barracks rather than tearing my own throat in screaming until I break my own eardrums, since my heart isn't here to break instead. Because *that* is what I am feeling, Ashe. *That* is my need. Forgive me if I thought for a moment that you felt it, too. Forgive me if I thought that we could sate that need together, if only in a communion of bodies, rather than hearts and souls. My mistake."

The whine of the whipping wind rose angrily, punctuating her final words.

Rhapsody turned once more and started off into the night.

Only to be grasped harshly by the arm and spun around again.

Ashe glared down into her eyes, his searing blue gaze meeting the green fire of hers.

"You don't think I loved my uncle? You don't think I am mourning him as well? You don't think I feel the void in the very *world* at his loss?"

Rhapsody returned his stare without blinking.

"Actually, I *know* you do—that is not in question. The only question is how we cope with that loss. I thought we would do it together, in a reunion that might not be what we want, but what we need."

Ashe's voice fell to a barely controlled whisper, thick with elemental lore.

"And do you understand the ancient powers you are prodding within me at this moment? I have told you my fears, my concern for your safety, my terror of what I might do to you upon our reunion—"

"I don't remember any of that, but I believe I do understand, Ashe.

I also believe there is nothing you can do to me at this moment that will cause me any more pain than I am already feeling. *Nothing.* I just suggested how we could give vent to that pain, that mutual pain. But since you are afraid, or reluctant, I understand. I will find the quartermaster and start packing—"

Her words were choked off as his lips crushed harshly against hers.

In a silent roar of elemental power that drew strength from the now-howling wind, Ashe tore forward and pulled her roughly into his arms, ripping her from the ground on which she had been standing, and carried her gracelessly into the darkness of the mountain pass, away from any noise or presence of those guarding the encampment.

Instead of struggling or knocking his head back with her impressive right cross, as he had braced for, Rhapsody wrapped her arms tightly around his neck and her legs around his waist, clinging to him as if to life itself, returning his kiss with similar desperation and lips that held heat but no real warmth.

Distantly Ashe marveled at the strength of her musculature; when they had parted she had still been weak and frail from Meridion's difficult birth and the ordeals she had endured prior to it. His dragon senses noted the sinew that had returned to her legs, the corded muscles of her arms and shoulders tighter than had been evident in the past, even when she was still in fighter's trim before her pregnancy. Her back, pressed now against his forearms, though still lithe, was wider and stronger than it had ever been, and the breasts crushed to his chest, which had been softer, riper, and full of milk when they had said goodbye, now were dry and firm.

His building arousal, and the loosing of the bonds of control, gave him time only to vaguely note the changes in her body as he had in her spirit, rather than to luxuriate in the minutiae of detail available to his dragon senses.

He was too far gone to feel anything resembling regret.

Clenching his upper body and torso as she was, she proved light enough to carry one-armed; Ashe loosed the grip of his left hand and ran it roughly through her shorn hair, now barely reaching her shoulders. He felt a twinge of loss for the long waves of golden silk he had cherished so dearly, but a moment later that thought fled as he clutched her shorter tresses, winding his fingers tightly through them.

The fire that shot through him at the feel of their softness almost caused him to drop her.

As he pressed her up against the rock face of the mountain wall, he wondered dully for a moment if he was hurting her. Then her mouth broke with his; the heat of her lips sank into the fold of his neck, and any trace of that thought vanished.

The chill of the night wind on his hands disappeared and was replaced with glorious heat as he tore the bottom of her shirt loose from the waistband of her trousers and ran his palms up her torso, brushing aside the muslin camisole as if it were nothing more than a coating of dew on grass. She arched her back at his touch, her breasts filling his palms, sending blissful waves of shock through him, followed by tremors as the movement of her hands mirrored his own. The rough calluses on her fingertips and palms, juxtaposed with the silky warmth that her hands exuded, caused him to gasp aloud.

The clutch, the tugging of both of their hands on the laces of the garments that separated them, straining the fabric that kept them apart, tore at the inside of his skull. And then, freed from the interference of their clothing, a heat unimaginable, another kind of grip, overtook him; the return of the physical connection he had missed so deeply consumed his conscious thought.

The human soul within him was distantly aware of and essence of the dragon slightly amused by the banging together of two elemental swords of ancient manufacture and immense might, his the blade of water, hers that of starlight and fire, their scabbards clashing against each other as he delved euphorically into this woman, a woman who didn't have the same scent he remembered, both alien and completely familiar to him at the same time.

All finesse, all care and detail was lost to the eddies of power rushing forth from both of them; no tenderness, no gentleness of caress was evident in the pounding, blasting need that consumed them both.

The darkness of rage and lust was closing in at the edges of his consciousness.

Overwhelmed now, he was only dimly aware of the woman in his arms propped against the rock face, wrapped as he was in furious heat, the beautiful, desirable, compelling warmth of the elemental fire raging within her, pulling him ever more deeply into her.

He felt not a trace of his beloved Emily.

He was too far gone to care, even as he sensed that he was breaking faith with her.

The woman in his arms leaned forward as she tightened her legs around him.

"Drive it out of me," she whispered. "Drive yourself into me, and drive the pain out. Make it go away—*please*."

"Happy to—do so if—it helps us—honor—Anborn's memory—"

"Shhhh," she said into his ear as she caressed it with the warmth of her mouth. "Shhhhhh."

His last conscious thought before succumbing to what she had called sweet oblivion was of the opposing notions of the overwhelming relief and thrill in being reunited with his treasure again, while at the same time feeling as if he was betraying her with a woman he barely recognized.

And then all thought ceased, blotted out in the flood of frenzied carnal need.

60

Then it was over. Cold reason returned in the passage of the night wind through the mountain pass.

Rhapsody leaned back against the rockwall and exhaled deeply.

"I have changed my mind. You have my permission to touch me after all."

Ashe chuckled, trying to keep the sense of loss that was impending at bay. "Let me catch my breath, and I will endeavor to make up for my ham-handedness and—"

"That's not necessary. I wasn't looking for finesse or romantic nice-ties, just release—and you gave it to me," Rhapsody said. She slowly let go of his shoulders, smoothing the surface scratches where her battle-ragged nails had dug into his skin, even through his shirt. "Thank you."

"Believe me, it was my pleasure," Ashe said ruefully. He swallowed, noting a lack of the warmth in her eyes that always had been a part of their afterglow.

"Please put me down, then." She pulled the loose, scattered locks of short hair from her face with her fingers as he stepped back and lowered her to the ground. "I'm not sure how that honored your uncle's memory."

Ashe struggled to slow his breathing. "Oh, believe me, Anborn would have loved knowing that his death was being mourned, or rather celebrated, in the heat of raunchy, glorious fornication and panting debauchery, in the open air, amidst the detritus and smoke of the aftermath of battle."

Rhapsody loosed a ragged sigh. She pushed away from him and started to put her clothing back in place.

"It's certainly pleasant to believe that, whether or not it is true."

Ashe nodded. His heart was still racing, but it had begun to slow along with his breath, leaving him feeling bereft already.

"The only thing that would have pleased him more is if we had managed to do it on horseback," he said, beginning to put himself back to rights as well. "Wherever he is, he is smiling right now." He paused from tucking in the shirt beneath his studded vest and let his hand come to rest on Rhapsody's face.

She smiled slightly. "Well, next time the grief threatens to consume us, we can try that if you like, but only on a horse that you don't."

Ashe chuckled in spite of himself and caressed her cheek. "Two comments of levity in the same number of minutes; can it be that your humor, and therefore your old self, is returning?"

"No," Rhapsody said. Her expression and word were not unpleasant, but they felt like the slap of a cold ocean wave nonetheless; Ashe dropped his hand. "Namers are trained in the use of humor as a tool. I am not ill or just feeling grumpy, Ashe; the things about me that you are not happy with cannot get better on their own. I'm missing a rather significant piece of my name, tied to the part of me that you remember most fondly. Until I get that piece back, assuming I even can, I'm bound not to measure up to what you remember. I am sorry for that."

Her husband eyed her silently. After a long moment he spoke.

"Please don't ever believe you don't measure up to anything in my expectations or my memory, Rhapsody," he said quietly. "While I miss the part that you left with Meridion desperately, I still love the woman who was willing to make that sacrifice with everything I am, even if you don't feel the same thing in return. I have never deserved you; the fact that you even glanced in my direction a second time, let alone married me, is the greatest miracle I have known. I confess that I am sad, but the waiting will be well worth it once we have been reunited with our son, and you have recovered your name."

The woman who resembled his wife looked steadily at him. She sighed, then let her hand come to rest on the side of his face.

"For your sake, even more than my own, I hope you are right," she said.

She patted his cheek, then took down her hand. "Now, go attend to your injuries and get your wounds dressed, unless you want me to do that for you."

"I told you, my injuries are minor, bordering on nothing."

"And *I* told *you* long ago, if I am remembering correctly, that the Lord

Cymrian should put in an appearance at the medics' tent, even if his wounds are minor, to set an example for those who might be similarly inclined to ignore their injuries, but do not have the constitution of a dragon and the stamina of a man of your strength."

"What about you? Should you not be addressing your own wounds?"

She shook her head. "I have nothing but bruises, and there is nothing the medics can do for them."

"Can't you use your powers as a Namer to heal yourself?" Ashe pressed. "You still have that part of you, don't you?"

Rhapsody smiled ruefully.

"The part with the power of Naming, yes. But in order to heal myself, I would have to know my own name. And, as you are aware, I do not. So, until I have it back, I will just have to live with the bruises."

61

$\mathcal{L}$ater, once his wounds were dressed, Ashe sought his wife in the massive encampment in the lee of the mountain. Had he not been blessed with the dragon's abilities of discernment, there would have been no way to locate her tent, identical to the tens of thousands of others in which the infantry had bedded down, but his senses led him to her sleeping place, slightly away from the masses and sheltered from the wind in a jutting crag in the cliff face.

He bent down and whispered her name, then, hearing nothing in response, pulled aside the tent flap and came quietly inside.

The peak of the tent was not tall enough for him to stand erect, so he crouched even further down.

Suddenly the tent was filled with blazing light pulsing in rippling flames to the silvery sound of a sword being drawn.

Ashe winced and shielded his eyes.

Rhapsody was on one knee, her bedroll flung aside, with Daystar Clarion in her hand. She stared at him for a moment, then sheathed her sword quickly.

"I'm sorry," she murmured. "I was asleep."

"I am the one who should apologize," Ashe said as his wife put her hand to her forehead, pressing the heel of her palm against her eyes. "I didn't mean to alarm you."

"It's all right," she said, gathering her bedroll and smoothing it back out again on the ground. "I was in the grip of a nightmare anyway."

Ashe sighed sadly. "I knew they would come back when you and Meridion left for the Bolglands."

Rhapsody shook her head as she crawled back into the bedroll.

"Actually, they only returned once I left him in the Nain kingdom," she said. "One of the few things I remember about him tonight is that he has his father's ability to guard me against the torment of bad dreams, even as little as he is. You and he have a lot in common."

"Indeed," Ashe said, smiling slightly. "We both love the same woman more than anyone in the world."

"Is everything all right? Did you get your wounds taken care of?"

"Yes."

"Then why are you here?"

Ashe felt his face fall in the dark.

"I didn't mean to be presumptuous," he said. "I was hoping I might join you in your tent."

"If you'd like. You are not being presumptuous. You're my husband; you are welcome. But it's rather small in here."

Ashe tried to keep his voice as light as he could.

"If you will allow me to hold you, if you will sleep in my arms, there should be plenty of room."

There was silence in the darkness of the tent. When she spoke, Ashe thought he heard a trace of sadness in her voice.

"If you wish," she said. "Come in."

Ashe unlaced his boots and pulled them off, leaving them by the tent wall. "I will keep the nightmares at bay for you once more, Aria."

"Then by all means, please do come in." Humor had replaced the sadness.

Ashe exhaled in relief, and followed his dragon sense in the dark to where her bedroll had been laid out. He pulled his own from over his shoulder and stretched it out beside hers, then carefully lay down on it, attempting not to disturb her.

She was already supine again, pulling the camp blanket back over herself.

Feeling strangely awkward, he put out his arms to her and sighed when she moved closer to him. He pulled her gently against his chest and wrapped his arm around her, brushing her forehead with his lips and running his hand through her hair as he had done on so many nights over the course of their marriage.

Only to feel her body stiffen and freeze.

"Rhapsody? Is something wrong?"

For a moment there was only silence in the tent.

Then he heard and felt her take a deep breath.

"Do you remember, long ago, when we were traveling overland together, when you took me to your house behind the waterfall?"

"Of course."

Silence reigned for another moment. Then she spoke again.

"On one of the nights we stayed there, when I was racked by a terrible nightmare, you took me in your arms and held me until I became calm again—do you remember?"

Ashe's eyes stung at the memory, and his throat tightened. It was one of his most cherished recollections, the first time he had been able to share a bed with her, if only in the most innocent of ways, the first time he had been able to hold her as he had dreamed about since they had met months before. Rather than risk choking up, he made a nonverbal sound to indicate that he did.

"Do you think that you could hold me as you did that night?"

Ashe swallowed. "Am I not?"

Her voice was soft. "If you would do me the favor of not caressing me, or kissing me, it would make me much more comfortable. I'm sorry to ask this of you, but—" Her voice failed.

"But what, Aria?" Ashe felt his stomach turn at the tone in her voice.

"Even—even though I know you are my husband, I—I don't remember you in that role," she said, her voice steady but quiet. "The first actual memory I have of you is meeting you in the market in Bethe Corbair."

Ashe exhaled painfully.

"I remember that clearly," Rhapsody continued. "I also remember you coming to visit in Ylorc, and our travels together when you guided me to Elynsynos's lair and to Tyrian to meet Oelendra. But after that, I have no actual memories of you. Since you are my husband, we must have had a wedding—"

"Two, actually," Ashe murmured. "One in secret, one publicly beneath the tree in what has now become our home, Highmeadow."

"I don't remember," Rhapsody said, her voice still soft. "I have been repeatedly told we have a son, and from time to time, I can remember his name for a few moments, but at *this* moment, I don't know what it is. I don't even remember giving birth to him. I believe you and I met in the old world, in Serendair, but I do not remember that, either. I don't remember what I called you there—"

"Sam," Ashe whispered, struggling to keep back tears. "You called me Sam."

Rhapsody fell silent. After a moment she spoke.

"Did you just tell me what I called you?"

"Yes."

"It's gone already. It won't stay in my head—none of these things will stay. The essence of my true name, who I was when I met you in Serendair, when we fell in love, when I married you, is gone—it's with our son now. It's been utterly stripped from me. And I am lost, Ashe; so lost that when the man I know is my husband but I can only really remember as a platonic friend, sometimes almost a stranger, touches me intimately, it harks back to a time in my life when I was forced to endure men who were *actual* strangers touching me intimately—I have clear memories of *that* time, and it makes me ill. I'm sorry—I'm so sorry."

Quickly Ashe removed his hand from her hair.

"Two hours ago you seemed more than willing to be touched intimately," he said, struggling to keep the bitterness out of his voice.

Rhapsody was silent for a long time. Finally she spoke.

"If we were not married, if I didn't know you, I would have still taken you behind that barracks, not as my husband, or my lover, but as a handsome stranger or a platonic friend, and knobbed you as I did. I was burning alive, and needed to vent my rage and pain—and I thought you might need to do so, too. But for me it was just a communion of bodies, as I told you at the time. Women need the release of sex as much as men do. What we did a few hours ago in the darkness was not intimate, it was almost faceless, anonymous—but when you touch me tenderly, when you kiss me gently—then I don't know how to react. Because that *does* feel intimate. I'm so sorry."

Ashe nodded abruptly and sat up, releasing her from his arms.

"I'll go now," he said as he pulled his camp blanket off and rolled it quickly. "The last thing I want is to upset you or make you ill."

"Please stay." Rhapsody sat up as well. "I'm sorry."

Ashe ran his hand angrily through his hair. "As I told you earlier, I don't know how to behave around you now, Rhapsody," he said, the bitterness now rampant in his voice. "I am doing everything I can not to seize you and hold you, touch you, as I have been doing for almost five years now, but I have not been able to find a way to keep from bothering or disquieting you. You cannot imagine how much I have missed you— have longed to be reunited with you—and all I can seem to do is upset you. I don't know what to do, and I fear the dragon will rampage if I stay a moment longer."

Rhapsody watched silently as he rolled his bedroll and started to pull his boots on.

"Did I ever tell you what I was dreaming about when you held me through that nightmare in the house behind the waterfall?" she asked quietly.

Ashe stopped. "No."

She wrapped her arms around her knees and pulled them up to her chest.

"A demon vine had reached down into my soul, like the root of a poisonous willow, stripping my heat and my music from me," she said softly. "It took my very voice, Ashe—I was gasping, unable to make any sound, when I woke in your arms. And I clung to you, because I felt that you were the only person in the world who could hear me, now that my music was gone."

Ashe stopped lacing his boots and looked at her in the darkness. His dragon senses were able to make out her form where his eyes could not, could feel the way she shaped the air around her, could feel the elemental fire burning low within her, like fading embers.

Her spirit seemingly dying.

Her eyes utterly dry.

"I remember that, Ashe. I remember clinging to you, even though I almost never got to see your face in those days, even though your mist cloak obscured everything you were then. I sought the comfort of your arms, even though I barely knew you, and did not know how you felt about me at that time. Of all the people in the world, you, the man I rarely saw, hardly knew, who was continually pushing me away, avoiding telling me anything about yourself—you were *the only one who could hear me.* I remember this, Ashe—when I can remember little else, I remember this. I had to be careful as you held me, because I had seen the horrific wound that sundered your chest, and I knew that if I inadvertently moved in the wrong way, or touched your chest by accident, I would bring great pain to you. And I knew you were being careful in the way you held me, too—probably to not cross the line that would have threatened our growing friendship."

Ashe smiled slightly in spite of the dragon's angst. "Yes."

"I remember that night, Ashe. And I still feel it—that if I were broken and vulnerable, if no one else in the entire world could hear me, that you still would—you alone. Not Achmed, not Grunthor, not Analise—just you."

Ashe exhaled deeply.

Rhapsody loosed a heavy sigh in a harmonic reply.

"So, please—can you please hold me now as you did then?"

"You forget, Rhapsody, that I was in love with you, even then. I am endlessly more in love with you now."

"Then it shouldn't be difficult to recall that time, if you are still in love with me." Even unable to see her in the absence of light, Ashe sensed her eyes darken. "I may not remember you as my husband, but I would die for you, Ashe—without hesitation, I would lay down my life to protect you, not because I feel the love I have for you, but because, even though I *don't* feel it, I know it's there.

"When I came to this side of the world, even before Achmed, Grunthor, and I emerged from the Root, I had already decided to be celibate, to live a chaste and uncomplicated life, without lovers or a husband—I'm fairly certain I told you that during our travels together. And yet, in spite of that decision, I find myself a married woman, with a child—a child I must have wanted desperately to have taken the risk of giving birth to wyrmkin. The only thing that could have caused me to change my mind and my plans is to have fallen deeply, unguardedly, ridiculously, irrevocably in love with someone who meant enough to me to alter everything I wanted for my life. In the absence of my memories, I still can gauge how completely I must have loved you to let this happen. Is this making any sense?"

Ashe let his head drop to his chest. "It is," he said quietly.

"So, please," the woman who reminded him distantly of his wife said, "please be patient with me. I don't know how to behave around you, either. I don't want to keep hurting you, but all that's left of me is the Namer, and I don't know how to lie to you to keep you from feeling pain. The best I could do was to order, while you were getting your wounds dressed, *two* shifts of the quartermaster's regiments to work through the night, preparing for us to leave at First-light to go to Undervale. If the quartermaster wants to keep his head, the task will be finished when we wake."

Ashe chuckled. He pulled off his boots and put them back up against the tent wall, then came to her, lay down again, and took her back into his arms.

"That's a wonderful start," he said. "I will endeavor to maintain a respectful distance this time."

"Thank you. With any luck, it will only be for a short time more."

Ashe closed his eyes and listened to the sound of her breathing until it became regular, the soft music of the night he loved so dearly to hear as she fell into the darkness of sleep. He felt the prickle of energy as the dragon came forth to wrap itself around her dreams, and let go of wakefulness himself.

"I cannot wait until you tell me truthfully that you love me again," he said aloud as sleep came for him, knowing she could not hear him. "Assuming you ever do."

Homecoming

62

THE SKELETON COAST, SORBOLD

Once Achmed had made certain that Rath had Grunthor well in hand to travel back to Ylorc, he walked out as far onto the beach again as he could without feeling nervous and felt around for a stiff breeze.

It did not come right away, or at least he was unsatisfied enough with the ones that did to keep from making a decision on one.

Finally, after watching the sun slide two hands down the welkin of the sky toward the horizon, he felt one steady and sure enough to trust, and, wrapping his now-dry cloak solidly around himself, he took hold of the updraft and allowed it to carry him, with a series of die-downs and updrafts, to the place he felt he should return to before he went home to the Bolglands for a decidedly long time.

He could not imagine the desire to leave there ever again.

The wind set him down a little farther to the east than he had expected, so Achmed waited, crouched on the canyon floor, until he was certain that he had not landed in the midst of hostile locals or Talquist's guards.

After more than an hour of waiting, the only entities to greet him were horned toads, salamanders, and a jurilla that came upon him quite by accident and had almost had a fatal fit upon discovering him. It had screeched at him in its characteristic defense mechanism, then leapt away in panic when it had done so.

Achmed remained amused for some time, wondering if every animal in the late emperor's realm was as pretentious and cowardly as he had been.

Once he had determined that he was very likely unseen, as he had been the entire time he had made his way across this canyon before, Achmed set to, aligning his course to the place where he had come upon a body some time ago.

Surprisingly, it was still there, unmolested by coyotes and carrion, dry and withered as it had been before, its empty eye sockets staring at the painfully blue sky.

When he came to a stop at her feet, Achmed exhaled and remained standing in as close to a respectful position as he could. He remained thus until just before dusk, then set to gathering the dry weeds and scrub he needed.

Achmed had built more than his share of pyres, and built another one now, fashioning it as cleanly as he could. Now he had soldiers to do such things; it was a good reminder of the value of humility.

When at last the bier was complete, he rose and went back to the Seer's body, unrecognizable in the arid heat of the canyon.

"There's no Time like the Present," he said wryly.

With an uncharacteristic level of respect and decorum, he hoisted the corpse from the cactus bed where he had set it, awaiting the arrival of this day, then carried the elderly Seer, Anwyn and Manwyn's fragile sister, to her ceremonial blessing ground.

He tried to remember the words to the Lirin death ritual he and Grunthor had observed many times. Finally, when they refused to return to his brain, he resorted to using the words to one of Grunthor's favorite marching cadences that the Sergeant-Major had used in the training and intimidation of his troops.

> This may be the day you die
> And if it is, that's fine
> It's a very mealy apple that
> Stays too long on the vine
> Don' be sad yer life ain't long
> Don't wish that you could stay
> 'Cause everyone'll take a turn
> At dying anyway.

A smile crossed his face, imagining what the dreamy Seer would have said.

Then faded quickly, knowing that it would have been irritating, no matter what it was.

He stood a quiet vigil until nightfall. Just before night came he struck the tinder against a rock, then ignited the pyre.

It never ceased to amaze him how much a Lirin funeral pyre and funeral, something Rhapsody had given him careful training in, could make him reach back to the times in his life when he was lonely.

Those times had been few and far between as well, not because he had benefited from the love of many friends and happy acquaintances; Achmed had rarely bestowed the honor of friendship on anyone he had run into since coming to the Middle Continent. Rather, it took a major life event, the significant loss of someone or something that mattered to him, that allowed Achmed to feel anything at all sometimes.

He lowered the stick he had used to light the fire, then maintained his respectful silence and waited for the smoke to take the woman's ashes into the sky.

It took less than the span of a dozen heartbeats.

Finally, when what had once been the Seer of the Present had been reduced to nothing more than ash and taken by the wind, the Bolg king waited until said wind had come and completely scoured that part of the canyon clean.

Goodbye, Rhonwyn, he thought. *Irritating as you were, I am always grateful to have known you, because now I can go back to my life knowing that the Present is as fleeting as the wind in more ways than one.*

63

UNDERVALE, THE DEEP KINGDOM
OF THE NAIN

The better part of eleven days' journey had them in sight of the Molten River.

Rhapsody had little to no memory of the place, so it was necessary for Ashe to use his dragon senses to guide them along the passageways, by which even he, with his superior sensing capability, was confused and disoriented.

Finally he was able to lead the way, through all the ferocious security checkpoints, to the chambers where her four friends had put their lives in abeyance in order to be able to help keep their child safe.

Just as they cleared the last checkpoint, Analise appeared at the end of the stone hallway.

A bundle was in her arms, not too much bigger than it had been when Rhapsody had said goodbye.

Ashe stepped forward eagerly, then reined in his excitement long enough to allow his wife to hurry ahead first. The wide smile that had come over his face faded at the look of stark terror on hers.

"Aria?"

Rhapsody stared down the hallway at her old friend holding her son. Then she inhaled slowly and gestured for Ashe to go on ahead.

Ashe looked at her for a moment, then made his way hastily down the hall. He took the blanketed baby gently into his arms, trying to ignore the look of surprise turning to shock on Analise's face as she locked eyes with Rhapsody.

Then all else faded into oblivion at the sight of his sleeping son.

Ashe turned Meridion toward him and gazed down at him, allowing his dragon sense to assess him as gently as it could so as not to wake him.

The child had obviously been fed recently, and had slipped even more recently into a deep slumber. His golden curls had grown longer; with his eyes closed, he was a miniature of his mother, with long black lashes brushing his rosy gold skin, his tiny mouth with lips shaped like a curved bow. His face was free from care, though the dragon could tell that within a short time it would be wreathed in the comic scowl Rhapsody had shown him on several occasions when she had brought the baby to visit him through the scrying power of the Lightcatcher.

Then the dragon's network of heightened awareness sensed warm saltwater on the surface of the child's skin; Ashe blinked, and felt the swell of tears that had crept into his own eyes, unnoticed, that were beginning to fall on the baby. A fondness beyond measure rose in his long-tortured heart, followed by a tide of unbridled love long repressed that almost overwhelmed him.

"Hello, my son," he said, too softly for the baby to hear. "I love you. You seem to have done a fine job of growing strong and healthy without getting too big too fast. I was afraid you would be riding a horse before I got the chance to see you again. I know that your forbearance will make your mama happy, too. Well done, Meridion." His ability to resist shattered, and he pressed a gentle kiss onto the baby's forehead, letting his lips linger there, breathing in the child's sweet scent.

Meridion slept on, oblivious.

Finally he forced his gaze away from the little boy and looked back down the hallway at the child's mother again.

Rhapsody no longer seemed terrified; her aspect had settled into a sharp look in her eyes set in a face that was otherwise expressionless. Ashe beckoned to her.

"Come, Aria—come see our boy."

She swallowed hard, then pursed her lips, as if thinking intently. Finally she came slowly down the hallway, coming to a stop a few steps away from her husband and child. Ashe started to put the baby in her arms, but she stepped quickly away.

"You hold him for now," she said quietly. "I'm still not sure what I have to do yet."

"All right," Ashe said, choking back his disappointment. "Take your time—we'll be fighting over who gets to hold him soon enough."

"Here," Analise said, opening the door through which she had come. "Come in here, m'lord, m'lady; you'll have privacy and safety in the rooms we have shared when taking care of your son." Ashe followed her, as did Rhapsody a moment later, into a large room full of Nain guards and through another doorway, bound in brass, with sentries on either side who opened it.

Beyond the second door was another, much smaller room furnished handsomely with a beautifully crafted cradle. An interior chamber contained an adult bed and a small sofa and chair, human-sized, as well as everything needed for the care of an infant.

Analise stepped aside to allow the royal couple entry; as Rhapsody passed through the doorway, Analise touched her elbow. The Lady Cymrian stopped for a moment, and a smile flickered over her face as she exchanged a glance with her friend. Then the elderly Cymrian woman bowed and withdrew, closing the door and leaving the young family alone in the room.

Ashe brushed another kiss onto Meridion's head as the baby stretched and yawned, then returned to sleep.

"He's starting to make intermittent suckling motions, and the scowl is coming," Ashe said gently. "Come, Aria—take back your name, so that you can be truly reunited with him, too, before he wakes."

Rhapsody watched for several long moments. Then, tentatively, she put out her hand, struggling to keep it from trembling, and touched the tiny pearl in the baby's earlobe.

Her index finger caressed the small jewel, and Ashe concentrated, waiting for the hum he had heard and the glow he had seen the last time he had watched her retrieve a memory in this way.

Nothing happened.

Rhapsody cleared her throat softly, turning away so as not to disturb the baby, then began to hum her naming note, *ela*, the sixth of the scale. Ashe smiled as it began to change the air around them ever so slightly, clearing it as if after a rainstorm. When her note was resonating strongly, she began to chant words in Ancient Lirin, then looked up at him.

"Do—do you remember my old name?"

"Of course I do," he assured her, trying to keep his voice low. "Better than I remember my own. You warned me once to be careful uttering it outright, however." She nodded. "So I will tell it to you in pieces, much as you once told it to me." Rhapsody nodded again.

" 'Rhapsody' is your middle name, given to you by your Lirin mother, a Lirin name, a musical name, because she wanted you to have a musical soul. But your human father wanted to name you after his mother, so the first name you were given was her first name also, 'Amelia.' Your family called you 'Emmy' for short, but your friends, and the people of Merryfield, where you lived as a child, called you 'Emily.' It was that name you gave me when I first asked who you were on the night we met in Serendair. And your patronymic, your family name, was 'Turner,' as in Earthturner, you said—a farmer's surname. I'm not sure which of these you gave to Meridion, however."

Rhapsody rubbed her pounding temples with her fingers.

"Probably all of them—I don't remember any of them. Why do you keep calling me 'Aria'?"

Tears welled in Ashe's eyes again.

"It's an endearment I have called you since the summer we became lovers," he said quietly. "It means 'my guiding star'—"

"I know what it means," Rhapsody whispered. "I just don't remember you calling me that in the Past, though I can remember you doing so since we were reunited. But I can't even remember the ones you just told me—it's as if they refuse to stay in my mind."

"Then I will say them to you again, and you should speak them immediately after I do," Ashe said, panic beginning to rise up inside his viscera. The baby may have felt the change, because he frowned intensely and squirmed, settling down a moment later as Ashe caressed his downy head.

"All right. Let me replenish the Naming note first." She hummed it again, and the air cleared around them once more. "Now tell me."

"Amelia," Ashe said.

"Amelia," Rhapsody sang hesitantly.

"Turner."

"Tur—" Rhapsody stopped and stared blankly at him.

"Turner," Ashe said again. His voice shook from the effort of remaining quiet for Meridion's sake.

"Turner."

"Good. Now, the nicknames?" She nodded. "Emily."

"Emily."

"Emmy."

"Emmy." Rhapsody exhaled, then blinked. "Thank you—they're gone again already." She touched the tiny pearl once more and whispered the words of Ancient Lirin, the commands for *release* and *return*.

She repeated the ancient words several times, then fell silent.

When she looked up at him, her eyes were dry, but the expression on her face was stricken.

"I'm sorry," she said quietly. "I've done everything I know how to do. But I don't feel anything. Anything at all."

64

"Look at him again, Aria," Ashe urged. "Pause in your Naming lore for a moment, and let your instinct as a mother take over. Look at our son—"

"You don't understand. I—I can't feel anything; I have no instincts. He doesn't smell right to me. I don't even recognize him."

Ashe was thunderstruck.

"What do you mean, you don't *recognize him*? He looks exactly like you! A stranger could discern which one he is out of a crowd of babies from one glance at you. How is it possible that his own mother cannot?"

Rhapsody lapsed into silence.

"How can you feel nothing?" Ashe demanded in a harsh whisper. "You're a Namer—potent and powerful enough of one to alter the fabric of Time, of the world itself. This is *your* name—your *child!* I cannot imagine it possible that it's not within your power to recall it, if it's important enough to you."

Rhapsody looked steadily at him, though her eyes narrowed slightly.

"Perhaps that power is the problem; I didn't rename myself, I gave my name away. Maybe my own abilities have made it impossible for me to take it back."

"So you can smile at Analise, but not at our son?"

"I knew Analise when I was just Rhapsody. Our acquaintance is from that time. But you, Ashe—you knew me by another name, the name I was given when I was forming my identity, when I learned to love. A name I pledged to you when we joined our souls in marriage. A name I don't remember on a level that surpasses the knowledge of my mind; it's been stripped from my very essence. I gave it to Meridion—I can't seem to take it back. I'm sorry—I don't know what to do."

"Are you telling me you don't love him anymore? I have already had to adjust to the possibility that you will not love me always, as you have promised over two lifetimes to do, but our *child*? You don't feel love for our *son*?"

The angry tears in his eyes were not mirrored in his wife's, though her expression was sad now.

"Do you think for even a second, even a breath, that I want it this way?" she asked quietly. "Everything I've done since this war began, I did for our son, Ashe. You should understand this. You sent us away to the Bolg kingdom for our safety, knowing what the cost would be to you. A man who battles daily with his nether side should be better able than most to understand the loss of an intrinsic identity like a true name; your sacrifice for us made the dragon in you rampant. Do you not remember telling me that we could never be together again because of that, for fear that you might harm Meridion and me?"

Ashe stared at her, the vertical pupils expanding in his eyes. Then, as her words rang with truth within him, he dropped his gaze and nodded reluctantly.

"So you are uniquely qualified to understand how lost I am, how numb, I would wager." She looked down at the baby again, then looked away.

"Even as lost and unfeeling as I am, I don't regret the choice I made," she said softly. "I had to go to war; I had to leave him, for his sake and the sake of the continent. I gave him my name to comfort him, to spare him the loss of both of us, to assure him, no matter what happened to me, that he had my love, and yours, through me. If I had died, he would have had it. Now that I have lived, he has it still. If I am diminished for the rest of my life, at least it seems that what I hoped for came to pass. It was worth the sacrifice."

"Perhaps," Ashe said.

The baby stirred, his eyes still closed, making the soft sounds of awakening. When Ashe looked up again, his eyes were still gleaming with tears, but his anger was gone, replaced by something much deeper, much more desolate.

"What can we do? What can I do to help you, Aria?"

Rhapsody fixed him with a direct look. "You can tell me the truth," she said.

There was a tone in her voice that resonated with Ashe; she was asking something that surpassed the ordinary meaning of her words. He nodded, holding his breath in dread of her question.

"You were a motherless boy who never knew the love of the woman who carried you and brought you into this world—you have said that was the source of a lifetime of loneliness for you before we met. You had a father who loved you, even if his love was odd and somewhat stunted by the lineage that was his heritage.

"I ask you this: if you had to assess and choose, which of these two choices do you think would have been better for you—to still have been motherless, but to have known your mother's love intrinsically, to have *owned* that love in as real a way as it is possible to have something, along with that of your father—or to have had your father's love and the living presence of a mother that did *not* love you, did not have any feelings for you whatsoever? To have grown up in her house, in her presence, feeling innately that you meant nothing to her? Would it have been better to have known such a mother—or to have never known her at all, while having her love to keep throughout your lifetime? Especially if your father had made your happiness his life's purpose, as I know you will for Meridion?"

All the sound went out of the windowless room.

Then, after a span of a hundred heartbeats, Rhapsody saw her husband's spirit break. He did not move, did not even breathe, but it was in his eyes. He bowed his head, his shoulders suddenly weighed down as if under a heavy burden. She turned away.

"I thought as much," she said softly. "Thank you; I'm sorry. I will leave now, before he is aware that I was even here."

She had caught a look of utter despair on his face and wondered dully if Ashe's own mother had seen a similar sight with her last breath: the image of her husband, Llauron, frantic, holding a squirming child he was ill-prepared to care for alone as the woman he loved departed from his life. Even as numb and unconnected to him as she was, Rhapsody could not bear the sight of such anguish.

She started toward the door as the baby in Ashe's arms stretched again and cooed. She came to a halt as her husband called to her in a voice that sounded as if it had been rent by shards of metal.

"Rhapsody?"

She turned back to him.

"Where will you go?"

"I don't know," she said nervously, watching Meridion kick his blankets off in Ashe's arms. "Ylorc, perhaps, Tyrian, more likely. I can't think clearly now. But I can't let him see me; I will send word to you when I get to wherever I am going."

Her voice grew softer.

"Goodbye, Ashe. I hope you will remember how much I loved you both when I still had my name, and that it brings you consolation."

She turned again and hurried to the door.

Meridion opened his tiny blue eyes. The dragonesque pupils contracted as he took in the light in the room and his father's face. His small mouth puckered in interest, then opened as the soft clicking sounds of vocal exploration came out in a greeting that rang with recognition.

Ashe smiled weakly through his tears. *He remembers me, at least,* he thought. *After so little time together, and so much of it apart. Thank the One-God.*

The baby turned his head toward the sounds of the opening door. He let out a squeal of glee.

"Mimen!"

It was a natural noise for a baby to make, and sounded for all the world like the burbling of any infant, but both of his parents recognized the meaning of the word in Ancient Lirin, the language of Namers.

Mama!

Rhapsody, her hand on the door handle, froze where she stood.

A wave of heat seemed to wash over her, leaving her light-headed.

Meridion let loose another squeal and a slew of meaningless babble.

His mother turned around slowly. Her face was white as milk and her hands went to her face, covering her mouth in shock.

Ashe coughed, then gasped, then laughed aloud. He gestured briskly with one hand to his wife, cradling their son in the crook of his other arm.

"Come," he said encouragingly. "He's calling you, Aria."

Rhapsody tried to comply. She took a step forward; then her trembling legs gave way, and she sank to her knees on the floor.

Where she proceeded to burst into tears, flowing in streams down her face, still shielded by her hands.

"Sam," she whispered. "Oh, my God. *Sam.*"

Ashe came to her side and offered her his free hand.

"Do you remember?" he asked, his voice breaking. "Do you remember your name now?"

Rhapsody nodded as the tears continued to fall, but now they were tears of joy that caused her entire body to tremble.

"Emily," she whispered. "Your Emily, Sam. I love you—I belong to you." She locked eyes with her baby, grinning toothlessly at her in his father's arms. "And to you, *y pippin.*"

My baby.

Meridion squealed happily again.

The agony that had clenched his heart shattered; Ashe took Rhapsody's hand and pulled her gently to her feet. He attempted to put the child in her arms, but she backed away again.

"I'm afraid to hold him yet," she whispered. "I want to, but I'm shaking so that I fear I might drop him."

"Here, you hold him, and I will hold you both," Ashe said, his grin matching his son's, but with teeth. "He wants desperately to be in your arms, Aria; I know exactly how he feels." He took her hand again and led her to the sofa, where he sat, then pulled her onto his lap and carefully gave her the baby. He drew her tightly to his chest, wrapping his arms around them both, and loosed a sigh of deepest relief.

My family, he thought. *Finally. My treasure has finally returned. I have my family back.*

The dragon within his blood sighed as well.

Rhapsody looked down into Meridion's tiny face and smiled.

"Why, you little Namer, you!" she chuckled. "I've always said you'll be a great one someday, but I didn't know you could do it yet."

She looked at his father, who was watching in awe, and her smile brightened, sending waves of cold thrill through Ashe's body. "How foolish of me, Sam. I should have known I couldn't take back the gift I had given him, but that he could return it to me if he wanted to. I am constantly underestimating this child."

Meridion was watching her solemnly as she spoke to his father. He blinked when she looked back at him, then let out a resounding belch that rattled the furniture, as if in agreement.

The tearful parents broke into sweet, healing laughter. They smiled at each other; Ashe reached up with one hand and cradled Rhapsody's face, drawing her into a kiss that was, for the first time since they had reunited, met by the tenderness and warmth he had known before they parted. Her skin glistened beneath his fingers; the sparkle that had been lost from her eyes was there once again. The sharp angles of her face had resolved into the soft perfection he had missed so terribly. His wife had returned. *Thank the One-God,* he thought again, beyond grateful.

"What—what are you doing?" Rhapsody asked, looking down as her lips broke from Ashe's.

"Kissing you, I believe. It has been a *very* long time; I'm not surprised you don't remember."

"I wasn't talking to you," she said.

Ashe followed her gaze; Meridion had rolled up against her on his side and was gumming her shirt.

"I think he's trying to nurse; I'm surprised he still remembers how."

"Oh, believe me, once a man has had his lips on your breast, he never stops dreaming of it, and trying to make it happen again, no matter how long it's been," Ashe said wickedly. "Just wait until he's asleep again; I'll show you what I mean." He received an elbow in the chest in response and laughed in delight at another sign of the return to normalcy.

"Poor *pippin*; I'm sorry, Meridion," Rhapsody said, stroking her baby's curls. "That's been gone for a long time, but I will go to Analise and get goat's milk from the nan—"

Her words trailed off and her face went blank with shock.

"What's the matter?" Ashe shifted her slightly in his lap, then noticed the wet trails dampening the front of her blouse. He touched one small pool and found it to be warm; the dragon within him recognized the liquid immediately as milk. He threw back his head and laughed uproariously.

"A Namer indeed! We'd best be careful with him, Rhapsody—I can only imagine what clever magic he will employ to get around our rules when he's older."

Rhapsody was unlacing her shirt.

"I'm happy to comply with his wishes now at least," she said, putting Meridion to the breast and sighing in relief herself as he began to nurse excitedly. "As taxing as being his source of supply can be, it's a joyful responsibility. I'm so grateful he's still small enough to want to; I was worried that he'd be walking when we returned."

She leaned back against her husband's broad shoulder and closed her eyes.

Ashe looked down at them both and smiled, content with his world. He put his lips to her ear, kissing it gently.

"I love you so," he whispered. "Welcome back, Emily."

She smiled up at him, then kissed him in return.

"I love you, too, *always*," she said. "Both of you." She winced at her son's enthusiasm. "And believe me, I can feel it."

65

The next morning, when the clock in the underground village square chimed, echoing beautifully through the underground palace, Rhapsody, Meridion, and Ashe were preparing to say their goodbyes to the Nain king.

They found themselves, as Rhapsody had done when she first came to Undervale, standing before Faedryth at the base of the dais on which his throne stood, waiting for an answer in the confines of his underground Great Hall.

"It has been my honor and my joy to have been asked to guard this beautiful child," Faedryth said. "You are right that he shows signs of his great-grandfather's inventive and architectural genius, which I recognize in him, tiny as he is, but I'm not sure I could put it into words. I do hope that you will do as you said you had intended when you brought him here, that you will allow him to come back here when he is older and learn both the stories and the skills that are all but forgotten now."

"That would be *my* honor and joy."

For just a moment Time seemed to slow. Both Rhapsody and Faedryth looked at each other. The Lady Cymrian was experiencing the flash of a sudden memory, the quick image of Black Ivory box in the nervous hands of the Nain king, containing a strange, fragile piece of fabric or shell that had a few faded images on it.

From the look on his face, it was clear that the Nain king was having a similar type of memory.

Finally Rhapsody shook off her vision.

"Thank you for coming to the aid of the Alliance when you had determined long ago to stay out of any military action. What changed your mind?"

"Watching you with young Meridion," Faedryth said quietly. "Disturbing as it was to see my Lady, my sovereign, kneeling to me in tears, pleading for her son's protection as she headed off to war, offering me anything she had to keep him safe, that sight jarred me completely from everything I have ever seen or known Cymrian leadership to be.

"Anborn, may he rest peacefully in the Afterlife, was one of my dearest friends. I attended his Naming ceremony when he was an infant, and even there his parents' willful neglect, bordering on disdain for him, was evident. He was an afterthought; Gwylliam, who had been my king even before we left the Island, was deeply enamored of Edwyn, his heir and fellow engineer, while Anwyn only had interest in Llauron, her fair-haired boy. Neither of them gave a roasted rat's damn about their youngest, who had little of his eldest brother's mathematical sense and less of his other brother's lofty scholarship, but he had more heart, valor, and brilliant, selfless leadership skill than all the rest of the members of his family put together, twice over. Whatever his crimes were that came later, Anborn, up to the moment of his death, remained by far the most beloved member of that family among those who fought in the Great War.

"Edwyn holds court among those who stayed out of it, and Llauron's followers as Invoker were mostly non-Cymrians and those who were born later. But those of us who bled with Anborn in that war, fought by his side, watched him lead several attempts at peace with his mother—we remember him as he was, before the hatred that was nascent in his parents took him over. We remember him as the cheerful, vibrant boy who, though he was never given a second thought by his own family, grew up into a great man who made a family of soldiers, brothers, comrades who felt it would be an honor to die for him. We remember, and we mourn."

Faedryth fell silent for a moment; Rhapsody and Ashe stayed similarly quiet in respect.

Finally the Nain king shook his head as if shaking off sleep.

"But you, m'lady, you came to me, knowing my anger with you and your Bolg friends, well aware that I was likely to spurn your entreaties, or at least torment you mercilessly before assenting. You sliced off your beautiful hair and tossed it to a dragon without so much as a backward glance, I'm told, knowing what the threat to you would be from such an act, to obtain his increased vigilance at the door of my realm, something that is already within his own goals, to help ensure your son's safety.

"Gyllian has also told me of what you sacrificed of yourself and your own peace of mind as you left your baby here. I'm not certain I understand; the ways of women, Lirin, and Namers are foreign and terrifying to me, to say the least. But again, when I try to imagine making the sacrifices you have, both for your child and your Alliance, knowing that I could have done neither, it stirred something in me again that has long been dead and buried, a valor of a sort, a loyalty to my Lady, my Lord, and my nation. It seemed petty and, frankly, cowardly for me to refrain from joining the cause, especially given that my friend and hero was leading the charge as Lord Marshal once again. I could not stay out of it. A long way of saying 'you're welcome.'" The Nain king leaned forward and fixed her with a direct look that was full of amusement.

"Just don't become accustomed to it, m'lady."

Rhapsody laughed. "Duly noted, Majesty."

"And I must thank you, as well," the Nain king continued. "The golden banner under which we fought is a possible sign of a new era of peace between the Nain and Witheragh, as well as a stronger and more vigorous participation of our kingdom as a member of the Alliance. Do you want to know the story of how that splendid flag came to be?"

"Of course," Rhapsody said.

The Nain king chuckled. "You completely flummoxed the beast," he said, clearly enjoying the memory. "Witheragh summoned me down to the border, more politely than ever in the Past, in a high state of frenetic energy, something I have never seen before. He was intent on discussing all of the ways we could ensure the safety of your child, in the course of which he revealed many hidden passages and a good deal about his own lair which I had not known before. We now have an even more impressive security plan than we did before you came to Undervale."

"Happy to hear that," Ashe said. He kissed Meridion's forehead gently.

"Yes—you will be glad to know that as a result I will not be asking tariff relief from you, Lord Gwydion," Faedryth said jovially. "At any rate, when Witheragh and I were done with an exhaustive review of our fortifications, he presented me with the fall of your hair, m'lady. He was feeling somewhat guilty for demanding a lock of it in the first place, and was still bewildered by your response to that demand. He kept only one small strand, and requested that upon his death, when his lair is opened, it be destroyed or returned to you, so as to maintain your safety."

Rhapsody chuckled. "Well, that's very nice."

"He seemed to be relieved to be rid of it, and asked if I could find a way to make use of the remainder of the hair to ultimately aid you in your battle and your survival. I looked at it, gleaming on the ground, and for all the world it resembled a war banner. It was as if it were mocking me for the cowardice of keeping my army back in the recesses of the Deep Kingdom, while the mother of the child we were both discussing was bleeding on the battlefield of the Alliance to which I am sworn.

"So I took it back to Undervale and had it woven into such a war banner while we made preparations to depart. It came off the loom at the same moment we were mounting up; it was our honor to fly it, to ride into battle beneath it. With your permission, I kept a small lock of your hair myself, m'lady, to remind me of the sovereign who taught me what leadership and sacrifice meant."

"I am well and truly honored, Majesty," Rhapsody said softly.

"My personal guard regiment will accompany you back to Bethe Corbair, the nearest station on the guarded caravan, so that you might begin your journey home. You are welcome to return at any time; I know that Gyllian is hopeful that your friendship will continue as the world returns to normal."

"Of course."

"And should anything you need come up, please let us know if we are in a position to address it for you."

"Thank you," Ashe said.

Rhapsody held out her hand to the Nain king, who took it and bowed over her ring, then forgot himself and pulled her into an enthusiastic embrace. He released her quickly and gave an awkward cough.

"Guard that beautiful child well, m'lord, m'lady," he said.

"We will, thank you again," said Rhapsody.

Ashe offered her his arm, and together they made their way down the long aisle of inlaid stone mosaics that led to the Nain king's black marble throne.

Rhapsody waited until they had passed through the double doors and out of the Great Hall before leaning close to her husband, who bent down to catch her words, softly but racily spoken.

"Rest assured that I also stand ready to address your need should it come up, m'lord," she said. "Unless, of course, you would prefer that Faedryth did—he has offered, after all."

Ashe reddened, more from humor than embarrassment. "You naughty thing. Oh, I am so glad to have you back again, my love."

The servants in the Great Hall and the Nain king blinked in surprise at the sound of raucous, merry laughter echoing in the corridor outside as the Lord and Lady Cymrian made their way back to the upworld again.

66

BY THE BANKS OF THE MOLTEN RIVER

On the way home from the kingdom of the Nain, the Lord and Lady Cymrian stopped at the entrance to Faedryth's lands to return what Rhapsody had borrowed and to pay their respects to the wyrm who had stood even more stalwart vigil at the entryway to the Deep Kingdom where their son had been sheltered throughout the war that had scarred the face of the Known World.

Melisande, Analise, and Krinsel were in their company, the Liringlas women and the human little girl laughing and joking often and regaling the royal couple with strange and humorous tales of life among the Nain. When the group approached the place where they had first encountered the irascible wyrm, the three women who had remained in the Nain kingdom throughout the war had fallen silent. They watched in an apparent state of discomfort as the Lady Cymrian kissed her son, then her husband, and, smiling encouragingly at them, turned and made her way down to the Molten River.

Rhapsody had asked Ashe to hang back with the baby, and he did, smiling in amusement and caressing his sleeping son's downy head as the little boy drowsed in the folds of his father's cloak of mist. He watched his wife wend her way along the rocks on the embankment, her dancing shadow tall and thin against the towering archways of the cavern that demarked the entrance to the dragon's lands.

She came to a halt beside an area of the river that was sparking occasionally with fire and put her hands to the sides of her mouth.

"Witheragh!" she shouted brazenly, much as she had when she and the women had first come to this place. "Hail, in the name of Elynsynos."

"Your pronunciation is just as appalling as it was before." The deep draconic voice echoed in the very stones of the cave, causing loose rock and grit to fall from the ceiling into the river, where it spat and hissed. "How disappointing for me, how embarrassing for you. I see you have brought along a nice repast, even if two of them are bound to be tough or chewy. Ah, well, at least there's a juicy-looking child."

The three women stepped even farther back.

"You must have received word about Elynsynos, or felt her return, or gotten some such dragon missive, or else you would be less concerned with my appalling pronunciation," Rhapsody called back, grinning. "Don't be peevish; I have come to return the property you loaned me and make good on a promise I made you."

An enormous shadow emerged from the depths of the cave, followed by a dazzling hail of sparkling lights glancing off the stone walls of the cave like fireworks. A moment later Witheragh's enormous reptilian head appeared from the darkness, glittering in the shadows from all the exquisitely faceted gemstones that had been set in his hide over the centuries.

"I don't suppose you remembered to bring your crown," the dragon said with an injured tone in the voice that his strength of will formed out of the air. "I was so looking forward to having it—er, having a look at it."

"I did not," Rhapsody replied. "But I did bring my husband and child."

The dragon reared up in surprise, then settled back to the wet ground of the cavern, a mixture of amusement and annoyance evident on his massive face.

"That cloak of yours is truly an irritation," he said. "The water interferes with reasonable dragon sense and makes it impossible to correctly assess one's surroundings. I am insulted that you chose to bring it into my lair again."

"Oh. Well, if you are offended, you will have to take that up with my husband. Ashe, this is Witheragh, from the second Clutch of Mylinmacr, son of Ylsgraith. Witheragh, may I present my husband, who has a very long and arduous name that would require me to take a nap if I had to intone it all, but who is, for your information, the only great-grandson of Elynsynos."

The great beast blinked as Ashe took down his hood.

"Well, well," Witheragh murmured. He rattled off a long train of words and sounds which Rhapsody found familiar but could not translate, to Ashe's amusement and response in exaggerated squeaks and hisses that she had never heard him utter before.

A giggle emerged from beneath the cloak of mist.

The beast's head ascended toward the ceiling of the cave.

"What an utterly charming sound," he murmured after his surprise had passed. "I want to see it. Please."

Ashe looked at his wife.

"What do you think, Aria? Can he be trusted?"

Rhapsody's face took on a considered mien.

"Witheragh? I believe so. He has guarded the Nain kingdom vigilantly while our son has been here—"

"Son?" The dragon's voice was almost giddy. "It's a *boy*? I was right, you know—I said it was a boy and you told me that perhaps it wasn't and—"

"I wasn't asking whether *you* could be trusted," Ashe said. "I am wondering what mischief my son might make with you, given that you are entirely too excited at this point, Witheragh. He is wyrmkin, you know, and his mother's boy; he has a level of grace, guile, and roguery similar to her own. He would have you helpless and at his mercy within a moment if he wanted to—"

Let me see him.

The words echoed through the cave in the multiple tones of soprano, alto, tenor, and bass, rattling the vault and causing the Molten River to flow momentarily faster.

Rhapsody laughed and walked back to her husband, who was the only other entity in the cave chuckling at the moment. She peeled aside the drapes of fabric coated in vapor to reveal a tiny glowing face wreathed in a wide grin.

Sporting a tiny tooth on the bottom gum.

"Oh, goodness!" Rhapsody exclaimed. "That's new. Thank you for waiting to cut that until after I returned." Realization came over her face. "Oh. Oh dear. That's going to hurt."

Ashe laughed, pulled the cloak away, and extended his arms, holding the baby out for the dragon to see.

The look of fond enchantment on the wyrm's face caused even the three women cowering out of the way to chuckle as well.

"It is my hope and expectation that when he is older, we might bring him back to this place," Rhapsody said as the dragon swayed his head back and forth over the Molten River, making his gemstones glitter for the baby's entertainment. Meridion's eyes brightened and followed the waves of colorful light intently. "Between the lessons in smithing and engineering he could learn from Faedryth, and the dragon lore he might be able to cadge from you—"

"Don't make promises you cannot or will not keep," said the dragon, still distracted by the little boy. "You absolutely should plan to bring him here. There are few enough of us left in the world. It would be uncommon wisdom to make a point of undertaking that sort of education."

"We will consider it seriously," said Ashe. He kissed Meridion on the glossy curls of his head, then tucked him under the cape again. "We must be heading out, so as to make the most of daylight. Rhapsody—"

"Say no more." The Lady Cymrian took the canvas sack she had been carrying and opened it. She pulled from it the coiled tongue whip that Witheragh had loaned her when she left Meridion, her heart, and her name behind in the Nain kingdom.

"I have tried to honor it as best I could," she said to the dragon across the Molten River. "It was invaluable in battle, allowing me to take beasts of monstrous strength and tainted power from the sky, and beating back charges in which we were gravely outnumbered." She fell silent suddenly. "And it snapped the life out of hundreds of crows."

The dragon nodded thoughtfully. "Always a good thing."

"I thank you for the loan of it," Rhapsody said. "Where would you like it?"

In the hands of those that care for the child, in safekeeping until he is old enough to wield it himself.

The words seemed to echo from the very air around them.

"Are you certain, Witheragh?" Rhapsody asked. "We agreed that I would return it to your hoard if it survived."

Witheragh was not moving.

"Those words were not uttered by me," he said quietly. "I believe, for the first time since it has been in my keeping, that we have heard the tongue of Mylinmacr. I told you my grandmother was a lore-tender, like you. There can be no doubt to the wisdom of its speech. You must take it with you and put it in safekeeping for your son when he is older."

"Thank you," Ashe said. "For this, and for everything else you have done for my son. Now, with our thanks, we must go. May the Earth guard what you love; guard the Shield while it does."

"You as well. Goodbye, Your Majesty. Do bring back the boy—and the crown. I have a great desire to see them both again one day."

"May it be so," Rhapsody said. "Goodbye, and thank you again."

She and Ashe headed up the tunnel, past the Molten River, to the air of the upworld again.

The three women less than a full step behind them.

67

ENTRANCE TO THE BOLGLANDS

The fields leading to the steppes of Ylorc had been meticulously cleared of the refuse of battle, Rhapsody noted as the armored caravan approached the checkpoint at Grivven Peak. Had it not been for the presence of ruts and divots pockmarking the ground and wide swaths of burned and fire-brutalized grass, black and crisp, there would be no sign whatsoever that an attack had been launched and repelled here.

"I'm glad to see that Achmed has chosen the higher path," she said, reaching over to adjust Meridion's blankets as he stretched, his hunger sated, and yawned in his sleep in Ashe's arms. "I did not know what to expect upon returning to the Bolglands; it would not have surprised me to see bodies strung from every peak and skulls on spikes set up as fence posts."

Ashe looked out the carriage window. "Achmed has worked diligently to build the Firbolg realm into what it is," he said, his eyes scanning the peaks. "Allowing it to devolve into what it was before would be self-defeating; once one has successfully undertaken to divert the sea, it is far more difficult to do it a second time. Additionally, he must know that he is not going to be around forever; it's best that he seek to make the Bolg forget those times past as much as he can, lest they revert to what they once were, without the guidance of a visionary after him to maintain the humanity they have achieved."

Rhapsody sat back against the cushion of the carriage seat and finished lacing her blouse.

"I'm not certain that Achmed has decided he is not going to be around forever," she said humorously. "He's fairly convinced that he, Grunthor, and I achieved the same immortality as the First Generation seems to have. When I met up with him in Tyrian, though, he did actually consider the possibility that the Three might someday become Two, or even One. I'm fairly convinced he was not talking about himself, however. He never mentioned it ever being Nil."

"Well, I am very glad that Fate has allowed it to be Three still," said Ashe, smiling. He took her hand with his free one and squeezed it gently. "Thank you for coming back to me, in all senses of the words."

Rhapsody's eyes sparkled; she opened her mouth to respond, but was cut short by the ragged blare of horns. She pushed the heavy velvet curtain at the exterior window aside to get a better view.

From around the back of Grivven Tower, a pair of horses emerged, galloping full out under the colors of the Bolg kingdom. One was riderless; the other was ridden by a Bolg Rhapsody recognized after a moment as Kubila, the Archon who was responsible for maintaining Achmed's livery and stables. The Firbolg army had a minimal cavalry—horses tended to be uncomfortable near members of the race—but what it had was well bred and trained by handlers from the province of Bethe Corbair, where stood the best horse breeders in the Alliance.

"Slow to a stop," she called to the driver through the carriage's interior window.

"Stay in the coach, Aria," Ashe said seriously. His wife considered, then assented, waiting inside the armored carriage until the Archon had brought the two horses to a halt a hundred paces from them. From every angle of the caravan she could hear the squeak of bending wood as scores of bowstrings were drawn.

"First Woman!"

The words in the harsh Bolgish tongue scratched in familiarity against Rhapsody's ears. She rolled her eyes in amusement, only to catch her husband's placid gaze hardening into fury. The title had been given to her by the Firbolg when the Three had first taken the mountains, indicating that they believed her to be Achmed's preferred courtesan. She smiled at him warmly, then pushed the curtain all the way open.

"Yes, Kubila?"

"Come with," the Archon said haltingly in the Orlandan tongue. "Please."

"What's the matter?"

"King—said. Please."

Rhapsody looked at Ashe. His face was expressionless but his eyes gleamed like the blue rippling waves of Kirsdarke.

"I will tell the sentries to speed the caravan through to the Cauldron," she said quietly. "You and Meridion can catch up with me there." Her husband exhaled but said nothing.

The Lady Cymrian rose and bent to kiss her sleeping son's head, then raised her face to Ashe and pressed a kiss onto his lips. His hand came to rest on her cheek and lingered there as she stood straight again.

"Promise me that when this is done, you will finally allow me to take you home to Highmeadow. I have already sent orders for the troops and all the infrastructure to be relocated to the provincial garrisons, so that it can at last be the home I've always intended it to be for you and Meridion."

Rhapsody took his hand from her face and kissed it. "There is nothing I could imagine that would make me happier." She released his hand, turned, and exited the carriage, trying to block the light that blasted through the doorway from falling on the sleeping infant.

"All is well," she called to Analise and Melisande, who were peering out the window of the carriage behind hers. "I'm just going on ahead." Analise nodded, Melisande smiled warily, and the two heads disappeared back into the darkness of their carriage.

The Archon began to dismount as she approached, but she waved him away and pulled herself easily into the saddle. "What's the matter?" she asked as he turned the horses in the direction of the main gate.

The Archon shrugged and urged his mount forward at an increasing rate of speed, Rhapsody barely keeping up, as they thundered across the battle-torn plain toward the entrance to Ylorc.

$\mathcal{H}$arran the Loremistress met the Lady Cymrian in the corridor outside the Great Hall and indicated that Rhapsody should follow her, so she did, anxiety beginning to take hold.

She hurried along the dark stone tunnels of what had been her home upon first coming to this land, her eyes adjusting to the darkness and sporadic dim illumination that had been the standard until she had reworked the lighting plan; clearly the Bolg had reverted to the level of brightness they had been more comfortable with before her.

She thought back to the day in spring, a lifetime before, it seemed, when Anborn had first come to Ylorc to set up defenses and arrange for Bolg supply lines. Her jaw tightened as she hurried after Harran, recalling the breakfast that morning on the balcony overlooking the Bolg mess hall before he set out to ride the Threshold of Death, the good-natured bantering of her Firbolg friends, the Lord Marshal laughing unabashedly, her son cradled in her arms, wide-eyed and gleefully observing it all.

She could almost hear their voices echoing in the halls of Ylorc now.

I'm actually shocked at the decorum of the troops, Anborn had joked. *It certainly is nothing like what passes for behavior in the mess tents of the army of Roland. Or a Cymrian wedding—this is a formal dining experience by comparison. I don't know if I can stand it, frankly.*

Achmed had turned a sour gaze on her in response.

Rhapsody insists on civility in all parts of Ylorc, even the privies. And, unfortunately for all of us, she generally gets it. At least when she's here she does. Everyone is painfully polite, refrains from public urination, and puts the seat down. Are you certain you don't want to take her with you, Anborn? She's a tremendous pain in the arse.

I guess they weren't joking, she thought as she struggled to keep up with the Loremistress, who was leading her through the barracks toward the hospice now. *I knew they had rescinded some of the programs I put in place, had furloughed the school programs and the like with the buildup to the war, but it seems they have completely eradicated much of what I undertook in this place.*

She was not certain why the thought made her so sad.

Anborn's voice echoed in her ears.

While your influence is evident in the more social aspects of the mountain, the hospitals and hospices, the schools and agricultural programs and whatnot, it is clear that military might and manufacturing are the priorities of the Firbolg king, and all resources are directed to those priorities. This cheers me more than I can say.

Rhapsody swallowed hard as Harran came to a stop before a wooden door with a barred window in the center of it.

She opened it and stepped aside.

Rhapsody walked slowly into the dark room where but one candle burned.

The Firbolg king was sitting in a chair at the foot of an enormous bed, his elbows on his knees, his fingers interlaced and resting on his lips. He did not look up as she entered, his gaze remaining on the figure in the bed.

Rhapsody looked to her left, dread taking root in her heart.

The figure in the bed was blanketed in shadow, tall and thin, it appeared, by the hills and hollows its body made in the blankets that covered it, with gray hair and wide shoulders evident on the pillows. Rhapsody had never seen a being like it before, its long limbs thin beneath the covers. She looked back at Achmed, waiting for him to speak, but he did not acknowledge her presence. Finally, as the silence grew too heavy to bear, she spoke in a whisper.

"Achmed?"

The Bolg king said nothing, but turned his head toward her, his mismatched eyes glittering at her in the light of the candle.

"You sent for me?"

Achmed inhaled, then let his breath out evenly.

"Is this someone who is in need of a healer?"

The Bolg king's eyes narrowed, his gaze unrelenting. He shook his head.

"What—what do you need, then?"

For a long moment, the Firbolg king merely stared at her. Then, when he spoke, his voice was toneless.

"I felt you should have time with him, undisturbed by your husband and son. For his sake, as well as yours."

"Him?" Rhapsody asked, her brows drawing together. "Who is this?"

"You don't recognize him?"

The Lady Cymrian looked at the figure in the bed again. Then she went to the table next to Achmed's chair where the solitary candle burned and picked it up. She held it aloft, then slowly made her way across the room.

The tall man's wide face was sculpted with great hollows along the cheekbones and chin, the eye sockets deep and dark. His skin was the color of parchment in the inconstant light, his hair coarse and almost white in the glow of the candle, his great jaw jutting forth beneath an enormous nose that looked strangely too large for the face. Wide, thin lips stretched across his mouth from side to side, from which a polished tusk protruded.

Rhapsody's eyes widened, and her hand went to her mouth.

"It—it isn't possible," she whispered. "Grunthor?"

The Firbolg king's interlaced fingers returned to rest against his lips again.

Rhapsody's stomach dropped into her feet, making them heavy as lead. She moved slowly to the bed and shielded the light with her hand as she held it up to illuminate her beloved friend's face.

The man in the bed bore little resemblance to the affable Sergeant-Major, the giant soldier who had offered himself as her first protector outside of her family from the moment she had met him, the man within whose greatcloak and upon whose chest she had slept through the endless, excruciating trek through the Earth they had undertaken to come to this world.

She had not recognized him with the loss of color to his skin and hair, skin that had always had a greenish tone, the color of old bruises, that reminded her of the clay of the Earth, hair that had been a mossy red-brown and coarse like straw, wrapping around his jaw in the fulsome beard that Meridion had loved to sleep beneath.

That beard was gray now as well, thinner and damp, it seemed.

Numbly, Rhapsody sat down on the edge of the bed and set the candle down on the table beside it.

Gently she brought her shaking hand to rest on the long, bony one that rested on top of the covers. It was cool and damp, unlike the warm, wide paw it had always been, its carefully maintained claws dull and papery like his skin. She could feel his great heartbeat thudding in the vein that ran, elevated, from his wrist up his thumb; it seemed regular, at least, though diminished from the ringing tone that used to echo brazenly in his chest beneath her ear in the dark.

"I—I thought I healed him," she said brokenly.

The Bolg king lowered his hands.

"You did," he said.

"But—what happened?"

Achmed rose silently and came to the bedside, stopping behind her.

"The battle with the titan took more out of him than we knew," he said quietly. "The shattering of his bones, the metaphysical assault was not the kind of damage you could sing back to wholeness, Rhapsody. You did heal him; he's not injured or bleeding internally, he's not sick or feverish. He's alive; he's just asleep most of the time—ironic, given his stalwart vigil of the Earthchild has made him more like her than ever could have been imagined."

"Oh God," she murmured, losing the battle to keep back tears. "It's as if he has aged all the years that our trek through the Earth seemed to hold at bay—as if Time has finally caught up with him."

The Firbolg king exhaled.

"This is the cost of it all," he said. His voice carried a little more of its sandy tone. "The wager that did not pan out, the bet that lost. You, he, and I have been thwarting Fate for a very long time now, and paying very little for it. I have almost lost both of you before, and yet somehow between us we have managed to haul each other back from the abyss, back from the brink of the unimaginable, to full health and vigor. The real tragedy is that death would have been a perfectly reasonable outcome for him. He has been facing it all of the time I have known him with no more fear of it than of falling asleep. But this—infirmity, this diminution, this is something he never would have wanted. You cried for the Earthchild when you first met her, and the Grandmother took you to task for it, telling you that her existence was what it was meant to be, that her path was nothing to be mourned. Perhaps that's true—but not for Grunthor. This loss is incalculable. I assume you agree."

Rhapsody nodded, her tears now falling like rain.

"Has he been awake at all?"

"Yes," Achmed said. "He is awake intermittently. If you want, I can wait until he has opened his eyes and seen you."

"Wait?" The tone in the Bolg king's voice caused her face to flush hot while her blood simultaneously took on a chill colder than the frost that had coated the ground of the Bolglands that morning. "Wait for what?"

A bony hand, sheathed in a leather glove, came to rest on her shoulder.

"We made a promise to each other a lifetime ago," Achmed said, his voice returning to the quiet state of a moment before. "We would never allow capture, or torture, or our own diminution—"

"You plan to *kill* him?"

"Well, when you say it like that, you make it sound like a bad thing." There was a note of humor in the otherwise toneless voice. "No, Rhapsody, I could never kill him, especially not once he survived being dragged back from the abyss, unless he was in agony, dying, and begging me to do so. Or thinking he might have been possessed, or carrying the equivalent of a demonic pregnancy, like you were when you asked me to do the same thing for you."

Rhapsody's terror of the moment before turned to cold shock.

"I—I never told you why I asked if you would—"

"You didn't have to. I saw your face when you were locked in a battle of wills with the F'dor in Bethe Corbair." Achmed smiled slightly at the expression on that face now. "You forget, we are the opposite sides of the same coin. I know you far better than you think I do—better in some ways than you know yourself."

The Lady Cymrian exhaled. "I do not doubt that."

The hint of a smile faded. "I plan to take him down to the Loritorium, and put him beside the Sleeping Child. He can sit vigil of a sort, keeping her company; it will ensure that I see her more, as I will need to go each day to bring him sustenance."

"But he's not an Earthchild," Rhapsody said, her voice clogging with emotion. "He wasn't conjured into life, as she was; he has lived in the world, Achmed. He was born of parents, he has friends—troops, who love him—"

"What we *did* promise each other is that we would not allow the other to live in a diminished state in the sight of the rest of the world," Achmed interrupted gently. "We witnessed that in the old world, and we each agreed, in a blood pact, not to allow the other to suffer that way."

"Let me take him home to Highmeadow," Rhapsody said through her tears. "He will have complete privacy, and care, and—"

"I know you think you are helping, Rhapsody, but you are not even listening to yourself. Grunthor is Firbolg—a son of the Earth. I know that you feel oppressed being inside the mountain, and you put a good face on being here, but you know how trapped you are in Ylorc. It is the same for Grunthor; being in the forest, in the loose air of the upworld, while not objectionable for a short time, can begin to make a cave dweller's skin itch after a while. Stop trying to make this better; it isn't going to get better. This is what it is. This, as I said, is the cost of war. Sometimes your card doesn't come up, and when it doesn't, the game is over."

A gentle knock on the door shattered the silence that followed.

68

$\mathcal{R}$hapsody lowered her head to the bed while Achmed crossed to the door in annoyance. He opened it a crack, then closed it again quickly.

"Your husband and brat are here," he said angrily. "I may have to strip Harran of her Archon status."

"Best of luck in training her replacement if you do—it took me three years to train her, and I'm a Namer. It will take you the rest of your immortal life."

Rhapsody rose, wiping her eyes, and went quickly to the door, opening it wide.

Standing in the hall, wearing the same expression of mild shock on their faces, were her husband and baby son, the younger of whom was leaning back against his father's chest, chewing on his own hand. Rhapsody took Meridion quickly into her arms and kissed her husband, then turned back into the room. Ashe closed the door behind her, remaining out in the hallway.

"And, perhaps, rather than *brat*, a term you know I despise, the word you are looking for is actually Grunthor's *godson*."

"Rhapsody, I told you I sent for you to have time with him alone, undisturbed. This is exactly what I was hoping to avoid." The Bolg king's voice carried the unmistakable ring of threat.

"If you are going to shut him away where no one who loves him will ever see him again, the least you can do is allow those people to say goodbye."

"I just told you, that was exactly what we both vowed to not let happen to the other."

The Lady Cymrian caressed her son's curls as she carried him to the bed and sat down again, ignoring the Bolg king's exhalation of annoyance.

"You remember Grunthor?" she asked Meridion softly. "Our sleeping partner, when we came to this place? Your godfather? Do you remember curling up against his neck, under his beard?"

Meridion let out a soft squeal, followed by a series of babbling sounds as his arms bounced up and down in excitement. Even without looking behind her, Rhapsody could feel Achmed's eyes smoldering.

She swallowed hard and gently laid the baby on the giant's chest at his neck, under his chin.

The infant giggled. He stretched languorously and waved his tiny hands about, then curled slightly against Grunthor's throat, patting clumsily at the ragged beard.

"You really feel the need to torture him more, Rhapsody?" Achmed said acidly.

Grunthor sighed raggedly, but his eyes remained closed.

Rhapsody sat back down on the bed, put her hand on the Sergeant's shrunken paw, and cleared her mind. She hummed her Naming note, *ela*, then began to softly chant the closest approximation she had to his true name, a harsh Bengard appellation full of whistling glottal stops and the abrasive sounds of the desert in which he had been born.

She closed her eyes, trying to evoke the starry sky of Serendair; she sang of the twisting canyons and the dry rocks of his birthplace, sculpted by the wind and a long-dead river in glorious colors and amazing shapes hidden within thin chasms, of the joys of the gladiatorial arena that had been his mother's domain, of the Earth through which they had passed together, melding his name into the song that still resonated, forever, within all of the Three.

It was the same healing she had attempted on the Skeleton Coast, in the foam of the rising breakers, in the trembling of the earth beneath the sand, in the screaming wind and the rolling thunder, but this time in the dark quiet of the inert stone of the mountain, the caves that Grunthor had loved, the tunnels he had paraded his troops endlessly through, singing bawdy marching cadences enthusiastically and grotesquely off-key.

She opened her eyes and looked at him.

There was no change.

Struggling to keep the song going as her throat tightened in despair, she glanced over to her son, whose eyes were fluttering on the verge of sleep. She caressed the top of his head with her fingers as she sang, sick at the loss of the man who had been so vibrant, so full of life, the godfather that her son would never know.

Meridion sighed as sleep took him.

Rhapsody sat up a little straighter. She looked at Achmed, whose posture had stiffened as well, and as their eyes met, a thought passed between them.

The baby had sighed in the exact tone as Grunthor had a moment before.

Rhapsody kept singing, her voice stronger now.

Achmed leaned over Grunthor and gently pulled aside the sheet that covered his chest. His shirt, vastly too wide for his now-skeletal body, was open at the neck and the top of his chest, close to where the baby lay. He took the candle from the bedside table and held it aloft as he pulled the shirt gently aside.

The skin nearest the sleeping infant had taken on the color of old bruises again.

The Bolg king nodded at Rhapsody, then withdrew his hand and stood erect, watching.

Slowly, as the song continued, the giant Bolg's breathing began to match the tides of the infant's breath, the rattling receding until his chest was rising and falling with the ease of that of the sleeping baby.

The greenish tone of his skin seemed to spread out from where Meridion lay, rejuvenating the parchment hue bit by bit. It slid down the length of one arm, and as it came to the end of the wrist of the hand that Rhapsody was still holding, she looked at her son again and gasped, dragging the namesong to a faltering halt.

Meridion's tiny hand was pale as parchment.

She looked down at Grunthor's hand.

The sagging and discolored skin was tightening somewhat, the color returning to it as blood spread through the capillaries. As Grunthor's hand lost the dry, pale coloring, Meridion's hand returned to the rosy skin of youth it had had since birth.

In silence now, she leaned over the Sergeant's chest and could hear the namesong, blending with the song of the Earth, resonating in the tides of his breath. With each inhalation, his body seemed to rehydrate, reinvigorate a little, clearing away some of the aspects of withering age that had been present the moment before.

"Grunthor?" she whispered as she watched the hollows beneath his eyes fill in somewhat, his cheekbones sink back into flesh that rose beneath the hanging skin that had covered them moments before. "Can you hear me?"

The Sergeant-Major did not move.

Rhapsody reached out her hand, shaking violently, and as it moved through the air it slipped without looking into the open palm of the Firbolg king, sheathed in the thin leather glove. She cast a glance to the right to see him, staring down at his oldest friend, lost in thought.

Grunthor's forehead, a moment before pocked and sunken, had begun to regain some of its tissue, its musculature, and those muscles wrinkled at his brow.

His lips, thin as paper a few moments before, swelled back into something resembling those that had for many years sat just above his jutting jaw, below his polished tusks, and opened slightly, moving as if in the attempt to form a word.

Both Rhapsody and Achmed leaned nearer.

"Rrrrr," the giant Bolg whispered. "Rrrraaaaa."

The baby beneath his beard slept on, oblivious to its thickening and losing some of its gray to mossy red streaks that spilled like ink from his chin to the ends of the coarse tufts of whiskers.

"What do you suppose he's trying to say?" Rhapsody asked Achmed softly. The Bolg king shook his head, raising a finger to his lips.

The tusked mouth opened again, forming a grotesque cave from which the smell of salt and blood and decay emerged.

"Ro—rocky," the Sergeant said softly, his voice harsh and ragged.

Achmed squeezed Rhapsody's hand, trying to quell its trembling. They waited silently.

Finally, Grunthor spoke again; it was a sound that, in the most imaginative of ways, resembled a song, deadly to the ears, agonizing in its slowness.

> Rocky-boye, baby
> So—tiny an' sweet
> Don't fall from yer—cradle
> You'll damage—the meat—

Against her will and her better judgment, the Lady Cymrian let loose a sound that was half chuckle, half choking noise. The Firbolg king smiled in relief for the first time since he had returned from the Skeleton Coast.

Eyes still closed, the Sergeant continued his painfully protracted lullabye.

'Ave—a nice morning
Enjoy all yer play
You'll be in—my—gut
By the—end of—the day

As the last plodding, off-key note sounded, the great amber eyes opened
slowly, the lids thin and wrinkled, the scleras shot with blood.

Rhapsody's left hand, still trembling violently, came to rest on the hair
of her beloved friend's head.

Grunthor's mouth pursed again as he prepared to speak.

"Sir?" The deep-timbered voice was a little stronger, though it still
sounded costly to his throat.

"Here," Achmed said, releasing Rhapsody's right hand and bringing
his own to Grunthor's wrist, which he encircled.

"Do—me—a favor?"

"Name it."

The Sergeant-Major cleared his throat; it sounded as if he had swallowed rocks.

"If you—please, sir, don'—be callin' the lit'le—prince a—brat no
more," he said carefully. "After all, 'im and—Oi been—sleepin' together—"

Rhapsody burst simultaneously into laughter and tears.

"As you wish," Achmed said in what for him could be construed to
be a pleasant tone.

They both smiled at their friend, whose color had returned to the hue
they had always known, whose hollowed features had thickened somewhat,
whose hair and beard had taken on some of their previous shades, but who
still seemed wan and spent, far older than he had been when the Three
had parted in the advent of war. There was no mistaking the toll his battle with the titan had taken on him, likely aging him by a generation.

But the pallor of death was no longer in his cheeks, with much of the
weight returned to his heavy-boned frame, his hands the broad-palmed paws
they had once been, the claws opaque once more.

Child of Earth.

The Child of Time, curled beneath Grunthor's red-brown beard with
streaks of gray, stretched languidly and opened his cerulean-blue eyes,
scored by vertical pupils.

And let loose a squeal of delight.

His mother quickly gathered him up and turned him vertical, holding him so that Grunthor could look up at him.

"'Allo, my lit'le friend," the Sergeant said fondly.

Meridion answered in a slew of cackles and buzzing sounds from the back of his throat, to the Sergeant's delight.

"Oi think—'ealing me must—be a—family tradition wi' you," he said as if the words pained him.

Achmed's brow furrowed. He looked at Meridion, who met his gaze solemnly.

"My thanks," the Bolg king said with equal seriousness.

The child stared at him for a long moment.

Then opened his mouth and belched resoundingly.

The recuperating Sergeant and the Lady Cymrian both laughed as the Firbolg king turned away in disgust.

"I had best get my little Namer back to his father," Rhapsody said, wrapping his blanket more securely around him. "Ashe will be none too pleased with what might seem like a risk I have just undertaken if I don't return him shortly."

"He would be right to be displeased," said Achmed evenly and under his breath as he took her elbow and led her to the door. "You had no idea what sort of damage your son could have incurred, even if he did bring Grunthor back somewhat from the brink. While I do not question your maternal instincts, I suggest that you consider whether the loss and return of your true name and your experiences in battle may have left your judgment slightly impaired.

"Go home, Rhapsody—go back to Highmeadow, to your family, to your realm, to your responsibilities for this battered Alliance. You have earned your happy ending; go enjoy it. Leave us to our aftermath; we will retrench within the mountains, rebuild, and take advantage of an extended period of silence from the ways of those who live in the upworld. Thank you for your ministrations to Grunthor, and those of your son. Go home."

The Lady Cymrian stared at him in shock. Then her eyes narrowed. She opened the door and handed Meridion to Ashe, who was pacing in the corridor, and who took him eagerly. She signaled that she would return in a moment, then closed the door and went back to the Sergeant's bed, where she whispered his true name one last time, then bent down and pressed a warm kiss onto his forehead.

"I love you," she said softly. "I love you. I love you."

Beneath her the giant Sergeant-Major smiled.

"Feelin' is mutual, miss."

"I will be back to see you no later than spring, or at Second Thaw if you need me earlier. You know how to reach me on the wind if there is a pressing need or something urgent; otherwise keep in touch with me by bird. If for any reason you want me here, let me know and I can be back in a sennight, now that I know all the liveries where Achmed keeps his Wings." Grunthor nodded as she squeezed his massive hand. "And any heartfelt poems you would like to exchange, I am more than happy to return in kind, but please, no more shrunken heads. The ones you sent me for my birthday two years ago were enough to last me the rest of my life."

The giant sighed dispiritedly.

"Give my love to the Sleeping Child," Rhapsody continued. "And tell her I will see her in the spring as well. Rest now, and regain your strength. Thank you for keeping the Three intact."

"Doin' my best."

She kissed him again and crossed the room, where she stopped before the Bolg king.

"If you think you can get rid of me that easily, you have misread the field reports badly," she said matter-of-factly. "You don't need to preach to me about the cost of war; I have lost my beloved knight, and almost lost one of my dearest friends; our continent has lost tens of thousands of innocent souls; hundreds of thousands across the world are dead. Alliances, kingdoms, dynasties, and friendships have been needlessly shattered. When I return to Highmeadow I will be undertaking a Lirin mourning ritual the likes of which has never been seen on this continent.

"But it is flagrantly stupid to have paid the cost of war and then to not relish the freedom that cost purchased. I am not leaving you and Grunthor for any 'extended period.' Ever. I intend to be a pain in your arse, a burr under your saddle, and the irritating other side of your obnoxious coin for the rest of my life. You will need me if you want to ever explore the other colors of the Lightcatcher, and to be the *amelystik* to the Sleeping Child, to check in on and oversee your schools and hospices, which you *will* reinstate now that the war is over, to monitor your agricultural program, to train the midwives, and to make certain decorum is being maintained in Ylorc—which means, in addition to all the other rules, no public urination, *whatsoever*. Make use of the damned privies—it took long enough to unclog and clean them. Don't eradicate or supplant everything I have done in this place, no matter how much you may want to. I'm not your bloody courtesan, I'm fucking Firbolg *royalty*. I was the duchess of Elysian long before I became Lirin queen or Lady Cymrian, and I will be damned if you think you can unseat me from my titles in and my responsibilities to Ylorc. Unless you want another war on your hands—"

Achmed laid a gloved finger on her lips.

"Enough," he said quietly. "Gained. Go home."

"I also love *you*," Rhapsody said. "Don't forget that. Behave yourself."

She stood on her toes and kissed him on the cheek, then opened the door and took her leave with her husband and son.

The Firbolg king listened until he could no longer hear the sound of her footfalls echoing quietly in the stone hallway. He followed her heartbeat until she had made her way out of the mountain and down to the scarred fields beyond the steppes, then turned back to the Sergeant, who was resting with his eyes open, staring at the ceiling.

"Still bossy, ain't she?" Grunthor said weakly. "That's a relief, at least."

"I don't expect even an intercontinental war could change that."

"You still 'aven't told 'er. Bad plannin', sir."

Achmed smiled slightly as he poured the Sergeant some water. "We will see. Before you get too opinionated, have a drink."

He held the glass to his friend's lips, banishing the thoughts that were crowding at the edges of his mind.

69

HIGHMEADOW, NAVARNE

Gwydion Navarne was just finishing his supper in the small private dining room in the residence quarters of Highmeadow when a tap came on the door. He wiped his mouth with his linen napkin, bemused at how life had returned from the horror of daily bloodshed and strife to elegant etiquette in a mindlessly quick time, knowing it would take far longer for his soul and memory to go back to normal.

"Come."

Manus Kral, the chamberlain, opened the door and stepped to the threshold without crossing it.

"M'lord—"

"Let me in—*now*." A harsh feminine voice assaulted Gwydion's battle-damaged ears; he looked questioningly at Manus, who was staring help-lessly at him in return; then the chamberlain was pushed aside as a familiar woman thrust herself into the room.

Gwydion's heart sank.

It was Lady Madeleine Steward.

The Lord Roland's wife.

Or, more correctly now, widow, even if she didn't know it yet.

"Lady Madeleine—" he began.

"Where is Tristan?" she demanded as she strode into the room and over to the dining table, where she glared down at the young duke in his chair. "Where is my husband, Gwydion?"

"He—he—" Words failed him utterly.

"I have scoured every brothel, every whorehouse, every tavern from Canderre to this godforsaken forest, to no avail. Where is he?" The woman's fashionably pale face was even more sallow than usual, and Gwydion recognized grief and fear in her expression beneath the hard mien she was wearing.

"Tell me, please, oh gods, tell me," she said, her voice breaking. "I've had no word for the longest time."

Gwydion tried to speak, but he could force no sound into his throat.

He thought back to his own father, who had had to break terrible tidings to Melisande and him several times before. Stephen Navarne had always seemed to know what to say, even in the most awkward, painful, or embarrassing situations. He thought back to the only piece of advice his father had ever shared with him on the subject.

Always tell the truth, Gwydion, no matter how ugly or hard it is. People deserve that at least. But, while you're doing so, remember how damaging words can be in times of tragedy, and be as gentle as you can be while not compromising your word. Try to gauge what is really being asked of you, and do not give voice to more than that. You can always elaborate, but you can never take back words someone didn't want to hear.

Gwydion cleared his throat.

And, pushing back his chair, he stood.

He reached out and took Madeleine's trembling hands.

"He's been in none of those establishments, I assure you, Lady Madeleine; I am sorry to tell you that he is in the Afterlife."

The Lady Steward let out a sound that reminded Gwydion of air leaving a bellows.

"How? Why—what happened? Why—why didn't someone—"

"It was a matter of the greatest security," Gwydion said, groping for words. "His whereabouts were a highly guarded secret of the highest order."

Madeleine's face, crumpling a moment before, froze.

"They were?"

Gwydion nodded a little too enthusiastically.

"Indeed. The—er, the very fate of the continent was determined by his, er, sacrifice."

Lady Madeleine, as talented a social climber as Gwydion had ever met, nodded numbly, though her eyes were beginning to shift from side to side.

"Is—is that something that can be shared in a proclamation? That Tristan Steward's last action was an enormous benefit to the Alliance, and, in fact, the Known World?"

Gwydion exhaled.

He thought back to the moment when the Bolg king had fired a crossbow bolt into the Lord Roland's skull.

Tristan had bled his life onto the floor without any hesitation.

Any number of people he knew would consider that an enormous benefit to the Alliance.

"Yes, I think that would certainly be appropriate," he said, taking the shaken woman's elbow and leading her to a chair near the fire. He uncorked the brandy and poured her a snifterful. "Have a draught, m'lady, and tell me everything you want to be undertaken at his memorial service."

Epilogue

The death of the instigator should mark the official end of a war. It almost never happens that way, of course.

For all that the presence of the Sea Mages and the naval forces of Manosse helped to quell and root out the occupation forces that Talquist had installed up the entirety of the western coast, the process of returning peace to the Middle Continent was a long and occasionally brutal one. Achmed commented later, at the signing of the final armistice, that half as many lives had been lost in the days following the death of Talquist as had been taken in the land war itself.

The only saving grace for the Alliance in the course of bringing the continent back from the war was the intervention of Fhremus Alo'hari, the supreme commander of the forces of the Empire of the Sun. In spite of knowing that his actions could qualify as treason under the military code of conduct, Alo'hari sent the remaining divisions of the Sorbold army to the Threshold of Death with the order to surrender, and rode with his own regiment under a flag of truce to deliver that notification to Knapp and Solarrs, now serving in Anborn's stead.

Upon receipt of the offer of surrender, word was dispatched by falcon to the Lord Cymrian and caught up with him as his regiment was crossing the Krevensfield Plain in the northeast. Ashe had sighed in both relief and frustration, then diverted the coach and its escort to Sepulvarta, where the Sorbold supreme commander was being held in military custody, and the Patriarch was in the process of resanctifying the City of Reason.

"It seems I shall never succeed in bringing you and our son home," he muttered to Rhapsody upon his return to the coach.

His wife had merely smiled and kissed his hand.

"Wherever we are all together, we are home. Tend to what needs your attention—we will be by your side."

$\mathcal{A}$ council of peace, comprised of many of the same members that had attended the war council held in secret prior to the conflict's commencement, met at the foot of the Scales in Jierna'sid within a turn of the moon of Fhremus's surrender. The Diviner of the Hintervold, absolved of his participation owing to Talquist's deceit, stood in attendance, along with Edwyn Griffyth and many of the Council of the Sea Mages; the upper rank of military commanders of the Second Fleet of Manosse; Constantin, the Patriarch of Sepulvarta; Gavin, the Invoker of the Filids; and the Lord and Lady Cymrian, the latter of whom also stood in attendance in the role of Lirin queen along with Rial, her viceroy.

Behind Fhremus stood some of the surviving counts and barons of the city-states of Sorbold, many of whom had gathered almost two years before to see the Scales select a new ruler upon the passing of the Empress Leitha. After a long and somber silence, and a prayer for wisdom offered jointly by the religious leaders, those noblemen who had once pressed for independence from the empire were allowed a place in the conclave which had assembled again at the foot of those Scales.

Talquist's broken crown, pried from his skull at the bottom of the canyon below the tower of Jierna Tal, was brought forth from a burlap sack and placed on one of the Weighing plates against the Ring of State, also harvested from his corpse.

After a few moments of imbalance, the arm of the Scales that held the Weighing plate with the crown swung violently and catapulted the crown into the canyon below the palace, beyond the sight of any but the raptors that plied the updrafts above the rocky crevasse.

In turn, the counts were Weighed singularly and found wanting.

Finally, at the suggestion of the Patriarch, they were led, shaking nervously from their first experience, as a group into the Weighing plate that was counterbalanced by the Ring of State.

And found to be in balance.

"The Scales have made a determination, clear of deception," Constantin intoned. "The Empire of the Sun is formally dissolved; the power of the state is now remanded to the provinces, to sort through and establish themselves as independent. I shall offer prayers this evening for the All-God's wisdom and guidance as you undertake this difficult task."

The counts looked at each other in stark terror.

After returning from the armistice signing, the Firbolg king disappeared from the common sight of the world for a long time into the depths of the eastern Teeth. The exterior gates of Ylorc were closed to international visitors, and the northern and western borders were politely but vigorously patrolled, all except for the single entrance that accepted and dispatched deliveries of trade. The Bolg, who had been hesitantly undertaking to be part of the common world, withdrew into the stone and silence of the mountains, lost once more from the sight of that world.

To all but the Cymrian royal family.

True to her word, Rhapsody stalwartly refused to be kept away from the other two of the Three. She returned routinely to Ylorc, sometimes alone, sometimes accompanied by her family, occasionally sitting in solitary siege, singing at the gate of Grivven Post until the sentries begged the Sergeant-Major for mercy and intervention. Finally, at Grunthor's plea, Achmed relented and allowed her in.

The result was the beginning of the return of peace and normalcy to the Middle Continent and the Known World, which undertook the path that more-or-less-peaceful historic eras bring.

And remained thus for a little over a thousand years.

GLOSSARY

THE THREE

Achmed the Snake: king of the Firbolg and lord of the realm of Ylorc (named so by Rhapsody); Child of Blood (from the Prophecy of the Three); Ysk (named at birth by the Bolg); the Brother (renamed in Serendair by Father Halphasion, his mentor); the Assassin King (called by Rath). The irritable warlord in this world, an unerring assassin in the last, half-Firbolg, half-Dhracian, whose hypersensitive skin is scored with veins and nerve endings by which he can track the heartbeats of those born on the Island of Serendair.

Grunthor, Sergeant-Major: the supreme commander of the Firbolg military forces, the Chief Archon; "The Ultimate Authority, to Be Obeyed at All Costs" (self-named); Child of Earth (from the Prophecy of the Three). The affable soldier, half-Firbolg, half-Bengard, admitted cannibal (though mostly for effect), seven and a half feet of well-trained brute strength but with a soft spot for Rhapsody, children, and people he likes. He is nonetheless single-minded when it comes to military tactics and issues of survival.

Rhapsody o Serendair: Lady Cymrian; Queen of Tyrian [Lirin]; Duchess of Elysian (a joking name given to her by Achmed and Grunthor); Amelia Rhapsody Turner (given name); Emily, Aria (to Ashe); Pretty (to Elynsynos); First Woman (to the Bolg); Child of the Sky (from the Prophecy of the Three). A Lirin Singer and Namer, she is trained in the use of music to affect the vibrations of light, color, and sound that make up the universe, and therefore able to alter reality by manipulating a given thing's namesong, its unique vibrational signature. She is the Iliachenva'ar, the bearer of Daystar Clarion, one of the ancient elemental swords [combined fire and ether].

THE CYMRIAN ROYAL FAMILY AND THAT OF THE DRAGON ELYNSYNOS

Merithyn the Explorer: ancient Seren; the first mariner to successfully approach the Wyrmlands, falling in love with the dragon Elynsynos in the Seren form she took to meet him, the father of the three triplet Seers, Anwyn, Rhonwyn, and Manwyn. Deceased.

Rhonwyn: the Seer of the Present

Manwyn: the Seer of the Future

Anwyn: the Seer of the Past; daughter of Merithyn the Explorer and the dragon Elynsynos. Wife of Gwylliam, trapped in dragon form with a cwellan disk embedded near her heart. The first Lady Cymrian, who waged a seven-hundred-year war against her husband.

Gwylliam ap Rendlar: the last king of the Island of Serendair, deceased; led the exodus of the Cymrian people from the doomed Island to the Wyrmlands, known as the Middle Continent now. An engineer and smith, known as the Visionary, designed and built most of the great buildings still standing from the First Cymrian Age, including the mountain citadel of Canrif, now known as Ylorc.

Edwyn Griffyth: High Sea Mage of Gaematria; Gwylliam and Anwyn's eldest son [father's favorite]

Llauron ap Gwylliam: the late Invoker of the Filids; Ashe's father; Gwylliam and Anwyn's second son [mother's favorite]

Anborn ap Gwylliam: Lord Marshal of the Cymrian Alliance; Gwylliam and Anwyn's youngest son; Rhapsody's sworn knight

Gwydion ap Llauron: the Lord Cymrian, leader and high lord of the Alliance of the Middle Continent; Ashe (to his intimates); Llauron's son; Rhapsody's husband; Gwydion of Manosse (his title from his late mother's line); Sam (to Rhapsody); Meridion's father

Meridion ap Gwydion: infant son of Rhapsody and Ashe; the Child of Time (from the Prophecy of the Child of Time)

THE CYMRIAN ALLIANCE

Analise o Serendair: Rhapsody's oldest living friend, the child she rescued from Michael, the Wind of Death

Constantin: the Patriarch, head of the Patrician faith, a former gladiator

Faedryth: Nain king; Lord of the Distant Mountains; semi-estranged from Alliance

Garth: one of Anborn's men

Gavin the Invoker: the forester who replaced Llauron as the head of the Filidic [nature] religion of the continent; residing at the Circle in the Great Forest; protector of the Great White Tree

Gwydion Navarne: seventeen-year-old duke of Navarne; Ashe's namesake

Gyllian, Lady: crown princess of the Nain kingdom; Faedryth's sensible daughter

Jal'asee: an ancient Seren ambassador from Isle of the Sea Mages

Knapp: one of Anborn's men; a First Generation Cymrian

Melisande Navarne, Lady: Gwydion Navarne's sister, an intrepid ten-year-old

Omet: a former slave child in the tile foundry owned by the Raven's Guild, rescued by Achmed and Rhapsody, now working for Achmed rebuilding his Lightcatcher

Rath: an ancient Dhracian, a demon hunter who seeks both his list of targets and Ysk, the name by which the Common Mind of Dhracians know Achmed, whom they also seek

Rial: the viceroy of the kingdom of Tyrian; Lord Protector; Rhapsody's right hand

Solarrs: Anborn's lead scout and longtime man-at-arms; a First Generationer of the Third Fleet

Tristan Steward: the Lord Roland, highest ranking duke in Roland; imprisoned by Ashe for unknowingly fraternizing with the F'dor demon Portia in case he is her thrall

THE MESALLIANCE, THE PERPETRATORS OF THE WAR OF THE KNOWN WORLD

Beliac: King of Golgarn, nervous monarch of the seafaring nation; fears being eaten by Bolg

Dowager Empress: Leitha, Empress of the Dark Earth; killed and usurped by Talquist

Dranth: guild scion of the Raven's Guild, an organization of assassins in Yarim

Esten: guildmistress of the Raven's Guild, deceased

Faron: the titan of Sorbold; a Faorina spirit, the denatured, bastard child of a F'dor demon and a Seren woman; now in a Living Stone body with the appearance of a titanic statue of a soldier, sharing it with Hrarfa

Fhremus Alo'hari: supreme commander of Sorbold's land force; uncle of Kymel

Hjorst: the Diviner of the Hintervold, a sophisticated and educated man in a primitive role; the religious and political leader of the Icemen in the north, who divines the future chiefly through animal sacrifice and other animist practices

Hrarfa: the F'dor spirit in the Living Stone body of Faron; of the Older Pantheon; one of the few remaining of the Unspoken, a demon that escaped the Vault

Kymel: a young soldier; Fhremus's sister's son; an idealist, fifth-generation soldier

Michael, the Wind of Death: soldier from the Lost Island, known occasionally as the Waste of Breath, a voluntary host to a F'dor demon; the seneschal; the Baron of Argaut, deceased

Stephanus: a second lieutenant and subcommander under Titactyk, army of Sorbold

Talquist Rev-Penthor: the Merchant Emperor of Sorbold, in possession of one of the oldest of scales from Sharra's Stolen Deck, who rigged the Scales to usurp the throne

Titactyk: a regimental commander in the army of Sorbold

Yabrith: second-rate member of the Raven's Guild of assassins

ADDITIONAL PERSONS AND MYTHIC BEINGS

Earthchild, the: a conjured being made of Living Stone and brought into life by a willing sacrifice of part of a dragon's soul, in eternal slumber in the Bolglands. The rib from such a child could be used as a key to open the Vault of the Underworld.

Evrit: slave in a Sorbold ore mine, shipwrecked with his fellow religious pilgrims and family only to fall into Talquist's hands

Grandmother, the: ancient Dhracian guardian of the Earthchild/Sleeping Child; deceased

Halphasion, Father: Achmed's mentor from Serendair, named him the Brother

Jacinth Specter: sailor on the *Flying Sails;* witness to the attack on Avonderre Harbor

Jarzben: the elder of Evrit's sons, enslaved in the same ore mine as he is

Lady Rowan, the: the Keeper of Dreams, the Guardian of Sleep; Yl Breudiwyr; a manifestation of Time in the world beyond Death but before the Afterlife

Lord Rowan, the: the Hand of Mortality; the Peaceful Death; Yl Angaulor; a manifestation of Time in the world beyond Death but before the Afterlife

Miraz of Winter: a lesser Diviner in the Hintervold

Portia: a chambermaid, also a First Generation Cymrian possessed by a demon in the employ of Tristan Steward, who brings her to the household of Rhapsody and Ashe

Selac: the younger of Evrit's sons, enslaved with his family, location unknown

Sharra: the ancient Seren Seer who read fortunes on the Island of Serendair from a deck of dragon scales (see Given Deck and Stolen Deck); believed to be deceased

Syrus Turley: captain of the *Flying Sails*; witness to the attack on Avonderre Harbor

Talthea: also known as the Gracious One or the Widow; the daughter-in-law of MacQuieth Monodiere Nagall; a First Generation Cymrian; deceased

Weaver, the: the manifestation of Time in history, found behind the Veil of Hoen on the doorstep of the Afterlife. She sits behind an enormous loom, weaving the tapestry of history. It is said that no one can remember what her face looks like after it is seen.

DUKES OF ROLAND/NOBILITY OF
CYMRIAN ALLIANCE

Baldasarre, Dunstin: younger brother of Quentin Baldasarre; duke of Bethe Corbair

Baldasarre, Quentin: duke of Bethe Corbair

Canderre, Cedric: duke of Canderre; the Baldasarres' uncle; Madeleine's father

Karsric, Ihrman: duke of Yarim

Ivenstrand, Martin: duke of Avonderre

Navarne, Gwydion: seventeen-year-old duke of Navarne

Navarne, Stephen: late duke of Navarne; Gwydion and Melisande's father; Ashe's best friend

Steward, Lady Madeleine Canderre: Cedric's daughter; the Lord Roland's wife; known among the nobility and the populace as the Beast of Canderre

Steward, Tristan: Lord Roland and Prince of Bethany

ARCHONS

Archon: a Firbolg child chosen from one of the clans by Achmed and Rhapsody, selected for special skill and intelligence and trained to be a leader in the society

Dreekak: the Archon known as the Master of Tunnels

Greel: the Archon known as the Face of the Mountain/Mining

Harran: the Loremistress

Krinsel: the Archon of the Midwives

Kubila: the Archon of trade and diplomacy

Ralbux: the Archon in charge of Education

Trug: the Archon of communications known as the Voice

Yen: the broadsmith; the Archon in charge of weaponry

RATH'S LIST OF F'DOR DEMONS AND OTHER PREY

Ficken: the greedy Glutton, preying on unsuspecting small folk, both of stature and spirit

Fraax: F'dor, loose in the upworld, unknown of character

Hnaf: the Outcast of Outcasts, mistrusted by his own kind, possessed of cheap malice

Hrarfa: the Liar of Liars, more scent than fire, beckoning with false promises

Sistha: F'dor, loose in the upworld, unknown of character

Ysk: the name the Firbolg gave Achmed upon birth, meaning spittle or vomit

DRAGONS

Dyancynos, Elynsynos, Marisynos (deceased), **Talasynos, Valecynos:** the Five Daughters, the firstborn children of the Progenitor Wyrm. Each guarded one of the five World Trees, the gigantic trees that grew in each of the places where Time began, as measured by the first appearance of one of the five elements on the Earth. Dyancynos (Frothta, Water); Elynsynos (Great White Tree, Earth); Marisynos (Sagia, Ether); Talasynos (Eucos, Air); Valecynos (Ashra, Fire). Their lost sibling, the sixth egg of the original clutch, is the Sleeping Child, the dragon within the earth comprising one-sixth of its mass. The F'dor seek to awaken the Sleeping Child so that it can consume the Earth.

Chao: a sparkling, evanescent creature from the bright lands of the rising sun

Mikanic: from the Great Overward, his hide like the sand of the desert in which he lives

Mylinmacr: a dragon lore-singer and historian; Witheragh's grandmother; deceased

Salinus: lives in great salt beds, his white hide streaked with yellow and gray

Sidus: a coal dragon from the lands of darkness beyond the sea

Sinjaf: the vaporous steward of poisonous swamps and everglades

Witheragh: the dragon who guards the Molten River of Fire in the Nain kingdom

ELEMENTAL BASILICAS

Abbat Mythlinis: the basilica of Water in Avonderre (name actually means *Father of the Ocean-born*, but is believed to mean *Master of the Sea*)

Lianta'ar: the basilica of the Ether, the Patriarch's basilica in Sepulvarta (name actually means *Bearer of Light*, but is believed to mean *Light of the World*)

Ryles Cedelian: the basilica of Air dedicated to the wind in Bethe Corbair (name actually means *Breath of Life*, but is believed to mean *Spirit of the Air*)

Terreanfor: the basilica of Earth/Living Stone at Night Mountain in Sorbold (name actually means *King of the Earth*, and is correctly translated from Old Cymrian)

Vrackna: the ringed temple of elemental Fire in Bethany (name is actually the name of a demon from the old world, but is believed to mean *Fire of the Universe*)

THE LIGHTCATCHER

Primordial lore, words of deep magic from the Dawn of Time, reveal the power of vibrational color and the properties that each wavelength of light possesses. Each note except the last in the scale has both a sharp and a flat property, usually the opposite of one another. The Lightcatcher was an enormous instrumentality built into the dome of Gurgus Peak, the tallest of the inner peaks of the Teeth, and through the use of colored light, the pitch associated with it, and a true name, the properties of the colors could be accessed. The specific properties and names of the parts of the light spectrum are:

Red: *Lisele-ut*; sharp: Blood Saver (healing); flat: Blood Letter (killing)

Orange: *Frith-re*; sharp: Fire Starter (ignition); flat: Fire Quencher (snuffing)

Yellow: *Merte-mi*; sharp: Light Bringer (illumination); flat: Light Queller (darkening)

Green: *Kurh-fa*; sharp: Glade Scryer (viewing within vegetation or terrain), flat: Grass Hider (hiding within vegetation or terrain)

Blue: *Brige-sol*; sharp: Cloud Chaser (making things clear); flat: Cloud Caller (obscurement)

Indigo: *Luasa-ela*; sharp: Night Stayer (holds off darkness); flat: Night Summoner (brings on darkness)

Violet: *Grei-ti*; the New Beginning (overturns reality in favor of a new version)

EXPLANATION OF THE SCALES OF THE STOLEN DECK

Nine dragon scales harvested from the sixth of the original clutch of dragon eggs, the infant wyrm taken by the F'dor and secreted in the cold depths of the Earth, eternally asleep, awaiting awakening. Each scale is one of the seven colors of light, with their powers noted earlier, plus black and white.

> The white scale, one of the two most powerful and awful of the Stolen Deck, was said to have no image inscribed upon it at all. It symbolized Life or Creation, and was thought by many to be a picture of the very face of God. Its counterpart, the black scale, had inscribed upon it a picture of a key, a terrible harbinger of its power to open the Vault itself. It symbolized Void or destruction.
> —Rath's explanation, *The Assassin King*

EXPLANATION OF THE SCALES OF THE GIVEN DECK

A larger collection of scales sacrificed by younger dragons later in history when the Vault was ruptured by a star known as Melita, later also called the Sleeping Child, which fell to Earth and impacted it. Weaker because they are younger, each of the scales is color-specific and has a lesser power associated with it.

Abbey of Nikkid'sar, the: a respite for lost or orphaned children and their caretakers

Argaut (continent of Northland): a seafaring city of dark intent and commerce

Avonderre Harbor: the largest harbor on the Middle Continent; on the central west coast

Axis Mundi: the centerline of power through the Earth, bisecting it

Bolglands, the: the former citadel called Canrif, carved into the mountains called the Teeth

Cauldron, the: part of the Bolglands that was Gwylliam's seat of power, now Achmed's

Cave of the Lost Sea: the lagoon of salt tears in the lair of the dragon Elynsynos

Circle, the: center of the Filidic religion, where the Great White Tree stands

Citadel of the Star (the City of Reason): Sepulvarta, the holy city of the Patrician faith

Cymrian museum, the: Lord Stephen Navarne's historical collection of Cymrian artifacts

Deep Kingdom, the (Undervale): the kingdom of the Nain

Dovecote, the: the name by which Anborn calls Elysian, warning Rhapsody away from it

Easton: eastern port city in Serendair where Rhapsody lived when she met Achmed and Grunthor

Elysian: the underground grotto with a cottage in the center of a lake in the Bolglands

Gaematria, the Isle of the Sea Mages: where magic and the sea are studied as sciences

Golgarn: the southeastern port kingdom whose king surrendered his ships to Talquist

Grivven: the tallest peak of the Outer Teeth; a command center and observation post

Gurgus: in the Bolglands; the highest mountain past the steppes and before the canyon that separates the Cauldron from the Deeper Realms in which the Lightcatcher is housed

Gwynwood: northern part of the Great Forest of the western continent

Haguefort: keep belonging to the family of Stephen Navarne

Highmeadow: the new fortress home Ashe built for Rhapsody in the forests of Navarne near Bethany, which becomes the central command center of the war

Hintervold: northern part of the continent beyond the Tar'afel River, mostly tundra

Island of Serendair, the: the homeland of the Cymrian people before the exodus

Jierna Tal: the palace of the emperor of Sorbold

Kraldurge (the Realm of Ghosts): canyon in Bolglands believed to be haunted

Krevensfield Plain, the: wide-open land running almost the width of the Middle Continent

Kurimah Milani: a mythic city of healing from before the Cymrian era, lost to Time

Loritorium, the: a cavern deep within the Bolglands where the Sleeping Child rests

Madame Parri's Pleasure Palace: Grunthor's favorite whorehouse in the old world

Manosse: major coastal realm on the eastern part of the continent across the Wide Central Sea where the Second Fleet landed; part of the Cymrian Alliance

Manteids, the: the Cymrian name for the Teeth, also the name of the three Seers

Marincaer: a neighboring nation to Manosse

Merryfield: Rhapsody's birthplace, a farming village on the Island of Serendair

Middle Continent, the: common name for the part of the continent north of Sorbold and south of the Hintervold; Roland and the Lirin lands of Tyrian, as well as the Bolglands

Mirror Lake: a reflective body of water in the lands of Elynsynos the dragon

Molten River, the: the river of fire and melted rock that separates the lands of the dragon Witheragh from the kingdom of the Nain

Nonaligned States, the: a collection of small nations to the southwest of Sorbold

Quieth Keep: the royal college of Serendair

Roland: the provinces that comprise most of the mass of the Middle Continent

Sepulvarta, the City of Reason: the holy city-state of the Patrician religion north of Sorbold and south of Roland

Serendair (the Lost Island of Serendair): the homeland of the Cymrian people, destroyed in volcanic fire subsequent to the exodus when the star known as the Sleeping Child rose

Skeleton Coast, the (of Sorbold): the desolate and foggy western coast of Sorbold where the Third Cymrian Fleet landed, now a graveyard of the bones of their ships

Sorbold: the vast united empire of city-states in southern desert and mountains beyond the Middle Continent

Spire, the: the immensely tall tower in Sepulvarta crowned with a silver star in which an actual piece of ether from the star Seren has been housed

Tar'afel River: northern river that forms the boundary of the Middle Continent and the lands of the dragon Elynsynos

Teeth, the: the Bolg name for the mountains in which they live, also called the Manteids

Tomingorllo: the palace of the Lirin kingdom

Traeg: windy northernmost port on the western coast of the Middle Continent

trans-Orlandan thoroughfare, the: roadway built in the first Cymrian era bisecting the Middle Continent; considered the jewel of roadways

Tyrian: also called Realmalir; the Lirin forest realm

Undervale: the kingdom of the Nain, also known as the Deep Kingdom

Vault of the Underworld, the: vault of Living Stone where the F'dor are imprisoned

Veil of Hoen, the: the mystical realm between life and death; home of the Rowans

Verne Hys: a port on the western coast of the Hintervold

Vornessta, Sorbold: area housing one of Sorbold's biggest iron ore mines

Wide Central Sea, the: the ocean that separates Manosse from the Middle Continent

Windswere: a southern coastal city southwest of Sorbold

Wyrmlands, the: the original name of the continent

Ylorc (was Canrif): the Bolglands

Haydon, Elizabeth,
The Hollow Queen

JUL   2015